Dark Secrets 1

ALSO BY
ELIZABETH CHANDLER

Kissed by an Angel

Dark Secrets 1

LEGACY OF LIES

DON'T TELL

Elizabeth Chandler

Simon Pulse
New York London Toronto Sydney

This book is a work of fiction. Any references to historical events,
real people, or real locales are used fictitiously. Other names, characters, places, and incidents are the product of the author's imagination, and any resemblance to actual events or locales or persons, living or dead,
is entirely coincidental.

SIMON PULSE
An imprint of Simon & Schuster Children's Publishing Division
1230 Avenue of the Americas, New York, NY 10020
This Simon Pulse edition August 2009

For information about special discounts for bulk purchases, please contact Simon & Schuster Special Sales at 1-866-506-1949 or business@simonandschuster.com.
The Simon & Schuster Speakers Bureau can bring authors
to your live event. For more information or to book an event contact the Simon & Schuster Speakers Bureau at 1-866-248-3049 or visit
our website at www.simonspeakers.com.
Designed by Mike Rosamilia
The text of this book was set in Adobe Garamond Pro.
Manufactured in the United States of America
8 10 9 7
Library of Congress Control Number 2009924774
ISBN 978-1-4169-9461-9
These titles were published individually by Simon Pulse.

To Bob,
You're the best!
Love you.

Legacy of Lies

one

Last night I visited the house again. It looked as it did ten years ago, when I dreamed about it often. I've never seen the house in real life, at least not that I can remember. It is tall, three stories of paned windows, all brick with a shingle roof. The part I remember most clearly is the covered porch. No wider than the front steps, it has facing benches that I like to sit on. I guess I was never shy, not even at six; in the dream I always opened the door, walked inside, and played with the toys.

Last night the door was locked. That's how I awoke, trying with all my strength to open it, desperate to get inside. Something was wrong, but now I can't say what. Was there something dangerous outside the house from which I was fleeing? Was there a person in the house who needed my help? It was as if the first part of my dream was missing. But one thing I knew for sure: Someone on the other side of the door was trying hard to keep me out.

"I'm not going," I had told my father back in June. "She's a mean old lady. She disowned Mom and won't speak to you. She has never had anything to do with Pete, Dave, or me. Why should I have anything to do with her?"

"For your mother's sake," he'd said.

Several months later I was on a flight from Arizona to Maryland, still resisting my grandmother's royal command to visit. I took out her invitation, the first message I'd received from her in my life, and reread it—two sentences, sounding as stiff as a textbook exercise.

Dear Megan,
This summer I will see you at Scarborough House.
I have enclosed a check to cover airfare.

Regards,
Helen Scarborough Barnes

Well, I hadn't expected "love and kisses" from a woman who cut off her only daughter when she had decided to marry someone of a different race. My mother, coming from a deep-rooted Eastern Shore family, has more English blood in her than Prince Charles. My father, also from an old Maryland family, is African-American. After trying to have children of their own, they adopted me, then my two brothers. It would be naive to expect warmth from a person who refused to consider adopted kids her grandchildren.

Now that I thought about it, the meaning of my dream the night before was pretty obvious, even the feeling that something was wrong. The door to my mother's family had always been closed to me; when a door kept locked for sixteen years suddenly, without explanation, opens, you can't help but wonder what you're walking into.

"Megan? You made it!" the woman said, crumpling up the sign with my name on it, then giving me a big hug. "I'm Ginny Lloyd, your mother's best old friend." She laughed. "I guess you figured that out."

When Ginny heard I was coming, she'd insisted on meeting me at the airport close to Baltimore. That October day we loaded my luggage into the back of her ancient green station wagon, pushing aside bags of old sweaters, skirts, shoes, and purses—items she had picked up to sell in her vintage clothes shop.

"I hope you don't mind the smell of mothballs," Ginny said.

"No problem," I replied.

"How about the smell of a car burning oil?"

"That's okay, too."

"We can open the windows," she told me. "Of course, the muffler's near gone."

I laughed. Blond and freckled, she had the same southernish accent as my mother. I felt comfortable with her right away.

When I was buckled in, Ginny handed me a map so I could follow our progress toward Wisteria, which is on the Eastern Shore of the Chesapeake Bay.

"It's about a two-hour drive," she said. "I told Mrs. Barnes I'd have you at Scarborough House well before dark."

"I'm getting curious," I told her. "When Mom left Maryland, she didn't bring any pictures with her. I've seen a few photos that my uncle Paul sent, showing him and Mom playing when they were little, but you can't see the house in them. What's it like?"

"What has your mother told you about it?" Ginny asked.

"Not much. There's a main house with a back wing. It's old."

"That's about it," Ginny said.

It was a short answer from a person who had spent a lot of time there as a child and teenager—nearly as short as my mother's answers about the place.

"Oh, and it's haunted," I added.

"People say that," Ginny replied.

I looked at her, surprised. I had been joking.

"Of course, every old house on the Shore has its ghost

stories," she added quickly. "Just keep the lights on if it feels spooky."

This trip might turn out to be more interesting than I thought.

Ginny turned on the radio, punching in a country station. I opened the map she had given me and studied it. The Sycamore River cut into the Eastern Shore at an angle. If you were traveling up the Chesapeake Bay, you'd enter the wide river mouth of the Sycamore and head in a northeasterly direction. On the right, close to the mouth, you'd see a large creek named Wist. The next creek up is Oyster. The town of Wisteria sits between them, nearly surrounded by water, the Sycamore River on one side and the creeks on the other two. As for my grandmother's property, it was the large point of land below the town, washed on one side by Wist Creek and on the other side by the Sycamore.

We crossed two sets of railroad tracks. I watched the scenery change from outlet stores to fields of corn and soy and low horizons of trees. The sky was half the world on the Eastern Shore. Ginny asked a lot of questions and seemed more interested in talking about life in Tucson than life in Wisteria.

"What's my grandmother like?" I asked at last.

For a full minute the only response was the roar of the car engine.

"She's, uh, different," Ginny said. "We're coming up on Oyster Creek. Wisteria's just on the other side."

"Different how?" I persisted.

"She has her own way of seeing things. She can be fierce at times."

"Do people like her?"

Ginny hesitated. "Have you spent much time in a small town?" she asked.

"No."

"Small-town folks are like a big family living in one house. They can be real friendly and helpful, but they can also say nasty things about each other and squabble a lot."

She hadn't answered my question about how others saw my grandmother, but I could figure it out. She wasn't the town favorite.

We rumbled over the metal grating of the drawbridge. I hung my head out the window for a moment. In Tucson, creeks were often just trickles. This one was the width of a river.

"We're on Scarborough Street now," Ginny said. "The streets off to our right lead down to the commercial docks, where the oyster and crab boats are. The streets to the left border the college. In a few blocks we'll be crossing over High Street, which is Main Street for us. Want to drive down it?"

"Sure."

We passed a school, went a block farther, then took a right onto High. The street had a mix of houses, churches, and small shops, all of the buildings made of brick or wood. Some of the houses edged right up to the sidewalk; a few had tiny plots of grass in front of them. Pots of bright chrysanthemums perched on windowsills and steps. The sidewalks on both sides of High Street were brick and ripply, especially around the roots of the sycamore trees that lined the street. But even where there weren't roots, the brick looked softened, as if the footprints of two and a half centuries had been worn into it.

"It's pretty," I said. "Are there a lot of wisteria vines around here?"

"People grow it," she said, "but actually, the parcel of land that became the town was won in a card game called whist. That was the town's original name. Some upright folks in the 1800s, who didn't approve of gambling, added to it. I guess we're lucky they weren't playing Crazy Eights."

I laughed.

"There's my shop, Yesterdaze." Ginny slowed down and pointed to a storefront with a large, paned window that bowed out over the sidewalk. "Next door is Tea Leaves. Jamie, the owner, makes pastries to die for.

"The town harbor is ahead of us," she went on. "Only

pleasure boats dock there now. I'm going to swing around to Bayview Avenue and show you where I live. You know you're welcome to stay with me if things get difficult."

"Difficult how?" I asked.

She shrugged. "I find it isolated out there on the other side of the Wist. And Scarborough House seems awfully big without a family to fill it up."

"Is that why my grandmother invited me? She can't get anybody else to come?"

"I doubt *that's* the reason. Mrs. Barnes has never liked company—whoa!" Ginny exclaimed, hitting her brakes hard, sending shoe boxes tumbling over the seat from the back of the station wagon.

A guy in an open-topped Jeep, impatient to get around a car making a turn, had suddenly cut in front of us. The backseat passengers of the red Jeep, two girls and a guy, held on to one another and hooted. The girl in the front seat turned briefly to look at us, laughing and tossing her long hair. The driver didn't acknowledge his near miss.

"Jerk," I said aloud.

Ginny looked amused. "That was your cousin."

"My cousin?" I twisted in my seat, to look down the side street where the Jeep had made another sudden turn.

"Matt Barnes," she replied.

"I thought he was in Chicago."

"Your uncle moved there, and Matt's mother is somewhere in the North, I believe."

"Boston," I told her. It had been an ugly divorce, I knew that much.

"Matt has spent nearly every summer in Wisteria. He transferred to the high school here last winter and is living full-time with your grandmother. You didn't know that?"

I shook my head.

"She bought him the Jeep this past summer. Rumor has it he's getting his own boat. Matt's usually carting around jocks or girls."

Spoiled and wild, I thought. But things were looking up. No matter what he was like, spending two weeks with a guy my own age was better than being alone with a fierce seventy-six-year-old. I'd just fasten my seat belt and go along for the ride.

"Does my grandmother drive?" I asked.

"Pretty much like Matt," Ginny replied, laughing.

When we got to Bayview, she pointed out her house, a soft yellow cottage with gray shutters, then returned to Scarborough Road.

We crossed the Wist, rumbling over an old bridge, drove about a quarter mile more, then turned right between two brick pillars. The private road that led to my grandmother's started out paved, but crumbled into gravel and dirt. Tall, conical cedar trees lined both sides. They did not bend gracefully over the drive, as trees do in pictures of southern mansions, but stood upright, like giant green game pieces. At the end of the double row of trees I saw sections of sloping gray roof and brick chimneys, four of them.

"We're coming up behind the house," Ginny said. "The driveway loops around to the front. You're seeing the back wing. That picket fence runs along the herb garden by the kitchen."

"The house is huge."

"Remember that you are welcome to stay with me," she said.

"Thanks, but I'll be fine."

Now that I was here, I was looking forward to the next two weeks. I mean, how much of a terror could one little old woman be? It'd be fun to explore the old house and its land, especially with a cousin my age. Four hundred acres of fields and woods and waterfront—it seemed unbelievable that I didn't have to share them with other hikers in a state park. A wave of excitement and confidence washed over me. Then Ginny circled the house and parked in front.

"Megan," she said, after a moment of silence, "Megan, are you all right?"

I nodded.

"I'll help you with your luggage."

"Thanks."

I climbed out of the car slowly, staring up at Grandmother's house. Three stories of paned windows, brick with a shingled roof, a small covered porch with facing benches—it was the house in my dreams.

I took my luggage from Ginny, feeling a little shaky. For the second time in twenty-four hours, I walked up the steps of the house. This time the door swung open.

two

"WELL, WHAT IS it?" asked a short, heavyset woman whose hair was tipped orange from an old peroxide job.

"I'm here to see Mrs. Barnes." My voice sounded timid as a child's.

Ginny climbed the porch steps behind me. "Nancy, this is Megan, Mrs. Barnes's granddaughter."

Nancy's response was to turn her back and retreat into the house. I glanced questioningly at my mother's friend.

"Nancy comes in three times a week to cook and clean for your grandmother," Ginny informed me in a low voice.

"Is she always this friendly?"

"'Fraid so."

Without stepping inside, I peered down the long, unlit center hall. Nancy stopped at a door near the foot of the stairway, knocked, then entered. When she returned to us, she spoke to Ginny. "Mrs. Barnes wants to know how much she owes you for bringing the girl and whether you'd accept a check."

A look of surprise flickered across Ginny's face. "Please tell her it was my pleasure."

"Thanks for picking me up, Ginny," I said, slightly embarrassed.

"Sure thing. You know where to find me." She squeezed my hand and left.

Score one for Grandma, I thought as I lugged my bags inside the house: I hadn't even met her and already she'd made me feel like an inconvenience.

Nancy, having emerged a second time from the room by the stairs, fixed me with her eyes, then pointed a thumb over her shoulder. I figured it was a signal for me to go in. There was no chance to ask, since the housekeeper exited quickly through a door at the back of the hall.

I stood by the front door, considering my options. What would happen if I simply waited here? Who would give in first, me or Helen Scarborough Barnes?

I decided to take my time studying the center hall, which ran from the front door of the house to a smaller door under the main stairs, its wide plank floor covered with islands of rugs. I had never been in a hall large enough to contain sofas, side chairs, and tables. Heavy wood doors led into four rooms, two on each side. The broad staircase rose toward the back of the house, turned and climbed several steps against the back wall, then disappeared as it turned again toward the front. A grandfather clock ticked on the stairway landing: 4:25.

"Megan."

The voice was low and firm, used to being obeyed. I took a deep breath and walked down the hall, stopping inside the frame of the door. The room was a library, its dark walls lined with shelves of books. It smelled of leather and old fireplace ashes. I liked it immediately; I wish I could say the same for the white-haired woman who sat stiff-backed behind a desk.

She rose slowly, surprising me with her height. I was three inches taller than my mother, and so was she. Helen Scarborough Barnes observed me so closely I felt as if she were counting the threads in my clothes, adding up them and everything else she saw to see if I passed. Fine. I could study her, too, and decide whether she passed as a grandmother.

She had pale skin and high cheekbones. Her hair, pulled back in a French twist, and tiny drop earrings gave her a kind of elegance despite the fact she was wearing jeans. I met her light blue eyes as steadily as I could.

"You may sit down," she said.

"I'd like to stand, if you don't mind. I've been sitting all day."

There was a slight pause, then she nodded and seated herself. "Just don't pace."

I felt an incredible urge to pace but kept it in check.

"How is your mother doing?" she asked.

"Good—*well*," I corrected my grammar. "Did you know she finished her master's degree? Last month she started a new job. She's at the same school, but as a reading specialist. She loves the kids. She's terrific with them."

I knew I was chattering.

"And your brothers?"

"They're great. Pete, who's twelve, is into music. Dave's ten and lives for sports."

"And your trip here?"

"My father's doing great, too," I said, though she hadn't asked about him. "He was honored by the Sonoran Desert Museum for his work with mammals."

"Please answer only the questions I ask," Grandmother told me.

"Just filling in the details," I responded cheerfully, though we both knew otherwise. I wasn't about to let Dad be cut out of the family.

"How was your trip here?"

"Fine."

She waited a moment, perhaps to see if I'd fill in the details. I didn't.

"I had expected you to come here in the summer, Megan."

"As Mom explained to you, I go to a year-round school and had already committed myself to working at a camp for my three-week summer break. October was the next free time."

"What is your parentage?"

The sudden question took me aback. I stared at her for a long moment. "My mother is Carolyn Barnes, my father, Kent Tilby," I said, as if that were news.

"You know what I mean, girl."

I pressed my lips together.

"Your coloring is . . . unusual," she observed.

I decided not to reply. I have straight black hair, which I keep shoulder length, gray eyes, and skin that refuses to tan. In the bronze land of Arizona, I stand out like a white mushroom, but I didn't think that was the point of her comment.

Correctly deducing that she wasn't going to get any information about my birth parents, Helen Barnes rose from her chair. "I will show you your room."

I followed her into the hall, fuming. I don't know what I had hoped for from her. An effort to get to know me, a conversation that lasted longer than three minutes and revealed some interest in me, other than genetic? Some shyness or awkwardness that told me that she, too, had intense feelings about this first meeting? There was no such sign. Her eyes could have iced over the Gulf of Mexico.

"You will see the downstairs first," she said.

I nodded. Apparently, "Would you like to?" wasn't part of her vocabulary.

She showed me the three other rooms that opened off the center hall. Like the library, each had a high ceiling and corner fireplace, but their walls were painted in bolder colors: peacock blue in the front parlor, bright mustard in the music room. The dining room, which was at the back of the main house and across the hall from the library, was blood red. All of the rooms had paintings with heavy gilt frames; the theme in the gory-colored dining room was animals and hunting. I hoped we ate in the kitchen.

"When was this house built?" I asked, abruptly turning away from an impaled deer.

"In 1720," my grandmother answered, "by a family named Winchester."

"When did our family move in?"

The Scarboroughs bought the house, the land, and the mill in the mid-1800s."

"Is that when our family came over from England?"

"The Scarboroughs"—she said the name clearly, as if to make a distinction between that family and what I called *our* family—"have been in Maryland since the 1600s. This land was purchased by the seventh generation as a wedding gift for a son." She led the way back into the hall. "Carry whatever luggage you can," she told me, resting a thin hand on the curved banister. "Matt will bring up the rest when he gets home from his study session."

Study session? I thought. Better not mention that my cousin had come close to hitting Ginny's car when he was supposed to be hitting the books. I carried all of my luggage.

The trim in the upstairs hall was the same blue as the parlor's, but the walls were softened by faded wallpaper. A mirror, darkened with age, hung on one wall; on another were several photographs, old tintypes. My grandmother grew impatient as I looked at them.

"Megan." She waited by the door at the top of the stairs, the only one open in the hall.

I entered and set down my bags. The square room had a fireplace in one corner and a four-poster bed in the center. Though the inside shutters had been pulled back and the windows opened, there was a musty smell, reminding me that a river was near.

"Where's the water?" I asked, quickly crossing to a window. "On the map it looked close to the house. Oh, my gosh, the trees!" I couldn't hide my enthusiasm. "I've never seen so much green, not in Tucson. Look, their tops are just turning gold."

My grandmother, not interested in looking, remained in the doorway. "You can see the creek and river when the leaves have fallen. These old homes were not built directly on the water because of the insects. Now they spray."

"Oh."

"I'll leave you to unpack," she said. "Your bathroom is through that door. Dinner is at six. If there is anything you need—"

"What am I supposed to call you?"

She hesitated.

"What does my cousin call you?" I asked.

"Grandmother."

"That's cool."

I don't think she thought so, but she didn't object. She reached back for the door handle to pull it closed behind her. "Just so we understand each other, Megan. I will respect your privacy and assume you will respect mine."

I gazed after her as she shut the door. What was *that* supposed to mean? I had been respecting her privacy for the last sixteen years. If she didn't want to open the door between us now, why had she bothered to invite me?

I glanced around the bedroom. The rooms in this house were big—formal downstairs, and simple, almost stark, upstairs. To my relief, they were nothing like the cozy room where I often played in my dream. That would have been a little too weird. There were explanations for the outward resemblance of the two houses. Mom might have described her home to me long ago, when I was too young to know I shouldn't ask about it. Or maybe I'd seen a picture of a colonial house that resembled this one. Now and then Mom subscribed to East Coast magazines that had photos of old homes. There were probably just a few basic styles.

I unpacked my clothes, then lifted out several small, framed pictures and set them on the bureau, smiling at the menagerie of people and critters. Dad's a veterinarian and Mom volunteers at an animal shelter. Our home is a small zoo, and I'm not just referring to my brothers.

I put on a clean shirt and took out a comb, running it through my hair, then looked around the room for a mirror. Above a dressing table, where a mirror usually would hang, was a framed piece of embroidery: the Ten Commandments. *Well, that's nice,* I thought, *a friendly reminder to guests to behave themselves!* I used the mirror on the medicine cabinet in the small bath attached to my room.

As I emerged from the bathroom, I heard my cousin's Jeep circling the house. I quickly finished putting away my things and headed downstairs. At last I had someone my age to hang out with.

When I reached the landing with the clock, I could hear his voice.

"She shouldn't have come. I told you before, Grandmother, it was a bad idea to invite her."

Surprised, I leaned forward to hear Grandmother's response, but she spoke too softly.

"It's just a gut feeling," my cousin said. "No, it's more than that. You haven't been acting like yourself since you first got this crazy idea."

I walked noiselessly down the steps, straining to hear Grandmother's answer, but the library door was partially closed and her voice muffled.

"I really don't care," Matt insisted loudly. "She's not my cousin—she's adopted—and you've always been the first to point that out. I can't believe you didn't tell me she was coming today. I don't know what you're up to."

This time I was close enough to hear Grandmother. "Worried?" she asked.

It was tempting to sneak up on them. But two long weeks loomed ahead and embarrassing Matt wouldn't make things easier. Give him a chance to change his mind, I told myself. I pounded down the last few steps, so they would hear me and have time to switch topics.

Grandmother was sitting at her desk again. Matt's backpack was on the floor, his back turned to me.

"Hello, Megan," Grandmother said, then glanced in Matt's direction.

"Hello," I replied, and followed her glance. Matt reached for a book high up on a shelf and began to page through it, keeping his back to me. I doubted he was as interested in the book as he pretended.

Well, okay. I could play this game. I sat down with my back to him.

"Grandmother," I said, "I was hoping you'd have some family pictures hanging up."

"There are three in the upstairs hall," she replied.

"The ones from the 1800s? They're cool. I was hoping you might have some of my grandfather and you. I'd love to see pictures of Mom and Uncle Paul when they were growing up." I glanced around the room. Despite the space available on the desk, the long fireplace mantel, and walls of shelves, there wasn't a family photograph in sight.

"I don't like to display photographs," she said.

"Oh. Well, do you have some picture albums?"

"No."

"How come?" I asked.

"I don't approve of taking pictures of ourselves. It's vain. It glorifies our own image."

I frowned. "It also allows us to remember the people we loved."

Out of the corner of my eye, I saw Matt turn his head slightly.

"You mentioned my cousin," I said. "Does he visit Wisteria often?"

Her eyes flicked sideways, watching Matt. "He lives here."

"Oh, good! Will he be here for dinner?"

I caught the look of amusement in her eyes. "Yes."

"What's he like?"

A sly smile lit the corners of her mouth, as if she were enjoying the game. "You'll have to decide for yourself, Megan."

"Good point. It's not fair to judge people before you actually meet them."

The pleasure she took in our rude standoff convinced me to put an end to it. I rose and walked over to my cousin. "Just so I don't misinterpret things," I said, "I want to know, are you shy or a snob?"

He carefully closed the book and set it back on its shelf, so I got a good look at his profile, a tanned face that was too strongly cut to be described as "cute." His hair was brown and thick.

When he finally turned to me, I was ready to glare back and treat him to what my brothers call "the hot coals." But his eyes took me by surprise. They were dark and beautiful, fathoms deep, like a river on a moonless night. Now I knew why three girls were riding around with him in his Jeep.

We both took a step back. His intense gaze made me unsteady. "I'm Megan," I said, anchoring my hands in my pockets so I wouldn't twist my hair.

"Matt."

He kept staring at me. I waited for him to say more, but he didn't. I wished he was either less good-looking or less of a jerk. I'd rather not be drawn to rude and arrogant guys. Until now, I hadn't been.

"Nice to meet you," I told him.

He nodded, then turned and walked past me to pick up his backpack. "Are we eating at six, Grandmother?"

"As always," she replied.

Apparently our little family reunion was over. "May I go for a walk before dinner?" I asked. "I'd like to look around."

"Keep the house in view," Grandmother warned. "We don't want to have to search for you."

"Would anybody like to come with me?" I added, giving friendliness another try. Maybe Matt would behave better when Grandmother wasn't around.

"No." Her reply was blunt, but it was more of a response than I got from my cousin, who left the room silently.

"Sorry, Matt," I called. "I didn't hear your answer."

He turned back in the hall, a flash of annoyance in his eyes. "No. No, thank you."

I shrugged, wishing it was as easy to toss off the strange attraction I felt toward him.

After promising Grandmother I wouldn't get lost, I headed outside. I made a circle of the house, awed by the expanse of lawn and even more, the tall trees. I found the herb garden, which fit neatly into the L-shape created by the main house and back wing. The brush of my fingers against the plants shook loose a dozen delicious smells. When I exited through the picket gate, I saw what appeared to be another garden, surrounded by a red brick wall with creamy roses tumbling over it. I hadn't noticed it when Ginny drove in, for it was on the far side of the circular drive and I had been focusing on the house. Curious, I strode toward it.

As I got closer, I could see that it was a cemetery, probably a family burial plot. I opened the wrought-iron gate and stepped inside. Some of the gravestones were extremely old, round-shouldered, and leaning forward as if they were tired, their names and dates no longer readable. There were new markers made of shiny granite and I walked over to look at them.

Thomas Barnes, I read. My mother's father. I touched his stone lightly, then turned to the marker next to his. It was fancier, with roses carved into it. *Avril Scarborough.* The name echoed in my mind, as if someone had spoken it from the end of a very long hall. I read her dates, then drew back. I did the math again: She was just sixteen when she died—she was my age.

The grave gave me an eerie feeling. I didn't want to touch her stone. I turned, suddenly compelled to get out of there. As I left I glanced toward the house. The lowering sun flared off the panes of glass; still, I noticed it, the movement of someone stepping back from a second-floor window, as if trying not to be seen. After a moment I realized the person had been watching me from my bedroom. I walked quickly toward the house, but the reflected light made it impossible to see in.

A vague uneasiness seeped into me. Since my arrival, neither Grandmother nor Matt seemed interested in getting to know me. But obviously, someone was interested enough to keep an eye on me.

three

I RETURNED TO the house forty minutes later, feeling a million times better, full of the clear blue and gold light of the river and setting sun. I entered by way of the herb garden, walking up onto a covered porch and opening a door that led into the back hall. The small hall, which ran under the stairs, connected the back wing with the center hall of the main house. It had service doors to the dining room and library, and steps leading down to the back wing.

There I found Grandmother in a kitchen with a huge open hearth. An old stove sat halfway inside the blackened fireplace. She stood next to it, stirring something in a pot.

"So you found your way back," she said.

"Yes. I saw the river. It's awesome."

"Then you must not have kept the house in sight," Grandmother observed shrewdly. "You cannot see it from any place along the riverbank, not this time of year."

"I, uh, guess I did lose sight of the chimneys. But I have a pretty good sense of direction."

She didn't reply.

"Shall I set the table?" I offered.

"It's set."

So we were eating in the dining room with all those appetizing paintings of dying deer and fox.

"You may carry out the meat and biscuits. The rest will get cold if Matt—well, it's about time," she told him as he came through the door.

"It's three minutes to six," he replied mildly, then joined her at the stove and began dishing out the greens. I may as well have been a kitchen stool he walked past.

I carried out the platter of meat, then biscuits. He and Grandmother brought the soup and green beans. Grandmother sat at the head of the table with Matt at her right, which left me the seat across from him. As luck would have it, I was also across from the goriest deer of the hunting series.

"We always pray first," Grandmother said as I pulled up my chair.

She folded her hands, resting them on the edge of the table, so I did the same. Matt stared down at his plate.

"Dear Lord," Grandmother began, "forgive us our trespasses this day. Though we lie with our lips and our hearts, call us back to your truth, and grant us mercy rather than the justice we deserve. Amen."

It was the gloomiest dinner prayer I'd ever heard. "Maybe we should give thanks, too," I suggested, "as long as we're praying before a meal."

Matt glanced up.

"You may pray however you like on your own," Grandmother replied, then handed me the ham. "I *am* relieved to see your parents didn't bring you up to be a complete heathen, though, no doubt, they've passed on some kooky ideas."

"No doubt," I said cheerfully. She wasn't going to drag me and them down. I took a little of the meat, more of the green beans, and one very hard biscuit. A bowl of thick soup was dished out for me.

What appeared to be ham was so salty I could hardly swallow it. It was as if someone had glued fake bacon bits together, then sliced them ultra thin. "What do you call this kind of meat?" I asked.

"Smithfield ham," said Grandmother. "It's a tradition."

I took a long drink of water, ate another mouthful, then bit into a rock-hard biscuit.

"Those are beaten biscuits," Grandmother told me. "Another tradition."

Some of that traditional airplane food I'd turned down

was looking pretty good now. I sampled the green beans, then gobbled them up.

"Try your stew," Grandmother ordered.

I pulled the bowl closer and spooned lumps of grayish-white stuff.

"They're not raw," Matt said, "not when they're in the stew."

"*What's* not raw?" I asked, setting down my spoon.

"The oysters."

I ate one mouthful. It was the slimiest seafood I'd ever tasted, swimming in heavy cream. "May I have the green beans, please?"

"You're not a vegetarian, are you?" Grandmother asked. "I refuse to feed you if you are."

"I'm trying a little of everything, Grandmother," I replied patiently, "but I have always liked green beans." *I* used *to like biscuits,* I thought, taking another bite of the hard, flat thing.

"It would be just like her parents to raise her as an animal rights extremist," Grandmother said to Matt. "The two of them have always had strange ideas."

It annoyed me to be referred to in the third person, and it hurt to hear my parents put down, but I kept my cool.

"Dad doesn't like hunting," I admitted, "which isn't real surprising since he's a vet. But as you know, Grandmother, his father was an Eastern Shore farmer. Dad was raised on meat and still eats it."

"It's unnatural to avoid meat," she went on.

"Look," I exclaimed, frustrated, "I am *not* a vegetarian! Though the paintings in this room are pushing me in that direction."

Matt's eyes flicked around the room, then came back to me. His dark gaze was unreadable, but at least he'd given up the pretension of not seeing me.

"So what is your mother up in arms about these days?" Grandmother asked. "Migrant workers, I bet."

She knew Mom better than I thought. Two letters on migrant living conditions had been sent to senators last week.

To Matt, Grandmother said, "Carolyn marched for integration, raising taxes for education, luxury condos for chickens—for everything but common sense."

"That's an exaggeration," I countered. "For the chickens she supported two-bedroom apartments."

Matt's mouth twitched, but he remained silent. Grandmother grimly ate her ham and biscuits. Obviously, she had no sense of humor, which meant I wasn't going to be able to joke my way out of an argument.

"College ruined her," Grandmother went on. "It made her a sloppy thinker."

"Mom says that when she arrived at college she found out how narrow-minded she was."

Grandmother laid down her fork. "There was nothing narrow about Carolyn's mind. When she left my house she saw the world clearly and knew right from wrong. After four years away she became hopelessly muddled."

"It is easy to see clearly, when all you see are black and white," I argued, "when you believe that everything has to be one or the other. But it doesn't."

"What is clear to me is that you weren't raised with manners," Grandmother countered, her eyes glittering. She didn't like me, but she liked conflict. "You weren't taught respect for your elders."

"I was. But I don't fake well, and despite what Mom and Dad say, I don't respect people who don't respect others."

A long silence followed. I chewed and listened to the clink of silverware.

At last Matt pushed back his chair. "I'm going to a movie tonight. Alex is picking me up."

"What movie?" Grandmother asked.

"*Sheer Blue.* It just opened at the theater on High Street."

"That film got a great review in the Tucson paper," I said. "I've been wanting to see it." Maybe he'd take the hint and ask me along. I was eager to be with kids my own age. "The chase sequence is supposed to be fantastic," I added.

"That's what everyone says," he replied. "I'll be home by one o'clock," he told Grandmother, then rose and picked up his dishes.

I wasn't going to be invited.

"You mean twelve-thirty," Grandmother told him. "Who's going besides Alex?"

"Kristy, Amanda, and Kate."

"Oh, the girls you were studying with today," I ventured casually.

He turned around, surprised.

"It's just Alex that he studies with," Grandmother informed me.

"Really?"

Matt gave me a look, which translated into something like *drop dead*, then left.

I sat sipping water, waiting for Grandmother to finish her meal. When she pushed back her chair, I did the same. "Do you have any special instructions for washing dishes?" I asked.

"We each do our own."

"I'll do yours," I offered. "You did the cooking."

"Nancy does the cooking," she corrected me.

"Well, I'm still glad to do them for you."

But, as she said, we each did our own. Grandmother could not bend in any of her ways.

When the kitchen was cleaned up, she told me it was her custom to read in the evening. I could sit in the library with her, as long as I did not talk or listen to music. Her invitation didn't give me warm and cozy feelings. And I doubted she'd approve of the book I'd picked up at the airport: The cover showed a woman with a torn dress and half-bared breasts running from a big house on a stormy night.

As it turned out, sitting inside a cozy circle of lamplight on the high four-poster bed, with the dense night falling around Grandmother's house, was the perfect way to read a gothic romance. When I heard Grandmother come up, I changed into my nightgown but kept turning pages. The face of the deranged housekeeper started to look like Nancy's and the warm-hearted cook spoke with Ginny's voice. The story melted into the events of the day and my eyes closed.

Two hours later I sat straight up, knocking my book off the bed.

I had been dreaming about the house again, playing in the same cozy room with the sloped ceiling and dormer windows. But my old dream had become so clear, so real, I could hardly believe I was awake in a different room. In the dream I had a new toy: a dollhouse that was a miniature of Grandmother's house.

I threw back the quilt and slid off the edge of the bed. The night was brighter than when I'd fallen asleep, the air colder. I pulled a sweatshirt on over my nightgown, then stood at the window that looked down on the herb garden. The late-rising moon silvered the roofs of the back wing, both the shiny tin over the kitchen porch and the duller wood shingles that peaked above each second-floor window. Dormer windows and a sloped roof! Was my playroom in the back wing? Was it real?

I snatched up my purse and dug for my key chain. It had a penlight anchoring it which, with the moonlight, was bright enough to show my way. I eased open the bedroom door. The hall was lit dimly by a lamp on a side table. All the doors were shut, just as they had been earlier in the day.

I glanced back at my alarm clock: 11:59. I doubted Matt would be home before curfew. I slipped down the wide stairway, hurrying past the grandfather clock. In the shadows it seemed like another person, standing stiff and tall on the landing, watching me with disapproval. Just as I reached the bottom of the steps, it began its long toll of twelve.

A lit wall sconce in the lower hall guided me through the door that led into the back hall. I passed the service entrances to the dining room and library and tiptoed down the steps to the rear wing. I walked through the kitchen and opened a door next to the big hearth, then followed a hall that ended at a corner stair.

As I reached the stair, the sound of an engine caught my attention. Matt was being dropped off. I quickly climbed the narrow, triangular steps.

The room at the top had a low, sloping roof, peaked in the middle, with dormer windows on each side, just as in my dream. But it was empty. I played my penlight over the walls. Its beam flashed off a bright object, a knob. I outlined the rectangle of a built-in cupboard, then walked over and opened it.

Something ran across my feet. I jammed my hand in my mouth to keep from screaming, and then to silence my laughter—nervous laughter. The mouse was probably just as rattled. I shone the penlight inside the cupboard and my grip tightened. There it was, the dollhouse, a smaller version of Scarborough House, accurate down to the dormer windows in the back wing where I was standing.

I slid the house out of the cupboard and into a pool of moonlight, then knelt before it. There were large hinges on the corners which allowed the entire front to be opened as one panel. I gently pulled it back. Inside was miniature furniture, replicas of that in the real house.

I sat back on my heels, trying to come up with a reasonable

explanation for dreaming about something I'd never seen, then seeing it for real. As a little kid, I used to pretend I was going inside the pictures of my books. I'd imagine fairy-tale castles in three dimensions and daydream about living inside them. Among the photos Uncle Paul had sent Mom, I remembered a picture of her Barbie doll. It was possible that the dollhouse was in those photos and that I had imagined going inside it, until it became a house in my dreams.

As for the similarity between this room and my dream room, there were many ways to account for that. The lodge where my family vacationed in Flagstaff had a sloping roof and dormer windows, and I'd always liked the place. It figured that I'd turn it into a playroom inside my dream house.

I closed the front of the dollhouse and slid it back inside the cupboard. When I stood up, I noticed a door that might lead back to my room by an upstairs route, but played it safe and left the way I had come. At the bottom of the narrow stairs I clicked off my penlight and walked noiselessly toward the kitchen. After making sure that Matt wasn't having a late-night snack, I tiptoed through the kitchen and up the steps connecting the wing to the main house. In the back hall I stopped abruptly.

Matt was in the library, sitting at Grandmother's desk, his back to me. He was leaning over a drawer, searching it, opening files and boxes, sifting through contents that I couldn't see. What was he up to?

For a moment I thought of bursting in and asking him, but then I'd have some explaining to do as well. I slipped down the hall and padded upstairs to my room.

four

SATURDAY MORNING MATT and I arrived downstairs at the same time, close to ten o'clock. Grandmother greeted me first. "You've wasted a fine morning."

And good morning to you, too, I thought. But it was a new day and I was determined to make it start out well. "I wish I'd gotten up earlier," I said. "I guess I'm still on Arizona time."

She turned to my cousin. "I don't like being left with the chores, Matt."

"What chores, Grandmother?" he asked, then leaned down from the waist in a runner's stretch.

He was wearing shorts and a T-shirt, which showed off the muscled body of a guy who worked out often. *Stop looking, Megan,* I told myself.

"You live here," Grandmother answered him sharply. "You know what has to be done."

"Yes," he replied, his voice patient, "but what exactly did you need done?"

"My car has to be washed."

"I did it Thursday afternoon, remember?"

"The house gutters must be cleaned."

"I've done most of that. I'll finish up after the football game this afternoon."

"There is raking."

"It would make more sense in another week."

"Is there something I can do?" I asked.

Matt gave me a cool look. I mirrored it, then saw the spark in Grandmother's eye. She enjoyed the fact that we didn't get along.

"I can handle things," he told me.

What *was* his problem? Did he think I was competing for brownie points? He seemed too sure of himself to worry about being anything less than "number one" with her. And even if some of that confidence was an act, he knew how Grandmother felt about adopted children.

As irritated as I was with Matt, I was even more annoyed with myself for continuing to give him chances to be rude. But something defiant in me, something that refused to believe this was the genuine Matt, kept trying.

"Are you going for a run?" I asked.

He nodded.

"Can I go with you?"

He picked up a plastic bottle from the kitchen counter and twisted off the top. "No."

"Why not?"

"I'm doing serious running."

I prickled. "Meaning you don't think I can keep up with you?"

"Maybe you can," he said with a shrug, then took a vitamin.

"Then why not? In twenty-five words or more," I added, tired of his short answers.

He gazed at me with dark brown eyes. "I work hard year-round to keep in shape for lacrosse. I run cross-country, not little loops around a track."

"At home my dad and I do trails through the Catalinas," I told him. "They're low mountains, but next to the Eastern Shore, they look like the Rockies."

He nodded, unimpressed, then opened a different bottle and took another vitamin.

"Tell me," I said, "what kind of supplement do you take to grow an attitude like yours?"

A crack of a smile, just a crack. Then he pushed both bottles toward me. "Help yourself, though I think your attitude's developed enough."

I glanced at the bottles, which contained ordinary vitamins, then sat down at the kitchen table to drink my juice. I wished I had a newspaper to read, something to page through casually while waiting for him to leave. I grabbed a cereal box and studied that until I heard the screen door bang shut. Out of the corner of my eye I saw Grandmother mark a page in her Bible, then put it on a shelf by the window.

She returned to the table, resting her hands on the back of a chair. "You're not at all like your mother."

I glanced up, surprised. What an odd comment from someone who never forgot I wasn't related by birth! "Did you expect me to be?"

"Children learn from the person with whom they live. Even as a teenager, your mother was sweet-natured and gentle with people. She never had a harsh comment for anyone."

"Still doesn't," I said, setting aside the cereal box.

"So where did you get that sharp tongue?" Grandmother asked.

I sighed and stood up. "Don't know. Where did your child get her gentleness?"

I went for a run by myself that morning, following Scarborough Road away from town, passing field after field of harvested corn. I knew better than to expect an invitation to the football game that afternoon. After a long shower and a quick brunch, I asked Grandmother if she wanted to do some shopping in town. She informed me that she only mixed with "the riffraff" when absolutely necessary.

"I shall tell Matt to drop you off," she added.

"Thanks, but I can get there myself."

I figured it was only a twenty-minute walk to the stores on High Street, and I was too proud to accept any ride she had commanded.

In the early afternoon I crossed the bridge over Wist Creek. When I turned onto High Street, I saw a sign advertising "Sidewalk Saturday." About four blocks from the harbor, the shopping district turned into one long sale. Paperbacks were piled in wheelbarrows by the steps of Urspruch's Books. Mobiles and wind chimes dangled from the sycamore tree in front of Faye's Gallery. Teague's Antiques had transformed its patch of bricks into a Victorian parlor with chairs and a sofa. Groups of people strolled in and out of the small shops, some of the crowd walking in the street. Cars crept along, apparently used to this weekend style of life.

When I arrived at Yesterdaze, Ginny barely had time to say hello. Her shop clerk had gone home ill, which left Ginny trying to guide shoppers and cover the register.

"Want some help?" I asked. "I work at Dad's animal hospital. I know how to count change and do credit card purchases."

"Oh, honey, it's your vacation."

"But I'd like to," I told her. "Matt doesn't want to hang out with me. Grandmother doesn't want to hang out with anyone. This would give me something to do."

Ginny played with the amber beads around her neck. "Well, I could sure use a hand," she admitted, her eyes darting after a customer. "You're on."

Wearing a work apron embroidered with the shop's name, armed with credit forms and a money box, I took my place at a table outside. I bagged and boxed. I read price tags and squinted at driver's licenses, copying their numbers onto checks. Some customers were locals, but more were visitors, many from Baltimore and Philadelphia. I enjoyed watching the parade of people and listening to the conversations around me. I learned that shoppers are not as easy to deal with as dogs and cats.

A senior citizen with salon-molded hair argued with Ginny for selling a jacket she had asked Ginny to hold over two months ago. Her nurse companion, a heavyset woman, forty-something, picked through the lace handkerchiefs on the table next to me. "She'll go on like this for another five minutes," said the aide. "Maybe ten. We've argued our way down two blocks of High Street. Always do."

"Sounds like you don't have an easy job," I replied sympathetically.

She shrugged. "Easier than the last one. Pay's better too. Mrs. Barnes thinks it's still 1950."

I looked up from the roll of quarters I had just cracked open. "Mrs. Barnes?"

"Out Scarborough House." The woman kept wrinkling her nose and sniffling, while looking at the elegant handkerchiefs. I was afraid she was going to use one.

"Guess you're not from these parts," she said.

"I, uh, just arrived."

"Well, let me put it this way. Mrs. Barnes makes *her*"—she gestured toward the older woman—"seem like a saint to live with. As for that spooky old house on the Wist, where she'll let you board 'cause she's paying you peanuts, well, I wouldn't live there for any amount of money."

"How come?" I asked, curious.

"It's haunted."

My eyes widened. The woman saw she had an interested audience.

"My sister warned me," she chattered on. "Said it wasn't just the house. It was the family. None of them Scarboroughs was quite right in the head. That's why Mrs. Barnes's daughter ran off like she did. She had to get away."

"From what?"

"Avril Scarborough, I suppose."

I recognized the name from the gravestone.

"She was murdered, you know."

"Murdered!" I repeated with disbelief.

The woman's head bobbed. "The family covered it up. Said it was an accident. It wasn't."

"How do you know it wasn't?" I asked.

"I've seen the ghost. In the rear wing, the room above the kitchen, the only night I stayed there. Say what you want, but happy dead folks don't come back to haunt."

"Alice," the older woman hissed. "I'm ready to go."

"Never asks if *I'm* ready," Alice muttered to me, then stepped forward to take the woman's arm and guide her down the street.

I stared after them. My mother would have told me if someone in her family had been murdered. *It's just gossip compounded by Alice's imagination,* I thought.

For the next hour we were extremely busy. Still, as I ran my finger down a tax table and stuffed tissue in boxes, I found myself wondering what could have spawned Alice's story. Small-town boredom? Jealousy of a family that had more money than others? Or was there a suspicious event that could be interpreted that way?

I became so lost in thought, I didn't hear what a customer had just said to me. "I'm sorry. What?"

The red-haired girl gazed back at me with wide, clear eyes and smiled a little. "I didn't say anything."

I was certain she had, but perhaps it was the blond girl who had stopped with two friends to sort through items on our sidewalk tables. She looked like the passenger I'd seen in the front seat of Matt's Jeep yesterday. Her two friends echoed whatever opinion she had. She liked the beaded purses, so they liked the beaded purses. She thought the jewelry was for old ladies, so they thought the jewelry was for old ladies.

I noticed that the redhead looked up at the girls once or twice, as if to say hello, but they didn't acknowledge her. *Snobs,* I thought. She seemed used to it and went back to her own browsing, lifting up a silver chain that dangled a clear blue stone. The gem had the same mystical look as her eyes.

"Try it on," I told her. "There's a mirror inside the store."

She quickly put it down. "I can't buy it."

"So? Doesn't mean you can't try it on."

She looked at me uncertainly, then smiled, picked up the pendant, and went inside.

When I turned to a woman waiting to buy a lace collar, I saw the two echoes watching me, but the blond quickly got their attention with a comment about the shop's ugly old jewelry. I focused on finding my customer the right-size box, pulling out a flat piece of cardboard, then fitting the tabs into their slots.

"Matt! Hey, Matt!" the blonde called out, and I glanced up.

My cousin and three other guys strode toward her and her friends.

So that's what you look like when you smile, I thought. It was a terrific smile, I noted grudgingly, then lined my customer's box with tissue.

"Hi, Kristy," he greeted the blond. "Amanda, Kate."

"We missed you," Kristy said to him. "We didn't see you at the game."

"Oh, I think you did," he replied lightly. "I was sitting with Charles, remember?"

"Your sports buddy." I heard the sneer in her voice; raising my head, I saw it on her face.

"He's my teammate," Matt said, still smiling. "You're always sitting with your teammates," he added, nodding at the echoes.

Boy, did he know how to flirt with those eyes! The girls on either side of her giggled.

"They're friends," she told him, in a fake, quarreling voice. "We don't play a sport."

"Partying," he said. "Isn't that one?"

They all laughed.

I stamped my customer's check with an irritated thump. Why was he so flirty and charming to some people and such a jerk to me? I handed the package to my customer.

"Thanks very much. Come again," I said quietly.

Apparently, not quietly enough. I was turning my George Washingtons face up, counting the singles when I realized that Matt's group of friends had stopped talking. I looked up to see him staring at me.

"What are you doing here?" he asked. He sounded as if he'd caught me trespassing.

"Working. You got a problem with that?"

The blond-haired guy next to Matt glanced sideways at him and smiled.

"You're supposed to be visiting Grandmother," he told me.

"I don't remember clearing my schedule with you."

His friend laughed out loud, which annoyed Matt.

"In fact," I added, "I don't remember *you* showing an interest in anything I was doing."

Everyone but the grinning guy looked uncomfortable. Kristy moved closer to my cousin. "Who is she?"

I prickled at her tone.

"Megan, my cousin, sort of," Matt replied.

"What do you mean by sort of?" asked the smiling guy.

"Matt's father is my uncle, sort of," I said.

The guy looked from Matt to me. There was a brightness in his blue eyes, a spark of laughter. I liked him immediately. "So, who are you?" I asked bluntly.

"Alex Rodowsky." He held out his right hand. "Your sort-of cousin's friend. I hope he's not grouchy like this at home."

"He is."

Matt scowled.

"When he starts it with me," Alex said, "I just ignore him."

"Is he like this a lot?" I asked. "How long does he stay this way?"

What a scowl!

"Don't you know? You're his cousin," Alex pointed out.

"We met for the first time yesterday. Though Matt has disliked me long before that."

Alex looked puzzled.

I heard Matt suck in his breath and let it out slowly. "Maybe we should talk at home, Megan."

"Why, that would be a nice change!"

He didn't reply.

"Megan?" Ginny called through the door. "Can you give me twenty singles?"

"Be right in," I said, banding the stack of bills I had just counted.

Matt's friends drifted off. The way the girls bent their heads together, I figured they were discussing me. I picked up the cash box to carry inside, but Ginny met me at the door. "Thanks, honey. I don't know what I'd do without you."

I returned to my post in time to see Alex pull Matt back from the departing group.

"What's this sort-of cousin stuff?" he asked, not bothering to keep his voice down, perhaps thinking I was inside. "Is she or isn't she?"

"Legally she is, but not really," Matt replied. "She's adopted."

"Which means you can date her," Alex said. "Are you interested?"

"No," Matt answered quickly.

"Good. I am."

"She's got a mouth," my cousin warned.

His friend shrugged. "Makes it easier to kiss."

Matt must have made a strange face because Alex laughed at him, then walked off to join the others. Matt glanced back over his shoulder. His jaw dropped a little when he realized I was standing there. I turned away just as the redhead was coming from inside the shop.

"Want to see how it looks?" she asked, smiling shyly. "Miss Ginny told me to try these earrings with it. The stone is aquamarine."

"I knew it would look great on you!"

She touched the stone lightly, then reluctantly, reached back for the clasp.

"Too much?"

"Yes," she said, handing it to me.

I glanced at the tag. "Whoa! That's a lot of Big Macs."

I put it back in the velvet case and she set the earrings next to it.

"I'm Sophie. Sophie Quinn."

"Megan Tilby," I told her.

"Nice to meet you. I, uh, was standing at the door when Matt was talking to Alex," Sophie said. "Matt's your cousin?"

"Legally." *Darn,* I thought; *now* I'm *making that distinction.* "I'm visiting for two weeks."

"I hope you have a real good time. I probably shouldn't ask this, but has Matt told you anything about the girls at school and, well, who he likes?"

I started to laugh at the thought of him confiding in me, then stifled it, realizing Sophie might have a crush on him. "Why? Are you interested in him?"

She blushed a little. "Every girl in the senior class is interested in him," she told me. "And Matt never lets on who he really likes, which makes all the girls crazy."

I shook my head. "Sorry, I don't have a clue. I don't really know him."

Sophie nodded. "I guess he's just one of those people who gets along with everyone."

Nearly everyone, I thought.

five

At four o'clock Ginny told me to take a break and sent me to Tea Leaves with some money. Figuring that tonight's dinner would be leftovers from last night's, I splurged and got a piece of chocolate cheesecake.

The café was a comfortable place with a worn tile floor and painted tables and chairs, none of the sets matching. At the back was a long glass case filled with bakery items, as well as a refrigerator case with yogurt and salads. A lady with fuzzy hair and a man who looked like a fifty-year-old Pillsbury Doughboy waited on customers. The man had a round, pleasant face that creased easily into a smile. He called many of the customers by name.

I carried my dessert to a table by the bay window, glad for a chance to sit down. There was a sign in the window, its letters faded but readable: FORTUNES TOLD HERE. Well, I didn't need a psychic to tell me I was headed for two tough weeks. *Why did*

Matt dislike me so much? I wondered. I had never had trouble making friends. It was as if he'd made up his mind about me before we'd met.

I took a forkful of cheesecake, then another. Stop trying to figure Matt out, I told myself. He's a jerk.

"Everything okay?"

The round-faced man had come from behind the counter to wipe down tables. "If you don't like your selection, help yourself to something else."

I realized I must have been frowning.

"Whatever you want. On the house," he added.

"Oh, no!" I said quickly. "It's the best cheesecake I've ever had."

He smiled. "And you know, it doesn't have a single calorie—as long as you just look at it." He laughed at his own joke and I laughed with him. "You're not one of my regulars," he observed. "Just visiting for the day?"

"For a couple weeks," I replied. "I'm staying with my grandmother."

"And who might that be?"

"Helen Barnes."

He stopped wiping a table and gazed at me with surprise. I readied myself for another strange Scarborough story, but as it turned out, I was the cause for amazement.

"I didn't know she had a granddaughter."

"And two grandsons," I said. "I mean in addition to Matt. I have two younger brothers."

He straightened up. "Really! So you all must be Carolyn's children."

"Carolyn and Kent Tilby." I worked hard to keep my voice from sounding brittle. It wasn't this man's fault that Grandmother never mentioned us.

"The Tilbys. They had a farm up Oyster Creek. But they passed away."

I nodded.

"Carolyn and Kent hooked up in college. I remember now. I just didn't know they had kids. Well, welcome. It's a pleasure to have you. Tell your folks Jamie says hi. Riley's the last name, though nobody calls me anything but Jamie." He held out a damp hand and I shook it. "Back when they knew me, my father ran this place, and I had dreams bigger than puff pastry. But it turned out baking is what I do well," he added.

"Really well," I agreed, sliding another bite of cheesecake into my mouth. "Who does the fortune-telling?"

"My mother." He glanced toward the window. I should get rid of that sign. She's getting too old. Of course she's always happy to do a reading for a local. How about it? I'm sure Mama would be interested to meet you," he added before I could refuse. "She's known the Scarboroughs all her life. When she was a teenager, she worked for them, even lived at the house for a while."

"She did?" His mother would probably know if there was anything to Alice's story. "I'd love to have my fortune told."

"I'll call upstairs and ask if she's free. We live right above here," he added, pointing to the stairway that ran up the side wall of the café. "Makes it an easy commute to work."

I smiled. "Thanks."

After finishing the cheesecake, I walked over to the bakery case to buy some pastries for Ginny and muffins for myself. I had just made my final selection when I heard Jamie's voice behind me: "Here she is, Mama."

I turned around. Mrs. Riley was a small woman with dark brown hair, my grandmother's age or older.

"Mama, this is Megan Tilby."

"Hi, Mrs. Riley."

She looked at me but didn't speak.

"This is Mrs. Barnes's granddaughter," Jamie added a moment later. "Carolyn and Kent's girl," he said, as if trying to nudge a response from her.

But she just stared at me. The hair dye she used made her face look pale. The lines around her mouth were deep.

"Hi," I said again, a little louder this time, in case she had trouble hearing. "It's nice to meet you."

I held out my hand. She didn't take it.

"Mama?" Jamie seemed as puzzled as I. "This is the young lady who wants her fortune told."

She turned on him, her eyes blazing. "You were a fool to say I'd do it. I will not look into the cards for her." Then she stalked across the room and up the steps, moving quickly for an old woman.

Jamie's face turned red with embarrassment. "I—I don't know what to say," he stammered. "I'm very sorry, Megan. She's not always agreeable, and hasn't been that well lately, but I didn't expect this."

"Don't worry about it," I assured him. "She's probably just tired. I'll come back another time."

He nodded, but still seemed concerned, whether for her feelings or mine, I wasn't sure.

"Really," I said, "it's no big deal."

I paid for my purchases and left, feeling like that woman in mythology—the one who had snakes for hair—Medusa. One look at me, and some people turned to stone.

Grandmother gave me permission to eat with Ginny that evening. We locked up the shop about six thirty and went out to dinner. During the meal, Ginny asked if I'd be interested in filling in for her sick employee starting Monday. I jumped at the chance. I loved all the activity of High Street and was relieved that someone in Wisteria wanted me around.

By the time I got home that evening, Matt had left for a school dance. I joined Grandmother in the library, eager to tell her what and who I had seen in town. But she responded so negatively to the first few things I told her, I gave up well before I got to the strange Mrs. Riley.

I crawled into bed that night exhausted. Even so, I tossed and turned. The tall clock on the stair landing chimed every quarter hour, telling me the amount of rest I didn't get. A cold front was passing through. It rattled shutters and windowpanes and sent wind diving down the house's chimneys. My bedroom door shook so hard it sounded as if someone was trying to get in. I got up and latched it firmly. Finally I drifted into sleep.

It was some time later, when the rough weather had settled down to an eerie silence, that I again became aware of my surroundings. The voice awakened me.

"My name is Avril."

My eyes flew open and I glanced around the room. The whisper lacked the warmth of a human voice. I wasn't sure if it was inside my head or out. I lay as still as possible, listening, my skin prickling.

"My name is Avril."

I sat up and pulled the quilt around me. My skin felt as if it were crawling off my bones. "Who's there?"

Silence.

I gazed at the bedroom door, waiting for something to happen, the knob to turn, the whisperer to whisper again. My breath felt trapped inside my chest, my heart pounded in my ears.

You've got a choice, I told myself. You can cower here for the rest of the night, or you can prove that it was nothing but a voice in a dream, your imagination playing tricks.

I climbed out of bed, then tiptoed to the door. Taking a deep breath, I cracked it slowly, then yanked it wide open.

No one. Nothing. Just the *tick tock tick* of the big clock. I walked quietly into the hall. The clock's white face showed a few minutes after one.

Matt's door was closed, as was Grandmother's—which didn't mean they were actually in their rooms. With the house's interconnecting chimneys and old heating system, it would be easy enough to whisper something downstairs so it could be heard upstairs. Was Matt having a little fun with me?

I walked quickly toward the hall window to check for his Jeep; he was home. Still, playing ghost seemed like too much trouble for him. Till now, his way of dealing with me was to ignore me and hope I went away.

I listened for a moment by the door of his room, straining for some hint that he was awake. There was no sound but that of the clock. Giving up, I headed back to my room. As I passed the hall mirror, I glanced at it, then froze.

There, in the antique glass, I saw her, more light than substance, a changing wisp of fog, the shape of a girl. I stared at the mist in the mirror, struggling to understand what I was seeing. Avril? I felt icy cold all over.

I ran for my room and pulled the door closed behind me. It didn't catch. When I reached my bed, I heard the door swing open again, but I was too afraid to look back. Hands shaking, I pulled down my quilt in a rush to get in bed, then gasped with disbelief. She was there! She was lying there in front of me! No, it was *me* I was looking down on. And I was dead! I squeezed shut my eyes and put my hands over my mouth, barely muffling screams that echoed deep within me.

When I opened my eyes again, I was lying in bed, warm and safe beneath my quilt. It was a dream, I told myself, just a scary dream. Then I turned my head on the pillow and saw the door I'd latched earlier standing wide open.

Six

As soon as I emerged from bed Sunday morning, I felt the draft, a river of icy air flowing between the fireplace and entrance to my room. I hurried across the chilly floorboards to close the door. Memories of last night washed over me.

It was just a dream, I told myself—the whisper, the ghost in the mirror—they were nothing more than a nightmare seeded by what a customer had said. As for the door being open, old houses weren't airtight; it wasn't surprising after a windy night.

I dressed quickly, glad my mother had made me pack a long-sleeved turtleneck and sweater. When I arrived in the kitchen, neither Grandmother nor Matt was around. I made a steaming cup of tea and took it out to the kitchen garden.

The river mist was suffused with early-morning sunlight. In the garden every dew-drenched leaf, from the flat needles of rosemary to the smallest teardrops of thyme, shimmered.

I walked to the picket fence that edged the garden, stopping at the gate, gazing toward the family cemetery. From a distance the roses looked like soft pink and white smudges against the brick wall. I thought of the voice from last night. Was it possible—had the girl buried there come up to the house? I shivered.

"Need another sweater?"

I hadn't heard Matt approach. "No, thanks."

"You look cold."

He was wearing a short-sleeved shirt with his jeans. I'd turn into an iceberg before admitting to him I had goose bumps beneath my sweater. "I'm not."

"How did you sleep last night?" he asked.

"Fine. Great."

I could see it in his eyes: he didn't believe me.

"Why wouldn't I?" I asked.

He shrugged. "If you're not used to an old house, it can be a spooky kind of place when the wind kicks up."

He studied my face, and I, in turn, studied his.

"Guess I'm a solid sleeper," I said. "How about you?"

"I'm a light sleeper. I hear just about everything."

Like a girl's muffled scream? I wondered. I took a sip of tea.

"So, did you have a good time last night?" I asked. "I mean at the dance, not afterward." I watched him over the rim of my cup. But if he had been up to something afterward, like whispering in a ghostly voice, he didn't show it.

"No. I've always hated school dances."

"Then why did you go?"

"Everyone expects you to," he replied matter-of-factly.

"Do you always do what others expect?"

One side of his mouth pulled up in that smirky smile of his. "Not always."

"You're right about that. Most people would expect you to be friendly to a cousin you'd just met, or at least polite to a house guest."

He glanced away.

"Listen, Matt, I didn't want to come here."

"Then why did you?"

"Grandmother asked me to," I replied.

"Do you always do what others ask?"

"Not always," I said, giving him the same smirk he had given me a moment ago. "My father talked me into it. And I'm not brownnosing Grandmother—I'm not here for her money, if that's what you're worried about. Dad's hoping I can heal things between Grandmother and Mom. I think he's wrong, but, as it turns out, I'm glad I'm here."

Matt remained silent.

"I believe in making the best of a situation," I added.

"Why do you keep trying to make the worst of it?"

He didn't reply, just stared down at my face as if he were searching for something.

"Too bad you have such beautiful eyes."

Seeing him blink, I realized I had said that aloud.

"You have no problem speaking your mind," he replied, those eyes now bright with amusement.

I turned away from him. "Grandmother's standing in the window, waiting for us to come in, and looking annoyed."

I headed toward the porch and Matt followed.

"Good morning, Grandmother," I greeted her as we entered the kitchen.

"Good morning, Megan. Matt, you're up early for Sunday. I heard you come in before midnight last night. Were you ill?"

"No."

"Well, for once, you can get a good start on your studying," she remarked.

He nodded, strode over to the kitchen cupboard, and got out a glass.

She turned to me. "Megan, your mother has written that you're an honor student. Perhaps you can help Matt."

I saw Matt's hand tighten around the glass and I shook my head. "No, he's a year ahead of me."

"But you're taking Advanced Placement courses and

getting straight As," Grandmother insisted.

I looked at her, surprised. Apparently she had more contact with my mother than I'd realized.

"Matt, most definitely, is not getting As or even Bs," she went on.

Why was she comparing us? I doubted it was grandmotherly pride in my achievements.

"He's never been a good student," she continued.

Matt poured juice in his glass, his face expressionless.

"Perhaps you can motivate him," Grandmother added.

This wasn't about motivation, it was a comparison aimed at making him dislike me even more than he already did.

"Thanks for letting me have dinner with Ginny," I said, deliberately changing the subject.

Grandmother nodded and began eating her banana. "She was impressed with the way you handled customers. Matt, did you hear that Megan was offered a job?"

He kept his back to us as he returned the carton of juice to the refrigerator. "I saw her working yesterday."

"Did you know she was asked to continue?"

"That's nice," he replied.

"I have wanted Matt to get a job since last spring."

"Well," I said lightly, "I can't really see him selling purses and lace handkerchiefs."

She didn't smile and wasn't diverted from her goal. "He claims he has enough to handle with athletics and school, and of course his social life. I suppose it's my fault for continuing to give him money."

I wasn't getting into that. And I wasn't going to allow her to play me against him.

"Anyone want a muffin?" I asked, retrieving the bag from the counter where I had left it last night. "They're from Tea Leaves."

Matt didn't reply. Grandmother glanced at the bag, then lapsed into silence, sipping her coffee. Had she said her piece, or was she resting before unloading another round of antagonizing comments?

She washed her dishes, then walked over to the shelf where I had seen her put the Bible the day before. "Where is it?" she asked, turning quickly to us.

"Where's what?" Matt asked casually and dropped a slice of bread in the toaster.

"My Bible."

"It's not on the shelf?" He craned his neck to look around her.

Her eyes bore down on me. "Which of you has taken it?"

"I haven't touched it, Grandmother," I said, surprised by her accusatory tone.

"And you know I never do," Matt added.

"Someone moved it. I put it here last night. It is always here," she insisted.

"Maybe you carried it into another room," I suggested.

"I did not. I know what I've done and what I haven't."

"But everybody misplaces things," I reasoned with her. "I'll look in the library." It was an excuse to get away as much as a desire to help. She seemed bent on raising a fuss this morning, and I didn't want any part of it.

I checked her desk first, then the tabletops and mantel. Matt came in and began searching even more thoroughly, beneath tables and chairs, under a pile of magazines. I returned to the desk and tried to open the drawers, the ones he'd been looking through Friday night.

"They're locked," he said.

"Where's the key?"

"I don't know," he replied. "Some things Grandmother tells no one."

Except you, I thought.

The Bible wouldn't be in there anyway," he added.

"How would you know, if the desk is locked?"

His eyes met mine steadily. "I've seen the drawers open when she's working. They're full of junk. There's no room for anything else." He turned to survey the shelves of books. "Are you sure you didn't borrow it or put it away for her?"

"I'm sure."

His eyes continued to travel over the volumes of books. "If she put it on one of these shelves, we'll be lucky to find it."

He was acting as if we had a major problem on our hands. "It'll show up sooner or later," I said. "And if it doesn't, she can buy a new one—it's still in print."

He didn't smile. "You look in the music room, I'll search the parlor."

I checked the room thoroughly; nothing but dust had settled there for a long time. I returned to the kitchen, figuring that Grandmother had found the book or decided it was not important.

She spun around when she heard me enter. "It is a sin to steal."

"I know, Grandmother. The Ten Commandments are posted in my bedroom."

She glared at me, then started pacing back and forth.

"We'll find it," I assured her. "Meanwhile, it's Sunday. Is there a church service you like in town? I'd be glad to go with—"

"I don't go to church," she replied shortly. "I refuse to sit among the town hypocrites. As for the ministers these days, they can't tell right from wrong."

Matt returned. "Should I check your bedroom, Grandmother?"

"You should check *Megan's* room," she replied.

I opened my mouth to protest. Her suspicion was insulting. But if a search put me in the clear—"Oh, what the heck, check it," I said.

All three of us climbed the stairs. Matt searched my room, taking too long I thought. Grandmother checked his room. I offered to search hers but was met with a look that could shear steel. I sat on the top step stewing, then got up and walked in circles. When I passed in front of the hall's antique mirror, I saw myself looking angry and on edge.

The two of them returned empty-handed.

"Someone will be punished for this," Grandmother declared.

She sounded absurdly serious.

"Maybe the ghost took it," I suggested.

"We don't have a ghost, Megan. I don't want to hear that kind of nonsense from you."

I was feeling defiant. "Someone named Alice, who used to work here, told me she saw it."

"Alice Scanlon is a liar."

"She said the ghost's name is Avril."

The pupils of Grandmother's eyes were jet black inside

their pale blue rims. Matt shook his head, signaling me to keep quiet.

"On my walk Friday I visited the family cemetery and saw Avril's stone. She died young."

"She was the same age as you," Grandmother replied. "And just as sassy."

"How did she die?"

Grandmother looked at me for a long moment, the pupils of her eyes unsteady. "You heartless, rude girl, asking me something like that. You're not part of the family. Why would I tell you?"

"So when people say things, like she was murdered, I know how to correct them."

She turned abruptly, strode into her bedroom, and slammed the door behind her. There was a moment of quiet, then I heard her lock the door.

I looked at my cousin, hoping he could give me a reasonable explanation for her extreme behavior.

"Good job," he said. "Next time you set her off, do it on a day I'm out of the house."

"She's already off," I replied in a hushed voice.

"Yeah, well, if you don't want her over the edge, you'll drop the ghost stuff."

"She overreacts to things," I argued.

"And you won't mention Avril again."

"Why?" I asked, following him downstairs. I caught his arm at the landing. "Tell me why."

"It upsets Grandmother. Avril was her sister and they were very close."

"*Sixty* years ago. She can't still be mourning her. Matt, is Grandmother losing it? Mentally, I mean."

He started down the steps again, ignoring the question.

I caught up with him a second time. "Why do you protect her? When she goes after you, why don't you fight back?"

"There are a lot of things you don't understand."

"No kidding. How about explaining them to me?"

He was silent.

"Couldn't you see what she was doing with that stuff about grades and jobs? She's trying to turn you against me. I don't know why, since you already don't like me. But she's making sure of it. What's eating her?"

For a moment the mask slipped from his face. I could see the uncertainty in him.

"Matt," I said, taking a step toward him.

He jerked away from me, picked up his Jeep keys from the hall table, and strolled toward the door.

"What are you thinking?" I called after him. "What?"

He didn't glance back, didn't break stride. "You should never have come," he said, and left.

seven

GRANDMOTHER EMERGED FROM her room at ten o'clock that morning, no longer obsessed with finding the Bible. She was unhappy because Matt had left the house on his study day, but he knew how to get back on her good side, returning with the Baltimore paper, as well as the Sunday *New York Times* and *Washington Post.* Her fingers smoothed the newspaper with the same pleasure that some women show when touching silk. Anyone peeking in the library door right then would have thought she was a perfectly normal grandmother.

"Are you calling your mother today?" she asked me.

"I was thinking about e-mailing my parents. Do you have a computer?"

"Matt has one in his room. You may use that."

"Is that all right with you, Matt?"

Grandmother replied before he did. "I gave him the computer. It is all right with me."

Still, I waited for my cousin's response.

"It's on," he said, which I took as permission and headed upstairs.

Matt's room was neater than I thought it would be, with just a few pretzels crunched into the rug and a small pile of clothes thrown onto a chair. Two pictures sat on a shelf above his desk. In one several lacrosse players wearing helmets and holding sticks grinned back at the camera. I thought Matt was the player on the end. The second photo was of a little boy and a big dog. I knew by the eyes that the child was Matt, but the sweetness of his expression surprised me. His arms were wrapped so lovingly around the dog, a golden retriever that looked old and patient, I got a lump in my throat.

I finally sat down, pulled up my e-mail account, and began to type. I had decided writing would be better than calling because I could choose what to say and what to leave out. There was no point in upsetting my mother by telling her about Grandmother's eccentric behavior. And I didn't want to be overheard when I asked about Aunt Avril and the dollhouse.

I was finishing the e-mail when I heard voices in the hall. Matt entered the room with his friend Alex.

"Almost done?" he asked.

"Just signing off," I told him.

Alex dropped down in the chair next to the desk. "Hi, Megan. I was hoping you'd be here."

I smiled. "Hi! Matt didn't tell me you were coming over."

Alex stretched his long legs out in front of him. "You must have figured out by now that if you want to know anything, you have to pry it out of Matt."

My cousin, standing behind Alex's chair, grimaced slightly.

"We study together every Sunday," Alex added. "Want to hang out with us?"

"No," Matt said.

Alex glanced over his shoulder and laughed. "I wasn't asking you."

"Even so—," Matt began.

I interrupted: "You must have figured out by now, I'm not one of Matt's favorite people."

"Yeah?" Alex replied, his dark blue eyes sparkling. "Why?"

I shrugged. "Let me know if he tells you first."

Matt stood silently with his hands on his hips.

"Don't worry about it," Alex said. "Sometimes he's just strange."

I laughed. Matt shifted his weight from foot to foot.

"Are you a lacrosse player too?" I asked Alex, pointing to the photograph. "Are you one of those guys in a helmet?"

"I play lacrosse, but that's not our team." Alex turned to

look at my cousin, waiting for him to explain the photo. "Did you forget how to talk, Matt?"

"That's my team at Gilman," Matt said, "the school I went to in Baltimore."

When he fell silent, Alex continued, "Matt and I got to be friends at lacrosse camp, the one Chase College runs every summer. A bunch of guys on our team go to it, so when Matt finally moved here last year, he fit right in. He's the strongest guy on our team and plays awesome defense. He set a school record for assists last season."

"Wow," I said, impressed.

One side of Matt's mouth drew up.

There was no use arguing my sincerity. "Was that your dog, Matt?" I asked, pointing to the other photo.

"Yes."

"What's his name?"

"Homer."

"Homer?" I repeated. "You named him after the Greek writer? The guy who wrote the *Iliad*?"

Alex threw back his head and laughed. "Yeah, and he had a cat named Shakespeare."

I saw the pink creeping up Matt's neck.

"Not exactly," he said. "When I found him, he was hungry and hurt and looked like he needed a home. So I called him Homer."

I felt that strange little lump in my throat again. I carefully took the photo from the shelf and studied it. In grade school I had one special cat who heard all of my secrets and sorrows. This dog had probably listened to a few as well, especially since Matt was the only child of parents who were always fighting.

"There's a lot of chatter in here, and it doesn't sound like schoolwork."

The three of us looked toward the door, where Grandmother stood.

"Then you must not have been listening real hard," Alex told her. "We were just talking about the famous Greek writer, Homer."

"I believe that, and you'll tell me another one," Grandmother replied.

"I heard someone mention Shakespeare," he added.

"Save your lines for your girlfriends, Alex."

To my amazement, she was smiling.

He grinned at her. "My father said to tell you he's still hoping you'll change your mind and let him interview you for his Eastern Shore history."

"Your father will be hoping till Doomsday, at which point no one will be interested."

Alex laughed. "He wants one of the professors in his department to have a look at the old mill."

"I don't know why your father persists in thinking of me as anything but a grouchy old woman, who means no when she says no."

"It's the newspapers," Alex replied. "You're the only person in town who reads as many newspapers and magazines as he does. No matter what I tell him about you, he's convinced you're not all bad."

Grandmother clucked.

She liked this teasing, I realized. In some ways she was like me, always ready with a comeback, enjoying the give and take. *Except* she didn't enjoy it with me.

"It's time to get to work," she said, her voice turning prim, like a girl who'd decided her flirting had gone on too long. "I want to hear lessons," she said as she exited the room.

Matt tossed several notebooks on his desk.

"Golden retrievers are terrific dogs," I remarked, looking again at the picture in my hands. "How long did you have him?"

"Two years."

"What happened?"

"When we moved out, my mother said I had to get rid of him."

First his parents separated, then his mother got rid of his dog? "That's terrible! Homer was yours."

"It was no big deal," he replied, shrugging it off.

"Faker," I said softly.

I saw a flicker of emotion in his eyes, then he reached for the picture. "We should put this back." He set it gently on the shelf.

"Well, thanks for the use of your computer."

"Sure." His voice was quieter than usual.

"Hope I'll see you around, Megan," Alex said.

"Yeah, me too," I replied, pretty certain I wouldn't, not if he hung out with Matt.

"When do you turn on the heat?" I asked, soaking my hands in the hot dishwater, wishing the rest of me felt as warm. I had taken a walk before dinner and come back chilled. The cold fried chicken and potato salad hadn't warmed me up any.

"November," Matt answered, "if we're lucky. It's a big house to heat and Grandmother watches her money."

I didn't complain further, not wanting to seem like a wimp from the sunny Southwest. But having left behind ninety-degree days, I was freezing when the temperature plummeted to the low fifties. The dampness here added a raw edge that went right through my bones.

Drying my hands, I went upstairs to put on a heavy sweater, then joined Grandmother in the library for an evening of reading the newspaper. A few minutes later, Matt came in carrying several logs.

"What are you doing?" Grandmother asked him.

"Building a fire."

She studied him for a moment, then looked at me with my turtleneck yanked up to my ears and my sweater sleeves down to my knuckles. "How thoughtful."

The sarcasm in her voice made me reluctant to thank Matt in front of her. Besides, Grandmother was wearing a thick sweater too; maybe he was doing this for her.

Matt built the fire, arranging the logs and stacking the kindling in a quiet, methodical way. He had rolled up his sleeves so I could see the muscles in his forearms. His hands were large, with the wide palms and long, strong fingers of an athlete. I wondered what it would be like to hold hands with him, then quickly squelched that thought.

He struck a match. As soon as it was dropped on the crumpled newspaper, I was down on the floor, close to the hearth. He dropped in another match. A piece of newspaper flared up, then collapsed quickly into ash. Small sticks caught and made crackling noises. Big sticks burned and the outside of a heavy log began to char.

Matt turned to me. "If you keep sighing like that, you're going to blow out the fire."

I covered my mouth with my hand. A smile touched the corners of his lips.

"I love fires," I said.

"No kidding." Maybe it was the hissing log that made his words seem softer.

I suddenly became aware of Grandmother observing us with a sour look on her face. I sat back quickly and spread the newspaper on the bricks in front of me, then lay on my stomach and began to read. The golden light flickered over the paper. I could feel its warmth on my face.

Matt found the sports page and lay on his stomach about a foot away from me. I didn't look back at Grandmother, figuring we would have heard if she had any objections to our reading on the floor. I was more relaxed than I'd been since leaving home. Soon the print in front of me got blurry and my head felt too heavy to hold up.

I don't know how long I slept, probably just a few minutes. The sound of a shifting log awakened me. When I opened my eyes, I saw that Matt had stopped reading. His face was turned toward me, his eyes, like dark embers, watching me.

Look away, I thought. *Turn away now before it's too late.*

But I couldn't. Gazing back into his eyes, I felt something stir inside me, some feeling so deep, so secret, my own heart couldn't whisper the words to me.

Grandmother coughed and Matt and I glanced aside at the same time. I sat up and moved over two feet, so I could sit with my back against a chair. Matt poked at the fire.

That's when I noticed it, above Matt's shoulder, on a shelf to the left of the mantel.

"Grandmother, look. Your Bible."

She glanced at me, then her head jerked in the direction that I pointed. Her mouth opened with surprise. She sat still in her chair as if she couldn't believe she was seeing it. I scrambled to my feet, retrieved the Bible, and carried it over to her. When she didn't take it from my hands, I laid it in her lap.

"Which of you wicked children put it there?" she demanded.

Matt and I looked at each other. "Neither," I said after a moment.

"Liar!"

I stepped back. Matt got a guarded look on his face.

Grandmother started paging through the heavy book, then looked up at the gap on the shelf where the Bible had been. The pale blue of her eyes thinned inside a ring of white. "Put something there, Matt. Now!" she cried. "Put it *there*!"

Matt picked up several magazines and stuffed them in the space. "Are you all right?"

Her hands were shaking badly. "I'm looking for Corinthians," she said.

"Can I help?" I asked.

"*You* stay away."

I retreated to a chair.

"I have it," she said, and began to read Paul's famous passage about charity—what love is and isn't. Her voice quivered when she read how all things but love would pass away. Matt stood close to her, his face lined with concern. Despite what he had said before, he must have been worried about her state of mind. It was her intensity, the anger and suspicion with which she spoke, more than what she said, that was frightening.

She looked up suddenly. "Finish it, Matt. Verses eleven and twelve."

"Why don't we finish it later?" he suggested quietly.

"I want to hear it now."

"You know I don't like to read aloud."

"Read it!" She shoved the book in his hands.

He hesitated, then took a deep breath and carried the Bible to her desk. Sitting down in front of the book, he focused on the page for a few moments, marking the place with his finger.

"When I was a . . . a child," he began, "I . . . played—"

"Spake!" she corrected him.

"I spake as a ch-child, I . . . understand—"

"Understood."

"I understood as a child." His face was tense with concentration. "I tough as—"

"Thought!"

"I thought as . . . a child."

I listened with disbelief. Matt could barely read.

"But where I because a name—"

"But when I became a man," Grandmother said in a low, ugly voice.

He nodded and swallowed. "I . . . put . . . away childish thoughts."

"*Things.* Give it to me, Matt."

"You wanted me to read," he said, his jaw clenched. "I'm going to finish it."

I closed my eyes, wishing I weren't there.

"For no, we see . . . uh—"

"'Through a glass darkly,'" I said softly.

"For now we see through a glass darkly; but the but then . . . fa-face to face; No I now—" He shook his head and started again. "—Now I know in part; but there—then shall I now—know—ever as also I am known."

The passage was finally over. Matt looked grim and humiliated; I knew anything I said would only make it worse for him.

Anger simmered inside me. I didn't know what made

Grandmother act the way she did. It was as if certain things could turn on a switch in her and make her cold and mean. What dark, distorted glass did she look through when she got this way?

I couldn't begin to guess. Only one thing was clear to me: Matt was dyslexic and Grandmother was trying desperately to shame him in front of me.

eight

I AWOKE MONDAY morning just as the sky was getting bright. I knew I was at Grandmother's house, but something was different about the pale gray light. It reflected off a ceiling that was too close. My eyes traveled down to the walls. Faded roses, huge as headlights, surrounded me. I wasn't in my room. I sat up quickly and realized the surface beneath me was hard. I'd been sleeping on the floor of a small room that was wallpapered in roses.

I scrambled to my feet and went to a window. Below me was the herb garden and the long tin roof that covered the kitchen porch. I was in the back wing, in the room next to the one with the dormer windows where I had found the dollhouse. The closed door to my right must have led to that room. Opposite from it was an open door that revealed five steps, which rose to the second floor hall of the main house.

I walked slowly around the empty room, trying to remember how I had gotten here. I couldn't recall waking up and moving.

Was I sleepwalking? I had done it once or twice as a kid. I struggled to remember last night's dreams, hoping for some clue as to why I had left my room. All I could remember was something round, a circle with bumps or marks on its circumference.

I wondered who had used this room and for what. Perhaps it was a housekeeper's or maid's room. Then I recalled what Alice, the customer at Yesterdaze, had said. "I've seen the ghost. In the rear wing, in the room above the kitchen."

The skin at the back of my neck prickled. Avril? I mouthed her name, afraid to say it aloud, as if I had the power to summon her. Had she been here last night? Had I followed her here?

"Get a grip, Megan," I muttered.

Wrapping my arms tightly around myself, I tiptoed back to my room. I didn't know what unnerved me more: the possibility that Avril was real, or the fact that I could do something and have absolutely no memory of it.

The second time I awoke it was after eight o'clock, and Matt had already left for school. In the bright light the objects in my room—my hairbrush, the romantic paperback, the sweatshirt I'd left draped over a chair—seemed startlingly normal. I got up and began to brush my hair, standing in a swatch of sunlight, hoping it would melt away my uncertainty and fear. Everyone has nightmares, I told myself. As for the change in rooms, I had been sleepwalking.

Arriving downstairs, I found Grandmother pacing. When I greeted her in the hall, she jumped.

"Is everything okay?" I asked.

"My clock is missing."

"Which clock, Grandmother?"

She looked at me as if I should know. "The antique that sat on my desk in the library."

"You mean the little gold one, the one with a picture painted on its face?"

"Where did you put it?" she demanded as if I'd just admitted guilt.

Indignation flared up in me. But I had moved myself without realizing it; how could I be sure I hadn't moved a clock? And the fragment of my dream, a circle with marks on it—wasn't that like the face of a clock?

"I don't remember putting it anywhere," I told her honestly. "Have you asked Matt?"

"No, of course not. I can't trust him anymore."

"Why not?" I asked, walking over to the library door, scanning the shelves and tabletops.

"He has other loyalties now." She said the words slowly, as if they held great meaning.

I moved across the hall to the dining room, my eyes sweeping that room—side tables, windowsills, mantel—any ledge that could support a small clock.

"Grandmother, it's obvious that he loves you and wants to help you however he can. Though I don't know why, when you're so mean to him."

I walked down the hall and looked in the front parlor. "You were awful last night," I went on. "Matt has a learning disability. It has nothing to do with intelligence, but it makes school hard. You had no right to embarrass him the way you did."

Grandmother raised her head, like a cat picking up a new scent. "Well, now, instead of going after Matt with that smart little mouth of yours, you're defending him."

"I can do both."

"Have you become friends? I believe you have," she said before I could answer. "You're working together, aren't you? He's siding with you now."

I shook my head in amazement and passed her in the hall, crossing over to the music room.

"You two are playing tricks on me!"

"No, Grandmother, we are not."

"Where is the clock?" she asked.

My eyes surveyed the room one more time. "I have no idea."

***

Fortunately, I had agreed to work for Ginny from ten to three that day and could get away from the house for a while. I didn't mention to her the strange things that had been happening, afraid that she might call my mother or insist I stay with her. I was spooked, but determined to figure out what was going on, which meant I had to stay at the house.

Before I knew it, it was three fifteen and Ginny was shooing me out the door of Yesterdaze. I walked up High Street and had just passed Tea Leaves, when I heard a girl's voice calling to me.

"Megan. Hey, Megan. Up here!" From a second-story window in the next building, Sophie's ponytail dangled like a fiery flag. "I want to ask you something. Can you come up?"

"Sure," I replied. "Is this where you live?"

Sophie laughed and I stepped back to look at the brick building. It was long, with a porch roof running from end to end, extending over the sidewalk. Next to the front door was a brass lantern and sign: THE MALLARD TAVERN, 1733.

"It's a B and B, bed and breakfast," Sophie explained. "Mom cleans it and I help out after school. Door's open."

I entered the front hall and climbed the carpeted steps, following the sound of a vacuum cleaner. When I arrived on the second floor, the machine shut off and Sophie stuck her head out a door. "The weekenders are gone," she said. "Mom's down washing sheets and towels. Come on in."

The room she was cleaning was homey, with red and white wallpaper, a canopy bed, and chairs pulled close to a small fireplace.

"I looked for you at the dance Saturday night," Sophie said.

I figured she had invited me up to ask about my cousin. "I'd like to have gone, but Matt doesn't want me hanging around his friends. Like I said before, there's really not much I can tell you about him."

"Her," Sophie corrected me.

"Excuse me?"

"It's a *her* I want to ask about." She shook out a clean bottom sheet. "Avril Scarborough. Do you know her?" She watched my face and waited for my response.

"You mean the ghost?"

"Have you seen her?" she asked.

I walked to the other side of the double bed, caught the edge of the sheet, and slipped it over two corners of the mattress. "Have you?"

"I asked you first," she said, then laughed. "Once I did."

"When? Where?"

"Back in sixth grade," she replied, tugging down her corners and smoothing the sheet. "I was still hanging out with Kristy then and she had a sleepover. We paid her older sister to drive us to Scarborough House at four in the morning. Avril usually shows up just before dawn in the back wing."

My breath caught. Then I reminded myself that people would expect to see a ghost in an abandoned part of a house, and people saw what they expected. I had seen what I expected after hearing Alice's story.

"It was a bust," Sophie continued. "Everybody got tired and whiney. Kristy's sister got mad, piled us back in the car, and headed toward town again."

"So when did you see her?"

"That same night, when we were crossing the bridge over Wist Creek."

Sophie shook out a top sheet. We worked together to slip it under the lower end of the mattress and pull it up evenly.

"How do you know what you saw?" I asked. "How do you know it was Avril, or even a she?"

Sophie tossed me a pillow, then thought for a moment. "I guess there was something about the shape. It was thin and moved in a graceful kind of way. She seemed more like a girl than a woman."

"Did anybody else see her that night?"

"Nobody. I got teased a lot," Sophie added, then shrugged.

"I've always seen things other people don't, now I just don't tell anyone." We pulled the spread up over the pillows. "I guess you know how that is."

"What do you mean?"

"You're psychic, aren't you?" she asked.

"Me? No!"

Sophie's wide blue eyes studied me. "I was sure you were. I felt a connection."

I frowned and saw the color deepen in her cheeks. She picked up her tray of cleaning supplies and reached for the vacuum. "I've got another room to do."

I followed her across the hall to a room that had different wallpaper but a similar arrangement of bed and furniture. Sophie snatched up a feather duster and began whisking it over frames and mirrors. She didn't look at me.

"I would never have said anything," she explained, talking a little too fast, "except I thought you were like me. That's why I hoped you had seen the ghost. Psychics seem to attract other forms of spiritual energy—they're like magnets to ghosts. And—well, that's all," she said.

I caught her peeking at me.

"Are you sure you're not?" she asked. "You've never been aware of things that other people aren't? You've never had an experience you can't explain?"

"No," I lied.

She shook her head. "I read you wrong."

"Except," I said, "some, uh, strange dreams."

"Miss Lydia says that dreams are shadows cast by truth shining on our darkest secrets."

"Well, mine aren't all that mysterious," I replied. "I can explain them—most of them."

I told Sophie about my childhood visits to a house that looked like Grandmother's and my recent dream of the dollhouse, along with my theories about seeing photos of Mom with the miniature house.

"You could be right," Sophie said, sounding unconvinced.

"You have a better explanation?"

"You're psychic—telepathic. When you were little, your mom was watching you play and thinking about herself as a kid at home. You picked up the images and made them your own."

"I like my theory better."

"Okay by me," Sophie said agreeably. She lifted a sheet from a pile on a chair, and we went to work making the bed.

"Who's Miss Lydia?" I asked.

The old lady who owns the café next door. Jamie Riley's mother."

"Oh!"

"When I was little," Sophie went on, "and Mom was working here at the Mallard, I'd go to Tea Leaves for my after-school snack. Miss Lydia liked me and talked to me a lot."

"She sure doesn't like me," I said, then told Sophie about my introduction to the woman.

"Don't be offended," Sophie advised. "Miss Lydia doesn't trust many people. A couple years ago she got in trouble for selling her herbal remedies at the Queen Victoria, the hotel across the street. Guests complained. A woman said she got sick, but that can happen with herbal stuff, just like it does with a prescription from a doctor. Anyway, now Miss Lydia only deals with locals and keeps thinking guys from the FBI are coming after her."

"If she's psychic, wouldn't she know they aren't?"

Sophie didn't laugh and didn't get annoyed. "No. Just because you're psychic doesn't mean you can see clearly. Sometimes the more you see, the more confusing it is. Images overlap and it's hard to sort them out."

We finished making the bed in silence. Sophie kept her head down as if she were deep in thought. When she looked up, her eyes were bright. "How about an O.B.E.? Out-of-body experience? Some people do that, you know. Their spirit breaks free of their body and travels around. Maybe you were curious about your grandmother and came to see her as a child."

"Without my body?" I said, looking at Sophie like she was crazy.

"Well, yes and no," she replied. "Your body would be back where you left it. But if your grandmother were psychically aware, she'd have seen an apparition of you that looked like your body."

I kept quiet.

"I'm making you uncomfortable," Sophie observed. She stuck the vacuum cleaner plug in a wall socket. "This is all I have left to do. Thanks for stopping by." She waited for me to leave, her finger on the trigger of the machine.

"Have you seen *Sheer Blue*?" I asked.

"The movie?" she replied. "No."

"Want to go?"

She looked surprised, then smiled. "Didn't scare you away, huh?"

"Not yet."

"How about Thursday night?" she suggested. "We're off school Friday."

"Great."

The vacuum roared to life and I left. As I walked up High Street, I wondered to myself what secrets were casting shadows long enough to reach into my dreams.

nine

WHEN I ARRIVED home that afternoon, I found my grandmother sitting in the kitchen, idly watching her housekeeper fix dinner. Grandmother's skin was so pale it seemed translucent, her hands clasped but in constant motion, as if she couldn't keep them warm.

"Are you okay?" I asked, quickly setting down my purse. "Has something happened, Grandmother?"

She didn't reply.

I glanced over at Nancy. "What's wrong?"

"Don't know. She won't say," Nancy replied, then shoved a runny casserole into the oven. "I've tried all afternoon to get her to see the doctor. No use wasting your breath—she won't go. She's been spooky ever since I found that little clock."

"You found the clock?" I asked, my mouth dry.

"Now, don't *you* get funny on me."

"Where was it?"

"On the hall table, behind the silk flowers."

I pulled a chair up close to Grandmother and sat down. "How are you feeling?"

"Fine."

"You don't look it. I want to call your doctor."

"I forbid you," she said.

Nancy gave me an I-told-you-so look.

"As you know, Grandmother, I don't always listen."

"You may call, but I won't go."

I stood up. "Matt should be home soon. He'll know what to do."

Nancy shook her head. "He called and Mrs. Barnes told him he could stay at Alex's." The woman sounded exasperated. "She could have told me earlier. All the time I put into that casserole, and her with no appetite and you a vegetarian."

"I eat meat," I said.

"Take it out when the buzzer goes off," Nancy went on. "You can dig around for the peas."

I didn't correct her a second time, just waited for her to leave, hoping Grandmother would talk to me then. But as soon as Nancy was gone, Grandmother retreated to her room. I followed her upstairs and told her I would check on her in an hour.

"You will not," she said, then closed the door. I heard the lock click.

I ate alone in the kitchen that evening, glad to be away from the gory deer in the dining room. Afterward I went to the library to see the antique clock. I weighed it in my hands and ran my fingers over its cold metal surfaces, hoping they would remember what my mind did not: Was this the first time I'd held it? Could I have moved it before I went to the rose-papered room? I set the clock down gently, knowing no more than I did before.

At ten o'clock Matt still hadn't come back from Alex's. I found the number and called to tell Matt the situation. He said he'd check on Grandmother when he got home. I went to bed, leaving my bedroom door cracked, knowing I wouldn't sleep.

Twenty minutes later Matt knocked softly on Grandmother's door, calling to her. The door creaked open. I slipped out of bed and went to the entrance of my room. Though I couldn't make out Matt's words, I knew from his tone he was asking questions.

Grandmother was upset and either forgot I was in the next room or didn't care. She spoke loudly. "I have brought it on myself, Matt."

He quietly asked her something else.

"I have brought it on myself!" she repeated, sounding frustrated. "Don't you understand? I'm being punished."

"But there's nothing for you to be punished for," Matt replied, his voice growing as intense as hers.

"God has chosen her as his instrument," Grandmother insisted.

"God hasn't chosen anything," he argued. "You were the one who invited Megan. Things are being misplaced, Grandmother, nothing more. It's all in your head."

Her response was muffled with emotion.

"Hush! Everything's going to be all right," he said. Then I heard him take a step inside the room. The door closed.

Cut off from their conversation, I closed my own door and rested back against it. Their conference lasted a long time. Finally I heard Grandmother's door open and close again, then Matt's footsteps in the hall, heading in the direction of the stairway. He stopped at my door. I knew he was standing on the other side and I waited for him to knock.

When I heard him walk away, I quickly opened the door. He turned around.

"Is she going to be okay?" I asked.

His mouth formed a grim line. "She's confused. If she doesn't get better, I'm taking her to a doctor."

"And you?" I saw how shaken he looked. "How are you doing?"

"You don't have to worry about me."

"Do anyway."

He looked away.

I stepped into the hall. "Matt, why is she acting this way?"

"You should never have come here, Megan."

"Are you saying it's my fault?" I asked. "Are you? Please look at me."

He did, and for a moment neither of us spoke.

"Are you asking me to leave?"

He took a deep breath. "It would be the best thing."

"Okay, I'll consider it, but first tell me why she's upset. I want to know what's going on."

He didn't reply.

"Matt, I can't help if I don't understand the problem."

Still he said nothing.

"So I guess you don't want my help."

"I don't."

I stepped back into my room and closed the door. The distance he kept between us no longer made me mad; it made me hurt.

We were playing a game, Matt and I. I was tiptoeing around an abandoned house—or maybe it was a barn. The walls and floors were made of rough wood, and the simple wooden stairs looked more like tilted ladders. We were playing hide-and-seek.

It was twilight outside. Inside, it grew darker with each minute. I knew we should stop the game before it got too late, but I kept on. I could hear Matt walking on the floor above my head, searching for me. I quietly opened a trapdoor and descended the stairs that led to the basement.

The air was cold and damp down there; it held the darkness like a sponge. My eyes adjusted slowly to the bit of light that came from the doorway above. Suddenly I saw huge wheels, wheels with teeth, one wheel interlocking with the next, like the gears inside a clock. The largest was as tall as I.

I heard a noise, a groan from the machinery. My eyes focused on the biggest wheel. It started to turn slowly, very slowly at first. The smaller wheels rotated with it. I had to stop them. I knew if I didn't, they'd turn faster and faster, shaking the old building till it flew apart.

I grasped the huge teeth of the main wheel and pulled back, dragging it in the opposite direction. But as soon as I stopped pulling, the wheel moved forward again, turning more quickly. I gripped harder, my hands slippery with sweat. Still, each time I pulled back, the gigantic wheel made up those inches and moved even farther ahead, pulling me with it.

I had to find another way to stop it. I tried to step back to study the wheel and discovered I couldn't move. I yanked my arm, struggling to pull it away, but the edge of my sweater sleeve was caught between the teeth of the big wheel and a smaller one. The speed of the wheels was steadily increasing. I called for help, called for Matt. I writhed and pulled and bit the threads of my sweater. At the last moment I slipped free of it.

Run, I told myself. But I stood there, fascinated, watching the wheels consume my garment. Then I felt the pull. The powerful teeth had caught my hair. I was being dragged toward the center of the wheels. I screamed for Matt.

I heard his footsteps cross the floor above me. I shouted his name over and over. Then I heard his footsteps fading and the door upstairs shut. He had left me.

I struggled to free myself, fighting for each inch against the powerful wheels, dreading the teeth that would crush whatever came between them.

I couldn't believe Matt had abandoned me. Then I thought, he knows what's happening. He started these wheels moving. That instant I was pulled into the darkness.

ten

IN THE MORNING light last night's dream had lost its terror but not its power to disturb. I recognized the exaggerations of a nightmare—huge wheels, like gears inside a gigantic clock, waiting to grind me up—it was surreal. Even so, I felt a sense of foreboding. What truth lay behind the images? In the dream I had been drawn into something I had no control over, something I couldn't stop, and Matt had walked away.

I dressed slowly, then went down to the kitchen. Matt was there, finishing a bowl of cereal.

"How's Grandmother?" I asked. "*Where's* Grandmother?"

Her Bible lay open on the table next to a half-drained cup of coffee.

"In the music room," he said wearily.

"Why?"

"Don't you know?" he snapped.

I bit back a sharp response. "Something else has been moved."

"How did you know it was moved, rather than missing?" he asked, as if trying to trap me in my words.

"Ease up, Matt. When we thought the Bible and clock were missing, it turned out they were moved."

He rubbed his head. He looked as if he'd barely slept.

"So what was it this time?"

"Paintings. An old painting of the mill was moved from the parlor to the music room and hung above the Chinese chest. The watercolor that was there was left facedown on the floor."

"When did this happen?"

"You tell me. You were here last night, alone in the house while she was up in bed."

"Are you accusing me?" I asked.

"I don't know what I'm doing," he mumbled.

I intercepted him as he walked toward the refrigerator. "You have as much access to this house as I do, and know the place better. We can point fingers at each other and refuse to trust or we can try—"

The kitchen door opened.

Grandmother gazed at the two of us, her eyes narrowing. Matt and I stepped back from each other.

"I have put the watercolor where it belongs," she informed us. "I need help with the landscape."

"I'll take care of it," I said. "You'll be late for school, Matt. Leave me the phone number of Grandmother's doctor," I added, when she had exited.

I followed her through the door and down the hall to the front parlor, where I helped her set the large painting back on its hook.

"Is there anything else I can do?" I asked.

"Haven't you done enough?" Grandmother replied sarcastically.

I stared after her as she left the room. If I didn't get some answers soon, I was going to be as paranoid as she. I needed information, and there was only one person I knew who might have it.

I arrived at Tea Leaves an hour before work.

"I don't want my fortune read," I said to Jamie. "Tell your mother I have some questions about my grandmother's house and the family. Strange things are happening, and I need her advice."

A few minutes later the door opened at the top of the stairs, and the old woman beckoned to me. Before I reached the entrance to the second-floor apartment, Mrs. Riley had disappeared around the corner. I closed the door behind me and followed her down a narrow hall that ran toward the front of the building.

The room I entered had three windows, all of them facing High Street. Heavy drapes hung lopsided from their rods but were open enough to let in light. To the left were two sofas with faded print covers, and to the right an alcove, a square area between the front wall of the building and the wall of the stairwell. A round table and several straight-back chairs filled that space. A silk lamp with fringe hung from the ceiling.

Mrs. Riley sat down at the table, facing into the room, and gestured to a seat across from her. I perched on it nervously, tucking my hands under my legs.

"You have questions," she said.

I nodded. "I'm not sure where to begin."

"Strange things have been happening at the house." Her voice was low, almost soothing. "What kind of things?"

"Well, objects are being moved. The Bible, for instance. It was missing from its shelf in the kitchen, and Grandmother became convinced that someone had stolen it. Later, I spotted it in the library. Instead of being glad I found it, she was angry and kept staring at the spot it had occupied."

"Which was on a library shelf," Mrs. Riley said.

"Yes, just to the left of the fireplace."

The psychic's head lifted slightly. "Tell me more."

Feeling a little more comfortable, I rested my hands on the table. "This morning we found that a picture had been moved from the front parlor to the music room. Grandmother started getting weird again—paranoid, as if someone were doing this to her, as if *I* were doing it."

"A painting," she repeated.

"A landscape," I said. "A picture of a mill."

Mrs. Riley didn't make a sound, but I saw the buttons on her dress move and catch the light as if she had quickly sucked in a breath.

"Yesterday a clock was missing from Grandmother's desk."

"A small clock . . . an old one," she murmured.

"Yes. It has a picture painted on its face, roses and—"

"Was it found on the hall table?"

I blinked. "How did you know?"

She sat back in her chair. "That is where it used to be kept. The Bible always sat on a shelf by the library's hearth. The mill painting hung over the Chinese chest in the music room."

"You mean things are being moved back to where they were years ago? To where they were when you worked there?"

She nodded her head slowly, rhythmically.

"But then why would Grandmother blame me? How would I know where those things were kept? I don't see how

Matt would know, either, unless Grandmother told him."

Mrs. Riley's eyes closed, then drifted open again. She looked past me as if she were looking into another world. She stared for so long I turned around to see what was there. Nothing extraordinary—a flowered sofa, a table piled with Baggies, her herbal stuff.

"The clock belonged to Avril," Mrs. Riley said. "She insisted on placing it in the hall. She hated the big grandfather clock."

"I don't blame her," I remarked. "It's like a guard stationed on the landing, watching you come in and out. You can hear it tolling wherever you are in the house."

"Avril called it the big bully. She would reset the small clock to whatever time she wanted it to be. Her parents played along, allowing her to come home long after she was supposed to. I'm surprised your grandmother didn't throw out that wretched little clock."

"It's an antique."

"What's one more antique?" Mrs. Riley said. "Helen has money to burn."

"Maybe she keeps it because it reminds her of Avril."

"That's precisely why she would throw it out."

I was surprised by the bitterness in Mrs. Riley's voice. "Did you work there when Avril was alive?" I asked.

"I was the personal maid of both girls."

"But you must have been their age."

"A year older than Avril," she replied, "two years older than Helen."

That couldn't have been easy, I thought, especially if Avril acted like a princess. "What were they like, my grandmother and Avril?"

Mrs. Riley took a deep breath and let it out slowly. "Avril was pretty, popular, and spoiled. She was always into something and got too much attention from her parents. Poor, serious Helen got almost nothing."

"That doesn't sound fair."

"Helen was a good girl. She read a lot and always kept her room neat. It was nothing for me to pick up after her. But Avril! She didn't care where she threw things, and her room was small and crowded. She insisted on sleeping in the back wing."

"The back wing?" I sat up a little straighter.

"Oh, I knew what she was up to, even if her parents didn't. She could get in and out of the house by way of the kitchen roof."

I put my hand over my mouth. Avril had slept in the room where I'd awakened, where Alice had seen the ghost.

"What is it?" Mrs. Riley asked.

"Nothing."

The pupils of her eyes were like dark pins tacking me to the wall; she wouldn't let me go until I gave a better answer.

"I've been in that room," I said at last. "It has roses on the wallpaper."

"Avril adored roses. She wanted them in vases, in her hair, in bouquets brought by her boyfriends, and she always got what she wanted. Poor Helen grew terribly jealous and angry. I didn't blame her, not after Avril stole Thomas."

"But my grandfather was Thomas." I said, puzzled.

Mrs. Riley nodded, her eyes long, dark slits, as if focusing on a distant memory. "He was Helen's beau first—at least publicly. There were other girls, many others. *Money* is what made up Thomas's mind."

It wasn't a flattering picture of my mother's father, but I had come for the truth.

"He was a young cabinetmaker from Philadelphia, an apprentice hired to do repair work at Scarborough House," Mrs. Riley continued. "Thomas was talented but had no money. He switched his affections from Helen to Avril, who, as the oldest, was supposed to inherit Scarborough House. When Avril died, everything became Helen's. Everything including Thomas."

I sat back in my chair thinking about how Grandmother must have felt, dumped, then picked up again, second choice. Still, it happened so long ago. "I don't understand why any of this would matter to her now, but something has set her off, and it seems connected to Avril."

"Some wounds heal, others fester," Mrs. Riley replied.

"Have you seen the ghost at Scarborough House?" I asked.

"No. Not long after Avril died, I married and left the house. I have never been invited back."

"Is it possible that my grandmother thinks she is being haunted by the ghost of her dead sister?"

Mrs. Riley ran her gnarled hands over the table, touching it with just the tips of her fingers, as if she were using a Ouija board.

"Why do you say *thinks*?" she asked. "Because you don't believe it's possible?"

"I don't know. I really don't. Can a ghost move things?"

"Yes," she replied.

"Can a ghost"—I hesitated—"lead a person somewhere, guide a person to a room or place?"

"Certainly you have heard accounts of ghosts revealing where they've hidden valuables," she said.

"How did Avril die?"

Mrs. Riley studied me long and hard. "Do you want the real story, or the one the family told?"

"Both."

"According to the family doctor, according to what Mr. and Mrs. Scarborough wanted him to say, it was an allergic reaction."

"To what?"

"Redcreep. It grows here on the Shore. Since colonial times, girls and women have used mixtures of it as a beauty potion. It dilates the eyes, brings color into the cheeks. They found a bottle on Avril's bureau."

"And the real story?" I asked.

"It was an overdose. Avril, like a lot of girls back then, had taken redcreep before. She wasn't allergic to it. She was sneaking out to see Thomas that night—Helen and I both knew it—and wanted to look pretty. She became ill at the mill, which was their secret meeting place. Thomas rushed her to the doctor, but she died on the way. An overdose of redcreep. Even good things can harm you if too much is taken at one time. So typical of Avril," she added, "always wanting to do more, try more, have more, always flaunting limits.

"The family did not want a cause like 'overdose' to be listed in the paper. That would make Avril responsible, and she never got blamed for anything. Of course, the Scarboroughs had their way, as money always does."

Mrs. Riley rested her chin on her hands. Her voice sounded tired, as if the bitter edge I'd heard earlier had turned, and all she could feel now was the flat of the knife.

"I guess that's most of my questions," I said. "How much should I pay you?"

"There is no charge for today," she replied, rising with me.

"Really, I planned to," I told her, but she refused the money and led the way to the door.

"I would send your grandmother my regards," she said, opening the door to downstairs, "but I doubt that would please her. It would be best not to mention that you saw me today."

"Why?"

"It's free advice, girl," she replied. "Take it or leave it."

"Thanks," I said, and took a step down, which was a good thing since she closed the door on my heel.

eleven

I GRABBED BREAKFAST downstairs at the café then headed for work at Yesterdaze. Ginny was incredibly patient with me that day. I had to count a pack of singles four times before I got it right and gave her nickels when she asked for dimes. At 3:10 I apologized for my mistakes.

She smiled. "Don't worry about it. Are we still on for Wednesday, Thursday, and Saturday?"

"Yup."

Ginny was giving me Friday off to rest up for "the weekend invasion."

Instead of going home after work, I wandered up and down High Street and the streets around it, thinking about the things I'd learned from Mrs. Riley. I didn't see the Jeep pass by, not until Alex hung out the back, waving and calling my name. It stopped a half block ahead of me and two girls got out, Kristy and one of her echoes. They looked in my direction, then quickly turned away and said something to the guys.

As soon as they started up the walk, Alex called out, "Hey, Megan, where you going?"

"Nowhere special," I answered as I got closer. "Just walking."

"Want a ride?" he asked.

I glanced at Matt, hoping for an invitation from him. He said nothing.

"Climb in," Alex encouraged me. "You can ride up front."

"I don't know if I want a ride that bad," I told him. "I saw how Matt drove the first day I was in town."

"How did I drive?" Matt asked.

"You nearly took Ginny's fender with you."

He frowned. "You sure? I didn't see you."

"No kidding!"

Alex laughed, then Matt smiled and reached across the seat to open the door. I climbed in.

We drove to a street of Victorian homes that faced the college campus, stopping in front of a tall white house with green shutters and a wraparound porch. Alex hopped out on the passenger side, then leaned on the edge of my door.

"Would you go out with me?" he asked.

I didn't expect the question. "Um . . ." I started to turn toward Matt.

Alex reached up and caught my face lightly with his hand. "You don't need his permission, do you?"

"I guess not." I heard my cousin's seat squeak. "It's just that I'm not here for very long, and I don't want to screw up the friendship you guys have."

"If Matt doesn't like me going out with you, then *he's* screwing up the friendship, right?"

I thought about it, then smiled. "Right. So when?"

"Thursday night? We don't have school Friday and there's a big party at Kristy's."

"Oh, no, sorry. Sophie and I are going to a movie."

He looked surprised. "Can't you change it? I thought girls had a rule that when one of them got asked for a date, all other plans were off."

"I don't go by that rule."

Behind me Matt laughed, a little too loudly, I thought.

"It's not fair to the other person," I explained. "Especially Sophie. She's got enough to do with school and work. I don't want to change plans on her."

"You mean Sophie Quinn?" Alex asked. "We used to be best buddies when we were in grade school. Why don't the four of us go to the party—you, me, Sophie, and Matt?"

Now I did turn to my cousin.

He shrugged. "Okay with me."

"I'll ask Sophie what she wants to do," I told Alex, though I was pretty sure she'd be thrilled to be Matt's date.

Alex probably thought the same thing, for he gave the door a satisfied thump. "See you Thursday night."

As we pulled away from the curb, I said to Matt, "Don't worry about me and your friends. I'll be on my good behavior."

"I was just getting used to you," he replied, "and now you're going to change?"

"I can't win with you!" I exclaimed.

"Didn't know you wanted to."

I shook my head and sighed. "Listen, Matt, before we get to the house, we have to talk."

"About Grandmother," he guessed, and slowed down a little. "Did she get worse after I left?"

"Not worse, but she's really starting to get to me, the way she blames me for the things that are moved. I needed some information so I could figure out what was going on. I went to see Mrs. Riley."

The firm set of his mouth and long silence told me he didn't like what I had done.

"She used to work for the Scarboroughs," I went on, "back when Grandmother and Aunt Avril were teens. Did you know that?"

"I knew she had worked at the house." He flicked the Jeep's

blinker with one finger, then made a sharp turn. "And I know better than to trust her."

"She told me that the Bible, the clock, and the painting were moved back to where they used to be years ago, when Avril was alive."

He glanced sideways at me. I couldn't see enough of his face to know if he was surprised by the news.

"Mrs. Riley has a way of coaxing information out of people," he said, "then feeding it back to them in a different form, so that they think she's telling them something new."

"But she guessed where the clock was found. And though I told her the landscape was moved to the music room, she knew it was hung over the Chinese chest."

"Megan, think about the size of the painting. Where else would you hang it in the music room? As for the clock, a lot of people keep them in entrance halls. Every old house in Maryland has a grandfather clock in the hall or on the stairway landing."

"It's too much of a coincidence," I insisted.

"Mrs. Riley makes her living off coincidences. I hope you didn't pay her a lot."

"She didn't charge," I replied somewhat smugly.

"She's counting on you to come back. Then she'll charge double," he said, sounding just as smug.

We rumbled across the Wist bridge. I turned back to look at it, remembering that Sophie had seen the ghost there. Didn't ghosts haunt battlefields and other places where they died? If Avril had died somewhere between the mill and the doctor's, could it have been while Thomas was driving over the bridge?

"Where's the mill?" I asked.

"On the creek. About a third of a mile beyond Grandmother's driveway there's a road to the left. It runs down to the mill."

"We've got some time," I said. "Let's go."

"No," he responded quickly.

"Why not?"

"There's nothing to see," he said. "It's been abandoned for years and is full of mice and rats."

"Okay, I'll go later without you."

He shook his head. "Pigheaded."

"Yeah," I agreed, "amazing, isn't it? We're not related by blood, but we share that family trait."

"Listen to me, Megan, you can't go inside the mill. Most of it's made of wood, and it's rotting. The structure's unsafe."

As he said that, he drove past Grandmother's driveway. I tried not to smile.

"Don't smirk," he told me.

"Another family trait."

"I'm taking you there so you don't go by yourself," he said. "Understand?"

"Yes. Thank you, big brother."

Mutual smirk.

The road down to the mill was bumpy, its stone and shell layer worn away, leaving long bare spots and deep ruts. Bushes and small trees grew close to the road and scratched the sides of the Jeep. Matt muttered a few choice words. Then suddenly we were in a clearing with a sea of tall grass washing around us. The soft weathered wood of the mill rose above it, two stories, topped by an attic under a sloping roof.

"It's the one in the painting," I said.

Matt nodded.

A structure like a dormer window projected out of the middle of the steep roof, but it was larger, framing a door. The roof door gaped open, leaving a dark cavity in the light gray building. The first and second stories had doors that lined up beneath the roof entrance, but they were closed, as was a side door. All the windows were shuttered.

"Where's the waterwheel?" I asked.

"Around the side."

I got out of the Jeep.

"Megan? Don't go inside."

"I'll be back."

A moment later he trudged behind me to the bank of a stream that ran toward the basement wall of the mill. The large, motionless wheel next to the wall looked like the rusty paddle wheel of a steamboat.

"Not exactly rushing water," I observed.

"The mill works from a pond," Matt explained, pointing toward a rise in ground on the other side of the road. "When the gates are opened, the water comes in over the top of the wheel, using gravity to turn it."

I nodded, then gazed up again at the dark entrance into the roof. "Have you ever seen a ghost here?"

"There is no ghost," he replied.

"This is where Avril came, the day she died."

He looked at me surprised. "How do you know that?"

"Mrs. Riley told me. She said Avril came with our grandfather. Thomas was Grandmother's boyfriend first, then Avril stole him from her. This was Thomas and Avril's secret meeting place."

"I don't believe it."

"Do you have any reason not to?" I asked.

"Mrs. Riley is a gossip and she's always been out to get our family."

"That's a pretty flimsy reason."

"We've spent enough time here," he told me abruptly, then started toward the Jeep.

I caught up with him. "Mrs. Riley said—"

"I think it'd be a good idea," he interrupted, "if you, Lydia Riley, and Grandmother started living in the present."

"Not knowing what happened in the past can keep you from living fully in the present."

"It's not relevant," he argued, and opened the door on my side of the Jeep. "Get in."

"No."

He reached for my arm.

I pulled back, but he held on, so tightly I winced. "You're hurting me!"

He let go.

"I have some more looking to do."

Matt leaned against the Jeep and said nothing.

I headed around the other side of the mill. As the land sloped down to the water the ground beneath my feet became soft and claylike, perhaps flooded by the creek, which was about twenty feet away. The mill looked tall from the creek side, four stories of it towering above me, the basement's brick wall exposed. At the base of the building was a Dutch door, its lower half open. It was an inviting mouse hole—and people hole.

I walked over to the double door and pushed on the top half. It didn't budge. I knelt and crawled through the bottom, tumbling into the darkness head-first—there were two steps down on the inside. The floor was wet, covered with gross stuff. Ahead of me I could see nothing but vague shapes. Standing up, I turned toward the door and ran my hands over the top portion until I felt a bolt. After several tries, I slid it back and pulled open the upper half of the door, letting in more light.

When I turned to face the basement again, I gasped. At the far end of the long room were wheels—big gears—one interlocking with the next, the largest as tall as I. I was in the basement of my dream, where I had hidden from Matt. I sank down on the doorstep, afraid to cross to the other side, afraid to get close to those wheels.

How had I come to dream of this place? I doubted I was reading the images of my *mother's* mind. The voice, the dreams, awakening in Avril's room, the movement of objects to where Avril would expect them—it was Avril I was connecting with.

My skin felt cold and clammy. I stood up quickly. "Leave me alone," I said, stumbling out of the entrance. "Just leave me alone!"

Matt, who had been hovering a short distance away, heard me. He stepped back, turned abruptly, and strode up the hill to his Jeep.

Neither of us spoke on the way home. I knew Matt thought that I was telling him to leave me alone, but there wasn't much

I could do about it. He wouldn't believe I had been talking to a ghost.

He parked in front of the house and got out of the Jeep without glancing at me. Following him up the porch steps, I noticed the clay and mud caked on the thick rubber soles of his Nikes.

"Our shoes are a mess," I said, sitting down on a bench to remove mine. He checked his, then sat opposite me. By the time he started unlacing his shoes, mine were off and I was carrying them into the house.

Grandmother met me, coming through the door from the back wing. "You're late."

"For dinner?" I glanced up at the landing clock. It wasn't five yet.

She stared at my shoes. "What were you doing after work?"

"Hanging out."

Matt came in the door and Grandmother's eyes darted to his shoes. Color rose in her cheeks. "Where have you been?"

Though the question was fired at him, I answered, since the trip had been my idea. "To the mill."

"Why did you take her there?" Grandmother demanded, still focusing on Matt.

I saw the wary look on his face. "I asked him to," I said.

"I'm not talking to *you*."

"Megan wanted to see the place," Matt replied, "and I thought it'd be safer if I went with her."

"Megan wanted to see the place," Grandmother mimicked.

"I did," I said. "I was curious."

Grandmother took a step toward me. "I told you the day you came that I expected you to respect my privacy. Didn't I?"

I nodded silently.

"I'm speaking to you now. Answer me aloud!"

"Yes, Grandmother." I couldn't snap at her. If I was feeling haunted by Avril's presence, I could only imagine how she felt.

"So now you're going to be sweet and soft-spoken," she observed, her lips curling. "Sweet and sneaky."

"Ease up, Grandmother," Matt said. "Did you ever tell Megan not to go to the mill?"

"Are you defending her?"

"All I'm saying is you're getting all worked up over a little visit to the mill," he replied.

"And Lydia Riley," she added.

I looked at Grandmother, surprised. "Who told you that?"

"It doesn't matter. What matters is that you promise not to speak to her again."

"Why?"

"Don't talk back to me!" Her voice was shrill.

I sat down on the steps, hoping to make this a conversation rather than an irrational shouting match. "I wasn't talking back," I explained. "I was just wondering—"

"You're living in my house, you'll follow my rules."

I bit my lip, then nodded.

Matt rested a hand on her arm. "Grandmother, be fair. Megan was just asking—"

She turned on him. "I don't have to explain my rules to anyone, including you, Matt." Her jaw began to shake. "I can't trust you anymore. Not since *she's* come."

"What do you mean?" he asked.

"You're loyal to her now."

He stared at Grandmother. It was as if he had to be on her side, or my side, and wasn't allowed to care about both of us at the same time.

"Get a hold of yourself," he said, and walked out the back door of the hall.

Grandmother stood in front of me, her head held high, then strode into the library and shut the door behind her.

I remained sitting on the steps, bewildered by her jealous suspicions. Some wounds heal, others fester, Mrs. Riley had said. Maybe Grandmother had never really healed from her first betrayal. Matt was the most significant person in her life now, and she the most consistent person in his. I wondered if she saw me as someone like Avril, putting myself between them. Maybe Grandmother was afraid of losing out again.

Well, that was her problem. She was the one who chose to spin her world around one grandchild, rejecting my parents and brothers and me. I rose and climbed the stairs, feeling torn between pity and anger. Then I heard the machinery of the big clock begin to wind. I took the steps two at a time, hurrying past before it could start its dismal tolling.

twelve

Wednesday morning I saw Matt just long enough to ask if I could check my e-mail from his computer. When he'd left for school, Grandmother informed me that she had an early appointment. I didn't ask where, not after yesterday's reminder about her privacy. She drove off and I went upstairs to retrieve my mail. I had several messages from friends at home, but it was Mom's e-mail I was most eager to open. I printed it out, deleted the electronic copy, then sat back to read.

Hi, Sweetheart!

Dad and I loved your e-mail. We felt like we were back on High Street again.

Life here isn't the same without you. Pete and Dave

have both said they miss you, though I promised them I wouldn't squeal (crossed my fingers).

In your note you barely mentioned Grandmother. I know you, Megan, and I worry when you get silent. I'm counting on you to let me know if there's a problem.

So you found the dollhouse! It was built for Grandmother and her sister. I played with it as a kid, but I can't find a photo of it anywhere. Why do you ask?

About Aunt Avril. Neither Mother nor Dad spoke much of her. I've never even seen her picture—perhaps they were all put away when she died. We weren't supposed to ask questions about her. Dad said it made Mother sad to think about her sister. I do remember putting birthday flowers on her grave in April—Avril is the French word for that month. In October, too—I think that's when she died. She had a close friend named Angel, Angel Cayton. Angel's father was a doctor, and someone told me that Avril was brought to him the night she died. That's as much as I know.

Everyone's well here. The Naughtons' spaniel had puppies. Write soon. And this time don't leave out whatever you were trying to skirt around in your last e-mail.

Love,
Mom

I printed out my friends' notes, then logged off. As soon as I got to work, I'd ask Ginny to help me find Avril's friend.

"Angel Cayton," Ginny said, stuffing tissue down the arms of a pale silk dress that was decorated with seed pearls. She and I had put the dress on a seamstress form so Ginny could photograph it for an out-of-town client. "I haven't thought about her in ages. She died fifteen, no, must be twenty years ago now. Angel was a character—very active in town affairs and generous with her money. She started the Watermen's Fund."

"Did she leave behind any family?" I asked, though I had little hope of someone remembering stories they were told more than twenty years ago.

"I don't think so. Evie?"

Evie Brown, one of our elderly customers who came by almost every day, was standing in front of a mirror, trying purses on her arm. "Evie, do you know if Angel Cayton has any family left around here?"

Miss Brown chewed over the name for a moment. "Nope," she said at last. "Angel was an only child and never married. Her sweetheart, Sam Tighe, died in the last war."

"That's World War II," Ginny whispered to me.

"Angel got killed in a car accident, didn't she—yes, I'm sure," Miss Brown answered herself. "Out Talbot Road on Dead Man's Curve. Though Angel was the only one who ever died there. Why we don't call it Dead Woman's Curve, I just don't know. The county never gets things straight."

"I don't think the county named the curve," Ginny said gently.

"State's just as bad," the woman responded, then reached for a red purse on a peg beyond her grasp. I walked over and lifted it down.

"Sorry we can't help you out," Ginny told me.

"What's the problem?" the old woman asked, taking the red purse from me, then looping the others she had tried on my arm, as if I were a store rack.

"I was hoping to talk to Miss Cayton," I replied.

"Then try Lydia Riley. She's good at ringing through to the other side."

I heard Ginny swallow a giggle.

"I'm surprised your grandmother didn't suggest that," Evie added. "Helen was over there today."

She added the red purse to my arm.

"Over where?"

"Seeing Lydia Riley. Right before my appointment this morning."

"Are you sure?"

"Are you saying I get mixed up?" Miss Brown asked, her eves flashing.

"No, no. I'm surprised, that's all."

"Me, too," she agreed amiably. "Far as I know, they haven't spoken for years. Can't imagine what they had to talk about." She peered up at me inquisitively. "Can you?"

"No," I said, imagining a *lot* of things.

Sophie dropped by the shop that afternoon. After finishing up with a customer, I joined her at the jewelry case. She was leaning on her elbows, gazing down at the aquamarine pendant.

"Guess what?" I said. "We have another invite for tomorrow night. A party."

She straightened up and smiled. "Whose? The only party I know about is Kristy's."

"That's it."

Her face fell. "I wasn't invited, and I don't think Kristy would be thrilled if I just showed up. I haven't been part of her crowd since middle school. You go to the party, and we can see the movie Friday night."

"But you're not crashing it," I told her. "Matt is asking you."

"Matt?" Sophie's cheeks grew pink. "Kristy will kill me!"

"But I thought you liked him. And I thought you said he doesn't date one person."

"I do like him. And he doesn't date one person. And she'll still be mad as anything."

"Who cares? You can talk to me at the party. I'm going with Alex."

"Oh! I have to think about this, Megan."

"Alex said you used to be best friends."

"Yeah, forever ago." Sophie went over to the silk dress Ginny had put on the seamstress form and traced its seed pearl design with her finger. Ginny came out of the storeroom, eyed Sophie, then eyed the dress. She held her head to one side and squinted, an action that usually meant we were about to rearrange a display.

Sophie turned back to me. "Alex and I used to spend every day together at school and during the summer, crabbing time," she said. "He could always convince me to chicken neck off the bridge at four in the morning. I was the only person who'd go out with him in his old boat in pouring rain to set a trot line. I really liked being around him and the water."

"Then this should be fun."

Sophie didn't look so sure. "I hope he's forgotten about the valentine I sent him in fifth grade."

"Why?" I asked.

"It was so embarrassing. Alex wanted to hang out with the guys, and they wouldn't let a girl tag along. I wanted him to know he was important to me, so I made him this valentine heart. I drew crab legs around it for lace, and a boat oar for the arrow."

I laughed out loud and Sophie blushed.

"One of his friends found it and showed it to everyone. They teased him awful. That was pretty much it for Alex and his *girl* friend."

She paused and watched Ginny, who opened the jewelry case and took out the aquamarine pendant.

"Listen, Sophie," I said, "if there's one thing I've learned about guys, it's that they don't remember sentimental things, not even a heart with crab legs for lace. Besides, that was fifth grade. I think Alex has changed his mind about hanging out with girls."

She laughed a little. "I guess so."

"So think about it," I told her. "We'll do whatever you want to do."

"Sophie, don't go anywhere," Ginny said. "I need a favor.

Would you put on this dress and let me take your picture?"

"The pearl dress? Oh, my gosh!" Sophie gasped.

"I think that's a yes," I said.

Ginny undid the buttons and removed the dress from the form. "Let's see now," she said, talking to herself more than us, "we're going to need some shoes, and let's put your hair up on your head, so a nice comb, soft ivory pearls for that red hair." Ginny picked up an armful of items, then ushered Sophie to the dressing room in the back.

I served two customers, waiting for Sophie to come out. When the bells hanging on the shop door jingled a third time, I looked up to see Alex and Matt in their running clothes.

"Let me guess," I said, "you're interested in lace hankies."

Alex grinned. "Do you have any that match our shorts?"

"White goes with everything," I replied.

Matt flashed a smirky, flirty smile.

"So, what's up?"

"Have you talked to Sophie?" Alex asked. "Does she want to go to the party?"

"She's still deciding." I heard Ginny's voice coming from the back. "If you wait a minute, you can ask her yourself."

Ginny emerged from the dressing room, followed by Sophie. I don't know who was more amazed at the sight of the other, Alex or Sophie.

"Nice dress!" Matt complimented Sophie.

The silk and slender pearls were as shimmering and delicate as Sophie herself. Her upswept hair showed off her high cheekbones and long neck. The aquamarine pendant was the same misty blue as her eyes. Neither Alex nor Matt could stop looking at her.

"Sophie," Alex said, "for a minute I didn't know you. You, uh, you've grown up."

She frowned. "Since math class? You saw me in math today, remember?"

"Oh, yeah." He reddened. "I guess it's the dress and all."

"No," Ginny corrected him, "it's the *girl* in the dress and all. Okay, honey, let's get your picture over here."

Alex, for once, had been left speechless, so Matt took care of their mission. "Are we on for tomorrow night?" he asked Sophie.

She glanced at me.

"It's your call," I said.

She smiled. "Sure."

Matt volunteered to drive and arranged pickup times, then the guys left. I watched Ginny pose Sophie, thinking that if her camera could catch the glow on Sophie's face, it was a sure sale.

When Sophie had changed back into her school clothes, I

took a break and walked her over to the Mallard. As soon as we were on the street, I told her about my conversation with Mrs. Riley.

"It's starting to really scare me, Sophie," I said. "I wake up in a room—I guess I sleepwalked—and find out it was Avril's. Things are moved to where they were when Avril was alive. I dream of a place I've never seen, then see it for real—the mill where Avril and Thomas used to meet, where she went the night she died. I feel like she's haunting me."

"I wonder why she'd choose you," Sophie mused, "other than the fact that you may be psychic," she added slyly.

"I think it's happening to Grandmother, too. I know the relocation of things is getting to her."

"And Matt?"

"He knows something he's not telling me. And he wants me to leave."

We were standing in front of the window of Tea Leaves. Jamie passed by inside and waved to us.

"Did Miss Lydia say anything about how Avril died?" Sophie asked.

When I recounted both versions of the event, Sophie's eyes lit up. "Maybe Avril is trying to set the story straight. There are lots of stories of murder victims haunting people and places until the truth is known.

"The death was an accident," I reminded her.

"Maybe," she replied, and walked on to a bench in front of the Mallard.

I sat down with her. There was one thing I'd been holding off telling her, and I needed to get it out.

"I saw the ghost."

Her eyes opened wide. "You did? When? Where?"

"A couple nights ago, in the upstairs hall. I saw her in the mirror."

Sophie got a funny look on her face. "In the mirror?"

I nodded. "She looked like a mist."

Sophie gazed down at the sidewalk, tracing the shape of a brick with her toe. "Have you ever seen her outside the mirror?"

"No, but I saw her only once."

"When you passed the mirror," Sophie said.

"Ye-ah . . ." She was making me uneasy. "What is it?"

"Megan, the way you talked about your dreams, I thought you were seeing the future or tapping into your mother's past. But maybe that's not it. What if you've been remembering places and objects that you saw in your own past?"

"What do you mean?"

"What if you're Avril—reincarnated?"

I pulled back. "Now you're getting weird."

"It makes sense," she argued. "When you returned to your old house, you instinctively went to your old room. You put your clock back where you kept it. Since the mill was important to you, you noticed a painting of it that seemed out of place."

"Are you saying I moved those things?"

"While you were sleepwalking," Sophie replied. "It probably happened more than once."

I shook my head.

"Avril died when she was a teen," Sophie went on, "and that makes it all the more likely. Reincarnation is a chance to complete what's unfinished in a previous life. For instance, if two lovers—"

"I've seen the movies and know what it is," I said, cutting her off. "A woman gets hypnotized, then remembers bizarre stuff from another century. I'm just having dreams."

"They're the same thing," she replied, "memories buried in the unconscious. They come out in different ways, that's all. Sometimes when a person has experienced a tragic death, there is a symptom of it in the next life. Say a girl died in a fire. In her next life, just seeing a candle being lit might frighten her. Her phobia comes from a memory buried in the unconscious.

"Well, I don't have any phobias," I told Sophie. "And besides, if Avril's spirit was reincarnated, I don't see how she could have a ghost."

"Maybe there isn't one."

"I saw her with my own eyes!"

"In a mirror," Sophie pointed out. "Maybe you had an out-of-body experience and saw your own spirit. Which is what others have been seeing just before dawn. That, too, makes sense—living in a different time zone, your sleep cycle is later than ours."

"No," I insisted.

"Think about the night you saw the mist in the mirror. Do you remember at any point looking down on yourself, looking upon your body as it is now?"

My spine tingled. "At the very end I—I thought I saw myself lying dead."

"Like the way people describe a near-death experience?" she asked. "Like when someone whose heart has stopped sees himself lying on an operating room table?"

I nodded slowly.

"It's an out-of-body experience."

"Or a dream," I replied stubbornly.

Sophie sighed and got up from the bench. "I've got to work. Talk to Miss Lydia. She'll help you understand."

I stood up. "There's nothing to understand."

She laid a hand on my arm. "Megan, listen to me. Sometimes a premature death keeps you from doing the work you were meant to do. Sometimes it separates two people meant to be together. Reincarnation isn't something to fear, it's a second chance."

"I never asked for a second chance."

"Okay, let me put it this way. Do you want the dreams to stop?"

"I want it *all* to stop."

"Then accept the possibility of reincarnation. Find out who you are and what you're to do with your second chance. Once you have, the past will let go of you."

I didn't know what to think. I wasn't the kind to run away from something and I certainly wanted the strange things that had been happening to end.

"See you tomorrow," she said softly, then went inside.

I walked down High Street and sat for a long time by the water. I knew that Grandmother was more than cold to me—she was jealous. Matt seemed confused, torn between protecting her and defending the time he spent with me. I, for some crazy reason, actually cared about Grandmother. And I was trying to overcome an attraction to Matt that I didn't want to admit. The parallels between the past and present were eerie. Were the three of us playing out parts in a triangle that had existed sixty years ago?

thirteen

I WASN'T READY to talk to Mrs. Riley Wednesday afternoon and didn't ask Grandmother why she had gone to see her. Obviously, she was feeling haunted. Questioning her would only make her more hostile toward me. That night I tossed and turned in bed. I discovered the one advantage to lack of sleep: lack of dreams. Still, my mind raced with thoughts as strange as dreams.

If Matt were Thomas, then he must have held me once, he must have kissed me. I quickly squelched that daydream. According to Mrs. Riley, there were a lot of girls in Thomas's life before he settled on Avril. It occurred to me that his love for Avril was not a proven fact. Mrs. Riley told me what she believed at the time, but for all she knew, Thomas may have been planning to break things off with Avril the night she had died. He and Avril might have had a terrible fight. Perhaps the negative feelings from that time had carried over; it sure seemed as if Matt had set his mind against me before we met.

By eight fifteen Thursday evening I had spun so many theories in my head I didn't know what I thought about Thomas and Avril. But my belief in the possibility that Matt and I had been reincarnated waned: The two of us meant for each other in a previous lifetime? No. He and I were nothing more than a pair of high school kids, cousins who occasionally got along, heading for a party. We set off in his Jeep to pick up Alex and Sophie.

"I hope Kristy won't mind Sophie and me coming," I said, when we stopped at a red light.

"She told us we could bring whoever we wanted," Matt replied. "Which doesn't mean she'll be nice," he added. "But you can handle her."

"Of course I can," I said, which made him laugh. "It's Sophie I'm worried about."

"I'll look out for her," he assured me.

We picked up Alex by the college.

"Stay where you are, Megan," he told me as he climbed in the back. "It's a short ride to Sophie's."

She lived on Shipwrights Street, in the middle of a block of small wooden houses, each one two stories high, two windows wide, with a porch spanning the front. Their tiny yards were neatly hemmed with picket fences.

As soon as we drove up, Sophie came out, followed by her three younger sisters, the oldest of whom looked about nine. The trio lined up on the porch steps to watch.

"Girls." We heard a voice coming from the house. "Gi-irls."

They made stretchy faces and slowly trooped back inside. Meanwhile, Alex had run around the Jeep to open doors.

"Hey, Sophie," I greeted her, about to climb out of the front seat so she could sit there.

I saw her hesitate.

"Oh, yeah," Alex said. "I forgot about that. Megan, do you mind riding up front?"

I looked at him surprised.

"Or I can," he offered.

When I saw Sophie blushing, I quickly pulled in my feet. "No problem."

As soon as she and Alex were settled in the backseat, she leaned forward. "Sorry, it scares me a little up there."

"Don't blame you, the way Matt drives," I replied.

Matt glanced sideways at me, one side of his mouth curling up. "Sophie," he said as we drove off, "have you been to Kristy's new house?"

"No. I heard it's awesome."

"It's got bathtubs big enough to row across," Alex said.

"Deep enough to drop a trot line?" Sophie asked.

He laughed. "No, it's nice, but not perfect. Hey, guess what I noticed tonight while getting dressed?"

"I don't think I want to," Matt quipped.

"Your valentine," Alex said to Sophie. "I had it tacked inside the door of my bedroom closet. You know, the card with the crab legs drawn around the heart and a boat oar going through it?"

She gazed at him, speechless, then turned to look at me.

"I was wrong," I told her. "I suppose one in a million guys is sentimental."

"Did I miss something?" Matt asked.

"How many things would you like me to list?" I replied.

He rested a hand on mine. "Glad you decided not to be on your good behavior tonight. I wouldn't know what to do with you."

I didn't answer. I was too aware of how his hand felt touching mine.

"You actually saved my valentine?" Sophie said to Alex.

"Is it too late to apologize for being a jerky fifth grader?"

Her voice was gentle. "You weren't jerky, just a fifth grader, a fifth-grade boy."

"How come you don't hang around with Kristy anymore?" Alex asked.

"I don't have the time," she replied. "I help Mom with her

job and take care of my sisters. After Mom and Ron had Jenny, I couldn't do all the things Kristy wanted to do. And with Kristy, you're either in or out. I'm out."

They continued to talk, catching up on news about his family and hers.

"Okay, guys, I'm going to need some help finding the turnoff," Matt said.

Only our headlights brightened the dark country road.

"It's about a half mile beyond Dead Man's Curve," Alex told him.

Dead Woman's, I thought, remembering Evie's annoyance with the name of the place where Angel Cayton had died.

I glanced back and saw Alex reach for Sophie's hand. It wasn't a friendly pat. He intertwined his fingers with hers and moved closer.

Matt glanced in the rearview mirror. "You taking two dates to the party, Alex?" he asked lightly.

"No, just getting beyond this curve."

"It's always scared me," Sophie explained.

"When we used to ride our bikes down here to fish," Alex said, "she'd make me go the long way so we wouldn't have to take the curve."

We started around the bend, which began slowly, then

sharply doubled back on itself. I looked over my shoulder and saw Sophie close her eyes.

"Thanks, Al," she murmured when the road straightened out again.

I stared at her wonderingly. I had been so caught up in Thomas and Avril, I hadn't thought about anyone else from their time. Avril's best friend had been Angel, and Angel had died on the curve that Sophie feared to the point of being phobic. Sophie said she felt a "connection" with me. Was it an old friendship she sensed? Angel had lost her love in the war, so she and Sam Tighe were another case of a couple separated too soon.

I felt surrounded by ghosts, trapped in the events of the past.

"Are you okay?" Matt asked.

When Sophie didn't answer, I did. "She's fine."

"I was talking to you."

I glanced up at him. "Me? Why wouldn't I be?"

"Megan," he said gently, "look at your hands."

I did, then made them lie quiet in my lap.

"I didn't think my driving was *that* bad," he remarked.

"Here it is," Alex called from the backseat.

The turn off took us all the way down to Wist Creek. By the time I climbed out of the Jeep, I'd pulled myself together.

Kristy's house was huge with long sloping roofs, wide wooden beams, and amazing spans of glass. The four of us walked into a two-story foyer lit by a globe chandelier.

"Hey, guys! Come on in," Kristy called, her voice carrying from another room. Then she came through the archway and saw Sophie and me. For a long moment she didn't say anything—she didn't have to. The dramatic way she stopped and blinked her eyes let us know she couldn't believe that we had come.

"Well, hello. This is a surprise."

"I told you we were bringing dates," Matt said.

"Yes, but you didn't—well, never mind."

Didn't say you were bringing *them*, I filled in the blanks.

"Come on, party's in the back. I haven't seen you for such a long time, Sophie," Kristy said and took her by the arm.

Alex and Matt waited for me.

The party, which started in the kitchen and family room, where Kristy's parents were, spread to a wide double-level deck, then spilled out on the lawn below, ending at the dock on the creek. Music blasted from the deck and groups of kids sat on blankets in the grass. It was all pretty laid back.

When Alex and I stopped to talk to some kids on the deck steps, Matt moved on with Sophie and Kristy. Alex introduced me to a guy and girl who had camped in Colorado and loved white-water rafting as much as I did, and after that, a girl who worked for a vet and wanted to be one. It would have been a great party if I hadn't had so many strange ideas and questions running through my mind—and if it hadn't been Kristy's.

"You're frowning," Alex observed, his eyes following mine.

I was watching Kristy. "You'd think she was Sophie's best friend," I said indignantly. "But I know what she's doing. She's using Sophie, and then she's going to ditch her. All Kristy wants to do is flirt with Matt."

"That's all a lot of girls want to do," Alex replied with a smile. We walked down the hill toward the creek. "How about you?"

"How about me what?"

"Are you interested in Matt?" he asked.

"He's my cousin."

"Sort of," Alex reminded me.

My laugh sounded fake. I quickly changed the subject. "Want to go out on the dock?"

"You're asking me? The closer to the water, the better," he said.

We walked to the end, about thirty feet offshore. The dock's pilings were lit with small lights that drew lavender circles on the dark water.

I asked Alex about catching crabs, about how you chicken neck and set a trot line, the things that Sophie had mentioned.

"You and Sophie really hit it off," he observed, sounding happy about it.

I nodded. "I've known her only a couple days, but it seems like we've always been friends."

I couldn't believe that had popped out of my mouth. *Coincidence,* I told myself; *you're reading into things.*

"She can be the best friend in the world," Alex replied fervently, then gazed in her direction.

She and Matt were standing by a table beneath a string of colored lanterns. Sophie talked and Matt bent his head, smiling, listening intently to her. For a moment I wondered what it would be like to have Matt smiling at me, as entranced as he seemed right then. I snuffed out that thought. Sophie was interested in Matt, and if the two of them got together, it would be the best thing that could happen.

At that moment Kristy moved in. Talk about rude! There were three guys standing close by, waiting to help her set up food, but apparently it was Matt's help that she wanted—Matt's attention.

Alex threw his head back and laughed. "Megan, if you were a cat, your back would be arched and your fur standing on end."

I grimaced. "My father says I wear my heart on my sleeve."

"No, just your thoughts," Alex replied softly. "It's pretty

easy to guess what you're thinking. But your heart, you keep that hidden."

"Sometimes even I'm not sure what's there," I admitted.

He smiled and gave me a friendly hug. "Whatever it is, I'm sure it's okay."

When Alex let go, I saw that Matt was staring at us.

"Hey, they're putting out food," Alex said. "Stay where you are. I'll get some and we'll have a picnic out here."

"Great!"

He started off and I turned away from the party to gaze out at the creek. With a late-rising moon and no street lamps nearby, the stars were brilliant. Close to the dock the water rippled, then lay quiet again, hiding the creatures that moved beneath its surface. The darkness was beautiful; the secrets it held, enticing.

A few minutes later I heard Alex coming back.

"I wish I could visit here in the summer," I said, "and swim in the creek at night."

"Do you?"

I turned around quickly when I heard his voice. "I thought you were Alex!"

Matt gazed long and hard at me. "He'll be back. I came out to let you know that Sophie is having a good time, so you can stop worrying. You can stop watching her."

"I guess I'm being obvious."

"I told you I'd look out for her," he said.

"I'm glad she's having fun. She's really nice and really pretty and, uh, Matt, mind if I give you some advice?"

"You're going to anyway."

"I know you're like—well—the main heartthrob of your school."

His expression changed. He seemed surprised, then amused. "Really," he said.

"I know you can have any girl you want."

"I can? I wish someone had told me that before. *Any* girl?" He took a step toward me. We were standing close, too close, but I couldn't step back—there was no dock left behind me. "Anyone at this party?"

"Well, just about," I told him.

"Wait a minute," he said. "A moment ago there weren't limits."

"Don't be greedy. My point is, there's Sophie." I gestured toward the shore, but he kept his eyes on me. "She likes you. She's gorgeous—I mean you must have noticed yesterday at the shop."

"I can see."

"Obviously, Kristy is too. Gorgeous, I mean."

He tilted his head to one side, frowning.

"The point is Sophie is not only pretty, like some girls, she is also nice, friendly, sweet, and—"

"Not my type," he said.

"And," I continued, undeterred, "she doesn't have a mouth."

His gaze dropped down to my mouth. I glanced to the side. When I looked back, he was still gazing at me, his eyes dark and mysterious as the creek. His lips parted slightly. He looked so long and so steadily at my mouth, my cheeks burned and heart pounded. I felt his eyes making my lips soft. I felt as if his eyes were kissing me.

"Not like yours," he agreed, then turned and walked back to shore.

fourteen

For the rest of the party I was careful not to look at Matt and Sophie, but Alex picked up where I had left off. I wondered if he was becoming interested in his best old friend. The ride home was awkward, our conversation mostly dumb cracks about Kristy's house. After dropping off Alex and Sophie, Matt and I rode in silence.

I was aware of his every movement, the way he shifted in his seat, how his hand rested on the steering wheel. Why did I respond to him so strongly? Even when Matt was his most obnoxious, the day I met him, his eyes had cast a spell on me. Had we once been in love? Was I falling for him a second time?

At home I thanked him for the ride and headed for the refuge of my room.

Having slept little the night before, I drifted off as soon as I lay down. When my eyes opened again, the sky was beginning to lighten. I heard the chime of the clock on the stairway landing and counted the hours—five, six, seven—I turned over—eight, nine, ten—couldn't be—eleven, twelve, thirteen. Silence.

My digital alarm read 5:00 A.M. I listened for a moment, then climbed out of bed and tiptoed to the door of my room. Opening it, I saw the stairwell was lit from below. I crept down the steps to the landing and gazed at the clock's pale face. Its hands pointed to a few minutes after midnight. In the window above the numbers, the picture of the moon was halfway up.

Using the key, I opened the glass door that protected its face. Though I could hear the clock ticking, its hands didn't move. With the tip of one finger, I tried to push the large hand forward. It would not move, so I eased it counterclockwise till the clock read a few minutes after five. I thought I had set things right, then I noticed the small second-hand dial in the clock's face. Its wand flicked backward over each lash of a second. Ever so slowly the clock's minute hand moved in reverse. Time was turning in the wrong direction.

I stepped back, afraid, and teetered on the edge of the landing. Strong hands gripped my arms and pulled me back to safety.

"It's only a clock," he said.

"Thomas!"

We were standing close, close enough to kiss, but I couldn't step away from him. If his hands hadn't held me, his dark eyes would have.

"I hate that clock," I said. "It is always telling us what to do when."

Thomas laughed. "And you certainly don't want to do what is expected of you."

"Do you?" I asked.

"I used to." His gaze dropped to my mouth. He looked so long, so steadily, my cheeks burned and my heart pounded. I felt his eyes making my lips soft. I felt as if they were kissing me.

"April," he whispered, "I can't stop thinking of you."

I didn't say a word—I knew the pain we could cause. But every time he looked at me, every time he spoke his special name for me, I wanted him more.

He laid his hand against my cheek, then touched my mouth with one finger, running it over my lip.

Just once, I thought, gazing up at him. One kiss wouldn't be so terribly wrong.

He bent his head and our mouths moved closer. His lips brushed my cheek, the lightest touch of him making me shiver. Then his arms tightened around me, and I felt the warmth and tenderness of his lips against mine.

"Thomas!"

We both pulled back. My sister stood at the top of the stairs glaring down at us.

Thomas let go of me. "Helen, I—"

"Don't try to explain," she told him angrily. "Don't make it any worse for me. Leave, Thomas."

"But I need to explain," he said. "I've let things go too long."

"Leave!" she shouted. "Now!"

He looked at me and I nodded.

"I—I'm very sorry," he told her.

My sister waited till Thomas was gone, then started toward me, her eyes burning with anger. "Is there nothing of mine you don't want, Avril?" she asked. "Is there nothing of mine you won't take for yourself?"

I bit my lip.

"Mama and Papa already give you whatever you ask for."

I closed my eyes, knowing what was coming next.

"The servants will do anything for you. Your friends cover for you. All the boys in this town wait on you."

"Helen, it's not my fault that—" I broke off.

"That you're everyone's favorite?" she finished for me. Her face was so pale, her skin so tight, I could see the bones moving beneath it. "Say it, Avril, it's the truth."

I looked away.

"You have everything. Did you have to take Thomas, too?"

"I can't help the way I feel about him," I said. "He can't help the way he feels about me."

"And what about good old Helen?" she asked. "Does it matter at all what I feel?"

Her eyes were bloodshot. I knew she was trying not to cry. My heart felt cut in two. I ached for her, but I ached for us as well.

"Do you think because I keep my emotions in check that I feel nothing?"

I was desperate to prove myself right. "If two people feel the same way about each other," I reasoned, "then that must matter more than what one person feels."

"I can't believe you'd do this to me!" she cried, her voice quivering with anger. "One day you're going to pay, Avril."

She took a step toward me, then another. Something in Helen had shattered, the lock she kept on her fierce passion had been broken. I could see the fury in her eyes, in the curl of her fingers.

"Mark my words," she said, coming toward me. "You're going to pay."

I stepped back quickly and missed my footing. I reached out, but couldn't stop the fall. My head snapped back and I tumbled downward, the edge of each tread banging against my spine. I heard Helen scream—scream as she did when we were children, "I didn't mean it! I didn't mean it!"

Then everything went black.

"Megan! Are you all right?"

My back hurt and my arm, jammed against the stairway banister, buzzed with pain. Matt knelt next to me, halfway down the flight of steps.

"Just a little bruised," I answered shakily.

He helped me sit up. "What happened?"

"I'm not sure." I struggled to put together the jumbled images in my mind. "I must have been sleepwalking. I did it a few nights ago. You didn't see me fall?"

"I was in the library," he said. "When I heard the noise, I rushed out and found you here."

"What time is it?"

He glanced over my shoulder. "About ten after five."

I turned to look at the clock on the landing and suddenly remembered the thirteen chimes and the scene with Avril, Helen, and Thomas. This time I wasn't dreaming simply of a place, but an event. Had it actually happened? Was I fantasizing, elaborating on the story that Mrs. Riley had told me, or was I truly remembering?

Until Matt touched my cheek, I hadn't realized I was crying. "What's wrong?" he asked. "Tell me." He gently took my face in his hands.

I didn't know how to begin to explain. "It was so real," I whispered. "But that's what crazy people always think, that what they imagine is real."

He put his arms around me and pulled me close. I buried my face between his neck and shoulder.

"You're not crazy." He smoothed my hair. "I promise you, you're not."

"I—I've had a lot of weird dreams since I've come here."

"Dreams about what?" he asked softly.

"Places, people. Thomas, Avril, and Helen—Grandmother. Dreams about the past."

His arms tightened around me. I could hear his heart beating fast.

"Were you dreaming when you fell?" he asked.

"Yes."

"Tell me about it."

"In the dream Grandmother was young, no older than us. And she was furious with her sister. She had walked in on Avril and Thomas."

I felt him swallow hard.

"They were kissing."

The motion was slight, but I sensed it, the way he pulled back from me.

"Grandmother threatened Avril," I added, then the tears streamed down my face again.

"Megan, you should leave."

"Leave?" That's not what I wanted to hear from him, not now that I was wrapped in his arms. "Why?"

"I think that if you leave, all of this will stop."

"All of this meaning what?" I asked.

"You know what."

Suddenly I wasn't in his arms anymore; he had let go and stood up. "Come on, I want to show you something."

Matt led me to the library, where the lamp on Grandmother's desk was already lit, and gestured for me to sit in her chair. After retrieving a key from a vase on the mantel, he returned to the desk and unlocked a drawer.

"I saw you in here," I told him, "the first night I came."

He laid several flat boxes on the desk in front of me. "I was looking at these. Have you ever seen a picture of Aunt Avril?"

"No."

"She's pretty." He lifted a lid and handed me a black-and-white photo. "Look like anyone you know?"

My breath caught. Her resemblance to me was striking.

He opened another box. "There's a colorized photo in here,

a portrait." He sorted through the pictures, then handed one to me.

"Gray eyes," I observed. "Her hair's lighter than mine, but her eyes are gray and the facial structure's the same."

"You see why Grandmother is going crazy," Matt said. "You look like her sister. You look like Avril the year she died, and it's spooking her."

I nodded. "The question is why. Sixty years is too long to be mourning a sister, to be upset about seeing someone who resembles her . . . unless there is more to the story."

I looked at him expectantly, but he said nothing.

"In my dream Grandmother told Avril she would pay for what she had done."

"So?"

"What did she mean by that?"

"Sounds like a typical fight between sisters," he replied, but he wouldn't meet my eyes. He knew more than he was saying.

"Mrs. Riley said the cause of death was an overdose."

His hand tensed till it creased the picture he held. What had Grandmother told him the night they had spoken in her bedroom?

"But," I continued, "who would know the difference between an accidental overdose and deliberate poisoning?"

"You can't be thinking—"

"Only Avril," I continued, "and the person who poisoned her, the murderer, if there is one."

"Megan, I told you not to trust Lydia. She makes her money off people's fears. She suggests things and lets people make themselves crazy wondering about them."

"So, why did Grandmother go to see her the other day?"

"You'll have to ask her," he said brusquely. His face was a mask. Grandmother had nothing to worry about—he wasn't telling her secrets. I was the one who should be wary of what I said to him; he probably told *her* everything.

"Does that key work on the other drawers?" I asked.

He unlocked them, and I started going through files and boxes.

"Look at these." I showed him photos of myself and my brothers, our names and ages inscribed on the back in my mother's handwriting. Grandmother never even sent us a Christmas card, but apparently my mother kept writing to her, kept trying to make contact.

Matt placed a picture of me on the first day of kindergarten next to a young one of Avril, then shook his head slowly. He cradled in his hand a photo of Avril standing by the gate in the herb garden. "It's scary how much you look alike."

"It's as if I've been here before," I said, watching his face carefully. "Have you ever felt like that, Matt, like you've been in this house some time long before now?"

"No," he answered quickly.

Perhaps I was reading into it, but it seemed to me that if Matt had never thought about reincarnation, my question would have drawn a different response, a slower one. He would have looked at me puzzled and asked what I meant.

"You should leave," he said.

"No way."

"Why are you so stubborn?" he exclaimed.

"It's you who are stubbornly refusing to open your mind to questions and explanations you don't like. I'm staying here till I find out what's going on."

"Nothing's going on," he argued, walking away from me. "You look like Avril. It's just a bad coincidence, and you're going to make both yourself and Grandmother insane over it." He started pacing the room.

"Did you move any of the objects in this house?" I asked.

Matt swung around. "I'm not the kind to play tricks."

"Then you must suspect me," I said. "But think about it. How would I know where those objects were kept when Avril was alive, unless—"

"Grandmother moved them," he interrupted. "Maybe she's gotten senile and did it without remembering, or this is just some crazy spell she'll snap out of. Whatever the case, you're not making things any easier for her."

He walked over to me. "Finished?" Without waiting for my answer, he put the photos and boxes back in the drawers and turned the key in the lock.

"Matt, those pictures mean that Grandmother has always known that I look like her sister. She knew and chose to invite me. I want to know why."

"Curiosity," he replied.

"Guilt," I countered. "Morbid curiosity and guilt."

Matt shook his head. "You're getting stranger than Grandmother. Take my advice, Megan. Get out of here. Get out before it's too late for both of you."

I got up from my chair. "Sorry. It already is."

fifteen

When I returned to my room, I couldn't get back to sleep, so I dressed and took a long walk, spending time by the water then stopping by Avril's grave. It didn't give me the same eerie feeling as the first time I saw it. Perhaps seeing your own grave is like looking at a gushing wound on your leg: Once you're over the initial shock, it seems natural enough. I knelt down before the stone and traced the name and dates with my finger. On the final date my finger stopped. Today. Avril had died sixty years ago today.

When I finally arrived back at the house, it was nine o'clock. I entered through the front hall, wanting to avoid Grandmother and Matt in the kitchen. I was angry with Matt for turning away when I needed his help. He had chosen Grandmother over me, determined to protect her at any cost.

I crept upstairs, stuffed some things in a backpack, and headed out again, leaving a note in the hall telling Grandmother

I'd be gone for a while. My first stop was the library at Chase College. I hoped to access local newspaper articles from Avril's time that might shed light on what had happened.

Three hours later, totally frustrated by the library's ancient and cranky microfiche machine, I'd found just one short piece on Avril that attributed her death to allergic reaction. It made no mention of the mill or Thomas. After searching online for redcreep, it became obvious that its local name would not yield information on the plant and its by-products. But I got lucky with Angel Cayton. She had not only started the Watermen's Fund but contributed to the college. A librarian directed me to a conference room where her portrait hung.

Angel looked like all the other matrons honored in the conference room, with gray hair, blue eyes, and a bustline that could amply support pearls and eyeglasses—only she wasn't wearing pearls. Around her neck hung a silver chain with a blue gem as mystical as the eyes of my newest and perhaps oldest—friend. It was the pendant Sophie loved.

I opened the front gate. "Is Sophie around?" I called to the group of little girls who were playing dolls on the porch. Barbie and Ken kissed with loud smacking noises, then one of Sophie's sisters turned to me. "Mom said we can only have one friend over at a time. Sophie's already got one."

"I'll be just a minute. Is she inside?"

"Around back," said another sister.

I followed a stone path to the narrow space between the Quinns' house and the house next door and emerged into a backyard.

"Oh," I said, though I shouldn't have been surprised. "Hi."

Sophie, who had been leaning over a tub of suds, leaped to her feet. A large black-and-white dog jumped with her. Alex caught the dog just before it escaped its bath. Soap bubbles flurried around them.

"Hey, Megan," Alex said, smiling. "Want to help us wash Rose? We'll throw in a free bath for you."

I laughed. "Thanks, but I've already had mine. I'll watch."

"Rose met up with a skunk this morning," Sophie told me.

"I'll watch from a distance."

"And Alex sort of stopped by to help," she continued, looking embarrassed.

"Glad he got here first," I teased.

"It was nice because he hadn't seen the girls for a while," she added, as if Alex had come by with the passionate hope that he could deskunk her dog and visit her sisters.

"Like I told you before, we're just old friends."

She was so worried that she was intruding on my dating territory, she missed the expression on Alex's face—the protest he almost spoke aloud. I saw it and smiled.

"You know, Sophie, I'm here for a two-week visit," I reminded her. "And I doubt Grandmother will be asking me back."

Alex realized that I was giving Sophie "permission" to go with whomever she wanted and glanced sideways at her, but she didn't get it. I don't think it had crossed her mind that her old crabbing buddy was falling for her—falling fast, I'd say.

"How's Matt today?" Alex asked.

"Hot and bothered, thanks to me."

"Any chance of you two cutting each other a break?" he asked.

"Don't think so," I replied, and tried to ignore the ache inside me.

I watched him and Sophie work the soap through the thick fur of the dog, debating what to say in front of Alex. How aware was he of Sophie's psychic side? He seemed an open-minded person; still, I decided to mention only what I had to.

"Listen, Sophie, I'm trying to get information on the plant called redcreep. Do you know its botanical name?"

"No, but Miss Lydia might."

"What do you need to know about it?" Alex asked.

"I was told that people used it as a beauty supplement. I

want to know if the processed stuff has any taste—or smell or color. Does it dissolve in liquid? What exactly does it do to you? How fast does it work? How much is too much and what are the symptoms of an overdose—uh, you know, that kind of thing," I added casually, after giving a list that belonged in a forensic lab.

"Why do you want to know?" he asked.

I glanced at Sophie.

"It's a long story," she answered for me. "How about someone at the college, Alex—would one of the biology profs know?"

"We can find out," he replied.

"Would you?" I asked quickly. "I've got some other things to do. Thanks. I'll catch up with you later." I started across the grass.

"Megan," Sophie called, hurrying after me. "Megan!" She waited till we were in the side yard, out of earshot. "What are you up to?"

"I have a lot to tell you," I said, "but not now. I want to talk to Mrs. Riley, then go to the mill."

"Don't."

"Don't what?"

"Go to the mill. I have a bad feeling about it." Shaded by a cedar, her blue eyes were a flicker of light and shadow.

"Look, Sophie, don't get prophetic on me. It's the past I need info on, not the future."

"I'm telling you, it's dangerous."

"I'll watch where I step and look out for rodents."

"You're asking for it," she warned.

"Is that a prediction?"

"Yes."

"Want to hear my prediction?"

She looked surprised, then smiled. "From the person who claims she isn't psychic? Okay."

"Before I leave Wisteria, you and Alex are going to be totally in love."

I left Sophie with a look of wonder on her face.

Mrs. Riley couldn't see me. At first I suspected that the purpose of Grandmother's visit had been to forbid the woman to speak to me, then I saw the worry on Jamie's face.

"She's had another bad night and is resting now. How about I fix you a late lunch? Some dessert?"

"No, thanks." Though I hadn't eaten that morning, I had no appetite.

"Try back later," he said. "I'm sure she'll feel better."

I wandered up and down the streets of Wisteria hoping for inspiration, some theory about what had happened sixty years ago that would help me understand what was going on now. Each time I tried to reject the idea of reincarnation, I came back to it. It was the one theory that explained all the strange things that had been happening. Sophie's suggestion made sense: While sleepwalking I had moved the Bible, the clock, and the painting to where they belonged when I was Avril. Small matters fell into place, such as Matt's reluctance to go to the mill. Did he remember something terrible happening there? Was he trying to get me away from Wisteria before I remembered?

On my wanderings I passed Tea Leaves, and Jamie flagged me down. He said his mother wanted to see me at four. I used the remaining time to look for Sophie, checking her house and Alex's, then the college, but didn't catch up with her. I browsed in a New Age bookstore, looking at covers and reading their fantastic blurbs, till the incense and tinkling music got to me—not to mention the weird shoppers.

They're probably all Mrs. Riley's patrons, I thought; *and now I'm one of them.*

At four o'clock the old woman was waiting for me, beckoning from the top of the café stairway. I climbed it and followed her down the narrow hall. When we sat at the table beneath the fringed lamp, I saw the deep circles under her eyes. There was a tremor on one side of her mouth that I hadn't noticed before. She lay her palms flat on the table in front of her. Her fingers looked sore, the nails bitten down to the pink.

"What is it you want of me?" she asked.

I hesitated, torn between my own need to get answers and the realization that she wasn't well.

"You want to know more about Avril and Helen," she guessed.

"You look so tired," I said, starting to rise.

"Stay!" She gripped my wrist with surprising strength. "I have been concerned about you and hoping to see you again. Ask your questions."

I sat down and carefully pulled away my hand, lowering it into my lap. "I want to find out about reincarnation."

"Go on."

"Sophie told me it's a chance to complete things that have been left undone."

Mrs. Riley nodded.

"She said that if a person died young, she might be reincarnated. Sometimes two people can be reincarnated together if they are separated too soon in a previous life."

Mrs. Riley studied my face. "And you think that has happened to you?"

"I think I'm Avril."

The old woman sat back in her chair. After a moment she

said, "Do not be misled by appearances. You look like your great-aunt, but that is not significant."

"It's not what I look like. It's what I dream about. It's what I seem to remember."

The shrill whistle of a teakettle sounded in another room. Mrs. Riley ignored it.

"What do you remember?" she whispered.

"Scarborough House. The dollhouse that looks like it. I dreamed about them before I saw them."

"And?" she asked, her eyes as bright and sharp as the whistling sound.

"The mill, its basement, the big wheels in it."

"And?" she pressed.

I bit my lip. "That's it." The dream about Thomas, Helen, and Avril was too uncomfortable, too personal to tell.

She looked at me doubtfully. "You must be honest with me if I am to help you."

I stared down at the table and said nothing.

She stood up. "Very well. Think about it while I get my tea."

As soon as she disappeared, I covered my face with my hands. What did I hope to prove—that Grandmother was guilty? Why reveal that now? It would only cause a lot of pain. Still, the doubt and suspicion that grew out of that dark secret were quietly poisoning the minds of Grandmother, Matt, and me.

Mrs. Riley reentered the room and set two cups on the table. "It's cinnamon apple."

"Thank you," I said, then sipped the fragrant tea.

"Do you know anything about karma?" she asked.

"I've heard of it."

"It is the belief that we are rewarded or punished in one life according to our deeds in a previous life." She held her cup in both hands and gazed at her tea as if reading it, then took a long drink. "Karma is just," she said. "According to it, the victim of an unnatural death will return in a later life and seek out the killer."

"Seek out the killer?" I repeated.

"It's justice, dear. If you take away someone's life, then in the next cycle, your life will be taken by that person. The victim will kill the murderer."

I stared at her. Did she know what I suspected?

"You're remembering, aren't you," she said quietly.

I sipped my tea, avoiding her eyes.

"What is it?" she asked, her voice soothing. "Avril, tell me what you are remembering."

"I had a dream," I said at last. "Helen was very angry at me. She threatened me, said I would pay. But that doesn't mean anything," I added quickly. "Brothers and sisters say that all the time without meaning it."

"True enough," the psychic replied. "Do you remember anything else—anything from the day you died?"

"No."

"And yet you are remembering more and more," she said. "I don't know how to advise you." She rose from the table and walked restlessly around the room. "I have my suspicions. To speak them may influence a clear memory. Not to may endanger you. You know that Helen came to see me yesterday."

I ran my finger around the moist rim of my cup. "Yes."

"I warned you, child, not to tell her you were here."

"But I didn't. Someone in the café must have told her."

"Can you trust your cousin?" Mrs. Riley asked. "You're hesitating. That tells me you can't."

"He's very protective of Grandmother."

Her hands worked nervously. "Then it would be foolish and dangerous to trust him."

"Why?"

"He's loyal to her, dependent on her money, and you fear the same thing I do—that you were murdered by Helen."

For a moment the raw statement of my suspicion shocked me. I struggled to think clearly.

"But if I was the victim in my past life." I reasoned, "I'm the one who is the threat now. According to karma, Avril would destroy her murderer—that's what you said. And I would never hurt my grandmother."

"The act does not have to be intentional."

"But what if I make sure I don't hurt her?" I argued. "What if I leave and never come back?"

Was that why Matt wanted me to go? Did he know more about this than he pretended?

"Karma is karma," Mrs. Riley responded. "There is only one thing that can prevent the victim from achieving justice."

"What?"

"Her own death."

I looked at her, startled. "You mean, dying a second time? You mean my death?"

"*Now* you understand why you must remember what happened that day. Just because you would not hurt others, doesn't mean others won't hurt you, not when it comes to saving themselves. You must find out your enemy."

My mouth went dry. I felt as if I couldn't breathe. "I can't will myself to remember. I'm not psychic like you or Sophie. I have no control—the dreams come when they want to."

Mrs. Riley came back to the table. "Today is the anniversary of Avril's death," she said, her voice calm, steadying me.

"There is a window of time when the past will be open to you. Can you get to the mill?"

"Yes."

"Go straightaway. Walk around it, breathe it, touch it. Listen to its sounds, let it become part of your life again. Go inside and make yourself quiet there, let the past come back to you. Your life depends on it."

I sat still as a stone.

Her brow creased, then she rested her veined hand gently on mine. "Finish your tea, child, then hurry. You haven't much time if you want to be home before dark."

sixteen

I DIDN'T RUN fast, but when I reached the mill, I was out of breath and had a stitch in my side. I walked slowly around the building, waiting for the pain to ease, mulling over what I had learned from Mrs. Riley. If Grandmother had murdered Avril, then I, the reincarnated Avril, was destined to take Grandmother's life. Did she know that? When she had gone to see Mrs. Riley, what had they talked about?

Grandmother would never harm me, I told myself. But then I thought, if she murdered her own sister, how hard would it be to do away with a grandchild, an adopted grandchild? With sixty long years in between, another accident would not seem suspicious. And she could count on Matt to protect her.

Matt's attitude toward me had changed in the short time between our first meeting and that moment on the dock. Had he exploited my attraction to him to keep tabs on me?

"Tell me," he'd said later, holding my face gently in his

hands, seeming as if he wanted to help. Perhaps all he wanted was information and to keep me from looking further. I was more determined than ever to find out what had happened in this place.

Breathe it, touch it, listen to its sounds, Mrs. Riley had said. I pulled on the long grass, feeling its sharp edges. I took a deep breath and smelled the salty water. The creek lapped gently, slipping between grasses and stones. The birds sounded exceptionally loud and sweet to me. I emptied my mind of everything but the mill and felt as if I were walking in a dream.

Since I had left both basement doors open, I entered the mill easily. I looked across the room at the wheels, then forced myself to go to them, to touch the biggest one. I wrapped my fingers around a metal tooth and gripped it hard. Rusted saws and metal circles that looked like disembodied steering wheels lay here and there. It wasn't a cozy place for two people to meet. The next floor up would be drier and brighter, I thought.

I saw the stairway along one wall, the same as in my dream, like a tilted ladder with wide wooden treads and no handrail. I walked under it and pulled on each step to see if it would support my weight. One split in half and two others cracked, but they were spaced well enough for me to climb to the trapdoor.

When I was near the top of the steps, I pushed against a square piece of ceiling. The trapdoor was heavier than it looked.

I managed to shove it up, swinging it back against a wall, carelessly assuming the door would stay. It slammed down on me. I was stunned by the force and clung to the top step, feeling dizzy. There were small, scurrying sounds—the mill's residents.

Determined to get to the next floor, I pushed against the trapdoor again. Then I grabbed a long piece of wood and placed it diagonally between the floor and the hinged door to prop it open. I climbed through and looked around the first-floor space.

Though the windows were shuttered, crooked seams of light shown through cracks in the plank walls. In one corner of the room was a round iron stove, missing its chimney pipe. Barrels and bins, burlap bags gnawed apart by rats, and frayed rope were strewn about. Narrow chutes built in long rectangular sections with elbow joints looked like the arms of wooden people coming down through the ceiling. The ceiling itself gaped with holes. The trapdoor above the stairs to the second floor appeared to be open. Gazing up into it, I suddenly felt light-headed.

I found a millstone, half of a pair used for grinding, and sat on it. Closing my eyes, I ran my hands over its rough surface, feeling the long, angled ridges. Waves of confused images and sensations washed over me: the sound of voices, Thomas's face, Matt's, the clock chiming, the sound of engines, my name being called, footsteps against a hard surface. I wasn't sure what was inside my mind and what was outside. I couldn't tell what was then and what was now, when I was Avril and when I was Megan. Everything seemed real but distorted, the sounds and images stretched at the edges.

Hunching over, resting my head on my knees, I saw moving lines of light. I struggled to focus.

Light between the floorboards—that was it. Someone with a flashlight was walking downstairs. Did the person know I was here? Instinct told me to hide. I crouched behind a pair of barrels.

Peering around the edge of them, I saw the orb of light dodge its way up the stairs, held by an unsteady hand.

"Child? Are you here? It's Lydia," she whispered as she climbed the last step.

I breathed a sigh of relief.

"I need to talk to you. I have seen something and must warn you."

Before I could emerge, another voice cried out. "Megan! Are you in here?"

It was Matt. At the sound of his voice Mrs. Riley moved quickly, hiding behind a bin.

"Where are you?" Matt called. I heard him walking below us, then hurrying up the steps. "Megan? Answer me!"

His words brought back the memory with sudden force. "Answer me! Answer me, Avril!"

Thomas's hands gripped my shoulders. He shook me so hard my head snapped back. He started dragging me down the mill steps. My chest hurt. It felt like straps of steel had tightened around it. Every breath was agony.

I pushed away from Thomas, gasping, desperate for air. He held me tighter. I tried to speak, but the darkness was closing in on me. I needed air!

I staggered to my feet, grasping the barrels to steady myself. Matt spun around. I was in the present again. I was Megan. But Matt's eyes were identical to Thomas's.

He started toward me.

"Run, child!" Mrs. Riley cried. "Run before he hurts you."

We both turned toward her. The surprise on Matt's face quickly changed to anger.

"Shut up, old woman," he said. "You've done enough."

"I'm not afraid of you," she replied, her eyes bright, challenging the fire in his. "Are you remembering now, Thomas?" she asked. "Are you remembering all of it now?"

"I don't know what you're talking about."

"That's why you came to me three years ago, isn't it?" Mrs. Riley continued. "You were seeing *her* face. She had come back to haunt you."

Matt glanced at me, then back at Mrs. Riley.

"But you didn't think you'd see her in flesh and blood again, did you?" she prodded.

"Your mind is twisted." he said. "It's been twisted for years. You've preyed on my grandmother's fears. You knew she wanted to make Avril sick that night so she couldn't meet Thomas. You gave her the redcreep and told her how much to put in the tea, but she cut that amount in half, and Avril was well enough to go. It was another dose, a later dose, that killed her. Still, you convinced Grandmother that she had given her sister too much, that she was responsible for her death. Grandmother had always been jealous, hurt by the attention Avril received, wishing that Avril would get out of her life. It was easy to change those feelings into guilt. You enjoyed torturing her with false guilt."

"I did enjoy it," Mrs. Riley admitted. "She was so self-righteous. But I believed it, too. I realized a second dose had been given"—her voice softened—"but I was *so* in love with you when you were Thomas."

Matt took a step back from her.

"I was so naive," she continued. "I couldn't believe you had done it. It had to be Helen, I thought. I couldn't accept that my Thomas was a cold-blooded murderer."

He was the murderer? Waves of fear and nausea washed over me. Matt, not Grandmother, was the one who should fear me.

Did he know it? I remembered the strange way he had looked at me the day we met. He had known from the beginning.

"I should have realized that it was Helen you wanted all along," Mrs. Riley continued.

Matt's dark eyes burned in his pale face.

"Avril was too unpredictable, too much of a flirt. But the fortune was hers. So you played up to her and killed her, then you and Helen got everything."

His fists clenched.

"Nothing has changed since then," Mrs. Riley added. "You still depend on Helen's money. You will be loyal to her till the end."

"You're wrong," Matt argued, "dead wrong."

"Even when the other boys would come here to swim," she said, "you couldn't bear to be in this place. You told me so yourself."

"I was an idiot to trust you."

"Karma," Mrs. Riley said softly. "Justice at last. Sixty years ago you wanted nothing to do with me, Thomas, not when you realized you could have the Scarborough girls."

Matt turned his back on her. "She's crazy, Megan. Let's get out of here."

"No." My tongue felt thick in my mouth, and I struggled to speak clearly. "Stay away."

"She's a liar, a troublemaker," Matt said. "I told you that before. You can't believe her."

"I do."

He took two steps toward me. One more and he'd trap me behind the barrels. I moved my hand slowly, then shoved a barrel at him and ran past his grasp.

He whirled around. I faced him, my back to the wall, inching sideways, feeling my way along the rough wood, trying to get to the steps that led down to the basement.

"Listen to me. You're not yourself," he said.

"I know who I am." The words came out slurred. "And who I was. So do you."

He looked at Mrs. Riley. "What have you done to her?"

"I told her about karma," the woman replied. "She knows what you know."

"Megan, come here." He held out his hand. "Come here!"

I shook my head and continued inching sideways.

"You must trust me."

"I trusted you before." My mouth moved slowly, my thoughts and words getting jumbled. "I trusted you when you were Thomas."

Matt's eyes darted around the room. His hands flexed, then he sprang at me. I lurched sideways and scrambled free. But he caught my shirt, yanking me back. Then something hissed and snapped between us. Matt let go, quickly pulling back his hand, burned by the rope Mrs. Riley had brought down like a whip.

I rushed blindly ahead, crashing into a plank of wood, part of the open stairs rising to the next floor. I clung to it. I had to get up. Had to get away from him.

Matt pushed back Mrs. Riley and came after me. "If you won't come, I'll drag you out of here."

I started to climb, but it felt as if the stair, the entire room, was tilting. I could barely hang on.

Matt stood at the bottom, studying me.

"No closer," I said. I didn't want either of us to die.

He put a foot on the bottom plank. "Something's wrong with you, Megan."

"No closer!"

I pulled myself up another step, then another. It was like moving in a dream, climbing in slow motion.

Matt started up the steps, but Mrs. Riley came after him like a cat. I saw something flash in her hand. Matt dropped backward. He turned and struggled with her, grabbing her wrists. A knife flew across the floor.

"What have you done to her, Lydia?" he demanded.

"Nothing."

"Liar!" he shouted. "You've poisoned her."

The woman fought to get free. He pinned her hands

behind her, then turned his face up to me "Don't run from me, Megan."

I took two more steps up.

"Can't you understand? You need help, medical help. Come down."

There was a pipe propping open the trapdoor. If I could get through the door and close it, I could use my weight to keep it shut.

"Please," Matt said, grasping the ladder with one hand, "don't let Lydia do this to us."

I reached up to pull myself through.

"April!" he cried. "Don't leave me again!"

It was the name he had written on my heart. I turned to look down at him. My foot slipped. Reaching out wildly, I grabbed hold of the pipe that propped open the door. For a moment it held me, then I felt its cold iron slide through my fingers, felt myself falling backward. I heard a rushing sound in my ears and plunged into darkness.

seventeen

I OPENED MY eyes in a white room with pale-striped drapes. It smelled like raspberry bathroom cleaner.

"Where am I?"

"With me."

I turned toward Matt's voice.

"How are you feeling?" he asked.

I lifted my head and glanced around. "Well, since I'm in a hospital, I can't be feeling too well."

He grinned. "You're talking like yourself, and you've been acting like yourself. The nurse said if you pulled out your IV one more time, she'd staple it to you."

"It's out," I observed.

"The doctor said that you'd come around soon enough, and then they'd irrigate you."

"Oh, that sounds like fun." I tried to sit up.

"Easy," he said, and slid his arm behind me to help.

I rested back against him. "Thanks. You don't want your arm back, do you?"

"Nah. Slide over." He sat next to me on the bed. It felt good, the way he kept me close.

"Do you remember anything?"

"Yeah." I took a deep breath. "If it was a dream, I'm crazy, and if it was real, some awful things have happened."

"Some awful things have happened," he said gently. "You may not want to talk about it yet."

"The sooner the better," I told him.

He leaned forward to study my face, then sat back again, convinced. "All right. You, Lydia, and I were at the mill, on the first floor. Do you remember our conversation?"

"You talked about who killed Avril, but it was confusing. The sounds and images kept overlapping. Sometimes I was in the past, sometimes the present."

"You were drugged."

"Drugged? But I didn't have anything to eat all day," I protested. "Just tea at Mrs. Riley's."

Matt said nothing, waiting for me to figure it out. I felt as if I'd just been punched in the stomach. "She did it. She did to me what she did to Avril."

He lay his cheek against my forehead. "I almost lost you a second time."

"I remember that she tried to keep you away from me. I thought she was protecting me."

"She didn't want me to interfere before the poison took full effect," he said.

I shivered. "She wanted to kill me, before I could kill her. I remember being at the top of the stairs. My foot slipped and I reached up for something. A pipe, but it gave way. I started falling. I don't remember landing, just falling."

One corner of Matt's mouth turned up in that smirky smile of his, then I noticed the wrap on his left ankle. "Oh, no! Tell me I didn't."

"Okay. You *didn't* come down like a ballerina," he said, then laughed at me. "It's just a sprain. But it's the last time I'm catching you, so don't try it again."

"Thank you," I said meekly. "How about Mrs. Riley—where is she? What has she told people?"

He didn't answer right away. I felt his arms tighten around me. "Megan, Lydia has died. The pipe struck her."

I went cold all over. "Oh, God!"

"It's all right," he said. "Everything's all right now."

"I did it," I whispered.

"It was an accident."

"But I did it!"

"You didn't mean to. You know that."

"Mrs. Riley said it would happen, intentional or not. Karma."

My eyes burned. Matt pulled my face against his and let my tears run down his cheeks.

Finally I reached for the tissue box.

"Okay?" he asked gently.

"For now."

"I'll be around later, too," he said.

I looked up into his eyes. "When did you know about us—about us back then?"

"I dreamed about you, saw your face, from the time I was nine or ten. When I got to high school, I talked to Lydia and she told me about reincarnation. I thought she was nuts. Then, when I described you, she said you looked like my great-aunt Avril. That's all I needed to hear—I was out of there.

"I dated every girl who'd go out with me, but I couldn't get interested in any of them. Finally—maybe it was sheer willpower—I stopped dreaming of you. A few months later Grandmother told me she had invited my cousin for a visit. I turned around and there you were." He framed my face with his hands.

"You looked stunned," I recalled.

"I was."

"I still find it strange that Grandmother asked me here."

"I know that she doesn't believe in reincarnation," Matt said. "Still, your resemblance to Avril unnerved her. Grandmother's a lot like you—she faces her fears—so she invited you. While we waited for you to come, she seemed so tormented, so obsessed with you, I disliked you before you arrived—at least I thought I did."

I laid my head on Matt's shoulder.

"Does Grandmother have any idea what's going on now?" I asked.

"She knows that Lydia killed Avril, that she shifted her own motive for murdering Avril to Grandmother. Earlier today Sophie and Alex came to the house looking for you with information about redcreep. When I put together what they had learned with what Grandmother had told me the other night, I knew the timeline didn't work out. Grandmother gave the dose too early—and gave too little. Someone else had a hand in it. We told Grandmother that and she called Lydia. Jamie said his mother had gone to collect some plants at the mill. Which is where you told Sophie and Alex you would be. Sophie was scared, said she had feared all day that something would happen there. I rushed to the mill. Grandmother called 911."

He buried his face in my hair. "I know I've been tough on you, Megan. I did whatever I could to keep distance between us. It was useless. At the party how do you think I knew you were watching out for Sophie?"

"I must have been pretty obvious."

"And I was pretty busy watching you and Alex," he said. "I was so jealous of him I thought I'd explode."

I laughed, then covered my mouth.

He pulled away my hand and gazed at my mouth, as he had that night. "And then you tried to sell me on Sophie."

"I didn't know *I* had a chance." I touched the curve of his lips with the tip of my finger.

"Megan, I love you. I will always love you."

I swallowed hard.

"Scared?" he asked.

"Yeah. How about you?"

"Even more than the first time," he said. "I know what it feels like to lose you."

Then he bent his head and kissed me.

Sometime after Matt left, Grandmother came in. I had dozed off and wasn't aware of her until I felt her hand touch my hair, brushing it back from my face.

"You must get well," she said, her voice shaking. "Megan, you must heal."

I opened one eye. "Are you telling me what to do again?"

Grandmother stepped back quickly. I tried to catch her hand but couldn't.

"Sorry. I was just being funny, just making a joke—trying to." I struggled to sit up. "You sounded so serious, Grandmother."

"I was serious. You nearly died."

We both looked away.

"Thanks for calling emergency," I told her. "I owe you my life."

"You owe me nothing."

I frowned at her. "Because you don't want me to? Because that connects us somehow?"

A long uncomfortable silence followed.

I sighed. "It's going to take a while for us to get used to each other, isn't it?"

"I am who I am, Megan," she replied. "I'm old. I can't change now."

"Change?" I repeated. "I wasn't even going to try. Can't we just stay as we are and get used to each other?"

I saw the small flicker of light in her eyes and the corners of her mouth turn up a little. "That," she said, "may be feasible."

eighteen

DESPITE WHAT I said about staying the way we were, I changed. I, who have always believed in speaking my mind and made it my mission to uncover the truth, have found myself keeping secrets. Sometimes life is more complicated than the simple rules we make for it.

In the morning that followed my poisoning, Grandmother, Matt, and I agreed to keep silent. Jamie believed his mother had become mentally confused, unintentionally giving me something that made me ill. He came to the hospital to tell us that, even brought the teacup from which I had drunk, so it could be tested and the doctors would know how to treat me. But I had already been diagnosed with an overdose of redcreep. We threw the cup in the trash.

Sophie and Alex came to the hospital together that day. I saw the brightness in Sophie's eyes, then the delicate chain around her neck.

"That pendant looks familiar," I said.

She smiled. "Alex bought it for me."

In the year since, they've become the best of friends again, and the best of sweethearts—again.

As for Grandmother, she, too, has changed, though I certainly wouldn't point it out to her. I suppose it's hard to keep your life the same when two extra grandsons, my rough-and-tumble brothers, come barreling through on holidays.

Matt's at Chase College now on a lacrosse scholarship. I'm applying to colleges in Maryland. And we're keeping another secret, though maybe not as well as we thought. Just the other day Jamie stopped me on High Street. "You know," he said. "I make wedding cakes."

Don't Tell

one

SEVEN YEARS EARLIER

THE SCREEN DOOR creaked open. I shut my eyes, hoping Mommy would think I was asleep and go away. I wanted to burrow under my bedsheets, but I lay as still as I could, hardly breathing.

"I can't sleep, Lauren."

I sat up. "Nora! Next time, say it's you."

She stood by my bed, looking like a skinny ghost in her pale cotton nightie.

"Someone keeps whispering. And Bunny is missing. I can't sleep," she said.

Bunny was a stuffed animal with fur worn flat as Aunt Jule's washcloths. Though Nora was twelve, two years older than I, she still took Bunny everywhere.

"I think he's on the dock. Want me to get him?"

Nora was afraid of water, this summer even more than last.

"No, I can go as far as the dock," she replied, then left my bedroom the way she had come, through the door to the upper porch.

I lay down, soothed by the sound of a sailboat line clanging against a mast. I came here every summer and loved Aunt Jule's big wooden house with its long double porches, the old boathouse on the river, and the overgrown gardens. Every year, as far back as I could remember, I came to play with my godmother's children, Nora and Holly, and their friend Nick.

Nick and Holly, a year older than I, had taught me all kinds of stuff Mommy didn't like. Aunt Jule never minded. She took care of us the way she took care of her house and garden—trusting somehow that we'd all survive. Being a kid was easy here in Wisteria.

But not this summer. Mommy had come, and she and Aunt Jule were fighting. It got worse at night, especially if Mommy drank wine. Afterward I would hear her walking the porches up and down, up and down. Sometimes she'd come into my room to talk to me.

"Someone has been in my room, baby," she'd say. "Someone has tied knots in all my scarves and necklaces. Someone hates me."

It scared me when she talked like that. When we were back in Washington, she often feared that people were following us. It was just reporters and photographers who wanted a picture of the famous senator's wife and daughter. I got used to it, but Mommy got more and more frightened by them. I thought it would be better at Aunt Jule's, but it wasn't.

She'd tell me things were moving in her room. "There's no hand touching them, baby. They move by themselves."

After a while she'd fall asleep, curled up on my bed. I'd lie awake for a long time, and when I finally closed my eyes, I'd dream of things moving with no hand touching them. In my dreams people chased us and tried to choke us with scarves and necklaces.

But Mommy hadn't come tonight, not yet. Maybe I'd fall asleep and feel safe and happy the way I used to at Aunt Jule's. The mist on the river was thick tonight, like a big soft comforter laid over the water, the edge of it lapping the house. I sank down in its friendly darkness, closed my eyes, and dreamed of playing treasure hunt with Nick.

In my dream the clank of a line against a sailboat mast became louder until it sounded like a bell being rung. The ringing wouldn't stop. I sat up suddenly. It was the dock bell—the big bell we were supposed to ring if there was trouble on the river.

"Nora!" I cried, then jumped out of bed and ran to the porch outside my room.

Holly, whose bedroom was next to mine, hurried out at the same time.

"Nora went down to the dock," I told her, panicky.

A light went on downstairs, cutting a path of white through the mist. Aunt Jule ran across the lawn toward the water, her bathrobe billowing behind her like a cape. Holly and I rushed to the end of the long porch and raced down the outside stairs.

The heavy mist blotted out the river and the dock. We paused for a moment at the top of the hill, straining to see, then ran down the grassy slope. I stepped on something sharp. Holly heard my cry and turned around. "It's okay. Okay," I told her, waving her on.

Close to the river edge she stopped and bent over. As I got nearer, I saw that Nora was safe, huddled on the ground.

"Where's Mother?" Holly asked her sister when I had caught up.

Nora pointed toward the water, her hand shaking.

Aunt Jule's voice sounded strange in the heavy mist, as if it were separate from her. "Holly, call 911."

Holly turned to me. "Lauren, go call."

"You run faster," I argued. "And you're wearing shoes."

"Go, Holly!" her mother shouted. She was wading in from the dark river, carrying something. I watched the way she swayed from side to side, as if the burden were heavy. I started into the water.

"Stay there, Lauren. Get back on shore."

I backed up onto the dry land, but away from the whimpering Nora, my stomach in a knot. I could tell from Aunt Jule's voice that something was wrong. The bundle she was carrying was long and limp. Even before I could see her clearly, I knew it was my mother. When Aunt Jule reached me, she laid her down in the grass. My mother's dark eyes stared up at me.

"Mommy?" I said softly. "Mommy? Mommy!" I cried. I picked up her hand and shook it.

Aunt Jule caught my wrist. "She—she can't hear you, love," she said, then closed my mother's eyes.

two

THE GRIEF COUNSELOR had said I would go back to Wisteria when I was ready. It took me seven years.

Sunday afternoon, as I stood at the top of High Street in one of the prettiest river towns on Maryland's Eastern Shore, I wondered why I had stayed away so long. Wisteria was not only the home of the godmother I loved, but the place where I was born. It was the summertime kingdom in which I had been allowed to run safe and free.

I walked down the sidewalk, enjoying the familiar feel of bumpy brick, hot beneath my sandals. Pots of red geraniums sat on broad steps. Impatiens tumbled over baskets hanging from painted wood porches. The Colonial Days Festival, held every June, was in full swing, and people crowded into shops like Urschpruk's Books. In front of Faye's Gallery wind chimes hung as they always had in one of the sycamores lining the main street.

Then the wind shifted. I smelled the river. Everything went cold inside me. Despite the sunlight, I started to shiver. For a moment I thought of returning to my car and driving straight back to Birch Hill Academy. This was why I hadn't come back here. This was why boarding with teachers and vacationing with my father and his political staff had seemed the better way to spend a summer.

I forced myself to keep walking and tried to focus on the present, making it a game to identify everything that was different: the new sign on Teague's Antiques, the dogwoods planted on the town hall lawn, the color of the window shutters along Lawyers Row.

"Are you lost?"

I turned around. "Excuse me?"

Two guys were sprawled on a bench close to the sidewalk. The one who had spoken wore tattered shorts and a colonial three cornered hat   nothing else. He had wide shoulders and long, muscular legs. He stretched dramatically, then lay his tanned arms along the back of the bench. "You look lost," he said. "Can I help you find something?"

"Uh, no, thanks. I was just looking."

He grinned. "Me too."

"Oh?" I glanced around, thinking I'd missed something. "At what?"

He and his friend burst out laughing.

Way to go, Lauren, I thought. He had been looking at *me*! He was flirting.

Feeling stupid, I stuck my hands in my pockets and kept walking. I knew I was blushing.

"Have a good time looking," he called after me.

I turned halfway around. "Thanks."

On the one-to-ten scale of the girls at Birch Hill, he was a definite *eight,* maybe higher if he took off the hat. I could see from the slight tilt of his head that he was assigning a number to me, too. I turned back quickly and kept walking.

"Make sure you stop at the dunking booth," he added. "It's part of the festival, two blocks down. See you in about ten minutes."

I glanced over my shoulder. "Okay . . . maybe." I felt the warmth spreading on the back of my neck and wondered if the backs of my legs were pink as well.

Would he really meet me there? But then what? Nothing, of course. I was good at math and English, and good at sports, but lousy at guys. Of course, a girls' boarding school didn't allow for much experience with guys, but the real reason was that when I got the chance, I ducked it.

I wondered if Aunt Jule's daughters were dating a lot now. My godmother visited me twice a year and downloaded me on everything I had done, but she always brushed off my questions about Nora and Holly with short answers. And she never remembered to bring photos, so I couldn't even picture them as teens. Maybe Nora and Holly knew this guy, I thought, then put him out of my mind.

The two and a half blocks from Washington Street to the town harbor were closed off to cars for the festival. I began to wander through the tents set up in the street. At a political booth I said a silent hello to my father. An unflattering picture of his face was blown up to beach-ball size and nicely framed by a red circle, a diagonal line drawn through it—the banning symbol. The farmers and watermen on the Eastern Shore hated his political agenda; if I were them, I would too.

I passed the Mallard, a colonial tavern converted to a bed-and-breakfast, then stopped in at Tea Leaves Café, where the best cookies in the world were made. Standing inside the door, I enjoyed the cool draft from the ceiling fans and the rich, familiar smells of brown sugar and butter. Then a feeling of dread spread through me. My skin prickled with sweat and turned ice cold. I remembered sitting in the café as a little girl, watching my mother slowly descend the steps from the second floor, where fortunes were told.

Mommy's face was the color of pale icing. Old Miss Lydia had peered into her crystal ball and seen grave danger and death. When my mother told me that—like a fact, not a prediction—I was so scared I cried. I didn't know how I could protect her.

Looking back on it now, I realized that Miss Lydia hadn't needed a crystal ball to make such a dark prediction. After a hundred tabloid stories about my father's romances and my mother's wealth, and having endured years of cruel comments from political advisers who saw my mother as a liability, she had come to believe that everyone was against her—everyone except me. She had clung to me as if I were a life preserver. Fear and anger had been written on her face, and that was all the fortune-teller needed to read.

I left the café and continued on, barely seeing the shops and booths I passed. Not until I crossed Cannon Street did I come back to the present, startled back into it by an amplified voice.

"Come on, all you spaghetti arms! Who's going to wind up and throw that ball? You there—come on, skinny. Put me out of my misery. Dunk me!"

It was the guy from the bench, still wearing his three-cornered hat. He razzed the fairgoers from a plank suspended above a vat of water. According to the sign, the dunking booth was raising money for Wisteria High School.

Two middle-aged men took the bait and threw at the target, a four-inch disk which, if struck, would upend the plank.

"Nice curve ball, buddy. Too bad it was five feet off. Come on, girls, your turn. Show that guy how it's done."

Several groups of girls about my age had gathered around the booth, and guys were hanging out to watch the girls hanging out. There was a lot of body language going on—a glance over a bare shoulder, the sweep of eyelashes, the lifting of long waves of hair. *I could learn something from these girls,* I thought—not that I planned to use it anytime soon.

"Come on, limber up those pretty arms," the guy with the hat urged. "Want me to make the target bigger? How big? Big as a beach towel? Think you could hit that?"

I could, I thought. I could peg that little red disk. But I stayed at the back of the crowd, observing the flirting.

"Hey, it's the looker!" he announced with delight. "I didn't think you'd show, looker. Step right up! Why're you standing all the way back there?"

I glanced to the left and the right, hoping someone would materialize next to me.

"You," he said.

Everyone in the crowd turned to me. I've been stared at in Washington, where people know I'm "Brandt's daughter," and I've learned to shut it out. But this was different. My instincts told me I couldn't shut *him* out.

"You're not shy, are you?"

"Shy of what?"

Some of the kids laughed. I hadn't meant to be funny.

"Shy of showing off that arm."

"No," I said.

He waited for me to say more. There was a long pause. I felt as if I were back in the days when my father would call me up to the speaker's podium and I was supposed to say something cute. I remained stubbornly silent.

"Then come on up. Do everybody a favor and shut me up," he said. "Put down your money, pick up that ball, and let it fly, looker."

"I'd rather not."

People laughed.

He flapped his arms and squawked like a chicken. "Afraid you can't throw that far?"

"I know I can."

He lifted his hat in a small salute to my claim. Blond curls slipped out, then he plopped the hat back on and said, "I dare you."

The guy with whom he had been sitting on the bench put down a dollar and motioned to me.

"Come on," the blond guy taunted from the dunking bench. "Show us some muscle."

This is what you find in a small town, I thought, *guys from the last century when it comes to their attitude toward girls.*

I made my way to the front of the crowd. The guy on the plank started singing what must have been the Wisteria High School anthem. His buddy handed me a softball. I focused on the target, imagining it was the first baseman's glove at Birch Hill and we needed one more out to win the championship. I planted my feet and threw.

Bull's-eye! He went down on a high note.

The crowd cheered loudly. For a moment all we saw was the floating hat, then his blond head popped up.

"Lucky shot," he said.

"No way," I replied.

"Law of chance. Eventually someone had to hit the target."

"Want to try for two?" I asked.

"Twice lucky? I don't think so."

I grabbed a ball and raised my arm, ready to nail the target.

"Hey—hey! Wait till I get back on the bench." He reclaimed his hat and climbed up onto the plank. "And somebody's got to pay."

I pulled a dollar from my shorts.

"Okay, girls and guys, let's see if this looker is—" He swallowed the rest.

There were more cheers and shouts of "Do it again! Do it again!"

People started laying down money. I had never been surrounded by so many cute guys. I lost my nerve and backed away from the booth. "Sorry, I, uh, have to go."

"Three in a row, three in a row!" someone shouted. Others picked up the chant.

"No, really, I have to go."

Out of the corner of my eye I saw a woman with camera equipment turn in our direction. I can pick out a press ID tag a mile away.

"Please let me through," I begged, but the crowd pushed forward. I glanced over at the guy standing waist deep in the water and expected him to start taunting me again.

He met my eyes, then reached for his megaphone. "I'm not getting back on that bench," he said, "not till little Miss Lucky leaves."

"Aw, come on," the crowd urged.

"No way." He set down the megaphone, then flopped on his back. With his hat resting on his stomach, he floated and sang "Yankee Doodle Dandy."

Two guys began to goad him. I slipped behind them, dodged three more, and made my escape, not stopping until I reached Water Street. There I leaned against a tree and silently thanked the tease for letting me off the hook.

A short block ahead of me was the glittering Sycamore

River. I gazed at it for several minutes, remembering long, lazy afternoons of watching it from Aunt Jule's porch, back when it sparkled with nothing but happy memories. A wet hand suddenly touched my shoulder.

"Remember me?"

I turned quickly and found the blond guy grinning at me, dripping on the ground around him, the corners of his hat sagging. I tried to think of something clever to say; unable to, I said nothing.

"Are you shy?" he asked.

"No, not at all, not around people I know."

He laughed. "That's brave of you. What's your name?"

"Lauren."

"Want to go out, Lauren?"

I blinked. "Jeez! No."

He blinked back at me, as surprised by my answer as I was by his question.

I fumbled for an excuse. "I'm not going to be here very long," I lied.

"Perfect!" he replied. "My dating policy is one date per girl. Occasionally, I go on two dates with the same girl, but that's my absolute limit. I don't want to get hooked. You like movies?"

"But I don't even know you," I argued.

"You want references? I have college recommendations. They don't talk about my excellent ability with girls, but—"

I glanced quickly to the right. A girl was watching us, most of her hidden by an artist's easel and the flap of a tent. All I could see were her dark eyes, eyes that were drawn together, as if in pain or anger. When she realized I saw her, she turned and disappeared.

"Hey," the guy said, touching me on the elbow, studying my face, "don't take me so seriously."

I glanced back at him.

"It's no big deal," he went on. "I can stand rejection. I'll just be crushed for months."

I smiled a little. "Maybe you know Nora and Holly—"

"Ingram?" he finished quickly.

"Their mother is my godmother."

His eyes widened. He took a step closer, peering down at me. I was very aware of the strong line of his jaw and the curve of his mouth.

Ten, I thought, he's definitely a *ten*.

"You're Lauren Brandt," he said. "I should have known it. You still have those chocolate-kiss eyes."

I took a step back.

"Here." He plunked his wet hat on my head. "Don't go anywhere," he told me, then turned away. When he faced me again, his eyes were crossed and his mouth stretched wide by his fingers. "Now do you recognize me?"

"Nick? Nick Hurley?" I asked, laughing.

He took back his hat. "You'll be sorry to hear I don't make gross faces as much as I used to. Now I'd rather smile at girls."

"I noticed."

He waved his hat around as if trying to dry it, his green eyes sparkling at me, as full of fun and trouble as when he was in elementary school. I relaxed. This was my old buddy. We used to fish and crab together and have slimy bait battles with chopped-up eels and raw chicken parts.

"You've changed," he said. "You're—uh—"

"Yes?"

"Taller."

"I hope so. I was ten the last time you saw me."

"And your hair's really dark now—and short," he added.

My mother had loved long hair and fussed with mine constantly. The year after she died, I cut if off and haven't grown it since.

"Other things have changed, too," he said, his eyes laughing again. "Where are you staying?"

"At Aunt Jule's," I replied. "Does your uncle Frank still live next to her?"

"Yup, and he and Jule still don't get along, my parents still live on the other side of Oyster Creek, and Mom still teaches at the college. Things haven't changed much around here." His face grew more serious. "You know, I waited for you to come back the summer after your mother died. And the one after that. When the third summer came and you didn't, I figured you never would."

I shrugged, as if things had just turned out that way.

"So why did you finally return?" he asked bluntly.

I told him the least personal reason. "Aunt Jule said she had to see me and insisted that it be in Wisteria."

His face broke into a sunny smile. "I'm glad she did. Listen, I have to get back. Tim is covering for me at the dunking booth."

I nodded.

"See you around," he said.

"Yeah, see you," I replied, and continued to watch him as he walked away. He turned around suddenly and caught me staring, then he grinned in a self-assured way that told me he was used to girls admiring him. I could never have predicted that the round-cheeked boy whose feet were always caked with river mud would turn out like this.

I glanced at my watch. Aunt Jule would be expecting me—not that she had ever stuck to a schedule, but she knew I did. I retraced my steps, pausing for a moment at a table of hand-made jewelry.

Her again—the girl I had seen before. This time she was hiding in the narrow space between two brick houses, watching me from the shadows.

Was she a friend of Nick's? I wondered, feeling uncomfortable. Perhaps she was someone who had dated him once and never gotten over him. Why else would she be watching me?

You're acting the way Mom used to, I chided myself; someone looks at you twice and you read into it. It's just a coincidence.

Wanting to avoid another scene at the dunking booth, I took a detour onto Shipwrights Street and stopped to admire an herb garden in a tiny front yard. There she was again! I found it disturbing that someone with such unhappy eyes would shadow me. At the end of the block I returned to High Street, feeling safer in a crowd.

I had parked my Honda in front of the old newsstand and stopped there to pick up a local paper. As I stood at the counter inside, I remembered buying a pile of magazines and comic books after my mother's funeral. My father, hoping to comfort me, had given me a twenty to spend and waited in the car, talking to his advisers by phone. I remembered looking at the tabloids that day, reading their glaring headlines: SENATOR'S WIFE MURDERED, SENATOR STOPS INVESTIGATION.

But it wasn't my father who kept the police at bay the

night my mother died and in the weeks following. Aunt Jule had argued fiercely with the sheriff and the state police, insisting the drowning was an accident, begging them for my sake not to stir up rumors with a pointless investigation.

Aunt Jule, whose long roots in this town gave her more clout than my father, had been my protector, and the house where my mother felt haunted, my refuge. The headlines made me cringe, but I had been taught that tabloids lied. And I never stopped to wonder if my mother's death was truly an accident or if Aunt Jule might have been protecting someone other than me.

three

I BOUNCED MY way over the potholes of Aunt Jule's driveway, past her rusty Volvo, and thumped to a stop. From the driver's seat I gazed up at the house, hoping it would look as I remembered. In most ways it did.

The long rectangular frame of the house was covered with gray clapboard. Its double set of porches, upper and lower, ran from end to end and a wood stairway led down from the upper porch. Along both porches there were doors rather than windows, each room having at least one exit to the outside. But unlike the pristine image I carried in my mind, the doors sagged with potbellied screens, and the paint was peeling badly. The river side of the house, which was identical to the garden side but exposed to the water, probably looked worse.

I climbed out of the car. The pungent smell of boxwood and the fragrance of roses surrounded me—just as I remembered! Between the house and myself were two big gardens, a square knot garden on the right, bristling with bushy hedges and herbs, and a flower garden on the left.

"Lauren! You're here!" Aunt Jule cried out happily, stepping onto the lower porch. "Do you need help with your suitcase? Holly," she called.

No matter what clothes Aunt Jule bought, she always seemed to be wearing the same outfit—a denim skirt or pants with a loose print top. Her long brown hair had streaks of gray in it now and fell in a thick braid down her back.

We met at the head of the path between the knot and flower gardens.

She threw her arms around me. "Hello, love. It's good to have you back."

"It's good to be back," I said, hugging her tightly.

"I've missed you."

"And I've missed you." I saw Holly emerging from the house. "But promise you won't make a fuss over me."

When I was a little girl, my godmother would welcome me like visiting royalty and wait on me for the first few days. Holly would get so mad she wouldn't speak to me. It was only when Nora and Nick did, and she felt left out, that she would warm up and assume her usual position of ringleader.

Holly strode toward us, taller now than both her mother and I. Her shoulder-length hair was almost black, a glorious, shimmering color that contrasted sharply with her blue eyes. She had the beautiful eyes and brows of an actress, the kind that caught your attention with their drama and careful shaping.

"You look great!" I said.

She hugged me. "You, too. Welcome back, Lauren. I was so excited when Mom said you were coming. Is there something I can carry?"

I opened the trunk of my car, took out a full-size suitcase, and handed her an overnight bag.

Aunt Jule hovered close by and touched the smaller bag's soft leather. "How nice!" she said. "You should get one of these, Holly."

"Right, Mom. Shall we put it on our credit card? Come inside, Lauren. You must be thirsty," Holly said, starting up the path.

"Oh, Lord!" Aunt Jule's hand flew up to her forehead. "I forgot to check what we have to drink. There could be—"

"Iced tea or lemonade," Holly told me, smiling. "I made a pitcher of each. Which would you like?"

"Iced tea, please."

My godmother and I followed Holly into the house, entering the back of a wide hall that ran from the garden side to the river side of the house. We set my bags at the foot of the stairs and turned right, into the dining room.

It looked exactly as I remembered—a collection of dark wood chairs scattered around a long table that was buried beneath mail, magazines, and baskets of Aunt Jule's craft stuff. The mahogany table might have been a valuable antique, but it was badly scarred by years of water rings and the grind of game pieces into its surface. One reason I had loved to come here was that, unlike my parents' elegant town house, it was almost impossible to "ruin" something.

In the kitchen Holly set four glasses on a tray and began to pour the tea.

"Where's Nora?" I asked.

"She'll come around sooner or later," Aunt Jule replied casually.

Holly glanced sharply at her mother. "I assume you told Lauren about Nora."

"Not yet. Lauren has just arrived."

"You should have told her before."

"I saw no point in saying anything until she came," Aunt Jule replied coolly, then smiled at me. "Garden room or river room?"

"Garden."

Holly picked up the tray. "Don't forget to turn out the light, Mom."

"Forget? How can I, with you always reminding me?"

"I don't know, but somehow you do."

As we left the kitchen I peeked at Holly, wondering what I was supposed to be told about Nora. She had not been the most normal of kids.

We passed through the hall again and entered the garden room. Aunt Jule's house was built in the early 1900s on the foundation of a much older one that had burned down. Intended as a summer home, it was designed for airiness. The dining room and kitchen lay on one side of the stairs and, together with the steps and hall, occupied a third of the space downstairs. On the other side of the hall were two long rectangular rooms, each with two sets of double porch doors, those in one room facing the garden, those in the other facing the river. Two wide doorways connected these rooms, allowing the breeze to blow through the house.

At Aunt Jule's you never felt far from the Sycamore River. Each time I took a breath I noticed the mustiness that shore homes seem to have in their bones. And I knew I still wasn't ready to face the dock where my mother had struck her head, or the water below it, where she had drowned.

We had just settled down in the garden room with its two lumpy sofas and assortment of stuffed chairs when Nora entered from the porch. I was startled at what I saw.

"Nora, dear, Lauren has arrived," Aunt Jule said.

Nora stood silently and stared at me. Her thin, black hair was pulled straight back in an old plastic headband and hung in short, oily pieces. Her dark eyes were troubled. The slight frown she wore as a child had deepened into a single, vertical crease between her eyebrows, a line of anger or worry that couldn't be erased.

"Please say hello, Nora," Aunt Jule coaxed softly.

Nora acted as if she hadn't heard. She crossed the room to a table on which sat a vase of roses. She began to rearrange the flowers, her mouth set in a grim line.

"Hi, Nora. It's good to see you," I said.

She pricked her finger on a thorn and pulled her hand away quickly.

"It's good to see you again," I told her.

This time she met my eyes. Locking her gaze on mine, she reached for the rose stem and pricked her finger deliberately, repeatedly.

Her strange behavior did not seem to faze anyone else. Holly leaned forward in her chair, blocking my view of Nora. "So, did my mother think to tell you I'm graduating?"

"Uh, yes," I replied, turning my attention to her. "It's this coming Thursday, right? She said this was Senior Week for you. Are kids getting all weepy about saying good-bye?"

Holly grimaced. "Not me. I'm editor in chief of our yearbook. And the prom's tomorrow, my swim party Tuesday night. I'm too busy to get sentimental."

"I can help you get ready for the party," I offered. "Cleaning, fixing food, whatever. It'll be fun."

"I wish you hadn't come," Nora said.

I sat back in my seat, surprised, and turned to look at her.

She said nothing more, continuing to arrange the flowers with intense concentration.

"Ignore her," said Holly.

"She'll get used to you," Aunt Jule added.

Used to me? I grew up with Nora.

"We had some hot days in May," Holly went on, "so the water's plenty warm for an evening swim party."

"Don't go near the water," warned Nora.

"The whole class is coming," Holly went on, as if her sister hadn't spoken.

I heard Nora leave the room.

"I'm borrowing amplifiers from Frank—and torches and strings of lights," Holly added.

"I told you not to," Aunt Jule remarked.

"And I ignored you," Holly said, then turned to me. "You remember Frank, from next door?"

I nodded. "Yes, I saw his neph—"

I broke off at the sound of a crash in the next room. Aunt

Jule and Holly glanced at each other, then the three of us rushed into the river room.

Nora was standing five feet from an end table, gazing down at a broken ceramic lamp. She seemed fascinated by it. I heard Aunt Jule take a deep breath and let it out again.

"Nora!" Holly exclaimed. "That was a good lamp."

"I didn't do it," Nora replied quickly.

"You should watch where you're going," Holly persisted.

"But I didn't do it." Nora glanced around the room. "Someone else did."

I bent down to pick up the pieces of the shattered base. The lamp's cord had been pulled from the wall socket and was tied in a knot. When I saw it, the skin on my neck prickled. I thought about the things my mother had found knotted in her room just before she died.

A coincidence, I told myself, then untied the cord.

When I looked up, Nora was watching me, her dark eyes gleaming as if she had just solved a puzzle. "You did it," she said.

"Of course I didn't."

"Then *she* did."

"She?" I asked. "Who?"

"Now that you're here, there's no stopping her," Nora whispered.

"I don't understand."

Holly dismissed our puzzling conversation with a wave of her hand. "Leave that, Lauren," she said. "Nora broke it and Nora will clean it up. Come on, let's take your things upstairs. I'll help you unpack."

I glanced uncertainly at Aunt Jule, but she smiled as if everything were fine. "That would be lovely of you, Holly. I'll handle things down here."

Holly and I picked up my baggage in the hall and climbed the steps, which rose to the garden side of the house, then turned in the direction of the river side. Arriving in the upper hall, I felt as if I were ten again, breathing in the sweet cedar scent of the closets and the smell of the river.

A door to the upper porch was straight ahead. Aunt Jule's room was to the right, her bedroom facing the water, her private sitting room facing the garden. The hall to the left of the stairs led to four bedrooms.

"You're in the same room as always. Is that okay?" Holly asked.

"Sure," I replied, not so sure.

We passed Holly's room to the right, facing the water, and Nora's, which was directly across from her sister's, looking out on the garden. The next door to the right was mine.

I entered the bedroom and turned away from the door-length view of the river, focusing on the furniture. The oak chest, dresser, and plain oak bed with a blue-and-white quilt looked just as I had left them. The varnished wood floor had the same braid rug coiled in a circle. A small fireplace, which had been walled up as long as I could remember, still had a collection of old paperbacks on its narrow shelf. We set my suitcases on the bed.

"Thanks, Holly. Thanks for making me welcome, fixing the tea and all."

"Are you kidding? I'm glad you're here," she replied, sitting on a straight-back chair, then quickly standing up again. Its cane seat was worn through. "I'm just sorry the house is such a disaster. You know my mother. Not exactly the queen of mommies and housewives."

I laughed. "That's why I loved it here. It always felt so free and easy. But I guess her way of living is not as much fun now, not if you're the one who has to handle everything."

Holly tilted her head to one side, as if surprised. "I didn't think you'd understand that. Not *you.*"

She had always said I was spoiled. My parents had certainly given me enough to be, and it didn't help when Aunt Jule would treat me like a little princess. My last visit to Wisteria had been particularly hard on Holly and Nora, with both Aunt Jule and my mother fussing and fighting over me. Worse, my mother, who could be quite snobby about the children with whom I played, had constantly criticized Nora and Holly.

"I guess you know money is tight around here," Holly said. "Mom should sell the place, but she won't. Frank's been making good offers. He's been doing a lot of real estate development, and, of course, he'd love to have property next to his own, but she won't speak to him. Meanwhile we have old bills to pay—gas and electric, phone, taxes. Our credit cards are maxed." She shook her head. "Sorry, I didn't mean to dump on you. Let's get you unpacked."

I opened my suitcase. "I can help you out with the bills."

"Oh, no!" she protested.

"Holly, you know my father—he gives checks, not hugs. I have a large bank account from him, and when I'm eighteen, I inherit all of my mother's estate. I didn't earn any of the money. It's just there—there to be used. How much do you need?"

I could see her trying to decide what to say. "Do you have access to the family account?" I asked. "Do you have a checkbook?"

She nodded slowly. "I'm the one who writes the checks now, when there's money."

"So figure out what you need and let me know. I'll transfer the funds tomorrow when the bank opens. Really, it makes sense," I argued. "You want to keep your credit good."

"My mother would kill me if she knew I—"

"So don't tell her," I said. "She probably doesn't even look at your bank statements."

Holly burst out laughing. "You've got that right." She plopped down on the bed and stretched back against the pillow. It seemed easier to be with her now that we were older.

"Holly, what's going on with Nora?"

She turned on her side and picked through my open bag the way she used to go through my Barbie carry-case. "I'm really worried," she said at last. "I'm sure you can tell she's gotten worse. I guess Mom told you she didn't finish high school."

I shook my head no. "Your mother can be very silent about some things."

"Nora barely made it to her sixteenth birthday. I think the teachers passed her each year because they wanted to get rid of her."

"But she's not dumb," I said.

"No," Holly replied, "just crazy. Do you remember when you were here how she had started to fear water?"

"Yeah. The last summer I came, she would go out on the dock, but was afraid to dangle her feet over it, afraid to be splashed."

"Well, she's totally phobic now—about water, about all kinds of things. She never leaves the property."

I frowned. "Not at all?"

"No. She needs a psychiatrist—badly—but Mom won't do anything about it. It seems like Nora is getting weirder every day. It's scary." Holly sat up. "I mean, I'm sure she's not dangerous. She wouldn't hurt anyone. But she doesn't reason like a normal person. She gets angry when there's nothing to be angry at, and she imagines people are after her."

Like my mother, I thought. It was as if something in this house—I banished the idea, reminding myself that my mother's problems started before we came to Wisteria.

"She's always had an active imagination," I recalled.

Holly let out a sharp laugh. "You sound like my mother. *Nora's just imaginative. Nora's just sensitive. Nora's just going through adolescence.* Remember how'd she say that the summer your mother was here?"

I nodded, recalling Nora's sudden outbursts of anger and tears and Aunt Jule's quiet explanations. I used to hear Nora on the porch outside my bedroom, talking to herself, answering questions that no one asked.

"Well," said Holly, "it's been a very long adolescence."

I tugged open a drawer and dropped in my T-shirts. "You said she's totally phobic. Is there anyone she trusts—anyone she can talk to?"

"Myself, Mom, and Nick. Remember Nick Hurley, Frank's nephew?"

"Yes. I—"

"You might want to steer clear of Nora except when I'm around," Holly suggested, rising, then walking to the hall door. "I know her better than anyone, and it's hard even for me to guess what will set her off."

I saw the shadow on the hallway wall, cast by someone leaning forward to hear our words.

"Just till she gets used to you being here, of course."

The shadow pulled back, as if sensing that Holly was about to leave.

"Do you remember where the towels are? Is there anything else I can get you?" Holly asked.

"I'm fine, thanks."

She left me to finish unpacking and to puzzle over the situation I had walked into. Maybe Holly did know Nora better than anyone, but she didn't know everything. Nora left the property sometimes; it was she who had shadowed me at the festival.

four

SEVEN YEARS AGO I awakened from what I thought was a horrible nightmare. I rushed to my mother's room, wanting her to tell me it hadn't happened, but she wasn't there. I ran to Aunt Jule's. She, too, was gone.

I raced downstairs, out of the house, and down to the water. It was barely dawn, with just a hint of pink in the pearl gray sky. Aunt Jule was standing at the end of the dock, staring at a piling, one of the weathered posts that supported the long walkway. When she heard my footsteps on the wooden planks, she spun around.

In her hands were a bucket and scrub brush. As I got closer to her, I smelled bleach. Aunt Jule opened her mouth as if to tell me to go back, but it was too late. I saw that the piling was stained—dark-colored, reddish. It was blood, my mother's blood. I threw up.

I haven't been back to the dock since that morning, though I'd spent three more weeks at Aunt Jule's, until my father could arrange for a baby-sitter in Washington. Now I needed to see the place where my mother had fallen, to walk out on the dock and touch the piling that had been scoured clean by Aunt Jule and years of rain. Still, the thought of it made my stomach cramp.

I stood on the porch outside my bedroom, gazing at the peaceful river, looking well past the dock, farther out to the misty line between bay and sky. It was that view that Aunt Jule loved and that made her property so valuable.

The Chesapeake Bay washes northward through the widest part of Maryland, and the Sycamore River branches off the bay in a northeasterly direction. Surrounded on three sides by water—the Sycamore and two big creeks—the town of Wisteria sits on a piece of land that appears to jut into the river. Because the town is close to the wide river mouth, you can see the bay from one side of it. Aunt Jule's house is on that side at the very end of Bayview Avenue, built on land that extends beyond the corner of Bayview and Water Street.

According to my mother, the Ingram family once had a ton of money. They had owned several houses and sent their children to exclusive schools like Birch Hill, which is where my mother and godmother became friends. But generation after generation had mismanaged the wealth. Now all Aunt Jule had was the house and the land, which is all she wanted, if you ask me. She had been married briefly to Holly and Nora's father, but he had wanted to see the world and she didn't want to leave her home. Several years after he left Wisteria, he died.

I had no idea how she paid her bills. Abandoned craft projects were strewn through the house. She was very talented, but didn't have the discipline to earn a living that way. Still, I had never seen her worry about money. Somehow, whatever she needed materialized.

I reentered the house and headed downstairs. When I reached the bottom of the steps, I heard voices in the dining room.

"It's just common sense, Mother," Holly said. "You know you've never been able to handle a camera. Remember the pictures you took before the Christmas dance? None of us had feet."

"I don't find feet all that interesting," Aunt Jule replied.

"They are when Jackie and I each spend big bucks on shoes," Holly countered. "I told you that at the time." Seeing me at the doorway, she gave a little wave. Aunt Jule glanced up from her quilting.

"Anyway, like it or not," Holly continued, "Frank's coming over and taking pictures before the prom. Nick's parents are going to want photos, too, and—"

"Nick?" I repeated, entering the room.

"Nick Hurley," she replied, smiling.

"Mr. Frank's nephew?"

"Yes. We're dating."

I looked at her, surprised. *Two's the limit,* I almost said, but maybe that was just a line he had given me.

"We've been friends forever, of course," she went on. "Now Nick has finally seen the light. And if he hasn't, he will," she added, laughing.

I laughed with her and squelched my disappointment.

"Wait till you see him," Holly said. "He's not that round-faced kid anymore."

"I know. I ran into him at the festival on my way here. I dunked him twice at your school booth."

"You were at the festival?" The smile disappeared from Holly's face. "At my school's dunking booth?"

"I was walking through town and happened to pass it," I replied. I didn't tell her that Nick had asked me to stop by, for I had just gotten the same chilly feeling I used to get around Holly, as if I were invading her territory.

But then she smiled. "He's coming around later. It'll be like old times."

"I guess you visited Sondra's grave," Aunt Jule said to me.

"I didn't, but I will tomorrow. I need to do things one at a time," I explained. "It—it's kind of hard coming back here. For me Wisteria is not all happy memories."

"We're well beyond those unhappy times," Aunt Jule observed. "Seven years beyond."

"Still, when I came back today, it seemed like yesterday."

"That's why you shouldn't have waited so long," she replied.

Her cool tone surprised me. "My mother died here," I said defensively. "You can't expect me to think of it as a great vacation spot."

"It's where you were born," Aunt Jule answered firmly. "It's where you had your happiest times."

"Yes, but—"

"It's time you got over Sondra's death, Lauren. She wasn't exactly Mother of the Year."

That stung. "I know, but she was my mother. Excuse me, I'm going for a walk."

I turned abruptly and exited through the dining room door to the porch. I had thought Aunt Jule would be more understanding, but a trace of that summer's bitterness had remained with her. It seemed to me that Aunt Jule, herself, hadn't completely left that time behind.

I took the three steps down to the grass, paused to look at the dock, then walked the long slope down to it. The river's edge was a spongy mix of mud, sand, and clay, tufted with long bay grass. Aunt Jule's property was probably the only shoreline in Wisteria unprotected by a sea wall. The dock no longer met the riverbank, the land having eroded from beneath it.

Planting my hands on the dock, I swung my feet up onto it, as if climbing onto a three-foot wall. I stood up slowly, my eyes traveling the length of the T-shaped walkway, then shifting to the far left side, to the piling where my mother had struck her head.

She may have been drinking. It was easy to trip on the uneven planks. The tide was high that night, the water just over her head. It took so little for a person to die. Aunt Jule had told me over and over that it was nobody's fault.

And yet, I felt responsible. My mother had refused to let me visit Aunt Jule that last summer. But the more clingy she had become, the more desperate I'd been to get away from her. I had thrown fierce tantrums until she gave in—gave in with the condition that she would accompany me. If I hadn't argued, if we hadn't come, would she still be alive?

I couldn't walk to the end of the dock, not yet. I jumped down and climbed the hill to the house.

My mother had become even worse in Wisteria, still clinging, not wanting me to play with Nora and Holly. She would blame them for things. She'd tell me I was too good for them, and say it in front of them. Poor Holly had been caught between snubbing me entirely and acting like my best and dearest friend—just to get my mother riled.

Both Holly and Nora had fought back with words, showing the anger that I myself felt but tried to hide. Then Mommy drowned. What do you do with your anger when the person you're mad at goes off and dies? Bury it? Bury it inside you?

I circled the house to see the gardens, hoping they could still give me the peace I had felt there as a child. I passed my favorite tree, a huge old oak with a swing. Someone had lassoed the high branch with a new rope. The gardens, too, had been cared for and looked better than they had seven years ago. My heart lightened.

A greenhouse stood not far from the garden, a long rectangular structure with a gambrel roof, built in the 1930s on the brick base of an earlier one. The roof vents were up and the door open.

When I peeked in I found Nora tending plants halfway down the main aisle, on one of the short cross aisles. Focused on her work, her fingers moving deftly among the shiny leaves, she didn't notice me. I stepped inside the door and she looked up. Her eyes darted fearfully around the greenhouse. I thought that she had heard me enter, but her gaze passed over me as if I were invisible. I, too, looked around, wondering what she sensed.

She started to tremble and shook her head with quick, jerky motions. It was as if she had something frightening inside it that she was trying to shake out. I remembered as a child how she hated getting water in her ears and would become frantic to get rid of it. I watched silently, afraid to speak and upset her more.

The shaking finally stopped, the fear in her easing into a quiet wariness. She tended her plants, neatly removing yellow leaves. I surveyed the greenhouse again. There was nothing there—nothing that I could see—triggering her emotions; whatever Nora was reacting to was deep inside her.

"Hi, Nora."

This time when she looked up, she saw me. "I don't want you here."

I walked toward her. "Here in the greenhouse or here at your mother's?"

She didn't answer.

"Why don't you want me around?" I asked.

She moved on to another bench of plants and began to snip off their tops.

"Nora, why don't you like me anymore?"

"I don't remember."

"Please try to."

She pressed her lips together and nervously fingered dark strings of hair. I wished Aunt Jule would make her wash it.

"I'm busy," she said. "I have to cut off their little heads. It hurts them. They hate it, but they will be better for it."

"You mean you're pinching back the plants so they'll grow bushier?" I asked.

"Do you want to see my vines?" she replied.

I wasn't sure if she was too mentally scattered to answer my questions or simply unwilling. "Sure."

She led me outside and showed me several trellises standing against the southern wall.

"It gets too hot in the summer, so I use the climbers to shade the plants inside. These are morning glories," she said, pointing to the heart-shaped leaves. "And over there is Lauren."

"Laurel?" I asked, misunderstanding her. "It looks like a climbing rose."

"It is. I named her Lauren."

"Oh." I wondered if it was a coincidence that she had given the plant my name. "Then we're called the same thing," I remarked cheerfully.

But Nora was frowning now, the vertical crease between her eyes deepening, the troubled world inside her more real to her than the one outside.

"Will you get me some fishing line?" she asked. "I use it to tie up Lauren. Morning glories will twine themselves. But roses have to be tied or else their arms will fall and strike you, and their thorns will make you bleed."

I mulled over her strange way of describing her work, trying to understand what lay behind the words.

"There's fishing line in the boathouse. Will you get it?" she asked. "I don't go in there. It's full of water."

"No problem," I said.

"You'll need the key."

"It's locked? Why?" I asked.

Nora twisted her hands. "Because she's in there. She goes there to sleep during the day."

"Who?"

"Sondra."

My breath caught in my throat. "You mean my mother? She's dead."

"She sleeps there during the day," Nora replied. "Be quiet when you go in or you will wake her."

She was serious. A chill went up my spine.

"I'll show you where the key is," Nora said, walking backward a few steps, then turning to hurry on.

About thirty feet from the boathouse she stopped. Standing next to her, I surveyed the old building, which was nestled in the bank where the river curved, straddling the border between Aunt Jule's and Mr. Frank's property. The boathouse had deteriorated badly. Its roof buckled, two shutters hung off their hinges, and many of the wood shingles were broken. As far back as I could remember, there hadn't been a boat in the house. We used to put our crab traps there and fish off its roof. Now we'd probably fall through.

"Do you see her?" Nora whispered.

"No."

"She's asleep," Nora said, her voice barely audible. "All night she swims out by the dock, then she comes here at dawn. She wants to stay in the darkness."

"That makes no sense," I replied in a voice too loud. "Why would she do that?"

"She's looking for her little girl."

My throat felt tight when I swallowed. I strode ahead and found both the land entrance and the doors to the river closed and padlocked. The shutters were loose, but the windows were boarded up.

"Where's the key?" I asked.

"On a hook behind the shutter," Nora said, hanging back.

I found the key and unlocked the padlock. Nora crept closer. I laid the padlock on the ground, pulled back the latch, then opened the door.

After being in the bright sunlight, I couldn't see a thing. Cautiously I stepped inside. The smell of stagnant water, earth, and rot was overwhelming. It wouldn't be hard to believe that someone was dead in here.

I remembered there was a narrow walkway lining three sides of the building, surrounding the area of water where a boat would float. Along the wall to the right there used to be a light with a pull-chain. I felt my way toward it.

"Where's the line kept, Nora?" I called out to her.

"In the loft," she answered softly.

Great. I'd probably climb into a rat colony. But I went on, hoping that in helping Nora I'd win her trust, as well as prove to her that my mother wasn't here. I felt the beaded chain and yanked down hard. Nothing. I reached up and touched an empty socket.

At least my eyes were adjusting. I saw the outline of the ladder to the loft just a few feet ahead of me and started toward it.

"Don't close the door, Nora," I called to her. "I need all the light I can get. Did you hear? I said don't—"

The door shut.

"Nora? Nora!" I shouted. "No-ra!"

five

It was pitch black inside. I kept my hands on the wall and took a step toward the door. "All right, Nora," I called, struggling to keep my voice calm, "what are you doing?"

Metal scraped against metal. She was fastening the padlock.

"Nora!"

I rushed toward the door. My toe caught on the uneven boards and I pitched headlong in the dark. My fingers touched the ledge of a window frame but slipped off. I teetered on the edge of the walkway, my ankle wobbling. I couldn't stand the thought of falling into the foul water, the water where Nora said my mother slept.

I caught my balance again and sank down on my knees. I didn't care whether Nora was playing a prank or truly afraid, I was angry. I banged my fists against the wall. "Nora! Let me out!"

Her voice was faint. "Lauren?"

"This isn't funny," I said. "Unlock the door."

"She's awake!" Nora cried out.

"What?"

"She's awake!" Nora sounded out of breath, as if she were running away.

"Come back here."

There was no reply. I rested my head against the wall, thinking about what to do. Then, in the oppressive darkness and silence, I heard it: the movement of water, its restless shift from side to side in the boathouse. I couldn't see the water, but I could hear it, slapping the walls, tumbling back on itself. Something was stirring it up.

I listened as it grew more turbulent. Was it some animal? Had one gotten through the tangle of nets abandoned at the entrance? Something was in the water, something Nora must have heard or seen before.

She's looking for her little girl, Nora had said. I shivered. My mother was always looking for me, panicking as soon as I'd disappear from sight. I cowered against the boathouse wall and flinched with each slap of the water, feeling—or imagining—water droplets on my arms.

Then the lapping grew softer. The water became eerily quiet again.

I took a deep breath. *Something ordinary is going on here,* I told myself. Figure it out, Lauren; two people out of touch with reality is one too many.

A boat wake—that would explain the sudden movement of water. I hadn't heard a powerboat pass, but I was focused on other things; perhaps I didn't notice it. I rose to my feet.

What was Nora thinking? I wondered. That she had gotten rid of me, locking me with my mother in the boathouse?

I called out several times and received no response. I needed something heavy to bang against the door. The padlock wouldn't give way, but the old hinges might. I glanced around. Small cracks of light between the boards allowed me to orient myself. I remembered that tools had been kept in the loft and made my way slowly down the walkway. Grasping the ladder, I began to climb it, hoping none of the rungs were rotted through.

When I got to the top, I reached out gingerly. My fingers touched something metallic and small—a chain, a piece of jewelry. I tucked it in my pocket and continued to search. At last I found an object with a long handle and a cold steel end. Perfect! An ax.

I carefully backed down the ladder and felt my way to the door. *Perhaps it would be smart to shout a few more times,* I thought, *before swinging away like Paul Bunyan.*

"Hey! Let me out! Let me out!"

I waited for two minutes and screamed again. Giving up, I raised the ax, then froze when I heard someone fumbling with the lock. The door opened and I blinked at the sudden brightness.

"Well, hello," a deep voice greeted me.

"I told you to be careful," said another voice—Nick's. "There could be an ax murderer inside."

I lowered the ax and stepped into the fresh air.

Nick looked amused. "What were you doing in there?"

"Building a boat."

He laughed and turned to the man next to him. "Recognize her, Frank?"

"Barely," his uncle replied. "You've grown up, girl. You've grown up real nice. Welcome home, Lauren."

"Hey, Mr. Frank. It's good to see you again."

"Please, just Frank," he told me. "Don't make me feel any older than I am."

I grinned. His face was lined from all the sun he got and his hairline receding, but his eyes were just as bright and observant, and his smile was the same.

"How did you get locked in there?" he asked. "You couldn't have done it yourself."

"Nora helped."

Frank looked puzzled. "What do you mean?"

"She asked me to get some fishing line so she could tie up her plants."

"You mean she set you up? She trapped you?"

"Oh, come on, Frank," Nick said.

"It's hard to tell with her," I replied.

Frank shook his head. "Jule has got to get that girl some help."

"Let's not get on that subject again," Nick told his uncle.

"But it's true, Nick," I said. "Nora has become really strange."

"She's crazy," Frank declared. "One of these days she's going to do some real damage."

"She's harmless," Nick insisted.

"Sorry, kid, but she's out of touch with reality, and that's dangerous."

"Well, if she asks me to get this ax," I said, "I think I'll say no."

Frank laughed. I set the tool inside, beneath the light chain, then closed the door. Frank put the padlock on and returned the key to its hook.

"Seriously, Lauren," he went on, "you need to convince Jule to get Nora to a shrink. Jule's got to stop acting so irresponsible."

I winced; I didn't want to think the godmother I had adored for so long was anything worse than lax. But in relying on Holly to figure out how to pay the bills and denying Nora's need for help, she was letting them carry burdens that shouldn't have been theirs.

"Maybe they can't afford a doctor," Nick pointed out.

Frank's cell phone rang.

"If Jule sold that land of hers, she could afford a lot of things," he replied and plucked the phone from his pocket. "Hello. You got me. Who's this? . . . Well, is it now? How much riverfront?" He gave Nick and me a salute and headed back to his house, talking real estate and prices.

"Still making those deals," I observed.

"Seven days a week," Nick replied, walking with me along the edge of the river toward Aunt Jule's dock. "I've been painting his living room—you know Frank, he likes cheap help—and he's been using every opportunity to talk me into a double major in business and pre-law. According to him, a law degree is better than a million lottery tickets, *if* you know how to use it."

"Meaning it's the road to riches?"

"*If* you know how to use it. He's probably afraid I'll turn out like my parents."

I laughed. Nick's father was an artist, his mother, a poet

and professor at Chase, the local college. I remembered their house as a cozy shore cottage stuffed with books and smelling of linseed oil and turpentine. Nick's father and Frank had grown up in that home, the sons of a waterman with very little money. But Frank had gone on to marry a wealthy woman who owned the house and land where he now lived. She had died several years after he'd completed law school. They didn't have any children and he never remarried. Having become a prosperous lawyer and real estate developer, I guessed the only thing he had in common with Nick's parents was their love for Nick.

"So *are* you turning out like them? Do you still write and draw?"

"Yeah, but I don't do anything personal or profound. My parents take life way too seriously. I like to make people laugh. I had a regular cartoon feature in the school paper and created some for the yearbook. Social satire stuff. I've done a couple political cartoons for Wisteria's paper and just got one accepted in Easton's, which has a much bigger circulation. Impressed?" he asked, grinning.

"I am," I replied. I didn't point out that cartoons can be profound and personal, especially if he was doing political and social satire.

"So explain to me," Nick said as we walked toward the dock, "how you can ever meet guys at an all-girls school."

"There aren't a lot of chances," I admitted, "but I like it that way."

"You do? You're kidding. You have to be."

"No. We have an all-boys school nearby, and there's a regular dating exchange going. I take guys to dances, like escorts, but I don't want to date—not till I'm in college. I don't want to get hooked like my mother did and become dependent on some guy to make me feel like a person. I'm getting my life and career together first."

He looked me as if I had just landed from Mars. "That doesn't mean you can't date," he said. "I'm not getting hooked, either, and I'm dating everybody."

I laughed. "And breaking a few hearts along the way?"

He peeked sideways at me. His lashes were blond. I always knew that, but I had never thought much about his golden lashes, or his green eyes, or the way they brimmed with sunlight and laughter. Now, for some reason, this was all I could think about.

"How can you be so sure," he asked, "that *you're* not breaking hearts by not dating guys?" He turned toward me, blocking my path. "How do you know you're not breaking my heart?"

His sudden nearness took my breath away. I stepped around him. "I'm not worried about you, just Holly, who's really looking forward to the prom."

He thought about that for a moment, then caught up with me. "I'll always be grateful to Holly," he said. "If she hadn't shown mercy, I'd be taking my mother to my last big high school event."

"What happened to all those others you're dating?" I asked.

"Well, Kelly invited me to the prom and I said yes. Then Jennifer asked me to the senior formal. And I said yes. I didn't know they were the same thing."

I laughed. "Moron!"

"Now neither of them is speaking to me, and their friends, of course, must be loyal. That kind of narrowed the playing field."

"You got what you deserved," I said, grinning. "Holly should have said no."

"Hey, does my stupidity give you the right to bruise a tender heart?"

"Yeah, yeah. I'm bruising a heart made of Play-Doh."

He laughed, then turned toward the water and whistled sharply.

I had been looking toward the house, my eyes avoiding the dock, but now I saw a dog in the river. He swam toward us, stood chest deep in the water, then came bounding forward.

"Put on your rain slicker!" Nick cried.

"What?"

The big dog stopped in front of us and shook hard, sending river water flying.

"Too late," Nick replied. "But you won't have to shower tonight. This is Rocky."

"Rocky. Hi, big guy," I said and knelt down. "Wow! What eyes!"

"Careful, he stinks, " Nick warned.

"All water retrievers do," I replied, running my hands over his thick coat. It was a rich brown and wavy. "He's a Chesapeake Bay, isn't he? His fur looks like it."

"Mostly—he's enough Chessie to swim in ice water."

"You are gorgeous!" I said, gazing into his amber eyes.

"Don't let it go to your head, Rocky," Nick told his dog. "She doesn't date."

I glanced up. "Now, a dog," I said, "that's something I miss, living at school."

"Maybe you can get an exchange going with a kennel," Nick suggested.

"No, no," I said. "I want a dog of my own to love and pamper."

Nick grunted. Rocky wagged his tail.

I petted around the dog's wet ears and scratched under his chin. "Such an intelligent face!"

"Yeah, but he's a lousy dancer."

I grinned and stood up.

"Are you headed up to the house?" Nick asked.

"Yes." As we climbed the hill, Rocky ran ahead of us, then circled back and ran ahead again. We stopped at the porch.

"You know the rules, Rock," Nick said to his dog. "No stinky animals inside."

"Are you kidding? Aunt Jule won't mind."

"I'm here to see Holly."

"Oh. Of course." She had told me he was coming. Why else did I think he was walking me to the house?

"We have yearbook work to do," Nick explained.

"At this point in the year?"

"The supplement," he answered.

"Well, Rocky can hang out with me." I stroked the dog's head. "Come on, big guy."

Rocky licked my hand and complied, walking next to me as I headed toward the side of the house.

A shrill whistle split the air. "Rocky!" Nick called, sounding exasperated. "Come here. Come!"

The dog trotted back to him.

"What's going on? You're not supposed to go off with anybody who pats you on the head. Where's your training?"

I looked back at Nick, amused. "Jealous?"

"Not of you," he replied, then motioned to the dog. "Okay, go with Lauren. Go," he commanded.

The dog raced toward me and I continued walking. With Rocky trotting beside me, I checked the greenhouse and garden in search of Nora. Though I wanted to question her about what she had done, part of me was relieved that she wasn't in either place. As strange as Nora was as a child, she had never given me the creeps. She did now. Before, when she answered someone who wasn't there, I figured it was an imaginary playmate. So what if she had one longer than most kids? But my dead mother, that was a different kind of invisible presence. I didn't want to think about it.

Passing the garden, I came to the old oak tree with the swing. It was tied the same way as always, with a loop dangling about three feet off the ground.

"What do you think, Rocky? Am I still the champion swinger of the group?"

I grabbed the rope and gave it a hard yank, then put my foot in the loop and pulled myself up with my hands, making sure the rope was as strong as it appeared. Jumping down again, I carried the rope to another tree and climbed to "the platform of death," as we used to call it—a wide branch on an old cherry.

"Here goes." I slipped my foot in the loop, grabbed the rope, and pushed off.

With the first swoop I remembered why I had loved swinging. It was wonderful! It was flying! It was being Peter Pan! The earth fell away, the sky rushed to meet me. I was free and flying high.

Then the rope jerked. It happened so suddenly it caught me off guard. The rope writhed out of my hands. I grabbed for it frantically, but I couldn't catch hold and fell backward. With my foot caught in the loop, I hit the ground upside down, back first. The rope snapped, releasing me from the tree and tumbling on top of me.

I lay on my back stunned, the wind knocked out of me. Rocky nosed my arm. I sat up slowly and gazed up at the tree, which still had a piece of rope dangling from it. The rope had been in too good shape to be snapped by my weight. I quickly examined it, the part that had fallen on me.

About four feet above the foot loop was a knot. My mouth went dry. I thought of the knot in the lamp wire, the knots in my mother's scarves and jewelry. I had assumed that someone tied those knots before they were discovered, but I hadn't seen this one when I grasped the swing's rope.

I just didn't notice it, I told myself. Still, an icy fear ran through my veins. I didn't know how to explain what had just happened. I didn't know who or what to blame. Then I glanced up to the second floor porch and saw Nora watching me.

six

Before I could call to her, Nora disappeared inside. I coiled up the rope and left it under the tree, then entered the house, slipping past the dining room, where Nick, Holly, and Aunt Jule were talking. When I arrived upstairs, Nora's bedroom door was closed. I could hear her moving behind it.

I knocked, lightly at first. "Nora? Nora, I want to talk to you." I knocked harder, but she wouldn't answer. I thought of opening the door myself or sneaking around to the porch and trying to surprise her, but I didn't want to do something to Nora that she could do back to me. I gave up. As soon as I got a chance to talk to Aunt Jule alone, I'd tell her that Nora needed help and I'd offer to pay for it.

After changing out of my grass-stained shirt, I took a paperback from the bedroom shelf and joined the others in the dining room. Aunt Jule was working on her embroidery. Nick and Holly had cleared space on the table and laid out piles of photos. They were going through them, laughing and arguing, as they did years back when playing board games. I threw some pillows in the corner of the room and curled up to read the battered Agatha Christie the way I used to read Aunt Jule's Nancy Drews. It was almost like old times.

After a while Rocky was admitted as far as the hallway door. Stretching out next to him, I continued to read. Once, when I looked up, I found Nick staring at Rocky and me, smiling.

Holly glanced up. "Phew!" she exclaimed, waving a folder in front of her nose.

"Shh!" Nick said in a stage whisper. "You'll embarrass Lauren. Just make sure she showers tonight."

"I was referring to Rocky."

Aunt Jule laughed. I saw the same content look on her face as she'd get when we gathered around her as children.

Nora came in twice and stayed no longer than five minutes each time. She would eye me warily, then sit by Nick. He was gentle with her, showing her a handful of pictures and asking which ones she'd choose for the yearbook supplement. Now that I thought about it, she had always sat near him when we played board games and defended his claims against Holly's.

Nick stayed through dinnertime, not that there was an event called dinner at Aunt Jule's. We simply helped ourselves to what we wanted, when we wanted it. About ten o'clock Holly walked

Nick to his car. I couldn't help wondering if they were outside kissing. Since tonight wasn't an official date but a yearbook meeting, I figured his policy conveniently allowed for as many of these nights as he wanted.

"Lauren," Aunt Jule said when we were alone, "I was hoping we'd have time together tomorrow after Holly leaves for school—to chat and all. But I have a shopkeeper breathing down my neck for overdue work and have to pick up craft supplies. I'll be gone till noon."

"No problem," I assured her.

"I could meet you at twelve," she offered, "and go with you to Sondra's grave. We could take flowers. If you like, we could plant some."

I knew she was trying to make up for what she had said before.

"Thanks, Aunt Jule, thanks a lot, but I need to go by myself." I walked over and sat on the chair next to hers. "But there is something I want to talk to you about."

She paused, holding her silver needle above the fabric she was embroidering. "Yes, love?"

"Nora."

She quickly pushed the needle through. "What about her?"

"I'm really worried about her. I think she needs help—psychiatric help."

"Do you," Aunt Jule replied coolly.

"This afternoon Nora—"

"Nick told us about the boathouse," my godmother interrupted. "It was a childish prank. Certainly you weren't frightened by such a silly thing?"

"I was bothered by the way she talked about my mother. She said—"

"Ignore her," Aunt Jule advised, making a knot and snipping the thread. "Nora is confused and easily frightened, especially when there are changes here at home. Your visit has upset her a little, that's all. She'll get past it. In the meantime, don't take her seriously."

"But what if she wants to be taken seriously?" I asked. "What if her behavior is a cry for help?"

Aunt Jule shook her head, dismissing the possibility. "You're tired, Lauren, and so am I. This isn't the time to discuss Nora. Get a good night's rest and let things settle for a few days."

"Is Nora the reason you asked me to come here?" I persisted. "Is she what you wanted to talk about?"

"There is much for us to talk about, *after* you've rested up," Aunt Jule replied firmly.

I knew that once my godmother tabled a discussion, it was useless to say more. I kissed her good night.

When I got upstairs, Nora's bedroom door was closed. Before entering my own room, I glanced at the door across the hall, next to Nora's. The summer my mother came, she had slept in that room. I was glad the door to it was also shut.

In my room I turned on a small lamp and lay back on my bed for a moment, listening to the familiar night sounds. A breeze wafted in through the screen door, pushing back the light curtains. I reached lazily into my shorts pocket to remove my car keys. My fingers felt something else—the chain I'd found in the boathouse.

I had forgotten all about it. I sat up quickly and opened my hand. The necklace was so black that for a moment I didn't recognize the small tarnished heart. When I did, I couldn't believe it. I had thought it was gone forever!

The silver necklace was a gift from Aunt Jule when I was born. I had loved it and worn it at the shore every summer, though on a sturdier chain than the original. The summer my mother had come, she had taken it from me after a fight with Aunt Jule. The next day I had sneaked into her room and searched for the necklace everywhere—her jewelry case and purse, her bureau drawers and suitcase. I didn't find it and feared she had done as she'd threatened—thrown it in the river.

So how had it ended up in the loft? Though the boathouse was in better shape seven years ago, I couldn't imagine my mother going in, much less hiding something there. But if Aunt Jule, Nora, or Holly had found the necklace, why wasn't it returned to me? Maybe they meant to, but forgot. A lot of things went undone and forgotten around here. Still, why keep it in the boathouse loft?

I hung the necklace on the wood post of my mirror stand, puzzling over the events of the day. I had come here to tie up my memories like a box of old photos, so I could put them away once and for all. But the memories would not be neatly bound up; questions kept unraveling.

I didn't know what time it was or where I was, except far beneath the surface of a river. The river bottom was thick with sea grass and I swam in near darkness. Someone called my name, *Laur-en, Laur-en,* the voice rising and falling over the syllables as my mother's once had. I followed the voice, swimming through the long weed, feeling it flow over my skin like cold tentacles.

"Lauren! Lauren!" It *was* my mother. She was panicking.

I swam harder, trying to find her. I needed air, but somehow I continued scouring the bottom. The sea grass wrapped itself around my arms and legs, entangling me.

"Lauren, come quickly!"

I broke free and kept swimming. I could feel her fear as if

it were my own. I knew she was sinking into a place where I couldn't reach her, an endless night.

The banks of the river narrowed. Both sides were walls of tree roots, roots like long, arthritic fingers reaching out to catch me. I fought my way through them. But as her voice grew near, the river walls pressed closer together, threatening to swallow me alive.

"Where are you?" I cried out.

"Here."

Ahead of me was a deep crack where the two banks joined, a long and jagged fissure.

"Here, Lauren," she called out from the fissure. "Lauren, dearest, come to Mother."

But I didn't want to go where she was. I hesitated, and the crack closed, sealing her in forever.

I woke up sweating. My heart pounded and I gulped air as if I were emerging from deep water.

Laur-en.

I turned my head toward the hall, thinking I heard the same voice. Silence.

I climbed out of bed and tiptoed to the door. When I opened it, the door to my mother's old room creaked. Someone had left it ajar.

I crossed the hall and laid my palms against the door, listening a moment, then pushed it open. At the other end of the room a glass door to the porch suddenly closed. I started toward it and the door behind me slammed shut.

I screamed, then muffled it. A draft, I told myself, a draft running through my room and this one blew the doors shut. I wondered if it had been caused by someone making a hasty exit through the porch door.

I strode across the room, opened the doors to the porch, and leaned out. No one was there. Of course, if it had been Nora, she could have easily slipped into her room, the next door down.

Inside, I turned on the floor lamp and glanced around. It looked as I remembered it, with oak furniture similar to my own and a red-and-green quilt on the bed. Spiders had made themselves cozy here and dust coated the bureau top, but the dresser had streaks on its surface, as if someone had been using it recently. One of its drawers wasn't closed all the way.

I walked over and opened it. Inside were several old newspapers, tabloids that were badly yellowed. I spread them out on the dresser top. I guessed what was in them; still, the pictures of my mother shocked me—those horrible flashbulb photos that could make the prettiest woman look like a witch.

Had she put them here? *Not unless she wanted to torture*

herself, I thought. The only other thing in the drawer was an empty packet of marigold seeds.

I opened the next drawer. My mother's favorite pair of earrings lay on top of a scarf she had loved. I touched them gently. At the town house in Washington, my mother's personal things had been put in safe storage or thrown out soon after she died. I still had her jewelry box in my room at school, but it seemed like mine now more than hers. These items were different—barely touched by anyone else. I half-expected to smell her perfume on them.

In the corner of the drawer were snippets of photographs. For a moment I couldn't figure out what I was looking at, then I saw they were pictures from that last summer, with my mother cut out. Not exactly subtle symbolism, I thought. In the third drawer there were more empty seed packets and a pile of plant catalogs that had been mailed to Nora.

Were all these things Nora's? Some of the garden catalogs were dated the summer of the current year, which meant Nora had opened the bureau recently; it wasn't as if she had forgotten these things were here. I found it unsettling to think that anyone would keep the rag-paper photos of my mother seven years after her death. Equally disturbing was the possibility that, after all this time, Nora could have mimicked perfectly the intonation of my mother's voice. This was the behavior of someone obsessed with a person, obsessed with a dead woman.

I left everything as I'd found it, planning to show it to Aunt Jule, then turned out the light and left.

"Is everything all right?"

"Holly!" I hadn't expected her to be in the hall.

Nora stood behind Holly, her dark eyes glittering in the soft light. I was too tired to confront her now and wasn't sure I'd get anywhere if I did. The person to talk to was Aunt Jule.

"Everything's fine," I answered Holly.

"Are you sure?"

"I had a bad dream and got up to walk around—to shake it off—that's all."

Holly turned her head, glancing sideways at her sister, as if suspicious of something more, then said, "Nora, go to bed."

Nora moved past her sister and peeked into the room from which I had just come.

"Nora," Holly said quietly but firmly. Nora returned to her bedroom.

Holly guided me into mine. "You look upset," she observed as she turned on the lamp. "Do you want to talk?"

"Thanks, but it's awfully late," I replied.

"I'm wide awake," she assured me, sitting on my bed. She must have wondered what was going on, especially if she heard my muffled scream.

"Nick told us Nora locked you in the boathouse," Holly

continued. "I don't know what to say, Lauren, except I'm sorry it happened. Please don't take it personally."

"What if it was meant personally?"

"Just do your best to avoid her," Holly advised. "And next time Nora starts making trouble for you, tell me. Someone has to keep tabs on her. Since Mom doesn't, I'm the warden of this asylum."

"Holly, what's going to happen to Nora when you go away to college?"

"I don't even want to think about it," she said. "But Nora is a long-term problem. Right now I'm more concerned about you. It has to be hard coming back and seeing things you associate with your mother's death."

I glanced away. "I thought that by now it would be easier, but I was wrong."

She rested her hand lightly on my shoulder. "Then tell me what I can do to help, okay? I'm not in your shoes, so I can't guess."

"Okay."

She stood up. "Well, get some sleep. Tomorrow will be better."

"Right. G'night."

After Holly left, I locked my door to the hall and latched the screen doors to the porch. It felt strange, for I had never worried about my own safety at Aunt Jule's.

Reaching for the switch on my bureau lamp, I noticed that my newfound necklace was twisted up. I touched it with one finger, expecting it to swing free from the mirror stand, but it didn't. Like my mother's necklaces, it had been tied in impossible knots.

seven

I DIDN'T FALL back asleep until dawn. Waking late on Monday morning, I found myself alone in the house. Two notes had been left on the fridge for me, one from Aunt Jule reminding me that she'd be out till twelve, and the other from Holly. She invited me to stop by the yearbook office so she could introduce me to her friends. The underclassmen were on a half-day schedule, so she suggested I come at noon.

A list of needed grocery and household items was also on the refrigerator door. When I tucked it in my purse I discovered a second note from Holly that contained a log of bills due and overdue, adding up to a cool $4,000. I knew that dropping a big check wouldn't solve the problem—Aunt Jule would continue to be Aunt Jule. But it would relieve the pressure for the time being and give Holly an easier summer before college.

When I left the house Nora was in the knot garden snipping a boxwood hedge with hand clippers. The square garden, started in the 1800s, was once an intricate green design of shrubs, herbs, and colored gravel. When I was a child it had grown into one large mass of green. But Nora must have been cutting back the shrubs little by little each year. Now they looked like lumpy green caterpillars and were starting to trace out a pattern.

"Good morning," I called to her.

She looked across the outer hedge but said nothing.

"I'm doing some errands," I told her. "Do you need anything?"

"No."

I watched her work for a moment. "Nora, why did you lock me in the boathouse yesterday?"

She raked the top of the boxwood with her fingers, brushing off the fresh clippings. "I don't remember."

"Why did you run from it? What did you see?"

"I don't remember," she insisted.

"The water was stirred up," I reminded her, "as if a boat were passing by. Did you notice a powerboat?"

Nora shook her head. "It was her. She was making the river angry. She wants to make the river come up."

"Who?" I asked, though I could guess the answer.

"Sondra. She wants it to go over our heads."

"No, Nora, it was just—"

"She wants to pull us down with her," Nora said, her eyes

wide, as if she were seeing something I couldn't. "She wants her little girl."

I gripped my car keys hard. "Listen to me. There is no one sleeping in there, dead or alive."

Nora's eyelids twitched violently.

"Wind, tides, boats," I said, "those are the things that make the water rise and fall."

She didn't reply.

"Nora, while I'm out I'm going to visit my mother's grave. She was buried in the cemetery at Grace Church—by the high school. My mother is not in the river. She's not in the boathouse. She's in a grave in the churchyard. The stone has her name on it to tell you that's where she is. Do you understand? Do you hear me?"

She turned away and resumed clipping the hedge.

There was no reaching her, no way I knew of. She needed professional help.

I continued on to my car, stopping at the big oak to look at the swing's rope, which I had left coiled beneath. I studied the knot, then touched it timidly. There was nothing unusual about it. It must have been there all along and I just hadn't noticed.

It was a quick drive to the bank. High Street had been swept clean after the festival and basked quietly in the morning sunshine. Its main bank was a small-town miniature of the kind you see in East Coast cities, with bronze doors and Greek columns. I think the teller I got must have been there since it was built. Her fluffy white hair flew in the breeze made by a little desk fan. Pursing her lips, she read my check and driver's license, then lifted her head to study me, pushing her heavy glasses up her nose, so she could get a clearer view.

"Sondra's daughter."

"Yes," I said.

"You're depositing this in the Ingram account."

I realized that teens didn't usually write a check as large as mine. "Here's my bankbook," I told her, sliding it under the glass. "It has phone numbers and an e-mail address if you want to verify the availability of the money."

"No. Your mama's checks were always good," she said.

I nodded, though I didn't know what she was talking about. My mother didn't bank here.

"And always on time," she added as she started the transaction. "The first of each month Jule would come in to deposit them."

I looked at the teller with surprise.

"I always wondered why," the woman continued. "Of course, I figured your mama was being blackmailed, but I wondered what for."

Blackmailed? I stared at the woman.

"When I told that to folks here at the bank, they laughed."

Small wonder, I thought.

"When I told the police, they said I read too many paperbacks. But the real reason they didn't believe me was Jule. She's golden around here. The Ingram family, they're like the Scarboroughs, Wisteria's royalty."

"I see."

"Just between you and me," the teller said, peering at me, her eyes magnified by her glasses, "why *was* your mama paying off Jule?"

"She was just helping out," I replied, "like I'm doing."

The old woman gazed at me doubtfully.

I wondered if my mother had been in the habit of lending money to Aunt Jule, and if my godmother had become dependent on her. I knew my mother was good at manipulating others with her wealth—I'd heard my father tell her that more than once. Perhaps money was the cause of her and Aunt Jule's arguments that summer.

The teller stamped my check and handed me a receipt. As I turned to leave, I heard raised voices in one of the bank's offices. A door with frosted glass swung open and Frank emerged, his face red with anger. He didn't see me and, given his scarlet color and indignant gait, I thought he might not want me to see him.

I turned aside and took my time putting my bankbook away, mulling over what I had learned from the teller.

My mother and godmother had been best friends since their middle-school years at Birch Hill and probably had known each other's deepest secrets. But the teller's suggestion of blackmail was absurd. So was my idea that my mother was controlling my godmother with money, for Aunt Jule had nothing to offer her in return.

Besides, my mother had loved Aunt Jule. In the will Frank had drawn up for my mother that summer, she had left her entire estate to me, to be inherited at the age of eighteen. But if I died before then, my inheritance was to go to Aunt Jule. Obviously my mother trusted her; there was no reason for me to doubt their relationship now.

"Lauren, you found us," Holly said, sounding pleased "Everyone, this is Lauren Brandt."

Kids looked up from two rows of computer screens, greeting me with a chorus of hellos. Nick sat at a drawing table fifteen feet away, ink on his fingers and balled-up sheets of paper ringing his chair. He flashed me one of those smiles a girl could believe was just for her; I was smart enough not to. I tried to spread my smile to him and those around him, then turned to Holly.

"You look like you're busy. I'll come by at a better time."

"No, no, stay," she replied. "Karen, would you show Lauren around the office, introduce her to people, and tell her what's going on?"

A girl pushed back from her desk, tucked a strand of hair behind her ear, and obliged. I felt self-conscious, like I was playing my father touring a factory. Nick looked across the room at me and winked.

The walls of the yearbook room were covered with schedules, posters, photos of school events, and cartoons—Nick's, I figured. My father was the star of several of his pieces. In the cartoon that hung above Nick's table, my dad's tooth-filled smile bloomed over a podium as he announced, "I promise to lead Maryland in the Industrial Evolution." Smokestacks rose in the background; three-legged frogs and two-headed geese applauded.

Nick caught me studying it, and I quickly glanced away. When I looked back, he turned away, both of us pretending that I hadn't noticed the drawing.

Holly saw us and her hand flew up to her mouth. "Oh, Lauren, I'm sorry."

"Don't worry about it," I replied, moving on hurriedly to sports photos.

"I didn't even think about it," she explained. "After a while, you forget what's hanging up."

Everyone in the room started checking the walls to see what was hanging up.

"No problem," I assured her.

Holly bit her lip and looked at Nick. So did everyone else, figuring out that it was something of his. Luckily, a guy with funky red hair and a lot of freckles came in right then and saved me from further embarrassment.

"Well, boys and girls, I'm back from the Queen," he announced loudly, then threw himself down in a chair as if he'd just swum the distance from England. "Got it all scoped out," he told Holly.

She turned to him, and Karen filled me in: "Our prom is tonight at the Queen Victoria Hotel. Steve's a photographer."

"So give me a list of your shots," Holly said to Steve.

"They're in my head."

"Put them on paper," she told him. "How's the entrance looking?"

"Very rosy," he replied, leaning back in his chair. "It clashes with my hair, but then, I'm not part of the scene."

"You mean it's red?" Holly exclaimed. "I told them to make the archway white or pastel."

"That's what happens when you're not running everything," he remarked. I heard a muffled laugh in the corner of the room.

"But we need contrast for the photos," she insisted. "I told them that. They'll be sorry when they see their spread."

"There's always Adobe Photoshop," Nick suggested.

"Yes, of course," Holly replied, "but that will take time."

Nick smiled at her. "I was joking, Holly. This is a yearbook. We're supposed to be preserving memories, not creating them."

"Some people just don't get it," she said. "Well, I warned them." She leaned back against a desk and drummed her fingers.

"Listen, Holly," I interrupted, "I have a few more things to do."

She hopped up. "I'll walk you out." When we got outside the room, she asked, "So, how's it going today?"

"Pretty good."

"Have you visited your mom's grave yet?"

"That's where I'm going next," I replied.

"Want me to go with you?"

I was surprised and touched by her offer. "Thanks, but no."

"I've got time," she told me. "The cemetery is right across the street. Don't get snowed by my busy editor-in-chief act. It just makes me feel important," she added, laughing. "Why don't I go?"

"Thanks, but this time I'd rather be by myself."

She studied me for a moment, then nodded. "Okay."

"Oh, and I transferred the money."

She grabbed my hand. "You're a lifesaver!"

"So I'll see you at home." I turned to walk away.

"Holly," one of the kids called from inside. "Holly, tell Lauren to wait. We've got a great idea!"

Holly raised an eyebrow at me, then stuck her head through the door.

"We're going to fix her up with Jason," a girl said. "What do you think?"

Holly was quiet for a moment, then smiled. "I think it's brilliant."

"They'll look good under the arch, red roses or not," the photographer needled.

Holly ignored him. "I'll dig up a dress for you, Lauren, so don't worry about that. Shoes, too. One of us will have something from last year that'll work." To the group she announced, "I'm taking one-night donations—formals and shoes."

"Whoa! Wait a minute, what are we talking about?" I said, stepping into the doorway.

Karen, my guide, pointed to a photo of a great-looking guy in a basketball uniform. "Jason Deere. Star forward for W. H., just ditched by his yearlong girlfriend. He needs a date for tonight's prom."

"Well, thanks, but I'm busy," I said.

"Doing what?" Holly asked. "Come on, Lauren. It will be good for you."

"It will be better for Jason," Nick observed.

I glanced at him.

"You date, don't you?" Nick asked with a sly smile.

"I go to dances."

"What's Jason's cell-phone number?" a guy hollered.

"Wait a minute," I protested.

He picked up the phone and someone called out a number.

I didn't want to talk to some guy I had never met in front of a room full of people.

"If he wants to, fine," I told Holly, walking away as fast as I could. "Tell me when you get home."

Just before the hall's double doors closed between us, she gave me the thumbs-up sign and called out, "I'll pick up an extra boutonniere."

My car was parked on the church side of Scarborough Road. I stopped there just long enough to open the trunk and throw in my purse, then followed a brick path that led past the church to the cemetery beside it. Grace Presbyterian, built in the 1800s, had a deep sloping roof and a simple bell tower on one corner. On a sunny day its graveyard, shaded by a huge copper beech and tall, lacy cedars, felt ten degrees cooler than the street.

My mother had been buried here because Aunt Jule had said it was her wish. The day of the funeral I'd been too upset to notice anything about her plot, including where it was. I knew the church office would have a map for locating graves, but I wandered up and down the rows, reading names and dates. The dappled light fell gently on stones smoothed by decades of rain. Old trees rustled soft as angel wings. I suddenly felt hot tears in my eyes. If only my mother could have known this kind of peace when she was alive.

At last I came upon her grave, a polished granite stone, and knelt in the grass beside it. For a moment I hurt so much I couldn't breathe. My heart felt squeezed into a small, sharp rock. Then the feeling passed. I wiped away tears I hadn't realized I was shedding.

I sagged back against the marker next to my mother's. How cold these stones felt on a summer day, I thought. I ran my fingers over her name, then turned to see who was lying next to her, for the marker was very close. It was pink granite and slightly smaller than hers.

DAUGHTER, I read.

Daughter! Me! This was to be my grave.

I felt as I did when I was a child—smothered by her. It was just like her, not caring who else might be in my life, counting on my coming back to her.

When had she made these arrangements? I wondered. When she wrote the new will? That had been a week or two before she died.

A terrifying idea crept into my mind. What if my mother's fears were not as groundless as we had thought? What if someone really had been after her and she, with no one to believe or protect her, had made these preparations?

That's crazy, I told myself, rising to my feet, heading back to the car. There was another explanation for the grave. My mother had given birth to me here, having left my father for a time and run to the sanctuary of Aunt Jule's arms. Perhaps she had made the arrangements then.

When I reached my car, I retrieved my purse from the trunk, then opened the driver-side door. A sheet of white paper lay folded on the front seat. I gazed at it, puzzled, until I realized I had left my window cracked for air. Someone must have slipped the paper through. I picked up the note and flipped it open. The message, written in block letters, was simple: YOU'RE NEXT.

eight

I SPUN AROUND to see if someone was watching from behind, then quickly surveyed the street, church lawn, and school area. Several groups of kids lingered on the school steps. Two people dressed like teachers leaned on a parked car, talking. No one appeared to be interested in me.

I stared at the note. Was it just a prank or a warning to be taken seriously? Was it Nora's?

She knew I was coming here, but then so did Aunt Jule and Holly, and I wasn't eager to blame either of them. Perhaps I was being unfair to Nora. Perhaps, but Aunt Jule and Holly hadn't locked me in the boathouse. They didn't keep a cache of my mother's things and didn't silently stand by as I fell from a swing.

I refolded the note and placed it in my purse.

When we were children, Nora had been a gentle friend; I could easily believe she was harmless—harmless in her heart. But people act according to how they see the world outside them, and she saw it in a very distorted way. In her mental state, would she understand the real-life consequences of her actions? Had Nora pushed my mother in anger and watched her float in the river, not comprehending the finality of what she had done until it was too late?

If that were true, I'd learn to come to grips with it and accept that Nora wasn't mentally responsible. But that wasn't the only thing troubling me now. How did Nora see me? What if I were an unnerving reminder of my mother and she needed to get rid of me, too, without comprehending all of what that meant?

I was more shaken than I realized—it took several tries to insert my key in the ignition. At the grocery store I had to check and recheck my list, unable to concentrate on the task. When I finally arrived home, I didn't see Nora in the garden or greenhouse. I called for her in the house but it was Aunt Jule who responded, saying she was somewhere outside.

Aunt Jule eyed the bags I'd hauled into the kitchen. "Good lord, what have you done?"

"Picked up some things."

"You didn't have to do that, Lauren."

"I wanted to," I said, and began to put the groceries away. "Is Holly home yet?"

"No, after yearbook stuff she has a manicure appointment."

Aunt Jule helped unpack the bags, setting boxes randomly on shelves, placing soap powder between instant potatoes and tea. "Tonight's the prom, you know."

I nodded.

"So what do you think of Nick?" she asked.

"Some of those boxes are upside down," I pointed out.

"Honestly, you're as compulsive as Holly," she said. "Soon you'll be reminding me to turn off the lights." Then she smiled slyly. "Or maybe you're just wiggling out of my question. What do you think of the grownup Nick?"

"He's gotten taller."

"He's gotten terrifically handsome," she said. "And either you're blind or you're faking it."

I laughed. "There's no need for you to be shopping guys for me, Aunt Jule. I stopped by to see Holly and was drafted to go to the prom with some jock—one that's terrifically handsome, as you'd say."

"You were always such cute little pals, you and Nick," Aunt Jule went on. "I loved watching you play together. You were friends from the start."

"It's nice to see that Holly and he are good friends now," I replied, reminding her of Holly's interest.

She nodded without enthusiasm, then picked up a basket of fresh strawberries and poured them into a colander.

"Listen, Aunt Jule, we really do need to talk about Nora. She needs psychiatric help."

My godmother carried the colander to the sink, turning her back on me.

"She needs it now."

"That's your opinion," Aunt Jule replied as she washed the berries.

"And Holly's, and Frank's. Frank says Nora is out of touch with reality and that it's dangerous. He said one of these days she's going to—"

"If you ask me, people out of touch with reality aren't nearly as dangerous as lawyers like him who manipulate it."

"At least have her evaluated by a professional," I pleaded, "then we can decide from there."

"We? You've become quite the grown-up, Lauren," she observed.

"I meant *you.* But I'll pay for it."

"How nice of you!" she replied sarcastically.

I was baffled by her attitude.

She shook the water hard from the colander of berries. "You stay away for seven years, Lauren, and after one day back, you start telling me how to fix things. You're here for twenty-four hours and you're cocksure you know what Nora needs."

"All I'm saying is get her checked out. If a doctor says she needs treatment, I'll pay for it, all of it."

"Will you now? Sometimes, Lauren, you act just like Sondra, believing your money makes you superior, using your money to make other people do what *you* think they should do."

"I care about Nora! I'm trying to help her!"

"You're just like Sondra," Aunt Jule went on, "deciding how other people should lead their lives, deciding what's normal, what isn't, what's to be admired, what's to be scorned. There are more ways to do it than *your* way."

"But—"

"You walk like Sondra. You talk like Sondra. I *hate* it when you act like her."

The bitterness I heard in Aunt Jule's voice amazed me. I felt torn between insisting that I wasn't like my mother—I had tried hard not to be—and defending her.

"Well, there is one thing my mother and I share," I told her. "Nora's intense dislike for us."

My godmother twisted plastic bags in her hands, then balled them up.

"Aunt Jule, have you ever thought about the fact that it was Nora who summoned us, Nora who said she found my mother floating in the water?"

I steeled myself, figuring my godmother would be

furious at what I was suggesting, but she answered with a flick of her hand. "Of course I have. Sondra's reckless death traumatized Nora as well as you, and I still haven't forgiven her for that."

I realized then that Aunt Jule would never consider the possibility that her daughter was responsible in some way. Pressing the issue wouldn't bring my mother back or get Nora the help she needed.

"Last night, after I was asleep, I thought I heard someone calling my name, calling it the same way my mother did. The door to the room where my mother had stayed was ajar and I went in. I found old tabloid pictures of her in the dresser, photos from that summer, her earrings, and her scarf, mixed in with items that belonged to Nora. Why would Nora have these things? Why would she think my mother is in the river or asleep in the boathouse? Don't you see? She is obsessed with her. She needs—"

"Perhaps you're the one obsessed," Aunt Jule countered icily, "hearing Sondra's voice calling you, reading into insignificant comments. It's time to move on, Lauren, and clearly you haven't."

I wouldn't give up. "Nora and I used to play together. We used to be friends. Why does she hate me now?"

"She doesn't hate you."

"Why does she act the way she does?" I persisted.

"Because you've grown into Sondra," Aunt Jule replied, tight-lipped.

I looked her straight in the eye. "I don't think so."

We turned away from each other and worked silently for a minute.

"Aunt Jule, why did you stop the police from doing a full investigation?"

"I'm sorry," she replied, setting down a bag of sugar, "I don't think I heard you right, Lauren."

I knew she had. "It would have been better to let them investigate my mother's death so we could rule out everything but an accident."

"You ungrateful brat! I was protecting you!"

She stalked out the porch door and slammed it shut. I stood quietly for several minutes, staring down at the cans I held, then continued to put things away. The tears were there again, burning my eyes, but I didn't let them fall.

I spent an hour in my room, untying the tiny knots in my necklace, polishing the silver links and tarnished heart. I had seen Aunt Jule angry before—furious the summer my mother came—but her anger had never been directed at me, not until now. I felt as if I were reliving my mother's stay here seven years ago.

I didn't see Nora that afternoon, but I didn't look for her, either. About five o'clock I took a walk and watched storm clouds mounting over the bay. Dinner was a sandwich alone in the kitchen. I didn't know if Aunt Jule was still angry at me or simply wary after the argument. Returning to my room, I heard the radio in hers, but I didn't stop by.

About six-thirty Holly knocked on my door, then entered, wiggling her fingers.

I admired her nails. "Fabulous!" I said.

"Fake," she replied, "but what the heck. I put the boutonnieres in the fridge. Do you know how many girls would like to go to the prom with Jason?"

"Well, if anyone wants to take my place . . . ," I began.

"Cut it out. You want the bathroom first? I've got to make sure these are dry."

"Sure."

"I'll hang your dress on the closet door. You've got a pile of shoes to choose from."

"Thanks for getting all that together."

"Glad to," she replied. "This is going to be great!"

When I returned from the bathroom twenty minutes later, I found the shoe boxes piled neatly and the dress hanging on the door. One look told me the gown wouldn't fit, though it would have been perfect for Holly with her tall model-like frame. I figured it was hers—its blue matched her eyes.

"Jason had better not be picky about his last-minute dates," I muttered as I unzipped the back.

When I put on the dress, I didn't know whether to laugh or cry; a sleeping bag would have been as flattering. I gathered the waist with my fingers, trying to shorten the dress and give it some shape, then padded down the hall toward Aunt Jule's room to find something I could tie around me as a belt. I hoped she was in a better mood.

"Good Lord!" she exclaimed before I could say a word. "Are you trying to be nominated for wallflower of the year?"

"I thought a belt might help."

She clucked and came toward me. "It's going to need more than that," she said, grasping the fabric, lifting the dress up from my shoulders. "Perhaps your date can bring football pads."

"I think he plays basketball."

"Then we'll have to use his shoes."

I laughed, glad to know she was back to her old self.

With her hands still on my shoulders, she turned me around, then shook her head. "I don't know why Holly thought her dress would fit you. Let's see what I've got. I may have to do some fast sewing."

I followed her into the walk-in closet, a pleasantly chaotic room, where Nora, Holly, and I used to play. Aunt Jule suddenly seized on something. "This is it! Perfect. Halter tops never go out of style, not when you have pretty shoulders."

She pulled out a rather slinky red dress.

"Wow."

"I *was* pretty *wow*," she said, "back in the days when I could fit in this. Now you can be."

"I don't know," I said, touching the stretchy red fabric.

She marched me out of the closet and turned me toward the mirror. "Lauren, look at yourself. Do you really want to go to a prom looking like you're playing dress-up?"

I shook my head.

"So give it a try. Don't be prim."

"I'm not prim," I argued. "I just don't want to call attention to myself, and red does."

"So does a dress several sizes too big."

"True."

"How about shoes?" Aunt Jule asked.

"Holly brought me several pairs."

"Do they fit as well as her dress?"

"I haven't tried them yet."

Aunt Jule disappeared inside the closet. Box lids started flying. "Here we are."

She emerged holding up a pair of red heels. "Okay," she

said, noting the expression on my face, "so they're retro. Trust me, when guys see you in these, they'll be falling all over you."

"Or I'll be falling all over them. How can you stand in heels that tall and skinny? I've got four-inchers, but they're not on pinpoints."

"Try them," she said.

I did, walking back and forth in my room, then up and down the porch, my heels clicking loudly, my bathrobe blowing in the breeze of arriving storms.

At eight-fifteen I was dressed and surveyed myself in the mirror once more. The red gown was the most sophisticated thing I'd ever worn. The slits up its sides did more than provide a view of my legs, they were necessary if I wanted to walk rather than hop like the Easter Bunny.

I picked up the little evening bag Aunt Jule had lent me and headed downstairs. When I reached the lower hall, I heard Frank, Holly, and Aunt Jule talking. I assumed the guys hadn't arrived yet. Relaxing a little, I entered the river room and strode toward the fireplace, where Holly was posing.

Frank glanced over his shoulder, then turned around and whistled at me.

"Really, Frank!" Aunt Jule said, but this once he had succeeded in pleasing her.

Holly looked at me with surprise. "Where did you get that dress?"

"It's your mom's."

"I lent you mine," she said.

"It was beautiful, but it didn't fit."

"Surely, Holly," Aunt Jule interjected, "a girl into details, as you are, would have noticed that you and Lauren are built very differently."

I heard the put-down in my godmother's voice and wished she'd act more like a mother and less like a goading sister.

"Holly, you look incredible," I said. She was wearing a silk dress that perfectly matched her sapphire eyes. Her long black hair swept down over thin straps and a low-cut back. "I want a picture of you for my room at school."

"Perhaps one of you gals together," Frank suggested.

"No," Holly said. "With our dates and individually."

I didn't argue. It was her prom, we should do what she wanted. I backed up and sat down on a hassock. With the height of my shoes and the low seat, my knees shot up. So did the tight skirt, its slit climbing three quarters of the way up my leg.

"I don't know about these shoes, Aunt Jule," I said. "You could use them for hole punchers."

A deep laugh sounded behind me. I jumped.

"Nick! I didn't know you were here."

"I came in from the porch," he said.

He looked terrific and surprisingly at ease in his tux.

"Why didn't you say something?"

His green eyes held mine for a moment, shining softly. "I couldn't think of anything."

"That's rather unusual for you, Nick," Aunt Jule remarked.

Frank agreed with a grunt.

Nick smiled and sat in the chair behind me. "Enjoy it while it lasts." His eyes dropped down to my legs.

I pulled on my dress, then self-consciously rested my hand on my calf. Nick watched Holly pose but kept stealing glances at my legs. I couldn't stand it, the funny, fluttery feelings I was getting whenever he looked at me. I turned to face him. "This is nothing new," I said quietly. "You've seen both my legs before."

He leaned closer. "Then why are you covering them up?"

"Okay, next beauty," Frank announced.

I looked up and discovered Holly glaring at us. I couldn't blame her.

"It's not my prom, Frank," I said. "I don't want any pictures of me." What I really didn't want was to draw attention away from Holly.

"Well, your godmother might. Jule?"

"Yes, definitely," she said.

I stood up reluctantly.

While Frank was taking my picture, Nora walked in and sat on the floor next to Nick.

"Hey, Nora girl," Frank greeted her.

She didn't respond.

"Frank, I want one of Lauren and me together," Aunt Jule said. "She looks so grown-up, so very beautiful."

Nora turned her head. Her eyes studied every detail of me, making me uneasy.

"And then how about some pictures of Aunt Jule with Nora, and Aunt Jule with Holly," I suggested.

"No, we have plenty of us already," my godmother replied, standing next to me, putting her arm around me. "You look absolutely stunning, love. You'll be the belle of the ball."

I stole a look at Holly, who, luckily, didn't seem to be listening. She and Nick were going down a checklist for the yearbook's coverage of the prom.

Aunt Jule and I smiled at Frank's command, then she suddenly bent her head close to mine, studying the chain around my neck. "You're wearing it!" she exclaimed. "The heart I gave you when you were a baby. I didn't know you still had it."

Holly glanced up.

"Look, girls," Aunt Jule said, lifting the pendant with one finger. "It's the little heart I gave Lauren. Do you remember it?"

Nora shook her head no.

"I think so," Holly said. "Is it gold?"

"Silver," Aunt Jule replied.

"I don't remember," Nora said.

"Of course you do," Aunt Jule insisted. "Lauren wore it all the time. She'd get a white mark on her little suntanned neck. Sondra took it from you, Lauren," Aunt Jule recalled. "I was so afraid she had gotten rid of it. Where did you find it?"

"Don't tell," Nora said.

"In the boathouse."

"Don't tell! It's a secret!" Nora cried out.

Aunt Jule and Holly turned to her, both of them frowning.

"Sondra wants the little heart," Nora went on. "Sondra will get it back."

Frank shook his head and sent Nick a knowing look.

"Nora, Sondra is dead," Nick said quietly.

The doorbell rang.

"Who's next?" Nora asked.

"That's Lauren's date," Holly replied sharply. "Now, keep quiet! Try to act normal and not embarrass us all."

Nora bit her lip and turned to Nick. He laid his hand on her shoulder. "Everything's all right." The expression on his face, the sound of his voice, was heartbreakingly gentle.

But it was my heart that had been broken the night my mother died, not Nora's, and everything wasn't all right.

nine

THE DOORBELL RANG for the third time.

"What do you think," Frank asked, "should we let in Lauren's date before he tries another house?"

Nora sprang up and ran upstairs. Holly answered the door.

"This is Jason Deere," she announced.

My tall, dark-haired date was extremely good-looking and knew how to make an entrance, stopping a few feet inside the room, smiling at me.

"Okay, let's not make like a *deer* caught in headlights," Frank said. "Line up next to this pretty girl so I can snap a picture and we all can move on."

Jason liked to have his picture taken. He also liked to look at my chest. I wished he'd stop.

"How come you're not covering up for *him*?" Nick whispered as we left the house.

"Excuse me?"

"You know what I'm talking about."

I folded my arms over my chest, but had to unfold them again to walk—it was too difficult to balance with the slim dress and spike heels.

Nick threw back his head and laughed. Both Holly and I glared at him. Jason looked a little mystified but had too much self-confidence to worry about what was going on. He took my hand and drew it lightly through his arm, escorting me to his car.

We arrived at the Queen Victoria just as Jason's ex-girlfriend and her date entered the hotel. Though it was about to pour, we had to wait in the car several minutes to make sure they were settled inside and could watch us arrive. When we finally got to the famous arch of roses, guys gave me the once-over. Girls whispered. Jason's ex checked me out and looked annoyed. Jason was very pleased with this and told me so. I should have realized then what kind of night it was going to be.

Wherever she was, we were, on the carved wood staircase, by the punch-and-cookie tables, near a screen of potted palms. Jason gazed deep in my eyes as if we were madly in love and told boring basketball stories. For the first hour my only real entertainment was watching two girls dump glasses of punch on Nick.

Karen, my guide from earlier in the day, was standing nearby and explained what I had already figured out. "Nick said yes to both of them when they asked him to the prom."

A half hour later he had danced with both of them, and a lot of other girls as well, while Holly directed Steve in his picture taking.

Occasionally Jason would wander off with one of his basketball buddies. Nick had at least two chances to ask me to dance, but didn't.

My feelings aren't hurt, I told myself. But they were.

I tried mixing in with the other kids, asking about their plans for the summer and college, but it was only natural at this last school-sponsored event that they would want to talk about their memories, rather than get to know an outsider. At a band break, while Jason and his buddies recalled another story in the series of their team's greatest moments, I slipped away. I found a velvet love seat, conveniently secluded by palms that separated it from the other chairs. I sank down on it, glad to give my feet and party face a rest.

The fan of palms split. Nick's smile appeared. "Having a good time?" he asked.

"Terrific," I lied.

"How do you like Jason?"

"He's a lot of fun."

"Yeah, I can tell. He's over there, you're here."

"My feet are tired," I explained.

Nick leaned forward, so his face came around the side of the big plant. "That's one of those things I've never understood, girls and shoes. Why are you wearing those instruments of torture?"

I shrugged. "They're Aunt Jule's. They match the dress."

"You could drive their heels through the heart of a vampire."

I laughed and he laughed with me, but his eyes were watchful.

"Sometimes you look so serious," he said.

I glanced away. "Some things in life are serious."

"Ignore them," Nick told me. "I always do."

I met his gaze. "You've been lucky in your life. So far you haven't confronted anything that you can't ignore."

His face grew thoughtful, his eyes a different shade of green. I knew I was looking at him too long. I wished he would take my hand and be as gentle with me as he had been with Nora.

"Jason's looking for you," Holly's voice cut between us.

I straightened up as if our school's headmistress had just walked in.

"For me?" Nick asked mischievously.

"For Lauren."

"Right," I said, standing up.

Holly's voice became warmer. "He's thrilled with you, Lauren. He says he's got the hottest girl at the prom."

"Great." I headed toward Jason without glancing back at her and Nick.

Jason lifted his arm and put it around me as if we had been a couple forever, then went right on talking. I noticed a man wearing rose-tinted glasses standing at the rim of the group of athletes, smiling and nodding. He looked like one of those teachers who wanted to be in with the kids, the kind who went by his first name and didn't realize he was hopelessly uncool.

But I had no one else to talk to. When he followed the cheese tray around the circle to me, I smiled at him.

"I'm Dr. Parker," he said, holding out his hand "Call me Jim."

"Lauren Brandt," I replied, shaking his hand.

He repeated my name slowly. "Now, how would I know you?"

Judging by his wide, flowered tie, sandals and socks, and the ecology button pinned cockeyed on his shirt, he wasn't a supporter of my father. "I'm staying with my godmother, Jule Ingram, and her daughters, Holly and Nora."

"Oh, yes. Holly and Nora. Two very different girls."

"Have you taught Nora?" I asked eagerly. A teacher's view of her might be helpful.

"No. I'm the school guidance counselor."

"So you have a background in psychology," I said.

"That's right."

I steered him away from the group. "I have some questions."

"But I have no answers," he replied, smiling.

"My questions are about Nora, not myself," I explained, when we were a distance from the others. "I've known her all my life and I'm really worried. Do you have any idea what's wrong with her?"

Dr. Parker leaned back against a dark wood pillar, crossing one foot over the other, tilting his head at me. I had a feeling he had seen that pose in a movie. "Are you asking for a diagnosis?"

"Well, yes."

"I can't give one without a thorough evaluation," he said.

"But you must have seen her behavior at school," I persisted.

"Yes. And several of her teachers recommended an evaluation. But her mother would not agree to it. And though I invited Nora to my office a number of times, she never came."

"I can fill you in," I told him. "She's totally phobic about water. My mother drowned here, and Nora says she is sleeping in an old boathouse on the property. She thinks that when the water gets stirred up my mother is doing it. She says my mother is looking for me. Wouldn't you call that crazy?"

He shook his head. "Lauren, it's like asking me if I'd call a painting good, telling me it is blue and red, but not letting me study it firsthand. The answer depends on how those colors are used."

"But my godmother *still* won't agree to an evaluation. And Nora is too confused to know she needs help."

He spread his hands. "Then there's nothing I can do. In my field, if the individual doesn't want help and the person legally responsible refuses to take action, no one else can, not until something life-threatening happens. But I'm glad to talk with *you* about your feelings toward your godmother and Nora."

"I don't want to talk about me!"

He nodded—a little smugly, I thought. "I didn't think so. But just in case you change your mind, here's my card with my summer address and phone. I won't be around school much longer."

I took it from him and read the purple print: *Dr. James Michael Parker, Paranormal Investigator.*

He laughed when he saw the expression on my face. "It's my hobby," he said. "But if you like, I can set you up with a therapist who's more of a straight arrow. Tuck it away in case you need the number."

I thanked him, perhaps not as nicely as I should have, and put it in my purse.

The music had started up again. Jason was in the mood to

dance and—what a surprise—found space on the floor next to his ex and her date. Even luckier for me, Nick and Holly were close by.

I knew we were headed for trouble when the slow dance began, but with Nick right there, I had too much pride to duck out to the ladies' room. As we danced, Jason kept moving his head. I figured I was supposed to move mine until our lips would just happen to come within an inch of each other's. I kept my cheek firmly against Jason's lapel, figuring the angle would make it harder for him to kiss me.

Meanwhile Holly had her head on Nick's shoulder, her eyes closed. I wondered what it would be like to stand that close to Nick, to feel his arms wrap around me and have him whisper something for my ears alone. I wondered what it would be like to kiss him.

I came back to reality just in time to see Jason's ex kiss her date. Not wanting to be outdone, Jason quickly pulled my face up to his and put his mouth firmly on mine. I turned away.

"Not now," I said, then wanted to kick myself for leaving it open for a later time. But I didn't expect him to interpret my statement as thirty seconds later.

He tried kissing me again.

"No," I said.

He persisted, his hands on the move.

I didn't want to make a scene and embarrass us both. "No," I said quietly, pulling back, "I don't want to make out."

He looked at me, incredulous, then tried again. I pushed him back with both hands. The couples around us started to watch. Holly and Nick stopped dancing.

"What's wrong with you?" Jason said. "Are you frigid? Been going to an all-girl school for too long?"

Now I was furious.

He reached for my arm, trying to pull me back into a close dance. I remembered what Nick had said about Aunt Jule's shoes and vampires. I stepped on Jason's foot, and not with my tippy toes.

Jason yelped and went flying backward. Unfortunately, the punch table was right behind him. It tipped, the huge bowl sliding off, thumping on the carpet, sending up a volcano of pink liquid. Plastic cups tumbled around his head. Nick hooted with laughter.

Humiliated, I hiked up my skirt and ran. I didn't notice the rain till I was halfway down the block from the Queen Victoria, my head swimming with what I imagined others were saying about me. I could hear Nick laughing his sides out. I was sure Holly wasn't happy after all she had done for me. When I'd left, Steve was eagerly snapping pictures that weren't on the approved list.

I held my skirt higher so I could take longer steps and strode for home. An old brown car cruised up beside me.

"Hey, there," Nick said, rolling down the window. "Nice night for a walk."

"Yup."

"Hope that dress doesn't shrink too much. Looks like it's getting shorter."

I silently marched on.

"Maybe you'd like a ride home," Nick suggested.

"I can get there myself."

"I know you can. I was being a gentleman, trying to save the reputation of the guys from Wisteria High."

"I don't judge a whole group by one person."

"Lauren, come on, get in. Like it or not, I'm going to follow you and make sure you get home safely. It will be a lot more comfortable if both of us are riding."

My dress felt like a soaked wool stocking. My hair was hanging in short wet strings, and I figured that my mascara was making black rivers down my cheeks. I had never been more miserable.

Nick got out of the car and ran around to the other side, standing in the pouring rain, gallantly holding the door open. I followed him and got in. By the time he was back in the driver's seat, he was thoroughly wet. His hair looked like it did when we used to swim together, turning into dark gold corkscrews, but his face was very different from the mischievous cherub I once knew. It was chiseled, the jaw line strong, the mouth sensitive—

I quickly looked down and buckled my seat belt. I had seen enough of mouths tonight. It was bewildering to me how much I wanted to avoid Jason's and *didn't* want to avoid Nick's.

"All set?" he asked.

"Yes, thanks." My voice shook a little. I hated it when this happened to me. I could get through all kinds of anger and frustration, but when a crisis was over, I wanted to cry like a baby. I blinked my eyes hard.

"Okay," Nick said. "I'll explain your job. See this string?"

I looked up. It ran from one side of the car to the other, disappearing out the side windows. Peering through the fogged windshield, I realized the string made a big loop and was tied to the wipers.

"The blades don't work," Nick said. "So you have to grab hold of this string and pull. Left, right, left, right. Got it?"

I looked at him for a moment, then moved the string to the left. In unison, the wipers moved to the right.

"You're going to have to do it faster than that," he said.

I started smiling. "This is crazy."

"Left, right, faster, faster—there you go."

"Why don't you get them fixed?" I asked.

"It's more fun this way."

"I hope you don't feel the same about brakes. They don't need fixing, do they?"

"Why do you think I wear these thick rubber soles?"

I laughed. "You're kidding."

"You can try dragging your foot," he continued, "but I don't think those heels will do much more than knock off menacing forms of life."

I laughed again. "They are pretty good at that."

I liked being in the old car with Nick. I liked there being nothing but rain and us. He turned on the radio, which had lousy reception. I didn't care. I could have ridden around with him for hours. Probably all his other one-night girls had felt the same way.

Nick pulled up to the edge of Aunt Jule's driveway. "Last time I went down there in the rain, I had to be towed out," he said.

"No problem. Thanks for the ride."

"I'll walk you to the door."

"No, you'll get wetter than you already are," I told him, "then drip all over the dance floor."

Nick reached over the seat. "I just happen to have a shower curtain with me."

"You do? Why?"

"It's showering," he said, then pulled it over his head and got out of the car. I watched him hop over the puddles to my side.

"I use it as a drop cloth when I'm painting at Frank's," he explained as he opened my door and helped me out. Still holding my hand, he used his other to grab an edge of the curtain. I did the same and we made our way down the driveway.

My slim skirt made it difficult. I needed a third hand to hold up my dress. Suddenly I lurched forward. My heels had stuck firmly in the mud, pitching me headlong.

"Whoa!" Nick cried, dropping his part of the shower curtain, catching me around the waist. He straightened me up like a toppled-over mannequin, trying to get me back in my shoes.

I felt my way with my toes and was standing squarely again, but Nick didn't let go. The shower curtain rested on our heads like a collapsed tent. He ignored it, facing me now, his arms around me, his eyes shining softly. My hands rested on his shoulders.

"Hi," he said.

"Hi."

"I'd like to kiss you." He waited a moment for my response, then added, "Or, if you'd rather, we can dance, as long as we can get you unstuck."

"I think I'm in deep."

"Me, too," he said, looking into my eyes.

His head moved closer to mine. Then he lifted his hand, cupping my cheek ever so gently. His lips touched my lips, light as a butterfly, once, twice.

The kisses were lovely, so lovely I couldn't help it—I did a totally stupid, uncool thing. I sighed.

I heard the laughter rumbling inside Nick and I started to pull away. But his arms wrapped around me. He held me close and pressed his lips against mine. A thrill went through me. I kissed him back—I didn't think about it, just kissed him with all that my heart felt.

Now Nick pulled back, looking at me surprised. I wondered if I had done something wrong. My only experience was a smattering of hardly-touch good-night kisses after dance dates. What if I had done something weird and didn't know it?

"I—I have to go," I said, ducking out from under the shower curtain, making a dash for the porch without my shoes.

When I glanced back Nick was wearing the curtain like a cape, watching me run to the house. He turned away slowly and walked back to his car.

I stood inside the door and ran one muddy foot over the other. Aunt Jule's red shoes were stuck in the driveway, like little memorials at the magical place where Nick and I had kissed.

ten

Aunt Jule looked up from her book, silent for a moment, surveying me. "Oh, dear."

"I hope I haven't embarrassed Holly," I said, entering the river room.

"What happened? Where's Jason?"

"I left him on the dance floor, sprawled on it."

She laughed and pointed to the chair next to her. "Sit. Tell."

I did. When I had finished, Aunt Jule smiled. "And you seem so sweet and innocent. I bet he was surprised."

Not as surprised as Nick, I thought, recalling the expression on his face a few minutes before. I decided not to tell Aunt Jule that Nick had brought me home. She'd want every detail.

After cleaning the mud from my feet and wiping up the tracks I'd left in the hall, I headed upstairs, reliving in my mind Nick's wonderful kiss. On the landing I stopped abruptly. Nora stood near the top of the stairway, as if waiting for me. Her hand gripped the banister, her fine bones exaggerated by the tension in her. The light shining from below threw Nora's tall shadow against the wall, trapping it within the bars cast by the railing.

"Is everything okay?" I asked.

Her voice shook: "Someone doesn't like it when you wear that dress. Someone doesn't like it when you wear that heart."

"I'm taking off the dress," I told her, "but not the heart."

"Someone will be very angry."

"Do you mean my mother?" I wondered if "Sondra's" feelings were actually a projection of Nora's.

"I won't tell," she whispered.

"Won't tell what?" I asked loudly, and she drew back as if I'd threatened her.

"Don't tell!" she exclaimed. "Don't even think the words!" She lifted her hands and held the sides of her head. "Thinking can make it happen," she moaned, then hurried down the steps.

I stared after her, trying to understand the darkness inside her. I'd lock my door again tonight.

Aunt Jule had laughed about the shoes stuck in the driveway and told me to leave them and trash them tomorrow. I had dumped my muddy stockings in the bedroom wastebasket and hung up the dress to dry. A long hot shower had washed away the last bits of mud and mascara, but not my apprehensiveness toward Nora.

I had to admit to myself that I wasn't simply afraid *for* her but *of* her. The fact that Aunt Jule and Nick saw nothing in her to fear, and even Holly didn't think her sister would harm others, made me feel alone. I worried that my own mind was playing tricks on me—perhaps I had never heard a voice like my mother's.

I tried to read myself to sleep, but it was useless. When the bedroom lights of Aunt Jule and Nora finally went off, I pulled on shorts beneath my nightshirt and went downstairs again. On the garden side of the house, I restlessly walked the porch.

My thoughts shifted to Nick. I couldn't believe I had kissed him, not just with my lips but my heart. Until now, it had been easy to blame my mother for her screwed-up life, labeling her as one of those girls who couldn't live without a guy, who set herself up for disaster. But here I was, falling fast.

And what about Holly? I had told myself that she wasn't really drawn to Nick—she wasn't hooked on him. But by nature Holly was cool and collected, so there was no way to tell. It didn't matter. Nick had clearly explained his dating policy: one girl after the next. After the prom he'd be working on whoever stood in line behind Holly and me. The red shoes seemed symbolic—abandoned in the mud.

I gazed out in their direction. The rain had stopped and the moon was peeking through quick-moving clouds, splashing silver on the soaked gardens and long path. What if Holly came home with Nick, found the shoes, and dumped them in the trash?

I had to have them.

I trudged through the mud, feeling foolish. The ruined shoes were useless—all I could do was display them next to my softball trophies. But I *had* to have them.

When I returned to the house, my feet looked as if I'd put on brown moccasins. I set down the high heels and headed for the greenhouse to fetch a bucket of water for dipping. I was just beyond the knot garden when I thought I heard a door open on the upper porch. Turning toward the house, I surveyed it.

"Hello," I called softly.

No one answered, but I saw the slight movement in the shadows. If it were Aunt Jule, she would have replied. *It had to be Nora,* I thought, and continued on, determined not to be cowed by her.

The air was still and heavy, as water-saturated as the ground. It was the kind of humid Shore night I remembered as a child, when a light left on became a halo of mist and insects. When I entered the greenhouse, I kept the lights off so I wouldn't be swarmed.

In the intermittent moonlight the glass house looked surreal. Plants, looming tall in the darkness, suddenly caught the light and seemed to bristle and straighten as I came near. Spider plants drooped long tongues over the edges of hanging pots. Short, thick plants reached out, then curled back on themselves with crooked stems.

Moonlit raindrops and condensation kept me from seeing beyond the glass panes. As I moved among rows of plants, I couldn't get over the feeling that someone was outside watching me.

Something brushed my arm and I jumped. *Just a branch, Lauren,* I chided myself. Watch where you're going and stop imagining things.

Still, the skin on my arms prickled as I moved toward the back of the greenhouse searching for a bucket. There was something in here with me—I could feel it—some disturbance in the air. There was no rational way to explain the sensation; the air didn't move, but something unseen moved through it. I walked in the center of the main aisle and kept my arms close against my sides, reluctant to touch any of the plants.

Along the back wall was a bucket and six pots of vines,

young plants that Nora was training on two-foot trellises. I leaned over to pick up the bucket. Something rustled. I glanced left, then right, and told myself I was acting paranoid.

I heard it again, soft but distinct, like leaves tussling in a breeze, though the air was as motionless as before. My forehead felt damp. A trickle of sweat ran down my neck.

I quickly picked up the bucket, then noticed the twisted shape of the vine growing next to it. The vine wasn't just twined around the trellis, but knotted to it, its delicate tendrils tied in minuscule knots. I shivered, and with my free hand touched my necklace, running my finger along its smooth chain. Last night it had borne the same kind of knots. I looked at the other young vines. They were all knotted, some of their roots pulled up as if the force used to tie them had yanked them from the soil.

Clutching the steel handle of the bucket, I walked quickly toward the greenhouse sink, wanting to get the water and get out of there. But when I reached for the faucet, I stopped. On the shelf above the sink sat a jade plant, its fleshy almond-shaped leaves glimmering in the moonlight. It moved. I took a step back, staring at it, knowing it was impossible, but certain I had seen it. The branches had moved, as if invisible fingers had riffled them.

I was going crazy. I was seeing what my mother had seen

before she died, things knotting, things moving. *"There's no hand touching them, baby. They move by themselves."* Maybe Aunt Jule was right: I was obsessed with my mother, so much so that I was imagining her experiences.

I fought the panic rising in me and reached for the faucet again, turning the handle hard. When the bucket was half full, I shut off the stream.

I thought I felt a trickle on my neck—spray from the faucet or my own sweat. Reaching up to wipe it, I touched dry skin and my necklace. It wasn't water, but the chain creeping along my neck. I looked down at the silver heart, rising like a slow tide, moving closer and closer to my throat. I dropped the bucket and spun around, as if to catch someone pulling the necklace, but no one was there. I clawed at the chain, grabbing it before it could choke me, and yanked down. It snapped. Holding it tightly in my fist, I ran.

When I was outside the greenhouse, nearly at the porch, I opened my fingers and gazed down at the chain. The end of it was tied in a tiny knot.

eleven

I SLEPT LITTLE that night. Whenever I did drift off, I slipped into dreams of swimming through dark water with rope-like plants winding around my arms and legs. The next morning, when I was fully awake, I thought I might have dreamed the events in the greenhouse. Then I found my chain on the bureau, broken and knotted at one end.

I had no idea how to account for what I had experienced last night. I didn't want to think that Nora's distorted perception of the world was infecting me, making me see things that weren't real. But I had never believed in ghosts or other paranormal phenomena. It was terrifying to think that a power I didn't understand was present when Nora was. How could I defend myself against something I couldn't see?

When I got down to the kitchen, Holly was sitting at the table writing up another of her lists, looking chipper as usual despite her late night. Her steadiness had a calming effect on me. I poured a glass of juice and sat down across from her.

"Listen, Holly, I'm sorry if I embarrassed you last night when—"

She held up a hand. "Hey, cut it out. We both know Jason was acting like a jerk. He asked for it and you gave it to him."

I relaxed. "I wasn't sure you'd see it that way."

"Are you kidding? I wish I had a couple girlfriends like you. You're sweet to a point," she said, smiling, "but then you deliver the news straight."

I was surprised and pleased.

"By the way, I put your purse on the hall table. You left it at the Queen."

"Thanks. I forgot all about it." I took a long drink of juice. "So what can I do for the party? Clean? Pick up groceries?"

"I'd love it if you'd get the party platters from Dee's. They'll be ready at two."

"Okay. How about before that?"

"Well, since you've offered," she said, "there's about a million things."

We were going over the list when Nick showed up with Rocky. I felt suddenly guilty. Holly might not wish she had girlfriends like me if she knew that I had kissed her prom date. But Nick gave no sign of anything special having happened between him and me. In fact, I got a much warmer greeting from Rocky—a joyful bark, several head butts, and a lot of tail-wagging.

"Are you giving him treats on the sly?" Nick asked me.

"No. I guess I just smell right to him."

"Like waterfowl?" Nick replied, laughing. "That's his favorite scent."

I noticed that Nick didn't behave in any special way toward Holly, either, which seemed to confirm my theory that at tonight's party she and I would watch him move on to the next girl—if there was one in the senior class whom he still hadn't dated.

Nora walked in while Nick and Holly were discussing what they needed to borrow from Frank.

"Hey, Nora," he said softly.

"Hcy, Nick."

"Hi, Nora," I greeted her.

She didn't respond.

Holly said nothing to her sister. Perhaps she was used to Nora's cold treatment and didn't try anymore.

"Nora, was that you on the porch late last night?" I asked.

She turned to me as if she had finally realized I was there. "I don't remember."

"Try to," I said firmly.

Nick and Holly glanced at me.

"It was someone else," Nora replied. "Someone else did it."

"Did what?" Holly asked.

"Don't tell," Nora said, fingering the collar of her shirt.

Holly gazed at me expectantly.

"Nothing really," I replied. "I was out walking and went in the greenhouse. I thought I heard something stirring in there."

"Like an animal?" Holly asked.

"I don't know what it was. I was curious if Nora saw or heard anything."

Nora turned her back on us and rummaged through the kitchen cabinets. Holly pressed her lips together, looking as if she didn't completely believe my story. She'd believe me even less if I told her that a plant moved on its own and my necklace tried to choke me. I needed to talk to someone about what was happening, but not someone practical like her, or emotional and defensive like Aunt Jule. I wasn't ready to turn my mind over to the psychologist in the pink glasses. Still, it scared me to be alone with Nora in these strange experiences that were somehow connected to my mother's death. I needed to talk to Nick.

My chance came about an hour later, when I had stopped hosing off lawn chairs to play with Rocky. After several retrievals of his soggy ball, Nick's dog was trying to con me into the water, not bringing the ball to my hand, but releasing it a few feet offshore. The river was plenty warm for swimming, but I still didn't want to wade in it. And I still hadn't walked to the end of the dock.

"He wants you to swim with him," Nick said, coming up behind me.

I turned. "So I can doggy paddle around with that disgusting ball in my mouth? I don't think so."

Nick grinned.

I glanced past him, surveying the lawn and porches. No one was in sight. "Nick, I need to talk to you."

I saw him tense.

"About Nora," I added quickly, afraid he'd think I was bringing up the kiss.

"Okay," he said after a moment of hesitation. "What's up?"

"I know you believe that Nora wouldn't hurt a fly," I began, "but some strange things have been happening and I'm getting scared."

"Scared of what?" he asked.

"Nora is obsessed with my mother's death. You heard her last night, talking as if my mother could come back from the dead."

He nodded.

"She thinks my mother is looking for me, that my mother stirs up the water in the boathouse, that she gets angry because I'm wearing Aunt Jule's necklace and dress."

Rocky raced over and dropped the ball at our feet. When neither of us picked it up, he ran off with it again.

"Nora is haunted by her," I went on. "It's as if guilt has kept my mother alive in Nora's mind."

Nick pulled back from me. "Wait a minute. You're not suggesting that—"

I rushed on: "What if my mother's death wasn't an accident?"

"The police said it was."

"But Aunt Jule stopped them before they investigated."

He shook his head. "No. You're way off base. Nora is neurotic and confused, but she's not capable of murdering someone."

"How do you know that?" I asked.

"It's just not in her to harm others."

"Nick, there are things inside of Nora that none of us understand."

"Like what?" he challenged me.

"Voices, for one thing. Even as a child she answered questions no one asked her—you must remember that. There are things she sees and hears that we don't."

I didn't add that I feared those things had a reality beyond the one we grasped and that I was starting to have experiences as strange as hers. His quickness to defend Nora had cooled my trust in his ability to keep an open mind.

"Lauren," he said, "I know how hard it must be for you coming back here. The memories are terrible. I've noticed how you look away from the dock and don't want to go into the water. You are haunted too."

"Yes, but—"

He rested a hand on my arm. "Hear me out. I understand why you'd want to blame another person for your mother's death. When we lose someone we love very much, we want reasons."

"Don't patronize me," I said, shaking off his hand.

"I'm not. It's just that I've seen this before. Years ago, the Christmas Frank's wife died in a car accident, her family couldn't accept it. They accused Frank, saying he was after her money and property. Aunt Margaret's death was painful enough for him without their making him a murder suspect. But I understand their reaction. Fate and chance—they don't seem enough to explain terrible losses. We all want someone to point to and be angry at."

I pressed my lips together.

"Even so, you can't go around blaming innocent people. Nora is very fragile. Be gentle with her. Don't do anything to make things harder for her."

It seemed to me that Nora was doing plenty to make things harder for me.

"Now hear *me* out," I replied. "Yesterday I went to see my mother's grave in the churchyard across from your school. There is another grave next to it. Its stone is inscribed with the word 'Daughter.'"

Nick blinked but said nothing.

"When I got back to my car, I found a note that someone had slipped through the front window, a plain piece of paper with two words: 'You're next.'"

"When did you go there?" he asked.

"Right after I left the school. Nick, I know that Holly thinks Nora never leaves home, but she does. She was shadowing me at the festival Sunday."

"That proves nothing," he said, "especially since what you just described is a prank that could be played on anyone walking through a cemetery. It happened after school let out. Someone hanging around saw you enter the place—they didn't know you—they just thought it'd be fun to leave the note and get a reaction," he reasoned. "It was nothing but a joke. You're reading into it."

"If the person didn't know me, how would he or she know which car was mine?"

"This is a small town. Everyone knows the visitors from the residents. You have a D.C. tag, don't you?"

"Yes."

"There you go. Did you happen to stop at your car between the school and cemetery?"

I nodded, remembering that I had put my purse in the trunk.

"Mystery solved."

"No," I told him, "there's something more going on, and I'm going to find out what it is."

He shook his head. "You're going to make yourself as miserable and crazy as Nora. Your mother is gone, Lauren. I know this sounds harsh, but you have to get over it." He turned away from me and whistled for Rocky.

I have to get over him, I thought, as the two of us walked off in opposite directions.

I was glad to get away from the house that afternoon. I picked up the party platters at two and paid for them, making them an extra graduation gift to Holly. She was probably hoping I'd do that, but I didn't mind.

Dee's was on the other side of Oyster Creek, outside of town. On the way home I passed the small road that led to Nick's house and started thinking about the way he protected Nora. I was glad I hadn't mentioned the knots to him, for he wouldn't have believed me. Why give him more reasons to claim that I was going to make myself as miserable and crazy as Nora?

A loud *crack* shattered my thoughts. I quickly veered to the right, not seeing what had struck my car, instinctively getting out of the way. My car flew over the edge of the road. The wheel jerked in my hands and I struggled to control it. I hit something, hit it hard, and heard the sound of metal bending and scraping. For a fraction of a second my body was thrown forward, then the airbag buffeted me back.

I sat there stunned, staring at the windshield, a spider web of cracked glass with a large chip at the center. After a few moments I unbuckled my seat belt, opened the door, and climbed out shakily.

My Honda had become wedged between two trees, entangled in barbed wire fencing. I leaned against the side of it, too limp to get my cell phone from my purse.

A car passed by, then its brake lights flashed on and the driver backed up.

"Lauren!" Frank said, pulling himself out of his tiny sports car. "What happened?"

"I m not sure."

He quickly strode toward me.

"As I was coming around the bend, something hit my windshield. I shied away from it and ended up here."

"Something like what?" Frank asked. "A stone, a bird, fruit off a truck?"

"I didn't see."

Frank walked around to the front of my car surveying it with a grim face and sharp eyes. He examined the windshield, then whistled softly. "I don't like telling you this, Lauren, but that was no pebble that ricocheted against your windshield. It was something heavy and I suspect it was thrown."

twelve

I GAZED AT the big chip in the glass and the splintered lines radiating from it. "I figured something had been hurled at me."

"Did you now?" he replied, studying me curiously. "Did you see someone by the side of the road?"

"No, but I was on automatic pilot," I admitted, "thinking about a lot of stuff." I retrieved my purse from the car floor. "I'd better call the police to report this and find out whose fence I've ruined."

Frank slipped his own phone from his pocket "Don't bother," he said. "The sheriff's a busybody. I can track down the owner and help you if your insurance doesn't cover the damages. Who do you want to tow your car? Pete? He still has the Crown station on Jib Street."

"That's fine."

While Frank made the call I examined the front of my car. By sheer luck it had run between two trees, plowing into the fence. The trees were planted in even intervals along the stretch of road, about a car width apart. If I had steered a little to the left or right, I would have hit a tree head on. Before braking I had been going the standard speed for country roads, 50 mph. The accident could have been a lot more serious.

Frank clicked off his phone. "Someone will be here in about fifteen minutes. Let's see if we can find what hit you."

It wasn't hard. Rocks don't abound on the Eastern Shore, and bricks aren't part of the natural landscape. The only thing on the road and its sandy shoulder was a half a brick. Frank picked it up and showed it to me, his face thoughtful, then placed it on my car's hood.

We transferred the party food to his car. Fortunately the cold cuts and bread had not been made into sandwiches and could be rearranged at home. We had just finished when a sheriff's car put on its flashers and pulled over. A small man with a round, sunburned face climbed out and ambled toward us.

"Frank," he said, nodding his head.

"Tom," Frank replied coolly, his tone indicating that this was the man he didn't like.

The sheriff introduced himself simply as "McManus."

"Now let's see," he said, "Blue Honda, D.C. tag. I don't have any report of this, and I just checked in."

"It just happened," Frank replied.

The sheriff asked to see my license and began to question me. It was routine stuff, but the last question caught me by surprise: "Is there anyone you're not getting along with these days?"

"Uh, no," I told him, "not really."

"And who would be in your not-really category?"

Nora, Jason. "No one," I said.

He studied me for a moment. I gazed back at him as steadily as possible.

"Kids," McManus said at last. "One day after school's out and they don't know what to do with themselves. I'm sorry about this, Miss Brandt. It doesn't make our town look good."

"It can happen anywhere," I replied.

"Hope your insurance covers most of it. Well, here comes Pete's boy." The sheriff gestured toward the tow truck as he walked back to his car.

Pete's "boy" looked about thirty and seemed pleased to be towing my Honda. "She's real pretty," he said, "even with barbed wire wrapped around her."

Frank winked at me, then helped the mechanic disentangle the car. I filled out a form and was told to check in with Pete after talking to my insurance company.

When Frank and I finally headed home in his car, I thanked him for helping me out.

"No problem," he said. "That's what neighbors are for." We rumbled over the creek bridge. "So, how's Nora?"

I could guess why he was asking. "She's not that good at softball, Frank."

He laughed. "Well put. I didn't think she had that kind of aim. Of course, she could get lucky." Then his face grew serious. "Does she have any friends nowadays? Could she have gotten someone else to throw the brick for her?"

"As far as I know she doesn't trust anyone but Holly and Nick."

"Are there any other candidates for Wisteria's Hoodlum of the Year? I know the sheriff already asked, but it didn't sound like you were saying anything more than you had to."

"I had nothing concrete to tell him," I explained. "It's possible my date for the prom decided to get back at me. I kind of landed him on the floor with the punch bowl."

"So I heard," Frank said, grinning. "Of course, Jason would have a good throwing arm," he pointed out.

I nodded, unconvinced Jason had done it.

We were silent the last few blocks home, then Frank suddenly swore and swerved, narrowly avoiding the deep mud of Aunt Jule's driveway. "You need a sled around here," he said as he parked the car on the street. "Why doesn't she pave the thing? Oh, I know. She can't afford it."

As we got out to unload the food Aunt Jule emerged from the house.

"Jule, come here a sec," Frank hollered.

I could tell from the stiffness in her back that she didn't like being summoned by him. Before she said something unfriendly, I interjected, "I had an accident, Aunt Jule, and Frank stopped to help me."

She hurried down the path in her bare feet, not caring about the mud. "Are you all right? What kind of accident?"

I explained what happened.

"It was a near miss," Frank told her.

My godmother reached for me and hugged me tightly.

"Jule," Frank said, "is there anyone you know out to get Lauren?"

She let go of me abruptly. "What a ridiculous thing to ask!"

"Maybe, maybe not," he replied. "The last time Lauren was here her mother met with a fatal accident. At least we called it an accident. The sheriff isn't calling this one anything other than deliberate. The only question is whether it was random or not."

Aunt Jule's eyes flashed. "No one who knows Lauren would want to hurt her. And I resent what you're implying about Sondra's death. It was an accident—just like Margaret's," she added slyly.

I figured the reference to his wife was meant to sting, but Frank responded mildly. "I guess that's why it's got me concerned. This was awfully similar to Marge's accident, and she was killed instantly."

The color drained from Aunt Jule's face.

The porch door banged back, and Holly stepped outside. "Hey, Lauren, did you get everything?"

"Yes, I'll bring it in."

"Nick, we need help," I heard Holly say. He followed her out of the house and down the path. "Where's your car?" Holly asked, when she and Nick reached us.

Frank filled them in on the accident. Aunt Jule listened to the details for a second time, rubbing one hand over the other. Holly grilled me with more questions.

"I can't believe it!" she exclaimed at the end. "People are such jerks!"

Nick stood next to her silently, a wary expression on his face. Perhaps he was waiting for me to blame Nora. But even if I were positive that Nora was behind this, I wouldn't have accused her. The more I tried to convince Aunt Jule and him that something was seriously wrong, the more they denied it.

"Well, let's get the food into the fridge," I said. "Thanks for stopping, Frank. I was pretty rattled."

"No problem," he replied. "Call me if you need anything."

***

I needed a clone—a look-alike who would go to the party, swim in the dark river, and act cool around Nick. It was nearly six o'clock and I still hadn't put on my bathing suit.

Holly stopped by my room to warn me that the entire class was invited, so Jason would be coming.

"I figured that."

"Do you need a suit?" she asked, noticing my shorts and shirt. Then she grinned. "Do we dare to see what Mom has in her closet? Maybe a crochet bikini with matching beach mules?"

I laughed out loud. "Think I'll pass on that."

"You know, I'm glad to have your help tonight, Lauren. Really, I'm desperate for it! But you're going to party, too, right?"

"Right," I replied, planning to keep a low profile.

It wasn't hard at a gathering attended by eighty kids. Jason, his buddies, and several girls passed by without noticing me while I was setting out trays of food. Rocky found me, but Nick was nowhere in sight. Frank came over about eight-thirty to munch and admire the work we'd done. He had lent Holly two dozen torches, which made a fiery trail down to the river. His strings of outdoor lights and electric generator had the dock glowing like Christmas.

"Doesn't it look terrific?" I asked.

"Yup! It's a perfect site for a party," he said, surveying the landscape. "Where's Jule?"

"Last time I saw her, on the upper porch."

"Great chaperon," he observed.

"Don't worry," I teased, "if there's any trouble I'll come get you."

"Will you?" he replied, grinning. "I'm locking the door and pulling the shades. I guess Nora doesn't show up for these things."

"She's probably hiding in her room."

Frank asked about the estimate Pete had given me on my car. "Not too bad," he said. "Not nearly as bad as I thought it'd be, but if your insurance company gives you any grief, let me know. I'll tell them what they need to hear." He moved on, then stopped twenty feet away to survey the partyscape again and smile at someone. I followed his gaze to Nick.

I thought I had caught Nick's eye, but he turned away and I didn't see him for another hour. Holly and I were kneeling on the ground, bent over bags of ice, trying to break apart the cubes.

"Muscles, just in time!" Holly said, smiling up at him.

He didn't smile back—barely acknowledged her—fixing his gaze on me. In the flickering torchlight he looked different, his jaw set, his eyes intense.

"I want to talk to you, Lauren."

I saw Holly raise an eyebrow. "Shall I leave?" she asked, a note of irritation in her voice.

"No," he replied quickly. "This isn't private. I want to thank you, Lauren, for getting my cartoon pulled from the newspaper."

"What?"

"The cartoon you saw hanging above my drafting table, the one I sold to the Easton paper."

I looked at Nick confused. "What about it?"

"Aren't they running it?" Holly asked.

"No."

She frowned. "Did they give you a reason why?"

"Oh, yeah, they gave me a reason. Editorial decision. Funny thing, the editors loved it last week."

"I don't understand," I said. "Why did they change their minds?"

He stared at me coldly.

I stood up. "You *can't* be blaming me."

"Who else on the Shore would want to protect your father?" he asked.

"I resent that."

"I resent your getting my cartoon pulled."

"But I didn't!"

Holly rose and stood next to me. "Perhaps, Nick, you should have asked for a more specific reason than *editorial decision.*"

"I did, several times, but they were evasive. Obviously, someone has put pressure on the paper. Maybe not you, Lauren, maybe it was your father or his supporters. But then, how would they know about the cartoon? Who would have seen it and told them?"

I shook my head at him, amazed that he would accuse me.

"Things like small publications may not seem important to you," Nick went on. "You've got connections—people will bend over backward for Senator Brandt's kid. But I have to earn my way. One publication leads to the next. Every acceptance is important to me."

"How can you think I'd do that to you?" I demanded. "I wouldn't do it to anyone! I thought you knew me better."

He glanced past me, then met my eyes with steely intensity. "So did I."

thirteen

NICK STRODE AWAY. I stood there dumbfounded. When I finally realized Holly's hand was resting on my shoulder, I turned to her.

"Don't worry about it," she said. "When Nick cools down, I'll talk to him."

"I didn't ask them to pull it, Holly."

"I believe you. And after I talk to Nick, he will, too."

"Maybe." I looked down at the lumpy bags of ice, then picked up one of the crab mallets that we were using as hammers. "Leave this job to me. I'll enjoy it."

She laughed. "Go for it, girl."

I banged away, feeling better with each shattering of ice. Several guys tried to help, but I politely declined their offers and filled up two cold chests by myself.

Karen, my guide at the yearbook office, stopped to talk. Redheaded Steve came by and told me he had a photo of Jason and me at the prom, posing inside the arch of roses, and several excellent shots of Jason lying among the punch cups. Steve was hoping Holly would okay his before-and-after idea.

I laughed in spite of myself.

A little while later Holly tried to get me involved in the party by asking me to help with the dancing-on-the-dock contest. We played music while blindfolded couples slow danced, trying not to fall in the water. Jason and a pretty girl went quickly. Nick and his partner didn't tumble over till near the end.

We awarded silly prizes and the party went on. Some kids hung out on the dock, some swam, and others sat in groups scattered over the lawn. I wanted to leave but was afraid I'd hurt Holly's feelings. I sat with Karen and her friends from yearbook, watching the party like a movie, trying hard to keep my eyes off Nick.

"Earth to Lauren," Karen said.

"Sorry, what?"

"We're going up on the dock. Want to come?"

I hesitated. "Okay."

I followed the group, wishing I had made myself walk to the end of the dock before the party. A tall guy, one of Jason's friends, was giving the girls a leg up, but when it was my turn, he withdrew his hand.

"Well, look who it is."

"Hi," I said, and climbed onto the dock unassisted.

Jason's friend leaped up behind me.

"Want to play tag?" he asked. "We're getting up a game of water tag."

"Thanks, but no thanks. I was following Karen."

When I tried to move on, he stepped on my heel. "Don't you swim?"

"I do, but I don't want to tonight."

"Why not tonight?" he persisted.

"I'm not in the mood. And I'm not wearing a bathing suit," I added, walking ahead.

He caught me by the elbow. "You know how to swim better than your mother, right?"

That didn't deserve a response. I strode toward the end of the T-shaped dock and tried to turn right, where Karen had gone. But Jason's friend followed and deftly stepped in front of me, separating me from my group.

"Come on. You can swim in what you're wearing."

"I really don't want to."

"Water's warm." There was no warmth in his voice.

He took a quick step toward me, and I moved away, toward the left side of the dock. Kids lined both sides of the walkway, dangling their feet over the river. As the guy pressed forward, the only thing I could do was continue to the left. We reached the end of that part of the dock.

"Hey, everybody, look who I found," he announced to the kids gathered in the water below us.

I gazed down at the place where my mother had died. For a moment all I could see were the dark river and blurs of swimmers looking up at me, the party lights turning their shiny skins green and orange. The faces of Jason and his teammates slowly came into focus.

"I tried to get her to come in, but she doesn't want to play with us."

"Aw," one guy said mockingly.

"Snob," said another.

"Step on her foot, Ken," Jason suggested.

Ken moved closer to me. Feeling lightheaded, I reached for a piling to steady myself. The wood was wet and I shrank from it. It was the piling on which my mother had bled.

With a sudden move Ken pulled my knees out from under me, flipping me into the water. For a moment I was stunned by the impact and cold. The black river rushed over my head. My ears felt swollen from the surge of water. I hit bottom, kicked hard, and surfaced.

Jason and his friends encircled me. They were tall enough to keep their heads above water, but I had to tread. Jason reached out, his wide hand coming down swiftly on my head, shoving me under. I pushed up, angry, gasping for air. Laughing faces surrounded me.

Another hand hovered, then pushed me down. I fought my way back to the surface and tried to swim away, going left, then right. Their circle tightened. They shoved me under and held me there. When I surfaced, I tried to call for help, but I didn't have enough air in my lungs. They kept pushing me down like a bobbing toy. I began to panic. The taste of river mud was in my mouth. I saw black spots, as if the darkness of the water was seeping into my brain. My stomach cramped and I doubled over.

Then a force came rushing through the water, scattering us. The circle broke. I swam through it and kept swimming, wanting to stop for breath, but not daring to. When I kicked my foot against the bottom I finally stood up, breathing hard, with the water just above my knees. Rocky was next to me.

I heard the raucous laughter behind me. "Dumb dog!"

"Smart dog," I whispered to Rocky as we waded to shore.

Holly and Nick were standing close together at the edge of the water.

"I knew you should have put on a suit," Holly said, smiling at me.

I stared at her. Didn't she realize what those guys were doing? Didn't she see how scared I was?

"They're a mean group," I said.

She frowned. "What do you mean?"

"They knew I was out of breath."

"Oh, Lauren, they were just having fun."

"Then their sense of fun is warped."

She didn't get it—she seemed amused. "The guys were teasing you. It's how they flirt."

I turned to Nick, but he said nothing. I wondered what he would have done if they had "teased" Nora like that. "I'm going in."

"You're coming back, aren't you?" Holly asked.

"No." The dog was still by my side. "Nick, I want to take Rocky with me. I'll let him out later, okay?"

"He's going to smell awful," Holly reminded me.

"Fine," Nick said with a shrug.

When I got to the kitchen, I gave Rocky a bowl of water and a piece of turkey. "Sorry I don't have any waterfowl to offer you." I found an old towel and dried him off as best I could. "I don't know what I would have done without you, big guy," I whispered.

Holding on to his tags so they wouldn't jingle, I led Rocky upstairs. I heard Aunt Jule's television and tiptoed past her bedroom. When I was a child, I told my godmother everything. It hurt not to trust her now, but I could guess what she'd say if I recounted the incident in the river. At best, she'd dismiss it, seeing it as Holly did; at worst, she'd say I was obsessed with my mother's drowning.

Nora's door was closed as usual. So was mine, though I didn't remember shutting it. I opened the door and flicked on the overhead light. Rocky trotted in happily. I stood frozen in the doorway, surveying my room in disbelief.

The curtains hung half off the rod, as if someone had yanked on them furiously, each panel tied in a knot. The sheets were pulled off the bed and twisted grotesquely, their corners in knots. My bedside lamp lay on its side, its shade bent, its cord knotted. My heart necklace, muddy stockings, and the bras in my laundry hamper were all tied in knots. Now I knew how my mother had felt—this attack was personal.

I pulled open bureau drawers. My clothes were a mess, rolled up on themselves as if someone had tried tying their clumsy shapes. In the closet, the arms of my long-sleeved shirts were knotted.

Just touching the knots made me feel creepy, but I had to get rid of them. As I untied my things, I reviewed the events of the last three days, trying to determine what was truly a threat and cause for fear. The water in the boathouse was probably stirred by a wake. The note left in my car and the brick thrown at my windshield could have been done by or for Nora, but they also could have been random pranks. It seemed likely that the harassment in the river was revenge for decking Jason at the prom. Setting aside those events, the strangest ones remained: the swing incident, the nighttime experience in the greenhouse, and these knots.

I thought about showing some of the knots to Holly, then I kept on untying. Like me, Holly saw that Nora had serious problems and she wanted those problems fixed, but the incident with Jason's friends had made it clear—Holly read only the surface of things. I was convinced there was a lot going on beneath it. As for Frank, I didn't see how I could talk to him about things that sounded so crazy.

I had untied everything but my heart necklace. I stared down at its tiny knots, thinking about the way the chain had crept along my neck, the way the jade plant moved on its own, and the swing rope snapped and knotted. What power was at work here? The power of my own imagination and fear—or something stranger—an invisible, dangerous thing?

I pulled out the card with Dr. Parker's number and reached for my cell phone. I was finally scared to the point of desperate. My mother had seen things knotted in the weeks before she died. Now I was.

fourteen

Dr. Parker's pink glasses looked like magic spectacles in the lava-lamp interior of Wayne's Bar. When he'd asked me to meet him there at eleven p.m., I'd wondered what I was getting myself into, but Wayne's turned out to be a health bar serving various flavors of springwater, herbal teas, and vegetable dishes, some of which looked suspiciously like cooked bay grass.

I was sipping my raspberry water and staring at Dr. Parker's glasses, as if an answer might suddenly rise to the surface of them the way it does on a Magic 8 Ball. He had listened without interrupting while I recounted some of the events of seven years ago and the strange things that had been happening recently. Now he was either thinking or asleep.

"An interesting image," he murmured, then opened his eyes. "Tell me, Lauren, tell me all about knots. What do they mean?"

I stared at him blankly. "I don't want to be rude, but I thought you were going to explain them."

"If you were writing a poem," he said, "and used a knot as a symbol, an image, what might it stand for?"

I gazed down at my hands, twisting my fingers around one another.

"Think of all the different kinds of knots you have seen," he prompted, "not just the recent ones—others. What do they do? How do they work?"

"Well, there are nautical knots," I began. "You could use one to tie a boat to a dock or make fast a sail."

"So a knot can link things and hold them steady," he said.

"Yes, like a knot that ties a plant to a trellis and gives it the support it needs."

"Good. Keep going."

I traced a shape on the table with my finger. "I've seen jewelry, silver and gold wires, that has been twisted into shapes called love knots. I guess they symbolize the linking of two people."

I drew the shape again, as if it were dangling from a chain, then thought of the heart necklace pulling against my neck. "There are knots that can be tied and tightened until they hurt you, even kill you. Like a hangman's noose."

"Keep going."

"You can be bound and gagged, kept prisoner by knots."

"Yes. Keep going."

"Knots can be hard to untangle, so they could be a symbol

of confusion. Sometimes a person will say her stomach is in knots—like before an exam."

"And what does that mean?"

"That she's anxious, scared, worried."

"Keep going."

"That's all I can think of."

Dr. Parker sat silently, chewing his sprout sandwich, sipping his tea.

"So," he said at last, "knots can be positive and negative symbols. They can represent a whole spectrum of feelings, and even those that seem opposite aren't really. For example, sometimes our ties with people support us and allow us to grow. But those same ties can restrict us, strangle us."

It was like that with my mother, I thought, but I would never tell him that. "So you're saying that Nora can be feeling any of these things and this is how she expresses it?"

"If she's the one tying the knots," he replied.

"But the strange thing is—I probably didn't make this clear—she's not always—that is, I haven't seen her—I mean sometimes things seem to move when—" I broke off.

"She's not touching them?" The psychologist picked up a honey scoop and slowly twirled the golden liquid off the stick and into his tea. "Lauren, do you know what RSPK is—recurrent spontaneous psychokinesis?"

I tried to string together the meanings of the words. "No."

"Do you know anything about poltergeists?"

"Poltergeists? I've seen the movie."

He poked the honey stick back in the jar. "Spielberg's, I assume. Well, that gives you a sense of what some poltergeist activity is like, objects moving around without being touched—sliding across the floor, flying through the air. It can also be noises, knocking, or voices calling out—some activity for which there doesn't appear to be a physical cause."

Things that move with no hands touching them, I thought. It was what my mother had described, what I had seen.

"In the movie," Dr. Parker went on, "a group of dead people were causing the commotion. In cases investigated by parapsychologists, this kind of activity has been attributed to recurrent spontaneous psychokinesis, RSPK. That is, we think it is caused by the recurring and spontaneous mental activity of a person who is alive.

"Many of the documented cases are traceable to an individual who is profoundly disturbed or under great stress. Some are children, a majority of them are adolescents. It's rare to find such ability in adults. The subject may have a history of mental problems, but not always. In any case, during a crisis of some sort, the phenomenon suddenly appears—it can be quite spooky. It disappears after the stress subsides, when the mental conflict is resolved."

"Can Nora control this thing?" I asked.

"I'm going to rephrase your question. Can the individual who is responsible control it? Some who have been studied in the laboratory can, but to a limited extent. Many are totally unaware of what they are doing. It is often an unconscious response to trauma in their lives. Do you understand what I'm saying?"

"Yes, that in a sense, Nora is telling the truth when she says someone else broke the lamp and tied the knot. She really doesn't know she's done it."

"Not exactly. What I'm saying is that if Nora is doing it, she may not know; if Holly or you are doing it, you may not know."

"But I—"

He held up a finger, interrupting me. "I haven't written down the poltergeist events you have related, but you should do that, noting who was in the area during the time each one took place. I'm suggesting you three girls because seven years ago and now, you have spanned early to late adolescence and, as far as I can tell, you have all been in the area of the activity."

"Is there a limit to the distance in which it can work? The night I saw the plants move in the greenhouse, Holly was at the prom."

"That would be stretching it," he said, "but it's possible."

"But it's got be Nora," I insisted, picking up my bottle of water, swirling it.

"She is an obvious candidate," he conceded. "But sometimes the individuals who appear the calmest on the surface don't know how to deal with their emotions and therefore express them unconsciously this way."

"So it could be Holly," I said.

"And it could be you. From what little you have told me, I gather you felt loved by your mother, but also bound by her, your freedom choked when she accompanied you to Wisteria. Those conflicting feelings could have, in a sense, tied you in knots. And returning to the scene of her death for the first time, especially after putting it off for seven years, has got to be stressful for you."

I rested my elbows on the table, my head in my hands, my fingers shielding my eyes from him. I didn't want it to be me. I didn't want Nick to be right when he said "get over it."

"I still believe it's Nora."

Dr. Parker finished the food on his plate and drained his teacup. "It could well be," he said, wiping the side of his mouth, missing the crumbs. "I have just one piece of advice. Keep an open mind, Lauren. A quick theory is a dangerous way to answer important questions."

***

Dr. Parker offered me a ride home, but even at midnight, Wisteria was a safe town to walk through. When I arrived at Aunt Jule's, the music was off, the torches out, and the cars gone, all but Nick's. Only Aunt Jule's sitting room light shone from the street side of the house. Since Holly was always turning off unused lights, I figured she and Nick were cleaning up on the river side.

Halfway along the path that ran between the two gardens I discovered I was wrong. Nick and Holly stood just beyond the roses, kissing. I stopped, transfixed, watching where Nick put his hands on Holly's back, studying how she put her arms around his neck. I tried to read the expression on his half-hidden face to see if this was the most spectacular kiss he'd ever had—the way his kiss had felt to me. I noticed he didn't suddenly pull back and look at Holly surprised. She was good at it, and he kept kissing her.

Her long dark hair looked gorgeous next to his blond. I saw him softly touch her hair. I felt as if I had swallowed glass, my heart cut into a million sharp pieces. Thankfully, they were too immersed in each other to notice me. Then Rocky barked.

Holly and Nick turned quickly and caught me staring. Rocky bounded toward me, his tail wagging, pleased he had spotted me. Holly smiled. Nick seemed stunned to see me and pressed his lips together. I could feel his displeasure from fifteen feet away, and I focused on Holly.

"Lauren," she said, "I was worried about you. We both were."

Both? I winced at the white lie.

"Where were you?" she asked.

"Nowhere special. I just went out for a while."

She studied my face. "Is everything okay?"

"Sure."

Holly's arm was around Nick's waist, her thumb hooked in his belt loop. "After you went in," she said, "I was afraid I had been insensitive, that I should have realized the boys were going too far. You're sure you're okay?"

"Yes."

"Where did you go?"

"To see a friend. Listen, I'm going to bed. We can clean up tomorrow."

I turned my back before she could detain me with further questions. Once inside the house I rushed through the hall and up the steps, slowing again when I reached the top to walk quietly past Aunt Jule's room. When I reached my own, I eagerly reached for the doorknob and turned it, but the door wouldn't open. Remembering that I had let out Rocky, then locked both the porch door and this one, I pulled the old-fashioned key from my pocket and inserted it.

The door swung inward, swung into darkness. I was sure I had left on the bedside lamp. Bulbs burn out, I told myself, and flicked on the overhead light. My chest tightened. Everything was in knots—everything that I had untied before seeing Dr. Parker.

I strode across the room and checked the double doors. They were still locked from the inside. My skin prickled. No one, nothing could have gotten in, except a power that wasn't stopped by walls. I nervously plucked at my bedsheets. I could untie the knots a second time, but then what? Even locked doors wouldn't keep me safe. I felt powerless to stop Nora from whatever she wanted to do to me.

I walked across the hall to the room that had been my mother's, wondering if I'd find knots there. The photos and other things pertaining to my mother had been removed by someone, but nothing else had changed. I saw Holly's door was open and checked her room from the hallway.

"Looking for something?"

I jumped at Holly's voice.

"You're awfully edgy," she observed. "Are you sure nothing's wrong?"

"Something is wrong," I admitted. "Go look in my room."

She did and I took another quick look at hers. Nothing had been disturbed.

"I don't believe this!" I heard Holly exclaim. She returned to the hall. "What is going on, Lauren? When did this happen?"

I told her about the knots that I'd found and untied earlier.

"So it's happened twice tonight?" She rubbed her arms. "That's creepy."

"Do you remember the summer my mother came, how she kept finding her scarves and jewelry knotted?"

Holly nodded. "I don't like it. I don't like it at all."

"That makes two of us," I replied.

She turned suddenly and pounded on her sister's door. "Nora!" she shouted. "Nora! I'm coming in."

Aunt Jule came hurrying from her room. "What's going on?"

"Look for yourself, Mom. Look at Lauren's room. I told you before, but you wouldn't listen to me. Nora is out of control."

Aunt Jule entered my room, and Holly opened her sister's door. Nora stood before us in a frayed nightgown. Her dark eyes darted between Holly's face and mine.

"I'm losing my patience with you," Holly said. "You're way out of bounds, Nora. Get in there and straighten up Lauren's room. And don't try something stupid like this again."

"Just a minute," Aunt Jule said, coming back into the hall. "How do you know Nora is responsible? There were lots of kids going in and out of the house tonight."

"Oh, come on, Mom," Holly replied, but then she turned to me for backup.

"I found the knots earlier," I explained, "untied them all, then locked both doors to my room. When I came back, the knots were tied again in the exact same way."

As I spoke, Nora slipped past us and entered my room. I followed her and watched from the doorway as she touched the knots in the sheets, then the knots in the curtains, fascinated by them, admiring them.

"Did you keep the key with you?" Aunt Jule asked.

I turned back to her. "Yes."

Her eyes flashed. "So why do you think Nora had a better chance of unlocking the door than anyone else?"

I glanced away. If I talked about poltergeists, I would probably lose Holly's support.

"It seems to me, Lauren, that if we want to start accusing people, you're the most likely candidate for this prank," Aunt Jule went on. "You're the one who has the key."

"But that doesn't make sense!" I protested. "Why would I mess up my own room?"

"For attention. You're a girl who is used to a lot of attention."

I saw Holly glance sideways at me; she was considering her mother's suggestion.

"I didn't do it!" I insisted.

"Someone else did it," Nora whispered, emerging from my bedroom. Her face was as white as a wax candle, her pupils dilated.

"Nora, you look ill," Aunt Jule said.

"She *is* ill!" I screamed. "And you're cruel not to get her the psychiatric help she needs!"

Aunt Jule gave me a stony look, then said in a gentle voice, "Nora, love, I want you to sleep in my room tonight."

Nora slowly followed her down the hall.

I shook my head, amazed at how my godmother could twist things to accommodate whatever she wanted to believe.

Holly sighed. "Come on, Lauren, let's take a walk. Then I'll help you undo this mess."

"Thanks, but you've got to be tired. It won't take long to untie things."

"Still, let's walk," Holly persisted. "You're not going to fall asleep in the state you're in now."

"I'll be okay. I'll walk and talk to myself until I bore myself to sleep."

Holly laughed lightly. "Well, you know where I am if you need me."

When I reached the hall stairs, Aunt Jule stood at her bedroom door. "It's late, Lauren. Don't go far."

I answered her with a slight nod.

Downstairs, I headed out the river side of the house, then turned toward Frank's. I walked his land along the river and sat for a while in one of his lawn chairs, thinking things over. I recalled what Dr. Parker had said at the prom and knew he was right: I could do nothing about Nora's illness; the one person in my power to heal was myself. I needed to go to the place where my mother had died, this time on my own.

fifteen

THE MOON WAS high, making the unlit dock stand out clearly in the water. I imagined it as my mother would have seen it that night, a vague shape in the river mist. The bank wasn't as eroded then, so she could have climbed up easily. Had she walked the dock the way she used to walk the porch? Had someone cornered her there?

I climbed up and walked to the end where she had fallen. I forced myself to touch the piling, laying both hands on it, then stared down into the river.

Had my mother known she was going to die that night? Had she blacked out the moment she hit the piling or did she sink slowly into watery unconsciousness? Did she cry out for me?

"Get over it, Lauren," I told myself aloud. "You have to let go."

But I couldn't, not until I knew what had happened then and what was happening now.

I mulled over the poltergeist theory. Perhaps Nora was so traumatized by finding my mother drowned that she believed and feared she was still in the river. But Nora's irrational fear would make more sense if she had actually murdered her. My mother's presence had brought plenty of anger and dissension to Aunt Jule's usually quiet house. Perhaps Nora, already unbalanced—more so than any of us had realized—had been pushed over the edge and, in a sense, pushed back.

If Nora were guilty of murder and trying to repress it, my return to Wisteria would be intensely disturbing to her and could evoke a response as extreme as poltergeist activity. The puzzle pieces fit.

Then Dr. Parker's words floated back to me: *A quick theory is a dangerous way to answer important questions.* But my experiences in the last three days, some of them spookily similar to my mother's, had convinced me that her death wasn't an accident. And if Nora didn't murder her, who else could have? Who else had a reason—or the momentary passion and anger—to push my mother against the piling and off the dock? I didn't want to suspect anyone I knew; the excuse of insanity was the only way I could deal with it being Nora.

I retraced my steps, then climbed the hill and circled the house. It was completely dark now. Passing by the greenhouse, I was surprised to find that a light had been left on. I didn't remember seeing it when I arrived home and it seemed odd that Holly, given her compulsion to turn off lights, hadn't extinguished it. I entered the greenhouse, a little timidly after last night's experience.

The place felt overly warm and stuffy. I wondered if Nora had forgotten to open the vents, allowing the day's heat to build up. The bare bulb hanging over the center aisle was out; the beacon I'd seen was a large plastic flashlight. Perhaps Nora had come with it tonight, planning to cool down the place, and been frightened away by party guests.

I knew that when the sun flooded the greenhouse tomorrow the plants would die in the accumulated heat. The wheel that opened the roof vents was at the end of the main aisle, where the small trellises were. As I headed toward it, I played the flashlight's beam over the plants, listening intently, watching, afraid to blink my eyes. But every leaf was still. At the end of the aisle I shone the light on the pots with the young vines. All of them were limp, hanging from the trellises by their knots.

Above them was the six-inch metal wheel that cranked open the house's high vents—that is, the axle from it—the wheel was gone. I was sure I had seen the vents open the other day. I reached for the switch that ran the big exhaust fan, flicking it one way, then the other. It wouldn't turn on. Stranger yet, despite the breeze that night, the blades were absolutely still. When I shone the flashlight on the fan, I saw that the flap behind it had been closed, which was done only in winter to seal out the cold air. I tried the smaller fans distributed along the plant benches. They didn't work, nor did the center light.

It must be the power supply, I thought, and searched for a metal cabinet containing a circuit breaker. I found an ancient box with two screw-in fuses. Both had been removed.

Still something was running—I could hear the quiet motors. Space heaters, that's what was making it hot. The heaters burned kerosene and were used in the winter to keep the plants warm. I found four of them in the side aisles of the greenhouse and turned them off, puzzled as to why Nora or anyone else would have them running.

There was little I could do to save the plants except open the door and hope some cool air would waft in. I decided to transport at least one of each kind outside and carried a heavy pot to the entrance.

When I tried to open the door, it wouldn't budge. I set down the plant and shone the flashlight on the lock. The door had a deadbolt, the kind that required a key and could be locked from inside or out. But I hadn't locked it and the key kept on the hook next to the door was gone. Someone had taken it and turned the bolt from the outside. I couldn't believe it—I had walked straight into a trap!

Nora's trap. She must have been nearby, waiting until I was at the other end of the greenhouse to lock the door. But she was supposed to have been with Aunt Jule. Again I considered the possibility of another person being responsible for my mother's death and the things that had been happening to me. Nora's crazy behavior would provide a convenient cover, and it would be easy enough to mimic her. Who knew about the boathouse incident? Nick and Frank, Holly and Aunt Jule—and anyone in the town whom they might have told.

I tried to illuminate the area beyond the door, but the flashlight's reflection off the glass surface made it impossible to see more than a foot beyond the greenhouse. I clicked it off and stepped back from the door, retreating farther and farther into the rows of plants, hoping that as I became less visible, I would detect some movement outside.

Something touched my neck. I pulled away from a bench of plants and clumsily banged into the one across from it. It was my own sweat trickling down, nothing else. The heat was oppressive. A dull headache throbbed behind my eyes. I wanted to sleep.

The obvious way to escape was to break the glass, but I was reluctant to. The large square panes were old and might be irreplaceable. I decided to rest there till Holly or Aunt Jule woke up and found me. I sat on the damp brick floor, longing to put my head down, but something kept nagging at me. The missing fuses, the sealed fan. I pulled myself to my feet again and waves of dizziness broke over me. I felt sick, as if I had inhaled fumes, but I could smell nothing but the rich earthiness of the greenhouse.

Lack of ventilation, space heaters, sleepiness, no smell—my muddled mind kept groping for the pattern it sensed but couldn't identify. Sleepiness, no smell—carbon monoxide! The gas could be generated by heating units. It was odorless. And it could kill.

I had to break a window. I remembered that there was a hand shovel by the trellises, but I was closer to the front of the greenhouse, and the path to the back seemed long to me now, wavering in front of my eyes like a distant patch of road on a hot day. The flashlight, that would work.

I had left it on the ground when I'd sat down. I leaned over to pick it up and pitched forward. It took all of my strength to straighten up. I discovered I couldn't look down—just moving my head made me dizzy. Crouching slowly, grasping the end of a plant bench with one hand, I felt with my other for the flashlight.

My fingers curled around its plastic barrel. I pulled myself up and moved uncertainly toward the front of the greenhouse, like an old woman feeling her way along the pews of a church.

The open area by the entrance would allow me to take aim at the glass from a safe distance.

I stopped where the benches ended, about six feet from the front wall, and hurled the flashlight toward a pane. But my body had become as sloppy as my mind from the poisonous gas. The flashlight glanced off the metal frame without making a crack in the glass.

Unable to walk without support, I got down on my knees and crawled to the flashlight. I knew I'd get cut, smashing the glass at close range; the best I could do was turn my face away. Kneeling close to the window, holding the flashlight like a hammer, I banged against the glass relentlessly.

Shards fell like a shower of prickly leaves, stinging my arms. I knocked the two-foot square out cleanly, then dropped the flashlight on the grass. Standing up, thrusting my head through the opening, I gulped my first breath of fresh air and felt the cold breeze on my sweaty skin. Then I blacked out.

"Lauren? Lauren?"

I opened my eyes and quickly shut them again, drawing back from the bright light shining in my face. It clicked off.

"Lauren, can you hear me?" Nick asked.

A long dog tongue licked my face. Reaching up, I put my arms around Rocky and sat up slowly. I felt sick and scared. I wished Nick would hold me and be as gentle as he was with Nora, but I wouldn't ask for his comfort. I buried my face in the dog's fur.

"Your arms are cut," Nick said. "I want to check them."

Without looking at him, I held out one, then the other, and felt him probing the skin.

"Nothing deep," he told me, "mostly scratches. Still, you should soak in a tub to make sure all the glass is out," he added, his voice sounding almost clinical. "What happened? Why did you break the window?"

"Someone was trying to kill me."

"What?"

I petted Rocky until I felt in control. "I was out walking," I said, "and saw a light on in the greenhouse, the flashlight you're holding. I went inside. It was hot and stuffy. I couldn't ventilate the place. The fuses were pulled, the fan sealed, the vent crank broken. Space heaters had been left on. When I tried to leave, I found the door locked, locked from the outside."

I gazed up at Nick's face, waiting to see the flicker of realization. Behind him, the house lights came on. Nick glanced over his shoulder, then back at me.

"Don't you understand?" I said, but I could see by his face that he didn't. He wouldn't allow himself to believe that someone in Wisteria was a murderer.

"Understand what?"

"Nick, someone tried to kill me—to poison me with carbon monoxide!"

Another light went on downstairs, and three figures came out on the porch.

"What's going on?" Holly shouted to us. "Is everything all right?"

"Fine," Nick called back to her.

Fine, I thought wryly. Aloud I asked, "Why are you here, Nick? Did they call you?"

"Someone did," he said.

"Nick, is Lauren out there?" Holly asked. "She's not in her room."

"She's here, she's fine," Nick replied. In a quieter voice he said to me, "After I got home someone telephoned my house three times and hung up. The Caller ID listed Jule's number. I thought Nora might be upset and trying to reach me."

"She was upset," I told him, "and sleeping in Aunt Jule's room tonight—at least, she was supposed to be." I saw Holly hurrying toward us, followed by Aunt Jule and Nora. "So why did you come to the greenhouse?"

He hesitated. "It made sense to check here first. Nora spends a lot of time here."

I gazed at him doubtfully.

"And I saw the flashlight on," Nick added.

"When I used it to break the window, it was off."

"I don't think so," he replied.

"I know so."

Nick glanced away. "You're too groggy to remember anything clearly."

Holly stopped a few feet away, noticing the broken pane in the greenhouse wall and the pile of glass shimmering in the grass. Her jaw dropped. Nick stood up quickly and went to her, but I was still too dizzy to move.

Aunt Jule caught up. "Oh, no!" she exclaimed. "Lauren, are you all right?"

"Yes."

"Nick?" Aunt Jule said, turning to him. "What happened?"

He repeated his story about the phone calls, then recounted what I had told him. Aunt Jule and Holly glanced back at Nora, who was peering at me from behind them.

"Lauren seems to be all right," Nick concluded. "I saw the glass shattering, then her head come through. I lifted her all the way out. She wasn't unconscious for long. And the cuts are superficial."

Aunt Jule leaned down and reached for my hands, stretching out my arms to study them. "I don't understand. What was the point of all this?" she asked.

"To kill me," I answered bluntly. "To poison me with carbon monoxide."

She let go and took a step back. Holly looked incredulous, but then her face grew thoughtful. If there was anyone I could make understand, it was she.

"I don't believe it," Aunt Jule said. "This is the nonsense Frank planted in your head after your accident. Who would want to kill you?"

"I don't remember," Nora said softly.

"The same person who killed my mother," I answered Aunt Jule.

"Don't tell," said Nora.

Aunt Jule ignored her. "No one killed Sondra, Lauren. It was an accident."

"I used to think so." Holding on to Rocky, I rose to my feet. "So why are you all here? Who got you out of bed?"

Aunt Jule glanced at Holly.

"Nora woke us," Holly admitted. "She said something was happening outside."

"How did Nora know that?"

"She always has difficulty sleeping," Aunt Jule replied defensively.

"Yes, she had difficulty the night my mother died," I said. "I went to see Dr. Parker tonight."

Holly looked surprised. "Is *that* where you went? Oh, Lauren, you should have told me. I didn't realize you were that upset."

"We talked about the knots," I continued.

Holly glanced at Nick, and he put his arm around her. Aunt Jule and Nora listened, both of their faces pale.

"Dr. Parker said the knot-tying could be poltergeist activity."

"What?" Holly exclaimed.

"He said that most of the time the phenomenon is caused by an adolescent, someone who is very upset. It's a way of dealing with intense, suppressed emotions. Often it's not even conscious. The person doesn't know he or she is responsible."

Holly frowned and shook her head slightly.

"My mother's things were tied in knots just before she died. Tonight, my things were."

"Lauren," Holly said, "I think you need to talk to someone else. Coming back to Wisteria has been a lot harder on you than any of us thought it would be. We need to find you another counselor, one who is more—"

"It's real! It's happening!" I exploded. "Accept it!"

"It's real, it's happening," Nora echoed.

The others gazed at Nora, then me with the same concerned, tolerant expression. I would have been angered by their patronizing looks, but I didn't believe they were thinking what their faces showed. I didn't trust any of them. Not Nora, not Aunt Jule, not Nick, not Holly. They knew things they weren't telling me. Maybe they had agreed among themselves not to tell me.

"I promise you," I said, "I'm going to find out what happened to my mother and what is happening to me."

"All right," Holly answered softly, soothingly.

"Nick, I want to keep Rocky tonight."

"If it makes you feel safer," he replied with a shrug.

"It does," I said, starting toward the house. "Rocky doesn't pretend like the rest of you."

sixteen

I FINALLY GOT some sleep Tuesday night, lying with my back against Rocky's, listening to his dog snores. Early the next morning I went outside with him. While he swam, I fell asleep again on the grassy bank. Holly awakened me.

"This doesn't look good," she said, smiling, "one of my party guests asleep on the lawn the morning after."

I sat up. "What time is it?"

"About nine-fifteen. How are you feeling?"

"Okay. My headache's gone and I'm not nauseated anymore."

She nodded. "I opened the greenhouse door and turned on the fans to air the place out. Did you realize there's a big exhaust fan at the back of the greenhouse? Of course," she added quickly, as if afraid she'd hurt my feelings, "it might not have helped last night."

"The exhaust fan was sealed," I told her, "as it is in winter."

"No, it's automated now. The flaps open when you turn on the fan."

"So you replaced the fuses?"

"The fuses?" she repeated. "I just hit the switch."

"Holly, there wasn't any electric power in the greenhouse last night. I couldn't turn on the fans or the light."

She bit her lip, then said quietly, "Sometimes, when people get frightened, they think they're doing something, but they're not thinking clearly so they're not doing it right."

"I was doing it right."

She didn't want to argue with me. "Well, maybe. Let's get some breakfast."

"You go ahead. I'm not hungry."

"Come on, Lauren, you'll feel better if you eat something."

I gave in and called Rocky. Nick's wet and fragrant dog made it as far as the hall entrance to the house. "Please, not on an empty stomach," Holly pleaded.

I brought Rocky's breakfast out to the porch, some of last night's meat and a piece of toast, though the toast was supposed to have been mine. Heading inside to make more, I entered through the dining room door and stopped in my tracks.

Aunt Jule's work lamp had been knocked over, its white globe broken, the fragments scattered on the table. In the basket next to it a dozen colorful embroidery threads were tied together in fantastic knots. I debated whether to call to the others. No, Aunt Jule might accuse me again of seeking attention. Let her find it and see how it felt when this strange phenomenon was directed at her.

I started toward the kitchen, then backtracked—there was something amiss in what I had just seen. While the lamp's cord was pulled from the socket, it wasn't knotted. The cord of my bedroom lamp had been yanked from the wall plate and knotted. The lamp broken the day I arrived had also had a knotted cord. Perhaps it was the process of making the knot, the psychokinetic force used to tie the cords, that caused the lamps to tip over, and similarly, the force exerted to knot the swing's rope that caused it to snap. But there was no knot in this cord. It was as if someone had added the lamp to the scenario, overlooking that one detail. Maybe someone *was* mimicking Nora.

But who—who would have a reason to hide behind her behavior and wait for a chance to kill me? The question I had asked myself at the bank two days ago flickered in my mind again, and this time I couldn't snuff it out. What *was* the nature of the relationship between my mother and Aunt Jule? Had it gone bad at the end?

My mother had died the summer she'd written the new will, which left everything to me, with that one provision. Aunt Jule had asked me here, knowing I was nine months away from my eighteenth birthday and that she would inherit the money if I died before then. But I couldn't believe that my own godmother would hurt me.

I wasn't naive. Life in Washington had taught me how the desire for money destroyed the values of all kinds of people. But while I could almost imagine that Aunt Jule only pretended affection for me—perhaps it wouldn't be hard, visiting me twice a year and seeing me now for just a few days—I couldn't believe that she would allow her own daughter to be blamed.

Still, some curious puzzle pieces fit. Perhaps Aunt Jule had been refusing to get help for Nora because she knew she would need her as a cover. If Nora were accused of murder, she would be helped rather than harmed, getting the psychiatric care she needed and eventually being released. In the end Nora would share in the wealth she had "earned." Aunt Jule had always had a knack for quietly getting what she needed.

Hearing footsteps on the stairs, I continued on to the kitchen. My godmother entered a few moments after me. "Good morning, girls."

"'Morning," we both murmured.

"How did you sleep, Lauren?"

"Okay," I answered.

"And you, Holly?"

She pulled her head out of the newspaper. "Not bad."

"Well," Aunt Jule said, "Today's a new—"

A long, plaintive whimper came from the next room. Holly quickly put down the paper.

"I didn't do it!" Nora cried. "I didn't!"

"Here we go again," Holly muttered as the three of us hurried into the dining room.

I watched Aunt Jule's face, searching for some sign that she already knew what was there. Both she and Holly noticed the lamp first, then the knotted embroidery silk.

Holly suddenly turned to me. "You don't seem very surprised, Lauren. Did you know this was here?"

"Yes," I admitted. "I saw it when I came in."

Holly frowned, silent for a moment. "I want to believe you. I really want to believe you're not playing pranks, but I just don't know what to think."

"I didn't do it!" I insisted.

"I didn't do it," Nora echoed.

"Then who did?" Aunt Jule asked, setting the lamp base upright.

Nora edged toward me. "It's a secret. Don't tell."

"Oh, shut up!" Holly said.

Aunt Jule fingered the knots, her lips pressed together.

"If someone tells, will Sondra wake up?" Nora asked. "I won't tell."

Holly whirled around and Nora winced.

"I hate this, Mom!" Holly exclaimed. "Can't you see that Nora needs help? She's making life miserable for all of us."

Aunt Jule stared coolly at Holly.

"Nora, you are so messed up!" Holly said. "You are *really* sick."

"Holly!" Aunt Jule chided.

"You're out of control, Nora," Holly went on, pacing back and forth, combing her hair with her fingers. "You need to be locked up! You belong in a lunatic—"

Suddenly Holly stopped, the color draining from her face. She yanked on her hair, then she reached back with her other hand. I saw her swallow hard. I thought at first that it was her hands flexing her hair, picking it up off her neck. I watched with disbelief as a long strand of black hair twisted itself into a knot. Then another, and another.

Holly clutched at her hair, her eyes widening with fear. She leaned over and shook her head, pulling on her hair, as if she were being swarmed by bees.

"Make it stop, Nora!" Holly screamed. "Make it stop!"

Aunt Jule stood paralyzed. Nora looked terrified.

I know what this is, I told myself; *there is nothing to be afraid of.* I reached for the frightened Holly, trying to steady her, then caught her hair in my hands and held it till the bizarre storm of energy had passed.

The hair fell limp, though still in tangles. Nora turned and ran out the porch door. Aunt Jule started after her.

"She's crazy, Mother," Holly said, her voice shaking. "She's psychotic. Lauren is right—that was no accident last night."

Aunt Jule looked silently at Holly, then continued after Nora.

Holly was trembling all over—with anger or fear—perhaps both. I felt bad for her but relieved for myself. Finally I wasn't alone.

"Sit down," I said gently. "Let's get you untangled."

It took a half hour to work the knots out of Holly's hair; for a few of the tangles I had to use scissors. I knew Holly was upset because she didn't say a word except yes each time I asked if I should cut out a knot.

Aunt Jule returned without Nora. Holly had regained her composure, but when she spoke she still sounded irritated. "I know where Nora hides. I'll find her when I'm ready."

That wasn't for another hour and a half. We cleaned up from the party, then Holly left me with the final task and went off in search of her sister.

"Where is she?" Aunt Jule asked, when Holly returned alone to the kitchen.

"I don't know. I checked all of Nora's hiding places twice. And I looked at Frank's."

"Did you call her name?"

Holly struggled to keep her temper. "No, Mom, I called out *Susie!* Let her be for a while, okay? Her behavior is outrageous. It will be good for her to think things over."

"She thinks too much already," Aunt Jule said, and retreated to the dining room.

Through the doorway I saw that a lid had been put on the basket of knots and the broken lamp cleared away. With the yard clean and the house quiet, it seemed like just a peaceful day on the Shore. But I knew all of us were waiting; it was only a matter of time before something else happened.

As I headed outside I heard Nick in the garden greeting Rocky. When he saw me, the warmth in his voice quickly disappeared. "How are you?" he asked tensely.

"Okay," I replied. "But we've had another incident."

"What kind?"

Holly emerged from the house carrying her school backpack.

"You want to explain?" I asked her, not wanting to be the only one relating bizarre events.

"You can," she said, "but he'll just defend Nora. He always has."

When I'd recounted what had happened, Nick put his arm around Holly. "Is Lauren exaggerating?"

I bit my tongue.

"No, it was just *so* freaky, Nick."

He touched her hair softly. "Are you okay?"

"Yes. Thanks."

He turned to me. "Where's Nora now?"

"We don't know. Missing, hiding."

"What happened before the incident?" he asked.

"What do you mean?"

"What did you say to Nora to set her off?"

The heat rose in my cheeks.

"Be fair, Nick," Holly interjected.

"I didn't say a word," I told him.

"You didn't bring up what happened last night?" he asked. "You didn't start talking about your mother again?"

"No!"

"Nick, Nora is crazy, as crazy as they come," Holly said.

"Maybe," he replied, "but it sure would help if Lauren forgot the past."

I looked him in the eye. "You're asking for the impossible."

"I'm asking that you think about the effect of dragging Holly, Nora, and Jule through a lot of pointless stuff. You're making it hard on all of them."

My eyes stung with tears, and I quickly blinked them away.

"Come on, Holly," he said.

She looked at me uncertainly. "Lauren?"

"Bye."

I walked back into the house. I thought I'd be relieved to hear the sound of Nick's car fade away, but it only made me ache. Why had he turned against me? There had to be more to it than the cartoon. Had someone told him something else that angered him or made him mistrust me?

I paced around the garden room, thinking about Nora. For her safety—and my own—I would feel better knowing where she was.

There was a jingling of tags, then a nose pushed in the soft screen of the porch door.

"Hey, Rocky. Wouldn't Nick take you to school?" I let him in. When I sat down, the dog rested his chin on my knee, wanting me to pet him. "Maybe you can help, old boy. How are you at retrieving people?"

He wagged his tail.

I wondered if Nora was hiding somewhere off the property. There would be plenty of places in town where she could melt into the surroundings undisturbed by others—the college campus, the docks. I decided to search for her and hurried upstairs to put on my running shoes. The phone rang and I picked it up in the hall.

"Lauren? Frank."

"Hi, Frank. What's up?"

"Holly was over here earlier, looking for Nora."

"Yes," I said quickly. "Have you seen her?"

"Just now. I was chasing an army of geese off my lawn and saw her enter the boathouse."

"The boathouse!" I exclaimed. "She's afraid of going in there."

"That's what I thought," he replied. "What worries me is that she, well—to put it mildly—looked disturbed."

"We had an incident this morning," I began.

"Holly told me about it. Is Holly there now?"

"No, she's gone to school with Nick. I'll check on Nora."

"Is Jule at home?" he asked.

"Yes. Do you want to talk to her?"

He was silent for a moment. "No," he said. "I was going to suggest that she accompany you to the boathouse, but on second thought, Jule doesn't handle Nora very well. Don't say anything to her—let's see what's going on first. I'll meet you there myself, in case you need a hand. In about five minutes?"

"Yeah, thanks."

Frank clicked off. I put the phone down slowly. Holly was sure that Nora didn't go off the property, and she was wrong. Maybe I was just as wrong about Nora's fear of the boathouse. Maybe Nora could pretend like the rest of us.

I went downstairs and called Rocky to take him outside with me.

"Who was that?" Aunt Jule asked as I passed by the dining room.

"Just Frank. I need to take some things back to him that were borrowed for the party."

She nodded and continued with her needlepoint.

Rocky followed me halfway down to the boathouse, where Frank was waiting for me, then went off for a swim.

"I'm sorry to take up your time," I told Frank.

"No problem. I thought about going in the boathouse myself," he said as we walked toward it, "but I didn't want to scare her and have her bolt again."

The door was halfway open. "Nora?" I called from the entrance. "Nora?" I thought I heard a whimper and stepped inside. "Nora, it's me, Lauren. Are you all right?"

My eyes slowly adjusted to the light. I saw a gray shape—Nora lying still on the walkway.

"Frank, something's wrong!"

I rushed to her. As I did, the boathouse door closed swiftly behind me.

seventeen

I FROZE. I couldn't see in the sudden darkness. "Frank?"

"Nothing personal, Lauren," he called from outside, sounding as easygoing as when he'd said, "No problem."

I heard him put the padlock on the door.

"Frank? Frank!" I shouted.

There was no reply. My mind raced, trying to comprehend the situation. Why would he do this to me? Why had he put me in here with Nora?

The thin slit between the river doors and the hairline fractures of light between weathered boards allowed me to see no more than her form. I took the last few steps toward her. If I touched Nora and she was cold—I laid my hands on her. She was warm and breathing, but unresponsive to my fingers.

People don't fall asleep naturally in places they fear, I thought. I debated which to do first, get her conscious or find a way out, then I rose quickly. If Nora awoke and went berserk, I'd be trapped in here with her.

I needed the ax, the one I had left beneath the light chain. Using my hands more than my eyes, I moved as fast as I dared on the narrow walkway, feeling my way along the wall until I touched the beaded chain. The ax was gone.

Frank knew it was here. He must have removed it—he or Nick. I was bewildered by his actions and sick at the thought that Nick could be involved, but I didn't have time to figure out the situation.

Maybe the loft would have another tool. I continued working my way to the corner of the building and along the back wall. The ladder should be soon, I thought, it should be now. I should have passed it. I touched the second corner and my heart sank. The ladder, too, had been removed.

I heard a soft moan, then Nora stirring. I held my breath.

"Mom?" she called.

If she suddenly got up and fell over the side, I'd never find her in the dark water. "Stay still, Nora. Stay where you are," I said, and began to retrace my steps.

"Mom?"

She might not become hostile if she thought I were Aunt Jule. "Yes, love. I'm here. Go back to sleep."

"Where am I?" she asked. "Is this the place for crazy people? Are you locking me up?"

I winced. "No, Nora, you're home."

"You're not Mom." Her voice sounded clearer. She would soon realize where she was.

I said nothing more until I was four feet from her. "Nora, it's Lauren."

I heard her draw back.

"Everything's okay. Just stay against the wall. Lean against it."

There wasn't a sound from her.

"Are you hurt, Nora?" I asked, moving closer to her.

She didn't answer.

I took another step and crouched down. "What happened?"

Still, she was silent.

"Do you know what happened to you? Tell me so I can help you."

"Don't tell," she whispered.

"It's all right, you can tell me."

"It's a secret."

"You can tell me the secret."

She said nothing.

I waited a few moments, then tried a different tactic. "What hurts?" I asked. "Does your stomach hurt? Your arm?"

"My head."

"Why does it hurt?"

"Because I'm crazy," she said softly.

I blinked away unexpected tears, imagining what it was like for her, trapped inside her own dark world. I felt for her fingers. "Take my hand and show me where it hurts."

She guided my fingers. When I touched the crown of her head, she cried out.

"Is it sore?" I asked. "Is it bruised?"

She whimpered.

"Did someone hit you?"

"Don't tell."

"You can tell me. It's okay."

"It's a secret."

"When did your head start to hurt?" I asked.

"I don't remember."

"Were you in a hiding place?"

She was quiet for a moment. "In Frank's garage. It hurts, my head hurts!" She whimpered like a small child.

In the distance I heard a boat motor. I hoped it was turning away from us and wouldn't create a wake. "Did Frank find you in his garage?"

She continued to cry.

I laid my hand cautiously on her back, then rubbed it, trying to soothe her. The boat engine sounded closer. "Is the garage one of your hiding places, Nora?"

"Yes."

Then either Holly or Frank could have found her there. After her hair was knotted, Holly was scared and angry. Had she lost her temper? No, it was Frank who had lured me here, and most likely it was he who had struck Nora.

I heard the boat zip past us. So did Nora—I could feel her body get rigid. "Where am I?"

"You're okay."

She heard the watery movement and her voice quivered. "I'm in the boathouse. Sondra is here."

"It's not Sondra. It's just a wake."

As soon as I said *a wake*, I realized my mistake. I quickly rephrased it. "It's the waves from a boat, a passing boat." I wondered if that was how these imaginings had started—someone saying it was "a wake" and Nora, haunted by the death of my mother, twisting the words in her mind.

She was shaking. I reached for her hands and felt the fear in her as she grasped mine with icy fingers. I wrapped my arms around her and held her tightly. The waves slapped against the outside of the building and rocked the water inside. But the motion of the water lessened quickly, the series of waves ending sooner than it had the last time.

And then it started, just as it had before, the slow rocking of the water back and forth, back and forth—*sideways*, I realized.

The direction of the flow was wrong—it couldn't be a wake.

"She's here," Nora said, her voice low and terrified. "She wants you. She wants her little girl."

The water slapped hard against the walls. Nora's arms wrapped around me, her fingers grasping my shirt, twisting it so hard I felt her knuckles digging into me. I braced myself, trying to keep myself from being pushed into the water. I felt her shifting her position, but before I could react and throw my weight against the wall, she did. She held me against it, as if protecting me.

At last the water grew quieter and settled into a dark restlessness.

"You're okay," Nora said. "She didn't get you. I didn't let her have you."

A lump formed in my throat. She had tried to keep me from being "taken" by my dead mother.

"Nora," I said. "Do you know how the knots happen?"

"I don't try to do them."

"Someone else does?"

"Someone else inside me. I can't stop her. Only sometimes."

Her unconscious, I thought. Sometimes she could control the emotions giving rise to the poltergeist, sometimes she couldn't.

"Listen, I think I know how this water gets stirred up. There's a lot of stuff in here, things we threw in the water years ago. There are old ropes and nets, especially around the doors, where we used to fish. I think this person inside of you gets angry or afraid and moves those things, whips them around and ties them in knots. That's what stirs up the water."

"No, it's Sondra," she insisted.

"Remember how the lamp in the river room broke?" I continued. "When that person inside you got upset, she tied the knot in the cord, which yanked on the lamp and made it tip over. The same thing happened to the lamp in my room. And the swing—with my weight at one end and the tree anchoring it at the other, it had to snap when it was forced into a knot."

The heart necklace, too, I thought; it had risen against my neck because it was being tied.

"Nora, we just have to talk to that person inside you, and tell her that everything is all right. It's not Sondra. Sondra isn't here."

"But she is," Nora insisted. "Holly said so."

I sat back on my heels. Holly, who said she alone knew how to handle Nora—perhaps she alone knew how to torture her. I wanted to blame Frank, Frank entirely. But as I went over the various incidents in my head, I could see how easy it would be for Holly to hide behind Nora's behavior. I reluctantly took the plunge. "Why did Holly hit you?"

"I didn't tell, I didn't!" Nora pleaded, like a child who had been suspected of telling a secret and threatened with punishment.

"Didn't tell what?"

She wouldn't answer.

"What did Holly hit you with?"

"I don't remember."

She might not, I reasoned, if she were hit on the back of the head. "Do you remember what Holly was carrying when she found you in the garage?"

"The lamp."

"The lamp that was broken? Your mother's work lamp?"

Nora nodded yes. "My head hurts," she whimpered. "Inside and outside it hurts."

The mental pain was probably worse than the physical, and I hated to cause more, but if I didn't know what had occurred and who the enemy was, I couldn't help either of us.

"How did she hold it?" I asked, wondering if Holly was simply dumping the lamp in Frank's trash or using it as a weapon.

"With a glove, my garden glove."

My breath caught in my throat. She'd wear a glove if it were a weapon and she didn't want her fingerprints on it. But why use something as traceable as a brass lamp—why not a block of wood that could float away in the river? Holly was too good at details and planning—something wasn't right.

I rested my hand on Nora's. "You and Holly have a secret," I said. "Holly thinks you told the secret. Now that she thinks you have told, you can."

I waited for a response, struggling to be patient.

"The secret is about the night my mother died," I ventured.

Nora didn't reply, but I took this as a positive sign. She said no quickly when she wanted to deny something.

"You came to my room that night," I went on, "looking for Bunny, your stuffed animal. You had left him on the dock. I said I would get him for you, but you said you could go as far as the dock. You left the house, and then what?"

She slipped her hand from beneath mine. In the dim light I saw her pull up her knees. She hugged them tightly.

"It's okay. I just want to know what happened next. Were you alone?" I changed the question to a statement. "You were alone."

"No. Holly was there, she was coming in."

"Coming in as you went out?"

I remembered then, running down from the house to the dock, stepping on something sharp, waving Holly on—she was in her nightgown but wearing shoes.

"Did you say anything to Holly? Did she say anything to you?"

"I don't remember."

"I know you do," I replied gently. "Did you tell her about Bunny?"

"Yes. I started getting scared about going out on the dock. I asked her to get him."

"And she said?" I laid my hand on Nora's arm and felt the tension in her muscles.

"She said I couldn't be afraid of water and I'd have to get him myself."

"And then?"

"I wanted her to come with me while I got him, but she said no."

"So you got Bunny yourself? Where was he?"

"On the dock. He was all the way at the end. I had to go all the way to the end."

I could hear the fear rising in her voice.

"It's okay. We're just remembering now. It's not happening now. Did you pick up Bunny?"

"Yes."

"Were you alone?"

"No."

I held my breath.

"Sondra was in the water," Nora said. "When I picked him up, I saw her floating in the water."

I sagged back against the wall. My mother had fallen in before Nora arrived.

"I killed her."

"*You* killed her!" I exclaimed, then softened my voice. "Did you push her? I thought she was already in the water."

"I didn't get her out. Holly said I should have pulled her out. Holly said I knew how to swim. I killed Sondra when I didn't pull her out. But I was too afraid. I knew I should go in, but the water was dark and scary. I thought the river wanted me, too. I rang the bell."

"Nora, listen to me. You didn't kill my mother. It wasn't your fault. You rang the bell. That was a good thing to do."

Clutching her legs, pressing her forehead against her knees, Nora rocked herself. "Holly said she wouldn't tell anyone I killed Sondra if I promised I wouldn't tell anyone I saw her outside. *It's a secret,* she said, *don't tell.*"

I bit my lip, bit back my anger at Holly. She could be innocent, I argued with myself; she could have been nothing more than scared. She was only eleven at the time. Perhaps she had set up Nora in case she herself were falsely accused, guilty of nothing more than looking out for herself at the expense of someone else. But she had used Nora cruelly, and today she had hit her, left her, and lied to Aunt Jule and me—at least to me.

Nora began to cry. "Holly said you were coming back to Wisteria because you were angry about your mother's death. She told me not to talk to you and said that you would hurt me if you knew."

"She was wrong. I'm not going to hurt you, Nora."

Nora sobbed loudly.

"And you must believe me—you didn't kill my mother."

The sobs grew uncontrollable.

"You didn't. I swear to you!"

Were Frank and Holly working together? What about Nick? I shrank from the thought that he was involved, but he was Frank's nephew and Holly's boyfriend, the link between them.

"Nora, why would Frank lock me in here? Do you know?"

Her sobbing grew less as she thought. "To help me?" she guessed.

I doubted it. What puzzled me was the fact that Frank didn't disguise his effort to trap me. No one would believe what crazy Nora might say, but why wouldn't Frank worry about an accusation by me?

The answer stopped my breath, shrank my stomach into a cold, hard rock. He wouldn't worry if I were dead. He planned to kill me.

He—or they—were setting up Nora, beginning to work on

her mentally by trapping us together. My death would be hung around her neck. It wouldn't be hard; she had shown herself confused enough to accept the guilt for my mother's.

I pulled away slowly from Nora. "I have to get us out of here. I'm going to look for a tool."

I walked all the way around the boathouse, feeling for something I could use to smash the hinges of the door. The place had been stripped clean.

"Okay, Nora, I'm on the other side now. Don't get scared. I'm going to scream for help."

I shouted till I tasted blood in my throat. It was useless. Who would come—Aunt Jule? She couldn't hear from the house. Besides, she could be part of the plan.

She'd have to be if my inheritance were the goal, and that was the only motivation for murder that I could imagine. Frank, as lawyer and executor of the estate, would be able to process the will as quickly as possible, using his local clout to pull strings if necessary. But Aunt Jule was the designated heir, so there would have to be some agreement between them. As for the tension between my godmother and Frank, partners can quarrel, especially when the stakes are high.

I heard movement outside. I screamed again. Nora started shrieking with me. I hurried around the walkway to her. There was barking.

"Rocky!" I shouted. "Rocky, get help."

Rocky, get help? What did I think he would do—run off like a dog in a Disney movie and fetch the police? I started laughing and crying at the same time, getting hysterical.

I heard noises at the back wall of the building, Rocky barking, Frank telling him to keep quiet. The noise stopped. I heard Frank leave, his voice fading as he called the dog.

I removed my shoes. "Nora, there's only one way out of here, under the doors to the river. I'm going to swim under and go for help."

I put my feet over the side of the walkway, then rolled on my stomach so I could slide into the black water.

"No," Nora protested. "No, don't!"

"I'll be back."

"She's in there. She'll get you."

Nora pulled on my arms. I was stronger than she and slipped free of her grasp, then thrust myself back in the water. When I straightened my legs and pointed my toes, they barely brushed the silty bottom. I tread water, trying to keep my mouth above it. Its slimy surface coated my arms and neck. Its earthy, sulfurous odor filled my nose and seemed to seep through the pores of my skin.

I turned my head, sniffing something different from river and rot.

"Nora, do you smell smoke?"

I heard her taking in deep, soblike breaths. "Yes."

For a moment I was so shocked I couldn't think what to do. It was too horrible—I could not believe that Frank would set the building on fire with us inside.

"Nora, get in. You have to get in the water."

I heard her pull back against the wall.

"The boathouse is going to burn down. We have to get out of here now. Now! There's no time. You must come with me."

"No!"

"I'll help you. I'll hold on to you."

"No!" she shrieked.

It was useless to try to convince her. She wasn't thinking fire, she was too afraid of water.

"Okay, never mind," I said quickly, and grasped the edge of the walkway. "Help me get out."

As soon as her arms were around me, I pulled her into the water. She screamed.

"I'm here. Float on your back. I'll help you."

But she was terrified. I fought to get her into a life-saving carry. She clawed at me and tried to climb up on my shoulders. Desperate to get herself above the water, she pushed me under.

I struggled to the surface. Her fingernails dug into my skin. She was much stronger than I'd realized and pushed me down again. I dropped way down, pulling Nora with me, hoping she would panic and let go.

It worked. I swam three feet away from her, then came up for air.

The smell of smoke was strong, smoke and lighter fluid. My eyes stung with it. Nora was treading water but was so frightened she kept gulping it down.

"Get on your back, Nora."

Her arms flailed wildly toward me, and I propelled myself backward in the water, out of her reach. She went under.

I dived and searched frantically for her, then grabbed her and pulled her to the surface, wrestling her onto her back. Out of the corner of my eye I saw a bright flame shoot up a corner on the land side of the boathouse. I heard the crackling. Another flame shot up the second corner, as if following a trail of lighter fluid. I thought I heard barking, but it was too late to hope Rocky would draw attention. Doused with an accelerant, the wood in this house could go up in a matter of seconds.

I swam, dragging Nora toward the river doors, then stopped in front of them. She was coughing and I had to make sure she had air.

"Come on, Nora. Deep breath in, deep breath out. Deep breath in, deep breath out. That's the way. Deep breath in—"

I sucked down my own lungful of air, then pulled her under

with me. I swam toward the light, one arm keeping her next to me, kicking hard for both of us. In the murky water I didn't see the net, didn't know I had swum into it, until it was around us. I pulled back quickly, trying to find its edge.

I had to let go of Nora for a moment. Using both hands I yanked on the netting in front of me, tearing at it with my fingers and teeth, making a hole just big enough for one of us. I swam through it, then reached back and pulled Nora to me.

Almost there, I thought, my lungs burning for lack of air. I took Nora's hand and curled her fingers around the waistband of my shorts, wanting her to hold on to me so I could use both arms to swim. Suddenly I felt her let go. She bolted like a frightened animal, driven by her instincts, swimming directly upward. I saw the net, but she didn't. She was caught in it—a new net—a plastic one, one that wouldn't tear.

Nora clawed at it, pulling it around her even more, getting hopelessly tangled inside. I tried to pull it off her. She writhed, desperate for air. My own lungs ached, my body began to cramp.

I felt the net twisting, being wrenched away from me, and I lost my grip on her. I spun in the water till I was sick and didn't know which way was up.

Then suddenly there was clear light around me. The air was cold against my face, and I opened my mouth and drank it down. Strong arms held my head just above the water. I gulped and coughed, bringing up river water and a bitter fluid from my stomach.

"Easy. Easy now."

It was Nick's voice. Nick's arms. He turned me on my back and swam with me, pulling me to the bank. I heard Rocky barking. Sirens wailed, were getting louder, coming closer.

I tried to speak. *Nora,* I wanted to tell him, *get Nora!*

I felt other hands take me from Nick. I reached back, but they carried me away from him and the water.

"Two hundred feet!" a woman shouted. "Get her away. Go!"

I was finally laid down in the grass. I tried to sit up. Everything slid past me, out of focus, the world running with water, smelling of river and fire. "Nora! Find Nora!"

Someone crouched next to me. An arm wrapped around my back supporting me. "She's safe," Nick said. "She's just a few feet away."

I reached out, trying to touch Nora, wanting to make certain she was there.

Nick caught my fingers. "The police are taking care of her," he assured me. "Paramedics are on the way."

I leaned back against him and rested my cheek on his shoulder. I could feel the river water dripping off him.

"Thank you," I whispered. When I looked up, I saw he was crying.

eighteen

I ASKED TO speak with the sheriff privately. I had left Nora sitting up, fully alert, and very frightened. It had taken the effort of both Nick and me to loosen her grip on my hand and wrap it around his. Aunt Jule was talking to the medics. The boathouse smoldered—what remained of it—and volunteer firefighters continued to work. McManus, the man who had questioned me about the rock-throwing incident, told another officer to take charge and walked with me toward the house.

"So," said the sheriff, sitting on the edge of the porch, pulling out a worn notebook, "I asked yesterday if there was anyone you weren't getting along with these days. Want to try a different answer?"

"It's a long one," I warned him, then recounted everything that had happened, including events from seven years ago, ignoring the strange look I got when I told him about the knots. I mentioned the will without telling him why it worried me. *If desire for my mother's money was a reasonable motive, he would see it,* I told myself. The truth was, now that I was safe, I didn't want to believe it. It hurt too much.

"I don't have any physical evidence against Frank," I concluded. "It's what I say against what he says."

"And Holly?"

I hesitated. "Like I said before, she could have been scared and protecting herself the night my mother died. The spooky stuff that's happened—I think that was all Nora. I think Holly hit Nora today, but she may have lost her temper without having any idea what it would lead to. I—I just don't know."

The light-haired sheriff pushed his hat back and forth, as if he were scratching his head with it. "Frank's not here. We checked next door—that's policy with fire. The house is locked up and his car gone. I've already talked to Nick and Jule."

"What did Aunt Jule tell you?"

He ignored my question. "They're fetching Holly now. And Nick's parents—I like a kid's parents to be around for these things. Why don't we just sit back and see what Holly has to say, without bringing up what you've told me?"

"So she doesn't shape her story around mine?" I replied. "Is that why you aren't telling me what Aunt Jule said?"

He smiled. "That wouldn't be too smart of me, now, would it?"

"What if we pretend Nora died?" I asked. "If we tell Holly that I found Nora unconscious and that Nora died in the fire, she'll think I know nothing at all about what happened earlier today or the night my mother died. There would be more chances of—" I stopped myself.

"Catching her in a lie?" he prompted.

Was that how little I trusted her now? "Or showing that she is honest," I replied.

Twenty minutes later we gathered in the garden room. While I was changing into dry clothes, McManus had told Aunt Jule and Nick about our plan and had instructed them not to contradict him. I felt guilty for setting up Holly and kept telling myself I was giving her the chance to demonstrate her innocence, but when I entered the garden room, I couldn't meet Nick's or Aunt Jule's eyes.

Holly had just come from the boathouse, her face looking pale and damp. "Are you all right, Lauren?" she asked.

"Yes," I answered, stepping back quickly when she reached for me, not wanting her to touch me.

She turned to Aunt Jule. "Now maybe you'll believe that Nora is out of control. I blame you for what has happened, Mother, all of it."

Without saying a word, Aunt Jule retreated to the river

room. Both sets of doors were open between that room and the garden room, and I watched her pace.

Holly walked over to Nick and took his hand. Seating herself close to one of the porch doors, she drew Nick into the chair next to hers. Though the doors were open, both sets of drapes that covered them had been closed halfway. Nora was on the porch outside with a police officer, so she could listen.

I sat opposite Holly and Nick, and the sheriff squatted on the hassock between them and me. He stared at his notebook for several moments, then removed his hat.

"Holly, I have some difficult news to give you. Your sister didn't make it."

Holly blinked. "What?"

"Nora died. You know that she and Lauren were trapped in the boathouse."

"Yes, a firefighter told me, but—"

"Lauren found Nora unconscious. She swam under the doors to get help, but the fire had started, and the place went up like a matchbox."

"Oh, God," Holly said. "Oh, God, why?" She turned to me. "How did this happen?"

I told her about the phone call, finding Nora unconscious, then the door being padlocked by Frank. A warning look from McManus silenced me before I said more.

Holly's eyes filled with tears. "Where's Frank now?" she asked.

"We're looking for him," McManus replied. "He's not home. Not at his office. It's starting to look like he's nowhere in town."

Holly frowned. "Why would he do this?"

"That's what we're trying to figure out," the sheriff told her. "Do you have any theories?"

"No. No, how could I?" Holly said. "It's horrible! I can't even imagine it."

I wanted to end this miserable charade. "Sheriff—" I began.

He cut me off. "I have some theories of my own and would be interested in any ideas or observations you have, Holly. Sometimes little things you notice can go a long way toward giving the big picture."

"Things like what?" Holly asked.

"A statement someone made that gave you reason to pause. An argument you overheard. Anything that can help us piece this together."

Holly stared at the floor, biting her lip, then looked up slowly. "Mother?"

Aunt Jule stopped pacing and came to stand in the doorway.

"Mother, what have you told them?"

"What do you mean?" Aunt Jule asked.

"I want to know what you have said to the police."

"The little I know," she replied, stepping into the room. "I was home. I heard Rocky barking, but didn't pay attention. Then I heard the sirens."

There was a long silence.

"Holly, do you believe there is someone else involved other than Frank?" McManus asked. "Have you seen or heard anything to make you think that?"

"No—maybe," she said indecisively.

"I'd like to hear about that *maybe.*"

Holly wrung her hands. "This is . . . really unpleasant." She looked down at her hands and made them still. "I think that Nora wasn't the one somebody was after."

McManus leaned forward.

"I think it was Lauren my mother wanted dead."

Aunt Jule's face went white. "What are you talking about?" she exclaimed.

Holly kept her eyes on McManus. "Before Lauren's mother drowned, she wrote a will with the help of Frank. She left everything to Lauren, but if Lauren died before she was eighteen, everything would go to my mother."

"Holly, what are you saying?" Aunt Jule cried. She leaned

on the wooden back of a chair, her arm rigid, the rest of her body sagging against it. "Do you think I would hurt Lauren? Do you think I would hurt anyone for money?"

Holly straightened her shoulders, steeling herself. "If her name was Sondra or Lauren—yes. I think that you killed Sondra first."

"I did not!"

"You fought with her constantly that summer," Holly said, her voice becoming stronger in response to her mother's denial. "The night she drowned, the arguing was awful." She turned to me. "Do you remember?"

I saw the curtains move and for a moment was afraid Nora would reply, but she remained quiet.

I looked from Holly to Aunt Jule, not sure whom to believe. Each seemed shocked by what the other had said. Then suddenly the piece that didn't fit, one tiny observation, slipped into place. Why would a person who planned as well as Holly use a traceable object to strike Nora? Because the lamp was Aunt Jule's and would have her fingerprints on it. What if it wasn't Nora who was to be framed for my death, but Aunt Jule, who had the most obvious motivation?

"Yes, there was a lot of fighting," I admitted, "but I know your mother wouldn't have hurt my mother or me. And I can't believe she'd ever hurt Nora. I won't believe it," I added, "not without some kind of evidence—stains or fingerprints."

"Did you look for the weapon?" Holly asked McManus.

"What weapon is that?" he asked.

"I thought that Nora was struck—" Holly stopped midsentence.

She had been too quick to point the investigation in the direction of the lamp, too eager for the sheriff to follow the plan she'd laid out for him.

When she didn't go on, McManus said, "I told you that Lauren found Nora unconscious. I didn't say how she got that way. She could have fainted, could have been poisoned."

I saw the curtain move again, its long cord swinging loose.

"She could have," Holly agreed. "But I figured it happened the way it does on TV."

The cord swung as if in a breeze. Nick turned his head slightly. Aunt Jule noticed it. But McManus's eyes were on Holly, and hers on him.

"I'm not a detective," Holly went on. "I'm not trained to think of all the possibilities. Like Lauren, I can't believe my mother would do this. It—it horrifies me. It doesn't seem real."

The cord swung like a pendulum, closer and closer to Holly's right arm.

"And Frank—he's like an uncle to me. I trusted him! I trusted both of them."

"Holly," Aunt Jule cried, "why are you turning on me?"

The tip of the cord curled upward as if invisible fingers had twisted it.

"You've got it backward, Mother," Holly argued. "*You* turned on us. My sister is dead. And if I don't say what I know, Lauren may be next."

Tears ran down Aunt Jule's cheeks.

Holly's face hardened. "Stop faking it, Mother. Who else would want to kill Lauren?"

The moving cord suddenly twisted upward and snaked around Holly's wrist. It coiled twice and knotted itself, tying Holly's forearm to the wooden arm of the chair.

McManus rose from his seat, his notebook sliding from his lap. "Good God!"

Holly sat still and appeared perfectly calm, but her arms prickled with goose flesh.

There was a long ripping sound. The curtains on the other door fell and the cord flew across the room. It twined itself around her wrist. Holly's skin paled, her eyes widened with fear. She struggled to get free of the rope, rocking back and forth in her chair, knocking into the glass door. "Stop it, Nora!" she screamed. "Stop it!"

Two officers stepped into the room.

"Move aside, Nick," McManus said.

Holly's eyes darted over the room, as if she expected Nora to come back from the dead.

"Nora, you can come in now," McManus called.

Holly wrenched around in her chair and stared at Nora as she came through the door, then she turned to me. "Witch," she said, with unnerving calm.

I didn't reply. I had no answer for the hate in her eyes.

"You're such a fool, Lauren," Holly said. "Did you really think that anything had changed between us during the last seven years?"

"I hoped we had both grown up."

"You will always be rich and stupid, just like your mother," Holly said. "You don't deserve what you have. You don't deserve your money and you don't deserve my mother's sickening admiration. I have always hated you."

"Enough to attempt murder?" McManus asked.

She ignored him. "I told Frank you were an idiot and would be easy to take in. You trusted him like a puppy dog."

"I guess I am naive," I answered. "I never imagined that you could hate me so much you'd make your mother and sister suffer for it."

"Who doesn't help me, hurts me," she replied coolly. "They stood in the way."

"Of the inheritance?" McManus asked. "Perhaps, Holly,

you figured that if both Lauren and Nora were dead, and your mother charged with double murder, the money would be yours. At least, you'd be given control over it."

"You're smarter than the rest of them," she said.

"Of course," McManus continued, "it would help to have Frank moving things along legally. What was he supposed to get out of this?"

"My mother's property for a good price." She sounded proud—she sounded absurd, as if there were no difference between a murder plan and a yearbook layout.

"The boathouse was Frank's idea," Holly went on. "He saw it was in his best interest to help out. I knew Frank was in bad financial shape—he leaves his papers all over his home office, like he thinks a teenager can't read. He's got several banks and some real unhappy investors breathing down his neck. He was desperate to have something to offer them.

"I want a deal," she told the sheriff. "I'll give you the evidence you need on Frank, but I want a lawyer with brains to represent me and a good deal from you."

"We'll talk about it back at the station," McManus replied.

Holly eyed Nora. "You let me down, Nora," she said bitterly. "You screwed your own sister."

Nora stepped behind me, as if needing my protection.

"I am the one who let you down," Aunt Jule said, "all three

of you. It's way past time that I tell you why I asked Lauren to come back to Wisteria.

"Seventeen years ago, when Sondra came here pregnant and terribly upset, I myself was pregnant for the third time. Sondra lost her child. Her baby is buried next to her in the churchyard."

That was the grave I had seen, the one I'd thought was mine.

"Meanwhile, I had a child I couldn't afford. We agreed that it would be best for all three children if Sondra took Lauren and pretended she was hers. I knew that Lauren would receive all that a child could want and that Sondra would love her dearly. Sondra sent money every month to help support us here. As part of the agreement, my little girl was to visit each summer.

"But as Lauren grew older and Sondra more troubled, Sondra and I began to fight about how Lauren was being raised. When they came that last summer and I saw how painfully confused Lauren was by Sondra's behavior, I was furious. We fought about Lauren day and night, as you all well know.

"It's hard not to be overly critical and jealous of the woman raising your child. But I loved Sondra. I did not kill her. Still, I knew Nora had problems and feared that she had. I was afraid that in therapy, that secret would be discovered and they would take Nora away from us. I thought if I could keep her safe here at home, everything would be all right.

"I knew I had to tell Lauren the truth about her birth, but the longer I put it off, the harder it was. When I finally made up my mind to do it, and Lauren came, painful memories were stirred up in Nora. I worried that Nora might hurt Lauren and was afraid to explain the past and make things worse. I didn't know what to do."

Aunt Jule gazed at Nora and me, then turned to Holly. "I have not been a good mother. I have made terrible mistakes. But I have always loved you." Her voice wavered with emotion. "I will never stop loving all three of you."

I wanted to put my arms around Aunt Jule, to reassure her, but I couldn't. I struggled to comprehend that she was my birth mother and to reinterpret all the things I had thought I knew about myself. Nick, who was standing a distance behind us, came forward and took Aunt Jule's hand.

I finally found my voice. "Nora is innocent of my mother's—Sondra's—death," I said. "Holly convinced Nora that she was guilty because she didn't go into the river to pull her out, but Nora wasn't responsible."

Aunt Jule closed her eyes and shook her head.

"Okay," McManus said, "I think this soap opera's over, at least for now. I'll be sending someone back to you folks for some more statements."

An officer cut the curtain cords around Holly's wrists. When

Holly stood up, Aunt Jule tried to put her arms around her, but Holly pushed her aside. "I hate you! I hate all of you."

"I want cuffs on her," McManus said.

"Traitor," Holly hissed at Nick, then moved toward me. Two officers moved with her.

"Excuse me," she said, "I have something private to tell Lauren."

They looked at me and I nodded.

She took a step forward and whispered in my ear, "I killed Sondra, but you'll never be able to prove it." Then she turned away laughing and was escorted out the door.

nineteen

As the police exited, Nick's parents arrived. They said a quick hello to Aunt Jule and rushed over to Nick. I don't know how the three of them understood each other, for they all talked at the same time. I turned to Aunt Jule—in my mind, that was still her name. I hugged her and Nora, then pulled away, feeling suddenly shy.

My godmother—mother—touched my cheek gently. "It's okay, love," she said. "It's going to take a while to get used to the idea.

"Your dad knows," she added, "he has since you were three. I didn't realize Sondra had told him, not until we spoke at her funeral. The loss of Sondra had upset you so badly, we both thought it best not to tell you about your birth until you were older. Whenever I visited you, your dad would call to find out how I thought you were doing. He may not have been an ideal father—he certainly wasn't a good husband to Sondra—but he does love you."

I nodded silently. There was so much to absorb.

Aunt Jule hugged Nora and smiled at me, as if to send me the hug vicariously, while giving me the space I needed at the moment.

"Do you want one of your walks alone?" she asked. "See, I'm learning that you're not a little girl anymore and like to work things through by yourself."

I smiled back at her. "Yes, but I want to take Rocky with me. Tell Nick I've got him, okay?"

The dog trotted next to me down to the boathouse. I kept a tight hold on his collar as we watched the firefighters continue to douse the grass around the burned-out structure. Fishing line, crab traps, and nets, some of which looked new, had been dragged out of the water. Yellow police tape surrounded the site.

"Come on, Rocky," I said and headed in the direction of the dock. He raced past me, then plunged into the water. I watched him swim and tried not to think about Nick.

I had discovered that there was something more painful than falling in love with someone who hasn't fallen for you: hurting that person—hurting him and not being able to do anything about it. I wondered if Nick suspected that Holly had killed my mother. I wouldn't tell him. Holly was just a kid then—maybe a heartless one, but a kid, and legally a minor. If I pursued the matter I'd create more pain, not achieve justice. I told myself it was Holly and Frank who had betrayed Nick; still, my return to Wisteria had triggered the whole disturbing chain of events. I wondered if Nick and I would ever be friends again. I thought about the way he had cried when he held me on the grass.

Think about something else, I told myself, think about Dad. In nine months I'd inherit my mother's money and wouldn't be dependent on him anymore. It would give me a better chance to strengthen our fragile relationship, to let him know I didn't need, but *wanted*, his presence in my life.

And the money would enable me to pay for the psychological care of Nora—for the care of my sister, I thought, trying out the new words. I'd stay the summer and, if she needed me, do my senior year in Wisteria.

"It's going to get better," I said aloud.

"It will."

I turned, startled by Nick's voice. He stood a foot away from me.

"Didn't mean to scare you," he said. "Can we talk?"

"Nick, I'm so sorry. I know how much it must—"

He reached out and touched my mouth with the tips of his fingers. "What I meant was—can *I* talk?"

"Okay."

We walked together, following the riverbank. After a long silence he said, "I'm trying to put it all in order."

"Don't try. Just begin anywhere."

"Do you know what it was like kissing Holly and looking up to see you?"

"What?"

"You said to begin anywhere."

But I hadn't expected that as a beginning, middle, or end. I felt my cheeks getting warm. "I guess it was pretty embarrassing for both of us," I said, and walked ahead of him so he wouldn't see my face. "I know, I just kept staring at you."

"What were you thinking?"

"I don't remember."

"Don't *you* start using that line," he chided.

"Then don't ask me, Nick." Did he suspect how I felt?

He caught me and turned me around to face him. I focused on his shirt.

"Okay," he said quietly, "I'll tell you what I was thinking. I couldn't believe that I, who was never going to get hooked, had fallen in love with a girl who didn't want to date, and she was watching me kiss somebody else."

I glanced up.

"Your turn, brave girl. What were you thinking?"

"That Holly looked beautiful in your arms and that you didn't pull away from her the way you had pulled away from me when I kissed you."

He drew me to him. "I'm not pulling away again," he said, holding me close.

I hesitated, then put my arms around him. "I thought I had done something stupid."

"No, you just surprised the heck out of me. I knew before then I was getting hooked on you, but I thought I could handle it. I didn't know a simple kiss could be like that. It was scary, what I felt. My heart was banging against my ribs. I don't know how you didn't hear it."

"I couldn't hear it over mine."

He tilted his head back to smile at me. "I love looking in your eyes," he said. Then the smiled disappeared and his face grew serious. "I found out right after that what *really* scary was—someone hurting you, someone trying to kill you."

"You mean today."

"No. I was suspicious before. I didn't think that Nora would hurt you, but I had begun to worry that someone was hiding behind her. The night of the prom I realized how jealous Holly was of you. When I returned to the dance—I don't know, I must have had a dazed look on my face—she knew something had happened between us. She started cutting you down, saying a lot of nasty stuff. No big deal, I told myself, girls and guys get jealous of each other."

"I was sure jealous of her," I said.

"Were you?" he asked, his eyes shining. "You don't mind if I enjoy that, do you?"

"I feel responsible," I told him, "as if all of Holly's life I've gotten the attention she wanted."

"Everyone wants attention, Lauren, and everyone gets jealous. But you didn't try to get rid of her, did you?"

"No."

He let me go, then put an arm over my shoulder and started to walk with me.

"The day after the prom you told me about the note that had been left in your car. I could explain it as an anonymous prank, but as I did, I remembered that Holly had left school for a few minutes right after you. It would have been easy for her to put the note in your car while you were in the cemetery.

"And the brick that was thrown at your car, I could explain that, too, but again Holly had gone out during the time it happened. She said she had been at Frank's picking up some party things. Afterward, Frank pressed me for details about how you were getting along with Holly, Jule, and Nora. He must have realized then that someone wanted to get you."

"I—I just don't understand Frank," I said. "I knew he loved money and thought you should love it, too. I knew he enjoyed using his clout as a lawyer and businessman, but I didn't think he'd hurt people. I didn't think he'd hurt me."

"Me neither. Maybe Aunt Margaret's family was right about him. It's scary to think how easy it is to be fooled."

"I feel so bad for you and your parents, Nick. Frank is family for you; for me, Holly is. And I don't know how anyone writes off family."

"Yeah," he said, "I think Nora will have a lot of company in the next few months. You and I, Jule and my parents, we'll all be sitting in Dr. Parker's office, trying to understand what happened."

I stopped walking and wrapped my arms tightly around him. "You know, I *can* hear your heart."

"Could you hear it breaking when I accused you of getting my cartoon pulled?" he asked.

I held my head back so I could look him directly in the eye. "I didn't pull it."

"You couldn't have," he replied, "because I did."

"You?"

"I was worried about your safety," he explained, "but I thought if I accused Holly, she would deny everything. The only way I knew to protect you was to stick close to Holly and try to anticipate her next move. After the prom, I had to convince her in a dramatic way that I had turned on you. The cartoon was the only excuse I could think of."

I dropped my head, resting my forehead against his chest.

"I'm sorry, Lauren. When I accused you, I saw how badly I was hurting you. At the party I noticed Holly talking to Jason. Not long after that he and his friends started harassing you. I couldn't break it up, not without making Holly suspicious, so I sent Rocky into the water. It was the best I could do."

I smiled up at him. "It worked."

"I saw Holly enter the greenhouse twice during the party and wondered what she was doing. After I left that night, I parked in Frank's driveway and waited a while before sneaking back to investigate. I arrived just as you smashed the window."

"So there were no phone calls to your house?"

"No. You remember my stupid excuse about why I'd come to the greenhouse—the flashlight, which, as you pointed out, wasn't on."

"When you lied like that, I was afraid that you were part of it."

"You looked so betrayed—it was awful," he said. "When I left the second time that night, I was terrified at what might happen to you and went directly to the police. I talked to McManus's deputy. He drove by the house, but everything was quiet. He promised that someone would talk to you the next day, but he wasn't as worried as I. You hadn't asked for their help, and there had been a big party. Pranks happen.

"Anyway, this morning, when I learned about the knots

and the fact that Nora was missing, I knew the situation was critical. I blamed you in front of Holly to make sure I was in solid with her. After we arrived at school, I made up a sudden errand. I called the police, talked to McManus, and rushed back here to talk to you. He, another officer, and I arrived at the same time. Rocky was barking and we smelled smoke. The woman officer and I ran to the boathouse, and McManus called for backup and fire equipment. You know the rest."

"I thought you had turned against me," I said, "and all the time you were trying to protect me."

We had reached the end of Aunt Jule's property and turned back.

Rocky emerged from the river and came galloping toward us. Stopping in front of us, he shook water all over. I backed into Nick.

"Good dog," Nick said. "That's one of the tricks I've taught him, shaking water on girls so they back into my arms."

"Really! How smart of Rocky—and you, of course."

"That's another thing I've been wanting to tell you," he said, turning me to face him. "I'm tired of getting jealous of my dog. I mean, he has nice eyes, but so do I."

I looked from Rocky's golden eyes to Nick's laughing green ones.

"I didn't enjoy the way Rocky got to stick close to you while

I played Holly's boyfriend. He's going to have some competition from now on."

"Oh, yeah? Are you good at retrieving sticks?"

"I'm good at stealing kisses," Nick said, then proved it.

TURN THE PAGE FOR A
SNEAK PEEK OF MORE MYSTERY IN

Dark Secrets 2:

The Deep End of Fear and *No Time to Die*

one

12 YEARS EARLIER

I huddled under the blankets in the backseat of the car. Wind rocked the body of our old Ford. Sharp needles of sleet beat against the windows.

"Mommy?"

"Hush, Katie."

I raised my head, peeking out of the blankets, wondering where we were going in the middle of the night. I could see nothing, not even the headlights of our car.

"Did you fasten Katie's seat belt?" my mother asked.

"She was asleep," my father replied, "so I laid her down on the seat."

"Luciano!" My mother always used his full name when he had done something wrong. "Stop the car."

"Not yet. We haven't cleared the estate. Do you see the main road?"

"I can't see a thing," my mother replied tensely. "Put on the headlights."

"And let everyone know we're leaving?"

My mother sighed. "Quickly, Katie, sit down on the floor. All the way down."

I wedged myself into the seat well, the space between the rear seat and front, where people place their feet. "Why are we leaving?"

There was no answer from the front of the car.

"When are we coming back?"

"We're not," my father said.

"Not ever?" I had liked it at Mason's Choice. "But, I—"

"There's Scarborough Road," my mother interrupted.

The car turned and headlights flicked on.

"I didn't say good-bye to Ashley."

For a moment all I heard was sleet and wind.

"Ashley isn't here anymore, remember?" my mother prompted quietly. "Ashley has gone to heaven."

That was what everyone said, but I had trouble understanding how it could be so. I still heard her and played with her. Sometimes I saw her by the pond, though Mommy said they had pulled her out of it. Ashley always scared me a little, but on the big estate there were no other children to play with, and that had made her my best friend. "I want to say good-bye to Ashley," I insisted.

"Luke! In the mirror, behind us!" My mother sounded panicky, and I stood up in the seat well to see.

"Get down, Katie!" my father shouted. "Now!"

I quickly dropped between the seats. Daddy sometimes shouted at the people who hired him to paint portraits of their pets. He'd scream at his paintings, too, when he got frustrated, but never at me. Our car suddenly picked up speed. I pulled the blanket over my head.

"There's ice on the road," my mother warned.

"You don't have to tell me, Victoria."

"We shouldn't have tried this."

"We had no choice," he said. "Do you remember the cut-off?"

"The one that runs by the Chasney farm—yes. About a hundred meters before it, there's a sharp curve."

My father nodded. "We'll get around it, I'll cut the lights, and he won't see us take the cutoff."

Our car picked up speed.

"But the ice—"

"Katie, I want you to stay on the floor," my father said, sounding more stern than I had ever heard him. I hugged my knees and my heart pounded. The car motor grew louder. The wind shrieked, as if we were tearing a hole in it by going so fast.

"Almost there."

I wished I could climb up front and hold on to Mommy.

Then the car turned. Suddenly, I couldn't feel the road beneath us. The car began to spin. Mommy screamed. I felt her hands groping behind the seat for me. I couldn't move, pinned against the backseat by the force of the rotating car.

We came to a stop.

"Katie—?"

"Mommy—"

The stillness lasted no more than a few seconds. The next sound came like thunder—I could feel as well as hear it.

"Behind us, Luke," my mother gasped.

"Yes."

"Oh, God!" Her voice shook.

I jumped up to see what was behind us, but my father drove on. All I could see were darkness and a coat of ice halfway up the rear window of the car. We turned onto another road.

"I've got to keep going, Vic. For Katie's sake."

My mother's head was in her hands.

"If we go back and he isn't injured, we'll walk into a trap. If he's badly hurt, there is not much we can do. The gas station farther up has an outside pay phone. It's closed now—no one will see us. I'll call in the accident."

My mother nodded silently. For a moment I thought she

was crying. But she never cried—my father was the emotional one.

"What happened, Daddy? Did somebody get hurt?"

My mother raised her head and brushed back her long yellow hair. "Everything's all right," she said, her voice steady again. "There—there was a herd of deer by the side of the road, and your father was trying to avoid them. You know how they do, Katie, bolting across before you can see them. Some of them crashed into the wood. One went into the little dip next to the road."

"Did the deer get hurt?" I asked.

"I'm not sure," my father answered.

"Of course not," my mother said quickly, giving me the answer I wanted to hear but didn't believe. She unfastened her seat belt and knelt on the seat, facing me, to buckle me into my restraint.

My father drove more slowly now. There was a long silence.

"Victoria," he said at last, "I'm sorry."

She didn't reply.

Sorry for what? I wondered, but I knew they wouldn't tell me.

A chilly loneliness had settled around me, the way a winter fog settles in the ditches along the roads on the Eastern Shore. The silence deepened as we drove north to Canada and, a few days later, flew to England, my mother's birthplace. My mother and father shared a secret—I had known that from the day Ashley died. It was a secret that I was left to discover twelve years later, after both parents had disappeared from my life.

two

My dearest Kate,

You are the most wonderful daughter a man could have. You can't possibly know how much I love you. I fear that the last few months of my illness have been very hard on you, and I hesitate to ask any more of your generous heart. Still, I must leave you with two requests.

First, do not forget that your mother loves you as much as I. I know you don't believe me—I see it in your eyes each time I say this—but I was the reason your mother left. It broke her heart to be separated from you. Below is the name and number through which you can contact her. Please do so, Kate.

Right, Dad, I replied silently to his letter, *as soon as the sky falls.*

Victoria, as I now refer to my mother, had left Dad and me the day after we arrived in England—left without explanation, simply walked out the door while I was sleeping. I was five years old then and needed her desperately. At seventeen, I did not.

I glanced back down at the letter.

Second, in the chimney cupboard, I have left a ring that belongs to Adrian Westbrook of Wisteria, Maryland. I took it the night we left the estate. Please return it.

I frowned and refolded the letter, as I had done many times in the three months since Dad had died. His second request, and the brilliant sapphire and diamond ring I had found in the cupboard, baffled me. In his career as a painter of animal portraits—horses, dogs, cats, birds, lizards, snakes, leopards—my father had worked for fabulously wealthy people, with access to the homes and estates where these pampered pets lived; as far as I knew, he had never stolen anything. I did not look forward to presenting this piece of missing property to Adrian Westbrook or to seeing a place that I connected so strongly with my mother. But I had to honor at least one of my father's final requests.

I carefully returned the letter to my travel bag and paced the room I had taken at a bed-and-breakfast in Wisteria, Maryland. After airport security, a six-hour transatlantic flight, customs, and a two-hour ride in an airport shuttle to the Eastern Shore town, I longed for a decent cup of tea, but the sooner I got this over with, the better. I headed downstairs to a small room equipped with a guest phone and punched in the number I had found in an Internet directory.

My call was answered on the third ring. "Mason's Choice."

For a moment I was confused, then I remembered that that was the name of the estate where Ashley had lived.

"May I speak with Mr. Westbrook, please, Adrian Westbrook."

"Who is calling?" asked a woman with a deep voice.

"Kate Venerelli."

"Excuse me?"

Aware that years of schooling in England had given me an accent more clipped than Americans were accustomed to, I repeated my name slowly.

"I'm sorry. Mr. Westbrook is not available."

"When may I call back?" I asked.

"You may leave a message with me now."

I hesitated. An image of a person I had long forgotten formed in my head: a cap of straight gray hair, a pale stone face, a mouth and forehead carved with disapproval. Mrs. Hopewell. It seemed as if the housekeeper should be 103 by now, but of course, when you are five, anyone older than your parents seems ancient to you. She was probably in her sixties.

"Thank you," I said politely, "but I would like to speak to Mr. Westbrook myself."

Click.

I stared at the phone—she had hung up. Quickly I dialed the number again. "May I speak with *Mrs.* Westbrook, please?" I knew from Dad's clients that rich old men always had wives, usually young, pretty ones. "Who is calling?"

"Kate Venerelli." There was no reason to lie—I was certain the housekeeper took note of the number displayed on her phone and realized the same person was calling.

"Mrs. Westbrook is not available," Mrs. Hopewell replied.

"Who is it?" I heard a younger woman ask in the background.

"Someone selling something, a marketing call," the housekeeper said, just before the click sounded again in my ear.

I put down the phone. My reluctance to carry out my father's request had melted in the low heat of Mrs. Hopewell's voice. I strode down the hall, hoping to learn something current about the Westbrooks from the owner of the Strawberry B&B.

I found Amelia Sutter in the kitchen, finger-deep in bread

dough. She was very glad to talk, but I discovered that conversation with her was harder to steer than a flock of birds. It took twenty minutes of kneading to learn that Adrian had married a young woman named Emily and now had a little boy. Both of Adrian's grown children, Trent Westbrook and Robyn Caulfield, had divorced and never remarried. Of course, there was much more to those stories, details worthy of a racy novel, but those were the only statements made by Mrs. Sutter that I believed to be facts.

As her stories wandered on to other subjects, so did my attention. I tried to think of a reason to show up at the gates of Mason's Choice, some excuse that would get me past Mrs. Hopewell. Until I understood why my father had taken the ring, I wasn't going to reveal it to anyone but Adrian Westbrook. I stared down at a college newspaper lying open on the kitchen table. CARS TOWED, a headline read. That was an idea—I could pretend I had a disabled car and needed help. I continued scanning the page, my eyes stopping at an ad with a familiar phone number—the one I had just called.

WANTED: TUTOR FOR 7-YEAR-OLD CHILD. DUTIES INCL. TRANSPORTATION TO SCHOOL, HOMEWORK, & SOME REC TIME. EXCELLENT JOB FOR COLLEGE STUDENT. ROOM, BOARD, SALARY DPDT. ON EXPERIENCE.

My ticket in! I thought, jumping up so fast, I startled Mrs. Sutter. I didn't actually want the job—I had plans to tour cross county before attending university—but an interview would get me onto the estate, inside the house.

"Oh, there I've gone and offended you." Mrs. Sutter sighed. "I forgot how proper you English folks are."

"I'm American," I said, bluntly enough to prove it, then remembered my manners. "Would you excuse me? There is something I need to do—to do as soon as possible."

I hurried upstairs and grabbed my coat. Certain that the vigilant Mrs. Hopewell wouldn't answer a third call from the same number, I headed out in search of a pay phone.

At 4:20 that afternoon, about ten kilometers outside of town, Mrs. Sutter—Amelia, as she had asked me to call her—pulled up to the iron gates of Mason's Choice. They swung inward, triggered by an electric eye, an orb less discriminating than Mrs. Hopewell's. My plan had worked. Having used a phone at the local college, a bad French accent (I was afraid my American Southern wouldn't convince a native), and a polite request to speak to Emily Westbrook, I had gotten past the housekeeper.

My job interview was at 4:30, but the gloomy weather of early March made it appear later than that. A chilly fog had settled over the Eastern Shore, turning even the small wood that shielded the estate from Scarborough Road into the forbidding forest of a fairy tale. Massive vines and dripping black branches crowded close to both sides of the private road that led to the house. Amelia sped up, as if eager to get through the wood. A broken branch whisked across the windshield. Past the wood was an open area of lawn, bounded by a long hedge, perhaps three times the height of an adult, with a keyhole cut through where the entrance road passed. As a child I had found this living wall rather menacing; it didn't seem much friendlier now.

Then I remembered and turned my head quickly to the right. "Amelia, could you stop for a moment?"

"Yes, of course, dear. What is it?" she asked.

"A cemetery."

She strained to see. Had I not already known it was there, I wouldn't have noticed it—the wrought-iron fence and weeping angels. It had been foggy like this the week Ashley had fallen through the ice. After her funeral, I had visited her grave with my mother.

I remembered gripping my mother's hand as I watched the wisps of mist slip between the leaning stones. Ashley had claimed that the ghosts in the graveyard whispered to her; even when we weren't together, she said, the spirits watched me and told her what I did.

I shook off the eerie memory. Every day had been exciting with Ashley, but she had also frightened me. That summer, autumn, and winter, she and I had had the entire estate for our playground—gardens, pool, docks, play equipment, an old barn, and deserted outbuildings. She had loved daring me to try the forbidden. Spoiled and hot-tempered, and two years older than I, she had known how to scare me into doing what she wanted.

"Thanks, Amelia," I said, turning back. "We can keep going."

Passing through the hedge, we drove through the formal gardens bordering the long drive. The flowering plants were clipped clean to the ground, and the boxwood was perfectly manicured in patterns that looked as if they had been formed by big biscuit cutters. The house lay straight ahead.

Like many homes built in the American Colonial period, it was brick and impressive in its simplicity. The house rose three stories, the third being a steep roof with five dormer windows across. A wing extended from each side of the main house. Structurally, the wings were smaller versions of the house, turned sideways and attached to it by small brick sections that had roofs with dormers as their second story. There were no outside shutters, which made the house's paned windows seem to stare like unblinking eyes. Its red brick was stained dark with moisture.

Amelia stopped the car and craned her head to see the house. "I've changed my mind. I don't want to live here after all," she said, as if she had been seriously considering it. "If I owned this place, I'd sell it and buy myself three cozier homes."

"I think it has a view of the bay from the other side."

"I'd never see it," she replied. "I'd always be glancing over my shoulder. I didn't realize there was a graveyard here."

"Most old estates have them."

"I'd dig it up."

I laughed. "Then you certainly would have something ghastly standing at your shoulder, looking for a new place to rest," I said as we climbed out of the car.

Fortunately, an older gentleman, an employee I didn't know, answered the door. Mrs. Hopewell might have recognized me, at least, recognized a young "Victoria." During the last year I had cut my hair several times, starting with it well below my shoulder, shortening it to shoulder-length, chin-length, and finally having it snipped to wisps of gold that barely made it to the tips of my ears. I told Dad it was "sympathetic hair," for he was bald from the cancer treatments. But actually, it was my resemblance to the woman I remembered from twelve years back, her green eyes and cascade of blond hair, that had motivated me.

Amelia was asked to wait in the library on the left side of the spacious entrance hall, and I was escorted to an office on the right. A few moments later, Emily Westbrook entered. She was a slender woman with strawberry blond hair—probably tinted, for her eyebrows were much redder. She moved quickly, elegantly, as if she had been raised on ballet lessons.

We sat in chairs placed by a large, mahogany desk. While she studied my hastily created résumé, I studied the family pictures displayed on the fireplace mantel, curious to see the people whom I knew only through a child's eyes. I spotted Adrian's children, who were close to my parents' age, now early to mid-forties: Robyn in her horse-show gear, and Trent on a sailboat. Emily Westbrook and a baby—perhaps the little boy in need of a tutor—were in a large photo at the center of the mantel. Brook Caulfield, Robyn's son, who I thought was the same age as his cousin Ashley—two years older than I—sulked in a photo taken during those "wonderful" years of early adolescence. We all have those photos—I burned mine. Adrian, handsome, physically fit, looked nearly the same in all of his pictures, except his hair had turned from black to silver-streaked to pure white.

I checked the pictures on the desk and those placed on shelves, disappointed that there were none of Ashley. Perhaps the family had found it too painful to display her photos. It occurred to me that the woman interviewing me might not know who I was or that I had lived here once. If her son was seven, she would have been part of the household for at least eight years, but it was possible that what had occurred four years before that was never talked about.

"So, you were educated in England," she said, looking up.

"Yes, ma'am, and sometimes, because of my father's work, we lived on the Continent, but I was born here and am an American citizen. As you can see from my résumé, I completed my A levels and will be applying for university next year. Because I learned through correspondence when we traveled, I was able to finish up a year early," I added as an explanation for my age.

"We have a number of paintings in this house done by a Luciano Venerelli," she said.

"He was my father. He died three months ago."

"Really! Are you an artist? Can you teach art?"

"I—I could teach some of the basic things my father taught me when I was a child."

"Do you play a musical instrument?"

"A little bit of piano."

"So you could teach it?"

"The basics," I replied, with the uncomfortable feeling that she was getting too interested in hiring me. "Of course, I have no experience in tutoring children."

"You say here that you have baby-sat quite a bit."

Yes, I thought, but that was to get me inside your front door, not fetch myself a job.

She picked up a desk phone. "Mrs. Hopewell, please send in Patrick."

I had to act fast. "Mrs. Westbrook, I need to explain why—"

"Let me tell you what we are looking for," she interrupted, with the air of someone who expected others to listen to her. "We call it a tutoring job because we want a nanny who is educated and can teach Patrick in a manner that is appropriate to his position in life. We want an employee who speaks English well and can correct Patrick's mistakes, someone who can assist in his studies, and introduce him to other things a well-bred person should know."

There was a light knock, and the door opened. The little boy who entered was definitely a Westbrook—dark hair, blue eyes, fair skin, with a child's smattering of freckles. For a moment I felt like little Katie gazing at Brook. Clearly, Patrick had already been bred in a manner "appropriate to his position in life": His walk and raised chin indicated that he believed he owned the place. I almost laughed.

"Patrick, darling, this is Kate Venerelli."

Patrick surveyed me, not like a curious seven-year-old, but like an adult who was deciding whether I would do. I surveyed him with the same measuring eyes, as if deciding whether *he* would do. He suddenly turned into a little boy, backing up and moving closer to his mother.

"Kate is going to be your tutor."

I swallowed my gasp. "I'm sorry?"

"I've made up my mind," Mrs. Westbrook told me. "You are educated, you are familiar with the arts, and you speak very well."

"But—but don't you think you should have references?" I asked.

"Do you have any?"

"No."

"It doesn't matter," Mrs. Westbrook said. "No one supplies *bad* references. Recommendations don't prove anything about a person."

"But I'm sure Mr. Westbrook would like to interview me too," I suggested. I considered explaining my ruse, but if she grew angry and sent me off, I'd have no excuse to return.

"Patrick's father has been ill. He will be returning Friday from Hopkins, where he has been receiving cancer treatments."

"Oh." I still winced when someone mentioned cancer.

I glanced at Patrick, but his expression didn't change. Either he didn't understand, or he was already proficient at wearing a public face.

"When he arrives, Mr. Westbrook will have many other things to tend to," she went on.

"I need some time to think about this," I said, hoping to keep the masquerade going for one more day and hand deliver the ring.

"Perhaps you would like to get to know Patrick a little better," she suggested. "Darling, be a good boy and show Kate your room and the rooms on the third floor. Would you do that for Mommy?"

Darling didn't answer right away. Perhaps he was thinking about refusing or, better still, driving a bargain with Mommy.

I wanted this chance to see the places in which I had once played. "I'm sure you have some smashing toys in your room," I said encouragingly.

Patrick looked at me with new interest. "I'm not supposed to smash them."

His mother laughed. "That's an expression, Patrick. She means wonderful toys, exciting toys."

I think he would have preferred that I meant smashable toys, but he nodded and started toward the door, calling to me over his shoulder, "Come on, Kate."

I followed him out of the office. The entrance hall, which was furnished to serve as a formal reception room, ended at a wide passageway that ran from one side of the house to the other—that is, to the left and right, continuing on to the wings of the house. The living room and dining room, the two large rooms at the "back" of the house, were behind the passageway—facing the water, I remembered. The main stairway rose to our right, running parallel to the passageway.

The house had other stairways, in both the main section and wings, back steps that wrapped around the corners of its many fireplaces. It was a perfect place to play hide-and-seek, with three floors and so many escape routes connecting them. But it had also made me uncomfortable. I never knew for sure where Brook was, because he could sneak up and down stairways without us seeing him. Ashley had loved to leap out from behind a door and make me scream, immediately after my mother, who earned extra money by babysitting her, would tell us we must play quietly.

Patrick and I climbed the wide stairway. Halfway down the second-floor hall I paused at a secretary filled with photos. I scanned them quickly, disappointed again to find none of Ashley. Amelia had said that Trent was divorced; perhaps Ashley's mother had taken all the pictures with her.

Patrick reached back for my hand, impatient with me. "It's

this way." He led me to the room at the front corner of the main house, the last doorway on the left before the center hall narrowed to connect the southern wing.

I stepped inside the door of his room and moved no farther. The drapes and comforter were green check rather than Ashley's pink, but the furniture was the same—dark, heavy, too large for a child—each piece in the same place it had occupied twelve years ago. I looked at the bed and thought of Ashley swinging like a monkey on its tall posters. I gazed at the bureau and saw her standing on top of it, performing for me. The two big chairs, if covered with a quilt, were the covered wagon in which she and I had "traveled west." To me, her presence in the room was so strong, I could nearly hear her speak.

Why, given the absence of pictures, would the family have kept her furniture? Perhaps the deep connections with objects that a child experiences are lost on an adult. Certainly, the Westbrooks would have sold it, if they had found the furniture as haunting as I.

"You don't like it?" Patrick asked. He had been watching my face closely.

"Oh, no. It's a very nice room. In fact, it's positively smashing," I added, since he seemed to enjoy that word.

He grinned. "Want to see some of my stuff?"

"Of course."

Patrick opened the walk-in closet, which was filled to the brim with toys. My breath caught when I saw the shelf of plastic horses. They had given him her toys! Then I remembered that these had been Robyn's horses, toys that had belonged to Ashley's aunt. Perhaps the toys and furniture were kept because they were regarded as an inheritance.

I lifted up a prancing dapple gray. *Hello, Silver Knight,* I said silently. That had been the toy's secret name, and I still found myself reluctant to say it aloud.

"Want to play?" Patrick asked.

I set down the horse. "Not now. We had better follow your mother's instructions and see the third floor."

"This stairway goes up to your room," he said, opening the door next to the fireplace.

"You mean if I take the job," I reminded him, afraid that he was starting to think I would.

"You don't like me?"

"Taking the job has nothing to do with whether I like you."

Patrick gazed at me silently, doubtfully.

"I mean it," I insisted.

His mouth tightened into a little seam. He led the way up to the room that had belonged to Ashley's tutor, Mr. Joseph. Directly above Patrick and Ashley's bedroom, it was on the corner of the house, with a dormer window facing the front and a smaller window facing the side. Icy air slipped in through their cracks. The two spindle-back chairs and iron bedstead were painted white. Without blankets, pillows, or any kind of fabric to soften the room, not even curtains, they made me think of bones picked clean.

"Do you like it?" Patrick asked, looking up at me with a hopefulness I wished I hadn't seen.

"It's quite nice."

We exited into the third-floor hall. At the opposite end of the rectangular hall were the main stairs with rooms on either side of them. He showed me the schoolroom first.

"This is where I do my homework."

The piano had been rolled to a different corner in the room, and the computer and printer were new, but otherwise, the tables, chairs, and shelf-lined walls looked just as I remembered them. Perhaps it was simply the dreary lighting and the familiar smells of the house, smells I connected with Ashley, but I couldn't shake the feeling that she was at Mason's Choice, in the rooms Patrick was showing me.

He led me to the playroom. "Want to meet Patricia?"

"Who?"

"My hamster."

I smiled. "It's a lovely name."

"I like Patrick better," he replied, "but she's a girl."

The large room was a kingdom of little-boy toys. Patricia's cage, an aquarium filled with wood shavings and covered by a weighted screen, sat in the corner.

"Hi, Pat," I greeted the silky brown hamster. Ashley had had hamsters and a zoo of other creatures. "Do you have a dog or cat?" I asked Patrick.

"No. I'm allergic to their fur. I'm not supposed to pick up Patricia, but I do. She gets lonely."

It's he who gets lonely, I thought, *though surrounded by every toy a kid could want.*

The walls were covered with sports posters, most of them showing ice hockey players. Patrick watched my eyes, reading every reaction. "You like hockey? We could go see the games. Wouldn't that be fun?"

"You have a team in Wisteria?"

"Of course." He pulled a high school sports program from beneath a pile of crayons. "This is Sam Koscinski," he said, pointing to a guy with a helmet, shoulder pads, and a manic look in his dark eyes. "He's the best. He . . . *smashes* people."

"Sounds like a nice chap. Patrick, do you have some friends? Do you invite them over from school?"

He shook his head. "Tim moved away."

"There's no one else?"

"Just Ashley."

"Ashley?" My voice sounded hollow. "Ashley who?"

"Just Ashley."

I regained my senses. "Is she a hamster too?"

Patrick shouted with laughter. "No. She's a person who plays with me. Would you play with me?" His voice pleaded. "You could visit and play. You don't have to be my tutor. Just come and play."

I sat down by a table overrun by plastic action figures. Patrick walked toward me, then lightly, tentatively, rested a hand on my knee. "We could have lots of fun together. I wouldn't be *real* bad."

I could see the desperation in his eyes and knew the feeling, the loneliness of being the only child among preoccupied adults. Before my father was successful enough to have his own studio, we had traveled from household to household. I had spent a lot of time in the kitchen with the help, who were busy with their jobs, waiting for my father to finish his job—waiting for someone to notice me. For a moment I considered taking the Westbrook position. Only a moment. After years of parenting my loving but inept father, I wasn't about to take on "another" little boy.

"It would be lots of fun, Patrick. But I've been thinking about doing some traveling."

"You can't. I want you here," he insisted. "Ashley likes you," he added, as if that would persuade me.

"How can she if she hasn't met me?"

"She has. She's watching you."

A tingle went up my spine. I glanced around. "I don't see anyone named Ashley."

"She sees you," he said with confidence.

I took a deep breath. "Why don't we go downstairs."

Had family members told him about her? I wondered as we descended the main stairs. The name was common enough; perhaps he simply liked it and chose it on his own for an imaginary playmate. Given his isolation on the estate, it would make sense for him to create a fantasy friend.

When we reached the landing between the first and second floors, Patrick pulled on my arm to keep me from going farther. Below us, women were arguing.

"It's Mrs. Hopewell," he said. "She's mean. She hates me."

"Oh, I'm sure she doesn't hate you, Patrick," I replied, then cringed at how I had sounded like a typical, patronizing adult.

"Robyn hates me too," he added. "We'll go a different way."

But I had just heard what Mrs. Hopewell was saying, and I wasn't going anywhere. I pulled him back and put my finger to my lips.

"You can't trust her," the housekeeper said. "You would be very foolish to hire that young woman."

"Hoppy is right," said another woman. "I'm sorry, Emily, but I simply won't allow it."

"Really. What makes you think you have a say in this, Robyn?"

"Adrian won't allow it," Mrs. Hopewell asserted. "He sent her family packing twelve years ago."

Sent my family packing? If Adrian had dismissed us, why did we sneak away in the middle of the night? Something wasn't right.

"Her mother was a strange woman, a very angry woman," Mrs. Hopewell went on. "She was supposed to be watching Ashley the day she fell through the ice."

Robyn quickly cut her off. "We don't need to go into that, Hoppy. The point is, Emily, this girl will bring back bad memories and upset Daddy and Trent. I can't allow it."

"Well, you talk to *Daddy* when he gets home," Emily replied, "and I will talk to my husband, and we will see if he chooses to listen to his daughter, his housekeeper, or his wife concerning the welfare of his son." The strength of Emily's words was betrayed by the high pitch of her voice. I guessed that she was intimidated by Mrs. Hopewell and Robyn.

But I wasn't.

"Who are they talking about?" Patrick whispered to me as I took his hand and started down the main stairs.

"Your new tutor."

Also available by Elizabeth Chandler

Kissed by an Angel

Turn the page to see how the paranormal romance begins. . . .

1

"I never knew how romantic a backseat could be," Ivy said, resting against it, smiling at Tristan. Then she looked past him at the pile of junk on the car floor. "Maybe you should pull your tie out of that old Burger King cup."

Tristan reached down and grimaced. He tossed the dripping thing into the front of the car, then sat back next to Ivy.

"Ow!" The smell of crushed flowers filled the air.

Ivy laughed out loud.

"What's so funny?" Tristan asked, pulling the smashed roses from behind him, but he was laughing, too.

"What if someone had come along and seen your father's Clergy sticker on the bumper?"

Tristan tossed the flowers into the front seat and pulled her toward him again. He traced the silk strap of her dress, then tenderly kissed her shoulder. "I'd have told them I was with an angel."

"Oh, what a line!"

"Ivy, I love you," Tristan said, his face suddenly serious.

She stared back at him, then bit her lip.

"This isn't some kind of game for me. I love you, Ivy Lyons, and one day you're going to believe me."

She put her arms around him and held him tightly. "Love *you,* Tristan Carruthers," she whispered into his neck. Ivy did believe him, and she trusted him as she trusted no one else. One day she'd have the nerve to say it, all of the words out loud. I love you, Tristan. She'd shout it out the windows. She'd string a banner straight across the school pool.

It took a few minutes to straighten themselves up. Ivy started laughing again. Tristan smiled and watched her try to tame her gold tumbleweed of hair—a useless effort. Then he started the car, urging it over the ruts and stones and onto the narrow road.

"Last glimpse of the river," he said as the road made a sharp turn away from it.

The June sun, dropping over the west ridge

of the Connecticut countryside, shafted light on the very tops of the trees, flaking them with gold. The winding road slipped into a tunnel of maples, poplars, and oaks. Ivy felt as if she were sliding under the waves with Tristan, the setting sun glittering on top, the two of them moving together through a chasm of blue, purple, and deep green. Tristan flicked on his headlights.

"You really don't have to hurry," said Ivy. "I'm not hungry anymore."

"I ruined your appetite?"

She shook her head. "I guess I'm all filled up with happiness," she said softly.

The car sped along and took a curve sharply.

"I said, we don't have to hurry."

"That's funny," Tristan murmured. "I wonder what's—" He glanced down at his feet. "This doesn't feel . . ."

"Slow down, okay? It doesn't matter if we're a little late— Oh!" Ivy pointed straight ahead. "Tristan!"

Something had plunged through the bushes and into the roadway. She hadn't seen what it was, just the flicker of motion among the deep shadows. Then the deer stopped. It turned its head, its eyes drawn to the car's bright headlights.

"Tristan!"

They were rushing toward the shining eyes.

"Tristan, don't you see it?"

Rushing still.

"Ivy, something's—"

"A deer!" she exclaimed.

The animal's eyes blazed. Then light came from behind it, a bright burst around its dark shape. A car was coming from the opposite direction. Trees walled them in. There was no room to veer left or right.

"Stop!" she shouted.

"I'm—"

"Stop, why don't you stop?" she pleaded. "Tristan, *stop!*"

The windshield exploded.

For days after, all Ivy could remember was the waterfall of glass.

At the sound of the gun, Ivy jumped. She hated pools, especially indoor pools. Even though she and her friends were ten feet from the edge, she felt as if she were swimming. The air itself seemed dark, a dank mist, bluish green, heavy with the smell of chlorine. Everything echoed—the gun, the shouts of the crowd, the explosion of swimmers in the water. When Ivy had first entered the domed pool area, she'd gulped for breath. She wished she were outside in the bright and windy March day.

"Tell me again," she said. "Which one is he?"

Suzanne Goldstein looked at Beth Van Dyke. Beth looked back at Suzanne. They both shook their heads, sighing.

"Well, how am I supposed to be able to tell?" Ivy asked. "They're hairless, every one of them, with shaved arms, shaved legs, and shaved chests—a team of bald guys in rubber caps and goggles. They're wearing our school colors, but for all I know, they could be a shipload of aliens."

"If those are aliens," Beth said, rapidly clicking her ballpoint pen, "I'm moving to that planet."

Suzanne took the pen away from Beth and said in a husky voice, "God, I love swim meets!"

"But you don't watch the swimmers once they're in the water," Ivy observed.

"Because she's checking out the group coming up to the blocks," Beth explained.

"Tristan is the one in the center lane," said Suzanne. "The best swimmers always race in the center lanes."

"He's our flyer," Beth added. "The best at the butterfly stroke. Best in the state, in fact."

Ivy already knew that. The swim team poster was all over school: Tristan surging up out of the water, his shoulders rushing forward at you, his powerful arms pulled back like wings.

The person in charge of publicity knew what she was doing when she selected that photo. She had produced numerous copies, which was a good thing, for the taped-up posters of Tristan were continually disappearing—into girls' lockers.

Sometime during this poster craze, Beth and Suzanne had begun to think that Tristan was interested in Ivy. Two collisions in the hall in one week was all that it took to convince Beth, an imaginative writer who had read a library of Harlequin romances.

"But, Beth, I've walked into *you* plenty of times," Ivy argued with her. "You know how I am."

"We do," Suzanne said. "Head in the clouds. Three miles above earth. Angel zone. But still, I think Beth is onto something. Remember, *he* walked into *you*."

"Maybe he's clumsy when he's outside the water. Like a frog," Ivy had added, knowing all the while there was nothing clumsy about Tristan Carruthers.

He had been pointed out to her in January, that first, snowy day when she had arrived at Stonehill High School. A cheerleader had been assigned as a guide to Ivy and was leading her through a crowded cafeteria.

"You're probably checking out the jocks," the cheerleader said.

Actually, Ivy was busy trying to figure out what the stringy green stuff was that her new school was serving to its students.

"At your school in Norwalk, the girls probably dream about football stars. But a lot of girls at Stonehill—"

Dream about *him,* Ivy thought as she followed the cheerleader's glance toward Tristan.

"Actually, I prefer a guy with a brain," Ivy told the fluffy redhead.

"But he's got a brain!" Suzanne had insisted when Ivy repeated this conversation to her a few minutes later.

Suzanne was the only girl Ivy already knew at Stonehill, and she had somehow found Ivy in the mob that day.

"I mean a brain that isn't waterlogged," Ivy added. "You know I've never been interested in jocks. I want someone I can talk to."

Suzanne blew through her lips. "You're already communicating with the angels—"

"Don't start on that," Ivy warned her.

"Angels?" Beth asked. She had been eavesdropping from the next table. "You talk to angels?"

Suzanne rolled her eyes, annoyed by this interruption, then turned back to Ivy. "You'd think that somewhere in that wingy collection of yours, you'd have at least one angel of love."

"I do."

"What kind of things do you say to them?" Beth interjected again. She opened a notepad. Her pencil was poised as if she were going to copy what Ivy said, word for word.

Suzanne pretended Beth wasn't there. "Well, if you do have an angel of love, Ivy, she's screwing up. Somebody ought to remind her of her mission."

Ivy shrugged. Not that she wasn't interested in guys, but her days were full enough—her music, her job at the shop, keeping up her grades, and helping to take care of her eight-year-old brother, Philip. It had been a bumpy couple of months for Philip, their mother, and her. She would not have made it through without the angels.

After that day in January, Beth had sought out Ivy to question her about her belief in angels and show her some of her romantic short stories. Ivy enjoyed talking to her. Beth, who was round-faced with shoulder-length frosted hair and clothes that ranged from flaky to dowdy, lived many incredibly romantic and passionate lives—in her mind.

Suzanne, with her magnificent long black mane of hair and dramatic eyebrows and cheekbones, also pursued and lived out many passions—in the classrooms and hallways, leaving the guys of Stonehill High emotionally exhausted. Beth and Suzanne had never really been friends, but late in February they became allies in the cause of getting Ivy together with Tristan.

"I heard that he is pretty smart," Beth had said at another lunch in the cafeteria.

"A total brain," Suzanne agreed. "Top of the class."

Ivy raised an eyebrow.

"Or close enough."

"Swimming is a subtle sport," Beth continued. "It looks as if all they're doing is going back and forth, but a guy like Tristan has a plan, a complex winning strategy for each race."

"Uh-huh," Ivy said.

"All we're saying is that you should come to one swim meet," Suzanne told her.

"And sit up front," Beth suggested.

"And let me dress you that day," Suzanne added. "You know I can pick out your clothes better than you."

Ivy had shaken her head, wondering then and for days after how her friends could think a guy like Tristan would be interested in her.

But when Tristan had stood up at the junior class assembly and told everyone how much the team needed them to come to the last big school meet, all the time staring right at her, it seemed she had little choice.

"If we lose this meet," Suzanne said, "it's on your head, girl."

Now, in late March, Ivy watched Tristan shake out his arms and legs. He had a perfect build for a swimmer, broad and powerful shoulders, narrow hips. The cap hid his straight brown hair, which she remembered to be shortish and thickish.

"Every inch of him hard with muscle," breathed Beth. After several clicks of her pen, which she had taken back from Suzanne, she was writing away in her notebook. "'Like glistening rock. Sinuous in the hands of the sculptor, molten in the fingers of the lover . . .'"

Ivy peered down at Beth's pad. "What is it this time," she asked, "poetry or a romance?"

"Does it make a difference?" her friend replied.

"Swimmers up!" shouted the starting official, and the competitors climbed onto their blocks.

"My, my," Suzanne murmured, "those little suits don't leave much to the imagination, do they? I wonder what Gregory would look like in one."

Ivy nudged her. "Keep your voice down. He's right over there."

"I know," Suzanne said, running her fingers through her hair.

"On your marks . . ."

Beth leaned forward for a look at Gregory Baines. "'His long, lean body, hungry and hot . . .'"

Bang!

"You always use words that begin with *h,*" Suzanne said.

Beth nodded. "When you alliterate *h,* it sounds like heavy breathing. Hungry, heated, heady—"

"Are either of you bothering to watch the race?" Ivy interrupted.

"It's four hundred meters, Ivy. All Tristan does is go back and forth, back and forth."

"I see. Whatever happened to the total brain with his complex winning strategy in the subtle sport of swimming?" Ivy asked.

Beth was writing again. "'Flying like an angel, wishing his watery wings were warm arms for Ivy.' I'm really inspired today!"

"Me too," Suzanne said, her glance traveling down the line of bodies in the ready area, then skipping over the spectators to Gregory.

Ivy followed her glance, then quickly turned her attention back to the swimmers. For the last three months Suzanne had been in hot—*heated, hungry*—pursuit of Gregory Baines. Ivy wished that Suzanne would get herself stuck on somebody else, and do it soon, real soon, before the first Saturday in April.

"Who's that little brunette?" Suzanne asked. "I hate little petite types. Gregory doesn't look right with someone petite. Little face, little hands, little dainty feet."

"Big boobs," Beth said, glancing up.

"Who is she? Ever seen her before, Ivy?"

"Suzanne, you've been in this school a lot longer than—"

"You're not even looking," Suzanne interrupted.

"Because I'm watching our hero, just like I'm supposed to be doing. What does *waller* mean? Everybody shouts 'Waller!' when Tristan does a turn."

"That's his nickname," Beth replied, "because of the way he attacks the wall. He hurls himself head first into it, so he can push off fast."

"I see," Ivy said. "Sounds like a total brain to me, hurling his head against a concrete wall. How long do these meets usually last?"

"Ivy, come on," Suzanne whined, and pulled on her arm. "Look and see if you know who the little brunette is."

"Twinkie."

"You're making that up!" Suzanne said.

"It's Twinkie Hammonds," Ivy insisted. "She's a senior in my music class."

Aware of Suzanne's continuous staring,

Twinkie turned around and gave her a nasty look. Gregory noticed the expression and glanced over his shoulder at them. Ivy saw the amusement spreading over his face.

Gregory Baines had a charming smile, dark hair, and gray eyes, very cool gray eyes, Ivy thought. He was tall, but it wasn't his height that made him stand out in a crowd. It was his self-confidence. He was like an actor, like the star of a movie, who was part of it all, yet when the show was over, held himself apart from the others, believing he was better than the rest. The Baineses were the richest people in the wealthy town of Stonehill, but Ivy knew that it wasn't Gregory's money but this coolness, this aloofness, that drove Suzanne wild. Suzanne always wanted what she couldn't have.

Ivy put her arm lightly around her friend. She pointed to a hunk of a swimmer stretching out in the ready area, hoping to distract her. Then she yelled, "Waller!" as Tristan went into his last turn. "I think I'm getting into this," she said, but it appeared Suzanne's thoughts were on Gregory now. This time, Ivy feared, Suzanne was in deep.

"He's looking at us," Suzanne said excitedly. "He's coming this way."

Ivy felt herself tensing up.

"And the Chihuahua is following him."

Why? Ivy wondered. What could Gregory have to say to her now after almost three months of ignoring her? In January she had learned quickly that Gregory would not acknowledge her presence. And as if bound by some silent agreement, neither he nor Ivy had advertised that his father was going to marry her mother. Few people knew that he and Ivy would be living in the same house come April.

"Hi, Ivy!" Twinkie was the first to speak. She squeezed herself in next to Ivy, ignoring Suzanne and barely glancing at Beth. "I was just telling Gregory how we always sit near each other in music class."

Ivy looked at the girl with surprise. She had never really noticed where Twinkie sat.

"He said he hasn't heard you play the piano. I was telling him how terrific you are."

Ivy opened her mouth but could think of nothing to say. The last time she had played an original composition for the class, Twinkie had shown her appreciation by filing her nails.

Then Ivy felt Gregory's eyes on her. When she met his look, he winked. Ivy gestured quickly toward her friends and said, "You know Suzanne Goldstein and Beth Van Dyke?"

"Not real well," he said, smiling at each in turn.

Suzanne glowed. Beth focused on him with the interest of a researcher, her hand clicking away on the ballpoint.

"Guess what, Ivy? In April you won't be living far from my house. Not far at all," Twinkie said. "It will be a lot easier to study together now."

Easier?

"I can give you a ride to school. It will be a quicker drive to your house."

Quicker?

"Maybe we can get together more."

More?

"Well, Ivy," Suzanne exclaimed, batting her long, dark lashes, "you never told me that you and Twinkie were such good friends! Maybe we can all get together more. You'd like to go to Twinkie's house, wouldn't you, Beth?"

Gregory barely suppressed his smile.

"We could have a sleepover, Twinkie."

Twinkie didn't look enthused.

"We could talk about guys and vote on who's the hottest date around." Suzanne turned her gaze upon Gregory, sliding her eyes down and up him, taking in everything. He continued to look amused.

"We know some other girls, from Ivy's old school in Norwalk," Suzanne went on cheerily. She knew that Stonehill's high-class commuters to New York City would have nothing to do with blue-collar Norwalk. "They'd love to come. Then we can all be friends. Don't you think that would be fun?"

"Not really," Twinkie said, and turned her back on Suzanne.

"Nice talking to you, Ivy. See you soon, I hope. Come on, Greg, it's crowded over here." She tugged on his arm.

As Ivy turned back to the action in the pool Gregory caught her chin. With the tips of his fingers he tilted her face up toward him. He was smiling.

"Innocent Ivy," he said. "You look embarrassed. Why? It works both ways, you know. There are plenty of guys, guys I hardly know, who are suddenly talking like they're my best friends, who are counting on dropping by my house the first week of April. Why do you suppose that is?"

Ivy shrugged. "You're part of the in crowd, I guess."

"You really *are* innocent!" he exclaimed.

She wished that he would let go of her. She glanced past him to the next set of bleachers, where his friends sat. Eric Ghent and another guy were talking to Twinkie now and laughing. The ultra-cool Will O'Leary looked back at her.

Gregory withdrew his hand. He left with

just a nod at her friends, his eyes still bright with laughter. When Ivy turned back to the pool again, she saw that three rubber-capped guys in identical little swimsuits had been watching her. She had no idea which, if any, of them was Tristan.

About the Author

A former high school and college teacher with a Ph.D. in English literature from the University of Rochester, Elizabeth Chandler enjoys visiting schools to talk about the process of creating books. She has written numerous picture books for children under her real name, Mary Claire Helldorfer, as well as romances for teens under her pen name, Elizabeth Chandler. Her romance novels include *Summer in the City, Love at First Click,* and the romance-mystery *Kissed by an Angel,* published by Simon Pulse.

When not writing, Mary Claire enjoys biking, gardening, and following the Orioles and Ravens. Mary Claire lives in Baltimore with her husband, Bob, and their cat, Puck.